T0195775

ALL THINGS BEING EQUAL . . .

Under the sandstone overhang, watching the rainstorm, India began to giggle. The sensation of having nothing on beneath a blanket was new to her. Her concern turned to Ransom.

"Mr. Ransom, aren't your clothes wet?"

"Yep."

"Why haven't you taken them off?"

"Huh?" Gat Ransom sounded confused.

"Because I'm a woman do you think I'm more susceptible to chill than yourself?"

"Ma'am, you're the weaker vessel."

"I would debate that. I think if I take cold it will be because I followed your advice and foolishly took off my clothes, not because I'm the weaker vessel. All things being equal, Mr. Ransom, you should take off your clothes too . . ."

Ransom was tired, hungry and strung out, but he wasn't a fool and he wasn't one to argue with a lady. "Ma'am, on the slim point of all things being equal . . . this one time I'll throw in with you."

He began unbuttoning his shirt . . .

Betina Lindsey

POCKET BOOKS

New York   London   Toronto   Sydney   Tokyo

An *Original* Publication of POCKET BOOKS

POCKET BOOKS, a division of Simon & Schuster Inc
1230 Avenue of the Americas, New York, NY 10020

ISBN: 978-1-5011-3384-8

First Pocket Books printing January 1990

10 9 8 7 6 5 4 3 2 1

POCKET and colophon are registered trademarks of
Simon & Schuster Inc.

Printed in the U.S.A.

Women dream many dreams and see many visions while bending over the washtub.

—Ann Ellis

In memory of

my great-great-grandmother, Isabella Graham Blaine (1817–1907), who in the true pioneering spirit emigrated from Carlisle, England, and settled in Spring City, Utah, in 1863. Being widowed, she made the journey alone. Well, almost alone: she brought her nine children with her.

Dedicated to

my husband, parents and family; the writers of the Utah Romance Writers of America Chapter; Gail Olsen; the sisters of the Mormon Women's Forum; and feminists everywhere.

Chapter 1

A woman's scream, magnified by night and the late hour, reverberated through the pine wood wall. India Simms's goose-quill pen stopped mid-stroke and her full lips clamped together in indignation. Last night it was weeping and the night before shouted threats, she thought. In good conscience she couldn't let another night pass with such goings-on. The lace apron of civilization might not have reached Cheyenne, Wyoming—but India Simms had!

Getting to her feet, she fastened her silk wrapper more tightly around her diminutive waist and strode out the door and down the boardinghouse hall. Locks of abundant auburn hair carelessly fastened in a top knot tumbled down her shoulders as her lively, blue eyes focused on her neighbors' door. Though barely five feet tall and weighing little more than a hundred pounds, India Simms was one to take hold of any situation with determination and bravery. Combine this with her youth, beauty and refinement, and any ruffian would be prepared to lift his hat upon meeting her.

She stopped in front of the door, and clearing her throat, she summoned her best finishing school manners while trying to recall the couple's name. Bramshill, yes, that was it.

"Mrs. Bramshill," she called out, "is there something

wrong?" Of course something dreadful was wrong, India thought. She just wasn't sure of the extremity.

In reply, she heard a crash and a shriek. Losing some of her composure, she raised her fist, and pounded urgently on the door. "Mrs. Bramshill!"

The door flew open under India's hand and she gasped at the sight that greeted her. Mr. Bramshill had his wife pinned against the bed, and was choking her to silence.

In her twenty-six years India had never witnessed such a thing. For a moment, etiquette and embarrassment nearly sent her back to her own room, but if she left, who would intervene and save the poor lady? No one will announced the voice of her conscience.

She rushed into the room. "Mr. Bramshill, I beg you, let her go!"

He ignored her plea as Mrs. Bramshill's face was purpling. In desperation, India ran to the man and tried to pull him away, but his fist flew out and knocked her aside. Gathering her courage she snatched an empty whiskey bottle off the floor and brought it down on his head. He released his grasp on his wife's throat, staggered sideways and, with a handful of gingham curtain, went down cursing.

India ran to Mrs. Bramshill and helped her to her feet. "Are you all right?"

Mrs. Bramshill panted hoarsely, unable to speak, while Indian unbuttoned the collar of her dress. But a hasty glance at Bramshill sent India into motion. He was groping for his holstered gun. Horrified, she pulled Mrs. Bramshill to her feet and shoved her though the door. The lady needed little encouragement and together they fled down the hall, taking the stairs by threes. The screen door banged behind them as they stumbled down the porch steps and out into the moonlit street.

"The marshall!" India cried. "Run to the jail."

Mud sucked at India's feet and clung to the lace hem of her wrapper as she ran down the street, pulling along her floundering companion. The screen door banged again and she glanced back to see Bramshill's bulky figure chasing after them. Hindsight was a great teacher, especially in the thick of things. Yes, she thought desperately, she should have minded her own business—or at least have hit him harder with the whiskey bottle.

With Bramshill roaring and running after them, they veered in front of an approaching horseman and made for the sanctuary of the jail. Together they flung their full weight against the split wood door, which quickly gave way, causing them to sprawl into the dozing marshall.

"Marshall Bassett . . . ," India wheezed between breaths, "her husband . . . is drunk . . . he's . . ."

The startled marshall had no time to hear the rest, for at that moment Bramshill loomed in the doorway.

"Our differences are our own, Marshall. My . . . ," his voice wavered into a hiccup, "my wife must return to me." He leaned forward with a watery-eyed stare. "Sarah, you must learn obedience to your husband. I'll not hurt you." Beneath the slur of drunkenness, the voice was educated, but even Marshall Bassett seemed doubtful of the sincerity of his promise.

Bramshill took a swaying step nearer. Before the marshall could right himself, Bramshill pointed his pistol.

"Release my wife, sir!" Like a dowsing rod, the pistol barrel oscillated in his hand. "I'll shoot, sirrr . . ." was his final threat, his face paled and his eyes glazed. He teetered forward and fell, landing face down with a thud.

Spurs rang outside. "Well, now, ain't that a stroke of lady luck if ever I saw one," drawled a resonant voice.

India's eyes lifted from the heap on the floor to the figure in the doorway. His spurs clinked on the dirt-streaked floor as he moved into the light for a better view. Tall, over six foot, angular and well proportioned, he bore a face marked by the strong jaw line and high cheekbones of aggressive daring. His self-satisfied grin matched his confident motions. Though she knew they must look like foolish ninnies, trembling in the marshall's arms, India resented the cowboy's amused regard.

"You wife-stealing again, Asa?"

"Why . . . why, Gat," Bassett stuttered, slightly perplexed. The marshall disentangled himself and rose to his feet. "Wipe that grin off yer face and help me lock this coyote up. Get his feet on yer way in."

India guided Sarah to a stool and put a comforting arm around her shoulders. Sarah's long fingers clutched spasmodically at her bruised throat while she attempted to gain some composure. Her black hair fell in tangled wisps over her heaving breast, and she averted her red-rimmed eyes as the two men carried her unconscious husband into the cell and dumped him unceremoniously on the floor.

The marshall's keys clanked against the cell bars as he locked the door. Another jug-bitten drunk, bewhiskered and wearing a stovepipe hat, a preacher's black frock coat, and trousers stuffed into high-topped boots, shared the cell. He leaned against the cracked mud and log wall mumbling snatches of inane verse. Suddenly, he reached a grasping hand through the cell bars and motioned to India.

"As a parson I ain't much, but as a drunkist . . . *hic* . . . I am a successist," he giggled throatily.

"Cork it, Thirsty," the marshall growled.

India turned her head, swallowing her revulsion. It was all such a sorry affair, quite out of her experience.

Sarah clasped India's hand tightly, her bosom rose and fell with a futile sigh. In a sweet southern voice she said softly, "I should never have married him. It would have been better to suffer the miseries of spinsterhood."

The marshall, overhearing, came over. "Now, now, ma'am. Your husband will be a repentant and sober man in the morning. No need to be too hard on him."

Sarah's long suppressed anger surged forth in a burst of unhappy words. "Mr. Bramshill has never been repentant in the morning!"

India's eyes skittered uncomfortably past the cowboy's circumspect gaze to the marshall while Sarah continued bitterly. "Y'all can't know that for a lady, marriage can be a purgatory with no escape."

The marshall rubbed the back of his neck uneasily. "Why,

4

ma'am, I've never thought about it. Most ladies I've met hunt down a husband like a wolf looking for supper."

India saw more tears flood Sarah's eyes, and she winced at his tactlessness. What a time to say such a thing! "Marshall, it might be best for us to go back to the boarding-house," she offered.

The marshall's jowled face brightened with obvious relief. "Yep, that might be best, don't you agree, Gat?"

The tall cowboy nodded, but said nothing. At least, India noted grimly, he wasn't grinning any more. He touched the broad brim of his hat and moved out of the ladies' way. India, passing with the grace of royalty, ushered Sarah to the door.

"I beg a favor of you, marshall." Sarah Bramshill paused momentarily, a hint of trembling touched her soft voice.

"Anything, ma'am," Bassett replied gallantly, though his demeanor belied the verbal courtesy. It was clear that get-ting tangled up in Sarah's marital differences was the last thing he wanted to do.

"Keep Mr. Bramshill in jail. You understand, Marshall? He needs time to sober up."

The marshall nodded sympathetically. "Ma'am, as you are a lady, you ain't expected to know the intricacies of the law. I kin guarantee one day fer disorder and another fer drunkenness, but a third might be stretching things a bit."

India sniffed. From what she'd seen of Cheyenne the only intricacy of law which determined length of sentence was the capacity of the jail. If it got too full, the marshall would take Bramshill outside, ask which way he was going and point him in that direction.

"Of course, Marshall," India said indignantly, "I forgot wife-beating is a husband's right. Too bad he isn't guilty of a *serious* crime, perhaps spitting on the boardwalk?"

She turned on her heel, leaving the marshall groping for a reply.

"Pardon, ma'am," the cowboy said, as India ushered Sarah out the door. "It's late. The marshall or myself could escort you ladies home."

India raised a delicate auburn brow, her eyes flickered measuringly over him. She was surprised by his courtesy. The West abounded with cowboys who looked as if they bedded down in a sage brush patch every night and rode through a dust storm everyday. He had the continual squint and the unshaven face that seemed to be the hallmark of the Wyoming cowboy, though he was distinguished by a scar running from his temple down the left side of his face and cheek. Despite his good manners, his rough, rangy appearance prevented her from accepting his offer.

"Thank you, sir. But we no longer need protection."

He started to smile, then seemed to think better of it. Instead he reached inside his boot and brought out a tiny pistol. "Ma'am, I wouldn't go out unarmed in the streets of Cheyenne this time of night. I don't suppose you should either. Take this," he offered her the gun.

At first she hesitated, then took the gun.

"It's loaded. Just pull the safety when you're ready to fire," he instructed with a nod.

India looked at the gun warily, turning it over carefully in her tiny hand. She knew the women of the evening carried them, and rumor had it that most were deadly shots. The West was giving her quite an education, she thought ruefully.

She was a bit confused. "Of course. Thank you, Mr. . . ."

"Ransom, ma'am. Gat Ransom," he said. Her icy-blue gaze focused on his full lips encircled by the shadow of a beard, then rose to his smoldering eyes beneath black, arching brows. There was a wildness about him that wrenched her stomach and alerted her senses. In the face of his help she felt annoyed and defensive, yet she couldn't think of a single reason why. He was disturbing, this Mr. Ransom; she wished they'd never met.

She quickly gathered up her muddy-hemmed nightgown and led Sarah out into the darkened street. The bullet-cracked face of the wall clock marked half-past ten, and the chime accented the ladies' exit.

A sorrel horse at the hitching post snorted and India swallowed uneasily when she saw a muslin-swathed corpse

6

on its back. A wild-looking dog kept guard beside the horse and eyed her steadily. Somewhere down the street whoops and hollers echoed through the spring night, punctuated by gunshots. She glanced back over her shoulder to Ransom uncertainly. "I'm sorry but . . . but exactly where is the safety on this . . . this . . ."

"Derringer, ma'am," Ransom said. He reached over and released the catch. She gave him a tight smile and a polite nod. Linking her arm through Sarah's, she began to walk down the dark street with the derringer hidden in the fold of her silk wrapper.

She heard Ransom's voice behind her saying, "I hope she doesn't shoot her foot off," followed by a chuckle from Marshall Bassett, but pride would not let her turn her head. Yes, she could just imagine Mr. Ransom's grin.

Chapter 2

Gat watched the ladies, the uppity one in particular, disappear into the night. At first he watched her because he hadn't seen a woman in a month and then because he'd never seen a woman like her. In a territory where there were six men to every woman, he wondered who would let loose such an innocent in Cheyenne. Don't need protection! He grinned at her audacity. She sure was all arrogance and bravado, and green to the frontier—as green as prairie grass. He couldn't help but savor a face worthy of a porcelain locket and the hourglass curves of her body silhouetted beneath her silk wrapper, a silk wrapper so fine that in the right lamplight it would be transparent. She looked as desirable as any woman could look.

He whistled under his breath and reluctantly pulled his eyes away, and turning to Asa Bassett he said, "That gal's a stunner."

"Looks ain't everythin'. I never took you fer one to go after a sharp-tongued shrew."

"Shrew? That little thing? Ah, she's just got a little spunk. There's nothin' wrong with spunk." Gat pursed his lips and bit back a smile.

"Listen, you ain't been here. That little thing is stirrin' up all the ladies in town fer votin'. Imagine lettin' ladies vote. It'll be degradin' politics to let 'em in. I fer one will be glad to see the hind end of that filly leave Cheyenne. No wonder husbands is beatin' their wives, the way she gets them all stirred up about wimmin's rights. Bullshit! Why, ever since my Caroline went over to the town hall and heard her spoutoff, I've had no peace at home. Caroline informed me that during the first territorial legislature, I was to support enfranchisement fer wimmin, er else.''

Gat continued to hold back a grin. His old friend could tame a boom town like Cheyenne, but was mush in the hands of his good wife, Caroline. "Or else what?" he prompted.

"If you was married you wouldn't ask." Asa drew up the only stool in the room and sat down. "I ain't aimin' to sleep with my horse this winter. Them days is over fer me. Give me the soft flank of a woman to a saddle any day.''

"Meanin' . . ." Gat prodded good humoredly, though he knew exactly what Asa meant. Even so, for his money he'd take a saddle over the hobbles of matrimony, and if a man wanted more he could buy it on the edge of town Saturday nights.

"Meanin', I reckon I'll vote fer *wimmin's enfranchisement*. Ain't that a mouthful of words. Trust the ladies to complicate somethin' as simple as *the vote*.''

Gat yawned, exhausted from a long day's ride. "If I'd known what I was missin', I'd have encouraged the governor to come back sooner.''

Asa took a pouch of chewing tobacco out of his pocket and bit off a chew. "What's doin' up at Fort Laramie these days?" He offered the pouch to Gat, but Gat declined.

"Same as always—Indian trouble. Rumor has it there's something besides Sioux in the Black Hills.''

"Gold?"

"Maybe."

From inside the cell the sound of retching interrupted the quiet conversation.

Asa muttered. "That damn infernal pukeface!" He gave an exaggerated sniff, got up, and went out into the street for fresh air. "Howdy, boy," he greeted Gat's dog, Coyote, with an ear-scratching rub. The dog nuzzled for more atten-

9

tion. "Who's this you've brought by?" He walked over to Gat's horse and circled the corpse. "A little rank, ain't he?"

Gat stood in the open doorway. "I don't know who. He pulled two Colt Lightnings on Governor Campbell at the Platte Waystation yesterday.

"You the one who shot him?" Asa spit aside into the street.

"Had no choice. He opened fire when the governor refused to drink with him. One bullet ripped through Campbell's coat, another hit his shoulder, and four others missed altogether."

"Fool. The poor, reckless fool," remarked Asa as he lowered the cloth to examine the face. He eyed the lifeless features and made a hard-luck click with his tongue. "That's all I do in this job, sort out gunfights between whiskey-fired heroes."

Gat nodded in agreement. It wasn't the first time somebody had taken a shot at Governor Campbell. Appointed by the president, the non-smoking, non-drinking Republican Campbell was a little too puritanical for the frontier and Gat supposed that's why he'd been hired as the governor's temporary bodyguard. That, and to more or less guide him around Wyoming Territory.

"Bad luck, Gat," Asa began with a frown. "This here's 'Cut-Off' Bitterman. See all that's left of his ear is the lobe. He got too friendly with a Ute squaw a while back and her brave cut off his ear. Anybody else know you done the killin'?"

"The Chew boys were passin' and I guess everybody else that's come through the waystation since."

"Will Noble will be sure to write it up in the *Argus*. Chic Bitterman is bound to find out. Chic ain't a bad man, he just ain't a good one. I wouldn't leave myself open if I was you."

"I'm a quick learner," Gat laughed. He fingered the scar on his face, a keepsake from the war. Since the war, he hadn't had to outright kill a man, even in self-defense until yesterday. Taking a life didn't set easy with Gat because by nature he was a peacemaker. He owed that to Emmeline

Carlisle, who had bloodied his nose and whipped his pride when he was nine years old. She was ten. A hard lesson. He decided then that there were better ways to settle differences, and he got even with Emmeline. When she turned fifteen he stole a kiss from her, and she sure wasn't in a fighting mood then.

He blinked red-rimmed eyes. "Guess I'll drop your friend here by the coffin maker and then try to get some sleep."

"When that deputy of mine shows up I think I'll do the same. Hasn't been the quietest of nights," Asa said. He retied the muslin around Bitterman's head and stepped out of the way. "Good night, then," Asa said as Gat unhitched the horses and led them down the street.

The stop at the mortician's done, Gat mounted his horse. He paused, and leaned down to smell the violets in a crockery pot resting on the window ledge. *By hell*, he thought, *tired as I am, I'm glad to be alive!* He nudged his horse forward along Sixteenth Street, the last leg of his journey. He'd ridden over half of Wyoming in the past months and now he welcomed the gentleness of the spring night air, relieved that the Wyoming winter had at last departed. He looked forward to the warmth and comfort of Heddy's boardinghouse. Heddy's was the closest thing to home he'd encountered since he'd left Oklahoma before the war.

He thought again about the uppity gal at the jail. Something about her reminded him of home; white picket fences and apple pie cooling on the windowsill. Some women did that to a man, yet for all he could see she was the ramrod type, raised hackles and touchy temper, but at the heart, all the softness a man hankered for on lonesome nights—like tonight. He'd gone a long time with no softness, no woman.

The town was winding down for the night. The saloons and gambling parlors would soon be rolling the drunks out the doors. Lamplight filtered into the street from the *Argus* newspaper office. Will Noble was up late working on the next day's edition.

Gat noticed that Professor McDaniels had a new advertising mural in front of his barroom museum. "Clark is not Dead," the mural read. "Come and see him—free." Gat smiled to himself, wondering if Professor McDaniels had taken to mummifying humans now along with the snakes, toads and birds in his menagerie of horrifying wonders. Coyote escorted Gat down the street to the boardinghouse, stopping now and then to sniff at a morsel of street garbage.

Having stabled his horse out back, Gat took the steps of Heddy's boardinghouse by twos, paused a moment to take off his spurs—house rule—then tried the door. Finding it locked, he thought better of knocking and walked around to the back door. A peek in the window told him things were still stirring in the kitchen. Heddy Pierre was on her hands and knees scrubbing the floor, and Yee Jim was bending over the boardinghouse laundry in the alcove, flatiron in hand. Gat lent Heddy a hundred and fifty dollars to help buy the boardinghouse three years before. She'd paid him back, and whenever he was in town he had a free room.

He took a penny whistle from his pocket and blew a few notes through the open window. Coyote echoed the light refrain with a howl. "You goin' to let me in?"

"Gat? You and yo' hound dog sure be a pair! I scrub the floor last thing so nobody walks on it till mornin' and you show up. No use, I guess. You take off yo' boots and git in. Mind me, just yo' stockin' feet. I ain't startin' over, not fo' nobody!"

Heddy unlatched the door as Gat pulled off his boots, and when he stepped inside she threw up a halting hand. "Yo' socks be as dirty as yo' boots. Take 'em off. And fo' two tunes on yo' bird whistle, Yee Jim kin wash 'em fo' you." She widened her black eyes. "Lordy, they kin stand and walk over to the kettle by themselves. Don't you ever change yo' socks, boy?"

Yee Jim, who was in the process of spraying water through his teeth on the linen he was ironing, almost choked with laughter.

"I give special on not clean sock today only," he sputtered.

"You ain't supposed to insult a bad hombre like me by askin' if my socks are clean," Gat threatened. "Don't you know your place, woman?"

"My place be scrubbin' the floor, you jackrabbit, and yo' place be the bathtub. I run a clean house here. Now git!"

"What about the songs?" He put the penny whistle to his lips. "I sure wouldn't want to wash my socks myself."

"Save it fo' afternoon parlor sittin'. I want to relax and enjoy it. Yee Jim, fix Mr. Gat a mighty big tub of hot water. Quick, quick. And don't forget the sheep dip fo' ticks."

"Ticks? Sheep dip? Come on. I ain't that dirty," Gat protested.

"You ain't goin' no further in my boardin' house till you have a bath *with sheep dip!*"

Gat sighed. Yee Jim nodded agreeably and made a joke by holding his nose as he set aside the flatiron and picked up a kettle of boiling water from the wood stove. He and Gat went down the hall to the bathroom beneath the stairway. Gat stooped from lack of headroom, but for the short Yee Jim it was no problem. Yee Jim poured hot water into the tub and Gat hefted a few more bucketfuls from the water barrel in the corner.

He took off his hat and holster, unfastened his concha-studded chaps, and unbuttoned his wool shirt. Like his socks, the rest of his clothing could probably stand up on its own from the dirt and sweat of the trail. But then, escorting the governor was an easy job compared to herding cattle, though he preferred the latter.

"I get more hot water. You have nice long bath," Yee Jim said as he backed out the doorway.

"Do me a favor, Yee, and bring me a change of clothes from my saddle bags."

"I get water and clothes quick, Mr. Gat."

By the time Yee Jim had returned with the clothes and two more kettles of hot water, Gat had managed to gingerly lower his lengthy frame into the copper tub. His knees almost hugged his ears. The room reeked from the smell of the sheep dip solution that Heddy insisted he use. Sniffing, he lathered up with the bar of lye soap, only to have it slip out of his hand and over the side of the tub, onto the floor. He reached over the side, feeling around the floor, and came up with a glass bottle of flower-scented bath salts. Not being able to read French, he wasn't sure what fragrance the bottle contained, but when he uncorked it he discovered it smelled like violets. Well, that certainly was better than sheep dip! He sprinkled the salts liberally into the water as the air muted into a garden of wild violets. Since Gat figured more was better, the jar of bath salts was soon emptied. Gat settled back, stretched out his long legs best he could in the water, and relaxed like a turtle floating on a summer pond.

14

Chapter 3

*G*listening tears trickled from Sarah Bramshill's swollen eyes. "Things will work out," said India, dipping a cotton hankie into cold water and giving it to Sarah to press on her blackening eye. Hunched over and willow-thin, Sarah sat on the sagging boardinghouse bed and faintly whispered words of gratitude. India could see that the discord of her marriage had rendered her despondent. She was a pathetic sight, though underneath the misery India detected a vibrant woman of unusual beauty.

"I don't know how," she shook her head, obviously overwhelmed by the circumstances that had brought her marriage to this nadir. In a slow drawl she chastised herself. "I should have known what kind of man he would turn out to be."

"It's not your fault. How could you have known?" soothed India.

"Maybe you're right. But I must accept some blame. It was like the marshall said. Toward the war's end there were no men left in the South and I thought there could be no worse fate than to be an old maid. When Huntington appeared with his charming manners and declared devotion, I succumbed. Our courtship consisted of church suppers and chaperoned dances and gave me little inkling of his penchant for drinking and gambling." She paused, remembering. "My inheritance did not last the first year. He lost it on riverboat gambling tables. He is incapable of slow, honest industry. His greatest delight is to lure hardworking men into a game of cards just as payday dawns. For he must make money and make it by quick strokes no matter how.''

Inwardly, India ached for her. It was not an uncommon story. Her inheritance squandered, Sarah was a yet another victim of the law denying a married woman the right of property.

Sarah sniffed and wiped her eyes with the hankie. ''Never a day passes that Huntington doesn't take his drink. He knows how bitterly I hate his drinking. But I let it go, for he is very hard on me if I speak up.''

India could see that Sarah had meekly borne his abuse, thinking it was her assigned lot as wife. Now, India could only sympathize with her misfortune and offer her a bit of optimism. ''Surely he loves you.''

''Loves me! Yes, as he would love a fine horse; just because it was his, and a little better than what anyone else owned. But he does not spare me in the least. There is not a profane, low, vulgar, filthy name he has not called me. His vileness is almost unendurable.'' Sarah shook her head in despair. ''His heartless treatment long ago killed my love for him.'' Then she gave India a concerned look. ''Oh, forgive me, I shouldn't be saying these things, especially to you. You're so young, on the threshold of life, and I'll make you fear marriage.''

Matching Sarah's gaze, India smiled encouragement. ''Don't worry about me. I've vowed never to marry. Instead of living a life of subjection, I've chosen to dedicate myself to women's suffrage.''

For a long moment Sarah looked at India strangely, as if she were seeing an oddity of nature. India was accustomed to such stares. Women were often her severest critics, and she knew she posed a threat to the woman who wished to be protected, idealized and dominated. Of course she understood that many women led lives of great happiness, protected and loved by generous, kind husbands. But this was like claiming that there was no need for abolition because most masters were kind to their slaves.

"I've heard some talk of women voting, but I do not understand the need, since I've been taught God intended woman to be wife and man to rule," Sarah said thoughtfully.

"Why did God give every woman a brain if he didn't intend for her to use it? You say your husband considers you his possession. If you had equal rights under the law that wouldn't be so. Your inheritance could still be in your hands." The stricken look in Sarah's eyes stopped India's speech. She knew her sentiments caused her to be excessive at times. Telling herself this was not a public debate, she slipped from her seat and knelt beside Sarah. "Now, you must forgive me, I've said too much."

Sarah shook her head in slow comprehension. "Maybe not. Certainly the law has made me a pauper, dependent upon my husband's good graces, of which he has none. As it is, I have no money."

"You have no allowance, nothing set aside?" asked India.

"My husband gives me nothing. He fears I would bolt."

"And would you?"

A long moment passed before Sarah answered. "I think about it."

India gnawed her lower lip thoughtfully. Perhaps it wasn't her place to interfere, but she was about to. If she could help Sarah, she must! All her battles thus far were verbal, but now she was faced with the reality of her efforts.

"I have money. Allow me to give you enough for train fare back to your family."

For a moment hope came to Sarah's eyes, but then it faded. "It will do no good. Huntington would follow me, and as long as the law says I am his, no matter the distance or the place, he'd find me."

"What if you were no longer considered his wife under the law?" suggested India.

"What do you mean?" Sarah tilted her head stiffly.

"Divorce," said India quietly. The notion of divorce was

extreme and India knew abetting the dissolution of a marriage was no light matter.

"Is it possible?" Sarah ran her tongue across her lips in a deliberate motion.

"Yes, but uncommon. Before embarking on such a course you must be sure. Divorce is final. If you should change your mind . . ."

Sarah squared her shoulders and a look of pure resolve came over her face. "I can't bear to live with Huntington any longer. One way or another, I intend to free myself of this miserable alliance." She reached out to India and clasped her hands tightly in her own. "And no matter the hardship, I will repay you. I barely know you, yet you have put within reach my most heartfelt desire." A sudden light touched Sarah's face. "Until now, I dared not hope."

"Of course you must hope!" India came to her feet to leave. "Sleep on it, and we'll discuss it further in the morning. Now get some rest, and hope!" India gave her a parting caress.

Back in her room India abandoned her nightly ritual of massaging her skin with a special concoction of lard, rose water and coconut milk. Though the hour was late, she sat down on the straight-backed chair, dipped her pen into the ink and continued her letter to her sister, Cordelia.

Nothing in the West is accompanied by the comforts of civilization. On the journey here, my passenger car carried railroad employees, land-seekers, furloughed soldiers returning to their forts, and me, the only woman among them. I have found the West to have two things in abundance, flies and bedbugs. Before registering in a hotel—even if it be the best in town—I ask to see the room, promptly remove the pillow and turn down the sheet in search of the West's most friendly inhabitant, Monsieur Bedbug. During my short stay in Cheyenne it has been my good fortune to find a clean boardinghouse whose proprietress is the best of cooks. However, the frontier has sorely tried my sensibilities and I have learned that all of life's choicest gifts have been mine. Papa has been so good and generous to us, Sissy. Indeed we have lacked for nothing. I nearly weep with homesickness at the thought of Rosemount House.

Nevertheless, I will not abandon the cause for genteel comforts. Our sisters in the West need what a college-educated woman like myself has to give, and give it I will! Most care not for equality but for day-to-day survival. This very night I've had an experience that has made me more determined. This evening, a woman in my boardinghouse was beaten by her drunken husband. I was obliged to intervene. I will never understand men. They pay us exaggerated respect, then slap us around when that seems the thing to do. They dream of creatures in lace and silk, when what they really want is a workhorse with two legs. It is a contradiction between reverence and contempt—protectiveness and brutality.

I know you think I'm extreme in this matter and I will say no more of it, but no one who neglects to do what she feels she ought can be truly happy. I've put aside romantic notions for higher aims and I will never marry. Clearly, I've dedicated myself to the cause of women's suffrage and my path is set—a path, particularly here in Wyoming, that is seldom adorned with flowers.

I am an Alexander with few soldiers. Though I always lecture to a full hall, my audiences are mostly men who, out of novelty, come to see a lady orator. But I will not be disheartened, for the cause is not without enthusiasts in Wyoming Territory. I've found two ardent supporters, Amelia Post, Cheyenne's foremost suffragette, and one William Noble, editor and owner of the Cheyenne Argus newspaper, to which I'm now a contributor.

But, Sissy, it is difficult. I know you are thinking that Papa warned me, that life would be harsh in the West and that no lady of virtue would travel alone. It's true. I've been the object of ridicule and rude comment. Of course, I steel myself with Christian patience and hold *my tongue, ever craving the comforts and conversation of genteel society. How I weary of tobacco-spitting cowboys and clapboard boom towns.*

I miss you, Sissy. Kiss our dear parents for me. Write me in care of the Cheyenne Argus *newspaper. Make it soon.*

Your loving sister,
India

India sealed and addressed her letter, snuffed out the lantern and slipped into bed. As time passed, a cricket in the wall board chirped, and no matter how often she fluffed her tick-feather pillow to comfort, her mind churned over the events of the evening.

In her more grandiose daydreams India had imagined herself a commander-in-chief, leading leagues of oppressed women to freedom. But in reality, she felt very inadequate and uneasy. Was she helping Sarah or just meddling? India prayed with all her heart that she was doing the right thing. But even with the utterance of prayer she couldn't put this night to rest. Sleep brought half-nightmares and a distorted dream in which again she was running down Cheyenne's main street, but this time it was the tall, black-haired cowboy who pursued her.

Wrapped in her silk robe, India peeked out her door and down the back stairway to see if the way was clear. After a brief lapse during the wild happenings of the night before, her usual modesty had returned. The voices of Heddy and Yee Jim filtered up from the kitchen as she moved down the stairway to the bathroom beneath the stairs. Her habitual morning bath must be quick, for she'd promised Sarah an early visit to a lawyer. Before dawn Sarah had tapped on her door and confessed that during a sleepless night she had indeed made the decision to divorce her husband. Sarah advised her that they must act that very morning, before Mr. Bramshill was released from jail.

India still worried if she'd been right in offering to help

20

Sarah, but who better than she could help someone in Sarah's unfortunate situation? After all, this is eighteen hundred and sixty-nine and we women should avail ourselves of every advantage! she thought.

India knocked on the bathroom door and listened for a response. "Anyone in there?" she asked as she touched the porcelain knob and found it to be unlocked. She opened the door and illuminated the small, windowless room. "Oh," she gasped when she saw someone occupying the tub. She started to leave before the encounter became awkward, but peering closer, she thought something seemed a bit odd about the posture of the man in the tub. He wasn't moving or . . . She stepped closer and recognized Gat Ransom. He didn't appear normal and he hadn't roused at her initial call.

"Good heavens, he's dead!" she muttered to herself, then with a cry of alarm she ran out the door. "Heddy, Heddy, come quick, a man has drowned in the bathing tub." This news took only a second to register in the kitchen.

"Lordy, what you sayin', Miss Simms?" Heddy huffed, hurrying through the door. "Nobody ever did that before." She shook the limp body. "Gat, you alive?"

Gat sputtered and opened his eyes. "What . . . somethin' wrong?" His face hazed in sleep looked up at the two women. "Uh, I must of dozed off."

"Dozed off, you been sleepin' here all night! You look like a white prune. Missy here thought you drowned. What kind of reputation be settin' for my boardin' house havin' someone drown in the bathtub?"

India was slowly coming to the realization that she was staring at Mr. Ransom and he didn't have a stitch on. Feeling the heat of embarrassment, she quickly turned away to follow Heddy out the door.

Apparently insensible to the awkward situation, Gat sat up. "Excuse me, ma'am. Would you mind handin' me a bath towel on your way out?" He gave a slight nod toward India, who was nearest the towel hook.

Looking everywhere but at Ransom, India quickly reached for the towel, but as she did, her foot knocked over a bottle beside the tub. It was her own bath salts, which she must have left in the room the morning before. Stooping to retrieve it, her nose caught the familiar fragrance of violets mixed with some other peculiar stench. In truth, the air was overpowered by the smells.

Usually, India was long-suffering, slow to anger, and agreeably forgiving, but this was early in the morning after a taxing night.

"You've used my bath salts!" She turned to Ransom in fiery accusation. "How could you be so . . . so unthinking? Don't you realize how dear a luxury this is? There probably isn't another jar of this in all of Wyoming. I brought it from Boston and have conserved it with the closeness of a miser, and you, you lackwit goatherd, have used it up in a single bath."

"Ma'am, my apologies, but I just helped myself to what was here. And I herd cows, not goats." His voice held more offense than apology.

"Don't you have any consideration for personal property? If it wasn't yours, you should not have used it," she yelled, castigating in schoolmarm fashion.

"This water's ice cold ma'am, and I have the queer feeling I'm dissolving" was his answer. He was fairly riled himself. "If you don't plan to hand me a towel, I'll just help myself."

India's breath caught as he began to rise up out of the water. She found herself face-to-bare-chest. Dark wet hair curled around nipples on firm mounds of muscle, while a matte-black shadow of hair tapered down his stomach lower than her wide eyes dare explore. But explore they did, eyes to naked form.

It was as if the heavens had opened and God said, "Miss India Simms, this is man!" In the charged silence the kitchen wall clock ticked rhythm with the slow igniting pulse deep within her body. As she drew in each fortifying breath of air, the dizzying fumes of violet bath salts, mingled with her simmering senses, fairly seared the nostrils of her refined nose.

Gathering her wits, she couldn't toss him the towel and

leave the room fast enough. It was evident his chivalry had disappeared with his clothes.

"So, Mrs. Bramshill, do you feel you have legitimate grounds for divorcing your husband?" Benjamin Sheeks looked up from a tidy pinewood desk, his eyes searching Sarah Bramshill's face.

India shifted slightly, wishing they had gone to the other lawyer in town. This one seemed less than eager to aid them, though by the appearance of his desk he needed the business.

As she focused on the nondescript features of Benjamin Sheeks, the morning's unforgettable vision of Gat Ransom rising from the bathwater like Neptune from the sea engulfed her.

In that moment her reaction to Ransom had not been voluntary; it had been instinctual. Experiencing Ransom in his natural state, she'd witnessed the explosive masculinity his powerful body emanated. Her own undeniably primitive response, bordering on the sinful, had momentarily caused India to doubt the very foundation of her ideologies—that man *alone* was not meant to rule.

Refocusing on the pencil-thin torso of Mr. Sheeks, India reconsidered. Not all men were endowed with the superior strength, size, and intellect that supposedly entitled them to natural dominance. In truth, men weren't dominant by nature or they would always be dominant in the way women always had babies. And, heretic that she was, she could never believe Eve was created from Adam's rib, for, to her thinking, it was physically impossible and went against the order of nature.

But try as she might, she could not intellectualize her attraction to Gat Ransom. Why did she still burn at the thought of him? Was her unexpected reaction to him a primal need to be ruled? A primal need to be loved? Whatever the answer, it was clear to India that you couldn't have one without the other. If a woman wanted a man's love, she must suffer his rule.

Sarah's words interrupted India's introspection. "Yes, I feel I do, Mr. Sheeks." As if intimidated by Mr. Sheeks's authoritative manner, she had clasped India's hand for support.

"How long have you been married to Mr. Bramshill?"

"Four years. We were married in Atlanta just after the war. We have no children."

"No children," he echoed.

"My husband did not want children," explained Sarah.

Sheeks lifted his eyebrows and then pursed his lips. "Well, your husband is your protector. His judgment must be submitted to in loving obedience."

India's jaw tightened, her teeth clenched in restrained disagreement. *Submission and obedience! Are there no other words to describe the woman's role in the marital union?*

"Obviously you feel you have just cause for divorce. Can you elaborate?" continued Sheeks.

Sarah did not speak at once and it wasn't India's place to speak for her, though India could not deny the impulse to do so.

Then Sarah spoke, as though tallying up the long list of Huntington Bramshill's shortcomings. "Would it be enough to say we are incompatible?"

"Ah"—Sheeks cleared his throat with a cough—"you see, in Wyoming territory the 'just' cause for divorce is adultery. Unless you have evidence of infidelity . . ."

Upon this revelation India's eyes left the rosebud pattern on her dress and darted to the lawyer's clean-shaven face. "Surely there are other avenues to dissolving this unhappy union," she said out of turn and was immediately sorry for, since she had only meant to accompany Sarah and not interfere.

Sheeks gave her a glance of dismissal, and India knew her reputation as a suffragette must have preceded her.

"No," began Sarah, "in truth he is fully against my leaving him."

India swallowed back the mounting dread that Sarah might

not be able to obtain a divorce after all. And if Sarah could not divorce Bramshill, she would have to return to his abuse.

"Well, I can do little for you then. Perhaps you could come back with Mr. Bramshill. Sometimes these matters can be solved in mutual agreement."

"Her husband is in jail," India interjected, extremely distraught with the turn of events.

"In jail?" Sheeks looked back and forth at the two women. "Whatever for?"

"Drunkenness," said Sarah softly.

"Well, silly women, why didn't one of you say so?"

India glared at him. Her flashing blue eyes betrayed her resentment and anger. India almost shouted, *We are not silly women!*

"Is he an habitual drunk?" Mr. Sheeks took out a paper and put his pen to the inkwell.

"Yes," replied Sarah.

"Your eye," he said. "Did your husband hit you?"

"Yes," returned Sarah. By now Sheeks was writing furiously.

"We will make your application on the grounds of habitual drunkenness and extreme cruelty. You'll have your divorce, Mrs. Bramshill. Of course, you have the five dollars for my fee?" He seemed to withhold his pen from the final signature as he awaited her answer.

"I hope so, sir." She looked to India, who opened her beaded handbag and put a five-dollar gold piece on the edge of the pinewood desk.

"Excellent!" said Sheeks as he reached for the coin and deftly slipped it into his own vest pocket. "Now, a brief note of caution. If you reunite with your husband within three months, the divorce is null. Neither are you permitted to remarry for one year after the divorce is granted."

"Yes, I am in agreement with those terms." Sarah came to her feet seeming anxious to be done with it.

Sheeks came around the desk with an overt show of courtesy, giving them a judicious smile. "If I can be assistance, please call again."

"You'll serve the papers soon?" Sarah asked, more as a request than a question.

"As soon as everything is in order." Sheeks moved to open the door for her.

"I think it would be wise. While my husband is still in jail, you understand." She quickly stepped past him, examining the muddy street to locate the driest footpath. "Good day, Mr. Sheeks."

Passing Sheeks, India saw a sudden uneasiness rest upon his face as his eyes moved down the street toward the jail. India knew that Bramshill wasn't without reputation in Cheyenne. The lawyer's hand went to his vest pocket containing the gold piece. Perhaps he wished he'd charged more for his services, India thought, as she leaped from one makeshift board bridge to the next.

"My stomach is filled with butterflies. One moment I am overwhelmed at my good fortune and the next I am terrified of the consequences. But the actual transaction was so easy," confessed Sarah, taking India's hand tightly as they stood at the Cheyenne train depot waiting for the conductor's boarding call.

"Yes," agreed India. Thinking it did seem too easy, but then that was the way things were evidently handled in the West where Judge Lynch was the order of the day. "I still think returning to your family in Atlanta might be best," suggested India.

"No, I would only bring shame upon them. They would think me better dead than divorced. Don't worry, my cousin in San Francisco will assist me until I become settled."

The conductor sang out his boarding call and Sarah stooped to pick up her carpet bag, but then dropped the handle and turned to India. "I intend to repay you as soon as I can, but until then I will ever be in your debt." She put her arms around India.

Tears clouded India's eyes. "Never mind paying me back. I'm happy I could help you. We must be united in these things. Good luck to you."

"Thank you. Thank you!" Sarah, wiping her eyes, turned, picked up her belongings and boarded the train.

"Write me!" called India. "I want to know how you're getting along. Send the letter in care of the *Argus*. Goodbye!" She waved a gloved hand and turned toward the street. The train eased away from the depot with a departing whistle.

Feeling as if she had won a skirmish, India quickened her steps. She veered past a wagon filled with cages of squawking chickens, and daring to lift her skirts knee-high she made an unladylike but successful leap to the boardwalk.

A sudden pain stung her neck. She stopped short and looked behind her, seeing two rapscallions dart around the corner of the mercantile. Oh, it wasn't the first time she had fallen victim to their peashooters. Since her arrival the pair seemed to take great delight in stalking the town suffragette and tormenting her. She continued down the street and then felt the thump of a mud ball on her skirt.

"Those little demons!" She whirled around and caught sight of them ducking behind a wagon. In a false start she pretended to chase them, and they scattered like scared jackrabbits.

Brushing off her skirt and muttering to herself she stepped inside the *Argus* office.

"Good morning, William!"

"India," greeted William Noble. "I was just editing the article on suffrage." He put down his pencil and looked at her. His face turned to concern. "Are you all right?"

"Of course," she said, examining the mud spots on her skirt.

"Not the local renegades again?"

"What else have they to do?"

"Become proper citizens so they can vote for suffrage for women." His jest lightened her agitation and a smile tugged the corners of her soft mouth. "Perhaps this will cheer you up," he began to read aloud. "What man of intellect, after understanding the many wrongs women have been obliged to endure in all this great and otherwise freedom-loving land,

27

would not but wholeheartedly support a law which gave both sexes the same right to vote in Wyoming Territory?''

He looked to India for approval. "I think ending it with a question will set the reader pondering. Yes, any man of intelligence cannot but be in favor of women getting the vote."

India had taken off her cloak and was hanging it on the brass wall hooks. She removed her gloves slowly. "It's wonderful, but I'm afraid that only a handful of men in the entire world understand the need for women's rights. To most men, women are dolls, vassals, or hopeless drudges without the ability to make intelligent choices of their own."

William smiled. "Certainly you do not accuse me of such an opinion? I consider myself a man of enlightenment."

"Of course not!" India returned softly. "I didn't mean to insult you." India studied William momentarily, noting the integrity of his gray eyes and the concern etched on his fine features. He was a handsome man. His face and physique held all the attractive qualities one might wish to find in a beau. This was the kind of man she had hoped to marry in the dreamy days of adolescence. Yes, it had been easy to grow up with such notions. Every girl did. But she no longer listened for the hoof beats of Prince Charming's steed, even though she had recently found the ring of spurs distracting.

"Forgive me, I'm not at my best this morning. How are the arrangements for my speaking tour coming?'' she asked, changing the subject.

"Splendidly! We've found supporters in the territory. Certain individuals have discovered they would benefit politically if Wyoming women had the vote. Of course the governor is against the notion, but the governor has many opponents who might like the opportunity for a showdown on an issue such as women's vote. We intend to make arrangements for a guide."

"A guide?" India questioned. "I see no need for a guide. I've come this far alone."

"Until now you have journeyed on the train. Wyoming is

the frontier. There are no trains or coaches to many of the settlements."

"Well, perhaps you're right. A traveling companion might be pleasant."

"I'm sure the tour will be a success. A pretty face will fill the halls faster and be more persuasive than a stuffed-shirt politician," Will assured her.

"But that's the problem. At times I wish I were a stuffed-shirt politician. I'd be taken much more seriously. Now, I'm just a genuine Wyoming Bluestocking. Soon Professor McDaniels will be signing me up to be in his museum of wonders."

Will laughed. "Be patient. Tomorrow night when you speak at the governor's welcome home banquet you'll have your opportunity to be more than a sideshow attraction." Will smiled.

"I hope so! I welcome the opportunity. Heaven knows we need the vote to right wrongs of laws made solely to benefit men." India flashed William a smile of camaraderie, took pencil in hand, and sat down at the copy desk with renewed enthusiasm.

Chapter 4

*W*eaving in and around the tables of the crowded saloon, the thick-waisted, bearded barkeep carried five crockery mugs of Professor McDaniels's famous Scotch ale in his large hands. A red-jacketed pet monkey jiggled on his shoulder. The barkeep plopped his load down before Gat Ransom, leaving him to slide the foaming mugs to each of his five companions seated around the table. Gat took a long refreshing gulp before speaking.

"You boys know the governor will never sign a bill to give women the vote. You're wastin' your time," Gat said.

Colonel Bill Bright took a handkerchief from his pocket to wipe the foam from his mustache. "Look at it this way. Such a measure would advertise the territory, attract women and bring commerce. If I'm elected to the legislature, I'll support the bill just because the governor is against it."

Ed Lee, the territorial secretary, sat directly across from Gat. He seconded Bright's argument enthusiastically. "A few of us are just itchin' to embarrass Campbell. He'd lose face if he went against the general sentiments of the legislature and vetoed a bill for women's enfranchisement."

"Sure he'd lose face, but he wouldn't sign it. I rode beside the man through the territory for months. He has his views and women votin' isn't one of them." Gat leaned back in his chair and turned toward Will Noble. "I like Campbell fine, but don't expect me to carry your cause to him. I'm out of his employ, and now that winter's over, I plan to go back to the Sweetwater for spring brandin'. Politickin' ain't in my plans.''

"Wouldn't you like to see women get the vote?" urged Will.

Gat gave a cynical half-laugh. "I've never given it much thought, and I ain't likely to persuade the governor to be sympathetic to the cause.''

"We don't want you to persuade the governor. We need you to help us in another way," Will Noble said. A fight broke out across the barroom and the men were momentarily distracted. A brass spittoon flew through the air above the table. Will took a moment to press home the idea. "You know, Wyoming isn't the safest place for a woman, particularly a woman alone.''

Gat wouldn't argue with that and nodded in agreement. Sipping from his mug he sensed something else was coming. The invitation for a drink had been more than a friendly gesture.

"We feel a need to gain more support throughout the territory for this measure before the legislature meets in November," Noble continued. "We thought if we sent someone throughout the territory on a speaking tour . . . someone who could enlighten and gain sympathy—"

"Wait a minute, Will. I'm not the man," Gat broke in with a chuckle.

"Hold it, Gat, don't misunderstand," interrupted Ed Lee. "We don't want you to be the one who gives the speeches. We just want you as escort, guide and bodyguard for the speaker.''

"Oh." Gat took off his hat with a show of relief. "Why me?"

"Well," began Noble, "you're experienced, you're unmarried, and"—he coughed slightly—"you're of good character.''

"That sounds like you, Will. You're unmarried and you have a good character," replied Gat with a glint in his dark eyes. Then again, Gat thought, when it comes to me, it all depends on what they mean by good character. He had a passable reputation in the things that counted, like good sense and judgment. Soldiering during the war had taught him to stand up against opposition until his duty was fulfilled, and he usually met and mastered most situations. But on bad days he could be as ornery, rough, insolent and quarrelsome as the next man. Nevertheless he wasn't stingy, everybody borrowed off him, and he hated counterfeit in anything. Did that qualify as good character?

"I would take the job if it weren't for certain complications, like the running of my newspaper, to name just one," Will said.

"Oh come on, Will, let's just tell him," interrupted Bright impatiently. "We want you to escort a *lady* around the territory."

"A lady? You boys serious?" Gat put his hat back on and gave a low whistle.

"We'll pay you. Name your price," said Bright. He nipped the end off a thin cigar and struck a match.

The sound of a piano from upstairs floated above the din of the barroom conversation. Gat listened thoughtfully to the familiar refrain, attempting to recall its name before he gave an answer. "Can you match what I'd make wranglin' through spring and fall?"

"Double it!" Bright pulled out his cowhide billfold and opened it. "It might seem extravagant to you, but I'm not alone in thinking Wyoming's future is worth the investment." He spread a fistful of greenbacks across the wood table. "This much now and a bonus if the governor signs the bill."

Gat picked up a fifty-dollar bill and studied the picture of Henry Clay on one side, and Lady Liberty holding a torch in her hand on the other. His mind was calculating what the money could buy. It was more than he could earn running cattle, but he wasn't sure he wanted to accompany some sour-faced old suffragette around the territory. "Can this lady ride a horse, or is she too decrepit?"

Bright looked over to Will Noble with a sly smile. "What would you say, Will? Do you think she is too decrepit?"

Going along with the jest, Will answered, "I think she can sit on a horse if we can fine one sturdy enough to hold her." The men circling Gat laughed loudly.

"Don't mind us," said Lee, grinning. "We forget that you haven't met Miss India Simms."

India Simms. Gat's eyes narrowed, his aspect suddenly sobered. He'd hardly forget *her*! "Sure, I've met Miss Simms." Then to Will, "In fact, escorting her around the territory might just test my good character." The boys all laughed again.

"The job starts right away," Will said.

"Right away, huh?" Gat was still mulling over India Simms. The memory of her in the bathroom, shocked and horrified, curved the corners of his firm mouth into a complacent smile. "Well, I hadn't planned on leaving Cheyenne again that soon. But from the way you describe it, the job might be a real vacation. It's hard for me to believe you boys would pay me this much money just to make sure that little gal doesn't go in the wrong direction. But I'm game." Gat reached for Bright's money and tucked it into his pocket. He pushed his chair away from the table. His eyes went slowly from one face to the next.

"See you tonight at the governor's welcome home dinner," Bright added. "Miss Simms is scheduled to give a short address after dinner."

"You ain't wastin' any time," Gat said with a smile. "The governor ought to like a speech on woman suffrage about as much as a calf likes a hot brandin' iron."

Bright exhaled a puff of smoke. "Maybe the governor will learn not to stay out of town so long next time."

"Maybe." Gat touched his hat in parting salute to his friends, inwardly meditating the possibilities of this new venture. As he turned away he heard Tom Douglass, who up until then had been silent, whisper to Bright, "Do you think its fair to Gat, askin' him to take on that she-male?"

"He took the money. He'll have to, won't he?" From

33

behind, Bright's words followed by a deep roll of laughter irritated Gat. But then, a woman was a woman, and Gat knew a little something about women. Sure he could handle her.

India put the finishing touch of a tortoiseshell comb into her upswept, plaited auburn hair, and turned to slip on the dress Yee Jim had spent the late afternoon hours pressing. The gown was India's favorite, since it had been her father's gift after his trip to the 1867 Paris exposition. The immensely full hyacinth-blue silk skirt was no less than twenty yards draped over a voluminous crinoline. The deeply cut neckline exposed her flawless shoulders, and the lace-sleeved bodice trimmed with blue satin bows celebrated the delicate contours of her arms. A bouquet of intermingling satin wildflowers embroidered the front inset, while fine lace ruching edged the neckline, which was teasingly immodest, revealing India's generous curve of bosom and a hint of cleavage.

Though he could well afford it, her father had refused to pay for her to attend college because he didn't believe women should be educated beyond their sphere in life. So she had taken her future into her own hands and financed her schooling herself. Now, the last of her trousseau treasures, the one item not sold off for her education, the gown, was her compromise with vanity.

There wasn't another such exquisitely made dress in all of Cheyenne, nor would anyone suppose that she, suffragette extraordinaire, would have the figure or flair to wear it. Quickly she added the last touch, the sash her sister had embroidered with "Votes For Women."

She pinched her cheeks to redness, picked up a tiny bottle of French *parfum,* and dabbed a few drops behind her ears and over her bare shoulders. Unfortunately, the fragrance revived in her mind the vision of Mr. Ransom in the bathroom. She could forgive him for pouring her precious store of bath salts all over his insect-infested body, but she'd never forgive his irresponsible behavior. She stepped back to view herself in the looking glass for final inspection and instead envisioned the rugged specter of Mr. Ransom. She tugged at the tiny sapphire earring on her right ear with apprehension. His imposing presence haunted not only her dreams but now, her mirror. She'd found his dangerous good looks disturbing, and for the first time in her life she found herself going all soft over a man. But no, she'd vowed never to marry, and that would be the beginning and end of it!

Taking a deep breath, she blinked his visage away and picked up the speech she had painstakingly prepared for the governor's welcome home reception, slipping the folded papers into her black-beaded, silk-tasseled handbag. A small knot formed in her stomach, and she felt a little dismayed knowing she wouldn't do justice to the roast beef supper which always seemed to be the fare for such occasions. Will Noble had offered to escort her to the hall and he was probably waiting down in the parlor that very minute. Draping her cashmere shawl over her shoulders, she hurried out the door.

The flow of male voices filtered up the stairway, and as India descended she saw Will and another man conversing in the parlor archway. Hearing the luxurious rustle of her cerise taffeta petticoat, they turned, both stopping in mid-sentence. Their eyes seemed to devour her every step downward.

"India, at last," began Will. "You look wonderful." His eyes lingered a moment before he turned to the man beside him. "Let me introduce you. Miss India Simms, Mr. Gat Ransom."

With the touch of Ransom's gaze a flush suffused her face and crept to the creamy skin of her shoulders. Without apparent embarrassment he smiled at her, a friendly smile that hit her somewhere in the pit of her stomach and spread round her chest with a suffocating sensation.

"We've met," India said curtly. Her appraising eyes swept over his shirt and leather vest down to his holstered hips to the toe tips of his hand-tooled boots. Though his face was clean-shaven, the scar made his appearance uncivilized and his curly-black hair still brushed his shoulders in the fashion worn by scouts and Indians. "At first I didn't recognize you. It must be the clothes."

Gat gave her an appreciative smile. "May I say your own getup is worth the view." Scarlet fired her cheeks as his deep-set eyes took in everything about her in a quick sweep. Then, with flattery that verged on insolence, he continued to study the entire length of her body, slowly and with decidedly lustful concentration. Even she, lost and unsure of herself where men were concerned, could not fail to interpret the desire in his smoldering, heathen black eyes. And for some queer reason which she didn't want to pinpoint, India suddenly wished she were as plain as paper.

"India, Gat will be your escort through the territory on your speaking tour," Will said.

The constriction in her chest gave way to heart-stopping anxiety and she had to make a special effort to keep her mouth closed. A perverse amusement marked every line of Mr. Ransom's face, but for her this disclosure was not a humorous surprise but a mortifying revelation. The vision of him in the bathtub came back full-blown in humiliating detail, stirring her with an intensity she'd never experienced before. How could he think it could all be wiped away by a nod of the head and a friendly "howdy do"?

"Why, I . . ." India searched for the proper words. "I thought you would choose someone . . . older . . . more experienced," she anxiously concluded. Her eyes moved over their faces, never resting on any point in particular.

"Ma'am, I'm experienced." His face was sincere but his eye held an elusive twinkle. "I don't claim to know it all, however; I'm wide open."

An unbelieving tremor ran through her and his audacious inference caused her already knotted stomach to twist one more time. If ever there was a man who wasn't born yesterday, it was Gat Ransom. Why couldn't Will have asked a man of the cloth, or a . . . No, she just wouldn't agree to travel with this Mr. Ransom and after dinner she would tell William!

"Well, with that settled, shall we go?" Will took India's arm and Gat moved to open the front hallway door.

Heddy rushed up the back hall from the kitchen waving a letter. "Gat, wait one minute. I'll forget if I don't give it to you now. My, my! Don't you look nice, darlin'," she complimented India as she pushed past her skirt. "I have a letter Miss Indy wrote for me to my son, Ty. When you go back to the Sweetwater, you read it to him. I want him to know his ma be thinkin' about him."

"Sure Heddy. I'll take it." Gat took the letter and tucked it into his coat pocket.

India moved toward the open door but found it somewhat difficult, because of the width of her skirt, to maneuver herself and to let Will through the door at the same time.

"After you," Will bowed and stepped back. India glided past, wondering if the Paris dressmakers ever took into consideration that not all of their hooped gowns would be worn through the wide corridors of Versailles. Once outside, the trio made their way to Will's buggy, but after an awkward tussle of hoop and skirt, there was hardly room for anyone inside besides India.

"She could drive herself over," Gat suggested with the wit of a folksy philosopher. "We could walk, Will."

"What a remarkable idea, Mr. Ransom," India said, smarting from the inconvenience her vanity was causing, yet irritated by Ransom's comment. "However, I believe there is just enough room for William." She pressed herself to one side of the buggy and smiled sweetly to Will.

Will welcomed the invitation. "Well, if that's fine with you, Gat, we'll see you over at the hall." Gat touched the brim of his hat in a salute of agreement, his black eyes on India. She pointedly avoided looking at him, and after clearing the path of hoop and skirt, Will climbed up beside her and flicked the horses into motion. Gat, followed by his faithful dog, Coyote, walked casually behind.

He kept a steady gaze on Miss Simms's profile as she turned to Will Noble's conversation. She was a beauty, porcelain-like skin, fine bones with features so symmetrical they seemed drawn on her face. Her blue eyes flashed wide with combativeness as if to say "Clear the tracks, I'm coming," "I will not compromise," "I will be heard!" Were she a man, she'd be a general. But she fairly wallowed in the shortsightedness of conviction without experience. During the war he'd been led into more than one foolhardy battle by fanatic temperaments like hers. It was clear to him her genteel upbringing had left her like a pruned hedge, but underneath he sensed a luxuriant growth of womanliness that could sate a man's thirst through a nighttime . . . maybe a lifetime. He'd never find out for sure.

Will and the boys had been fools to ask him to be her escort. He'd seen it in her face when Will broke the news to her. He reckoned she wouldn't let him guide her to the commode, let alone through the territory. It would have been a challenge to teach her that there was more to being a woman than getting the vote. He lifted his gaze to the evening sky and whistled away his disappointment.

"You can't imagine how I felt when that old Indian chief, decked out in blanket and war bonnet, got on the train and set himself and his dog opposite me. Why, I nearly fainted," Milicent Templeton splayed her fan across her breast. Her reddish curls jingled about her pretty face as she chattered animatedly, holding the people at the table in friendly attention. "At least back in Washington our Indians don't hang scalps on their waist in public. And let me tell you how he stared at my hair! He never took his heathen eyes off me."

"Did you ever think that he might have been staring at you because you looked equally strange to him?" asked Amee Bouvette, the actress and famous "Circassian Girl" who sat beside India at the dining table with her escort, Ed Lee.

Milicent cast the dark-haired beauty a glance which India thought befitted only annoying insects and slovenly servants. Certainly the hall was abuzz with comment while everyone wondered how a burlesque actress could manage an invitation to the governor's reception, but Milicent Templeton seemed to take personal insult at the "scandalous" way Ed Lee had walked in with the woman on his arm, paraded her through the hall, and sat her down at the governor's very own table. As for India, she saw no reason for condemnation. By now she was adjusting to western rustics and their aberrant behavior. Besides, she found Amee pleasant company.

Milicent put her hands to her pink cheeks and continued her hair-raising tale. "He pulled out a knife and started sharpening it. I had no doubt he intended to add my red hair to his collection."

"Why didn't you get up and move?" queried Amee, giving India a sly nudge.

India put her napkin to her mouth to hide a smile. Milicent Templeton had no idea she was being led. Her main intent was to impress Governor Campbell, and from where India sat, Milicent seemed to be doing an extraordinarily fine job of it. Campbell, a bachelor, attended to her story with the proper amount of admiration.

"I did attempt it, but every time I tried to move his dog would growl at me."

"Are you sure it was a dog?" Amee asked, fully aware that Miss Templeton found her company and interruptions distasteful.

"Of course I am sure," Milicent replied, irritated by the challenge. "I know what a dog looks like."

"Could it have been a wolf?" the dark-haired actress wondered.

"A *wolf*! My heavens, I was in more danger than I realized!"

India was certain that this new embellishment pleased Milicent and that by the time she arrived in Washington, her story would be more exciting than a dime novel adventure.

"So what finally happened?" the governor asked, adjusting his recently wounded arm in the sling, keeping his eyes on Milicent's charming face the whole time.

"Well, the Indian spoke to Kendrick. Didn't he, Kendrick?" She turned to her brother beside her.

"Yes, in quite clear English. He said, 'woman have fire in her hair. I like.' Then he pointed to my gold watch with his knife tip and said, 'I like, too.' Well, I took the hint and gave him my watch. Soon after, the old fellow stood up and left the train at the next stop."

Everyone at the table laughed.

"Why, that was nothing short of outright robbery!" Will Noble exclaimed, pushing his empty plate away and shaking his head.

"Yes indeed. But thank goodness for Kendrick's quick thinking, or I might not have my hair now." Milicent took her brother's hand and gave it a gentle squeeze. "A woman needs a man's protection." Her calf's eyes rested on Governor Campbell coquettishly.

"Perhaps, but who's to protect the woman from her protector?" India asked offhandedly, thinking of Sarah Bramshill. Laughter rang out again.

"I suppose you think once women get the vote they'll be able to take care of themselves," said Gat, his cynical gaze aimed directly at her.

Plucking at her earring she looked past him to the waiter. She'd suffered Ransom's gaze on her throughout the meal, and in her opinion, his attention bordered on rudeness. The back of her neck prickled and again she fought back the vision of him standing in the bathtub. The heat of the overcrowded hall emphasized the mounting tension between them and she felt moisture breaking out on her body, trickling down the hollow of her breasts and collecting in the damp strips of the ribs of her corset. Every time their eyes collided the tension grew worse and the hall's temperature raised to boiling point. She'd never been this nervous before giving a speech.

She refused to look at Ransom, but replied in Will's direction. "Many women already take care of themselves. Unfortunately, most professions men enjoy are closed to women—"

"For good reason!" Ransom interjected. "When push comes to shove, a woman's no match for a man!"

Before India could retort that all livelihoods weren't necessarily a matter of push and shove, she was interrupted.

"That isn't so!" Amee Bouvette affirmed in her accented voice. "I went on the stage out of necessity. My girlhood dream was to become a sea captain, like my father. I could have succeeded, but there is no way for a woman to enter that profession." She sighed.

"Why haven't you ever told me that?" Ed Lee turned to her with interest.

"Because, my champion of woman suffrage, you never asked. I suspect you are like most men, thinking that what is inside a woman's head is not half as interesting as what is outside." She flipped her long nails against his lapel in gentle chastisement.

Lee laughed self-consciously.

"Well, I agree with Mr. Ransom, women are different from men," Milicent announced firmly. "Holy Scripture establishes a different and higher sphere for women, apart from public life. Indeed, if we were given the right to vote, we might be expected to do things unsuited to our physical organizations."

"Certainly birthing fifteen children on a sod house floor is much less suited to our physical organizations than putting our opinion in a polling box," India retorted, perhaps a little too fervently. Her scorn for the Milicent Templetons of the world was searing. She felt justly angered that while toiling, reasoning women stayed home, a parasite like Milicent flirted with politicians at the capital, not caring a straw if women had equal rights.

"You broach the subject just at the right moment, Miss Simms," Ed Lee said as he glanced at his timepiece. He rose to his feet, picked up a spoon and clinked it several times against a crystal glass to gain the attention of the rest of the hall. Smiling at Governor Campbell, he said loudly, "I promised the governor an interesting after-dinner speech. I'd say the subject of woman suffrage is interesting." A ripple of laughter filtered through the hall. "Miss Simms, we await your address." He bowed slightly. India stood and moved to the podium.

The governor leaned to Ed Lee and Gat overheard him say, "You may be surprised, Ed, but I'm in sympathy with your cause." Ed gave Gat a brief look of surprise across the table. "However, my fear is that the right for women to vote will tend to disrupt the harmony of society, bring discord to the family and thus cause much greater evil than good."

Applause cut off any further exchange between the Governor and Lee, as India took the podium.

A female speaker was a genuine novelty and the hall, mostly male, waited with rapt attention. Along with the others, Gat pushed his chair back to see better, deciding Miss Simms in her fancy dress was easy on the eye, though he didn't like the way she'd plaited her shining chestnut hair into an aloof coronet on top of her head. It gave her the "don't touch me" look of a setting hen.

She shifted nervously, preparing herself, and Gat smiled as he noticed that at least on one base she was not in complete control. Her voice began in a pleasant lilt, but as far as he was concerned, the subject would put most of the audience to sleep, himself included. He thought if things got too deadly he'd go home early by way of the Red Dog Saloon.

"I have entitled my words, 'The Question of the Hour,' " she began, as her shaky fingers smoothed out her papers against the podium surface. "The unhappy war has settled two questions. First, that we are a nation and not a mere confederation of states. Second, that all 'persons' born or naturalized in the United States are 'citizens,' and stand equal before the law. The chief public question of the hour is the woman's claim to the ballot. The Federal Constitution, as it now stands, leaves this question an open one for the states to settle as they choose. Will the territory of Wyoming choose to give voting rights to those who have rights under the Constitution? I speak on behalf of the women of Wyoming—intelligent, virtuous, native-born American citizens, and yet they stand outside the pale of political recognition.

The Constitution classes them as 'free people,' and counts them whole persons in the basis of representation. Yet they are governed without consent, compelled to pay taxes without representation, and punished for violations of law without benefit of judge or juror. In this new era, in this new age of progress, should not the fairer sex receive the right of suffrage?''

Ransom listened attentively, surprised at her proficiency with words and graceful delivery, yet her sound arguments, eloquently drawn, would never persuade him to consider this cause. It was a man's world, always had been, and if she thought she could change that she might as well dance on the moon. A hint of wry humor touched him as he allowed his unkind assessments of her run wild. He still thought she was a little too uppity, even self-important. To his mind nobody was ever important enough to feel important. A tap on Gat's shoulder broke his undivided attention.

"Mr. Gat, Mr. Gat," came a distressed whisper. Yee Jim, huffing and perspiring, leaned toward Gat. "Heddy say tell you the *man* is loose."

Taken aback, Gat asked, "What man is loose?"

"Gamblin' B'amshill. He come, hot mad."

Gat didn't make the connection. "Why, his wife is gone—"

Two shots rang out, then a volley of shots. Around Gat, amid shrieks and gasps, people slid off their seats and dove to the floor. Everything came together when Gat saw Huntington Bramshill positioned in the doorway firing two Colt Lightnings at India Simms. Hell! She didn't even have the sense enough to take cover. Gat leaped past the governor, who was fanning the swooning Milicent Templeton with his good arm, and bounded toward the podium. He swept India hoop skirts and all over his shoulder and made for the rear exit. She screamed and pounded on his shoulders. Kicking her petticoats over his eyes, she nearly sent him headlong into the wall.

"Settle down, ma'am. Bramshill's on the warpath. I suppose you know why."

She didn't answer. But he felt her settle somewhat.

Once outside, he tossed her into the nearest buggy, whipped the horses into a run and headed them down the street to the train depot. Coyote ran in front barking, and Bramshill, pursued by a half-dozen men, ran behind shooting. The bullets zinged past their heads.

Well, Gat thought, Ed Lee had promised the governor an interesting after-dinner speech. But this was a little too interesting!

At the depot, steam clouded around the cowcatcher as the Union Pacific westbound evening train built up momentum to pull out.

"We're coming aboard," Gat called to the conductor who was waving a lantern signal of departure to the engineman.

India gasped. "Mr. Ransom! What do you think you are doing?" She clutched the sides of the buggy and looked about desperately for escape.

"Ma'am, I'm saving your life," Gat said, ignoring her resistance. He lifted his protesting baggage over his shoulder and up the steps of the passenger car. Accustomed to last-minute boardings, the conductor waved the engineman the go-ahead, swinging himself up on the caboose railings. With a shrill farewell blast, the Union Pacific locomotive pulled away from the Cheyenne depot.

Chapter 5

*W*hen Gat plopped India down on the leather seat it wasn't the curious stares of other passengers on the train that whipped India's agitation into full froth. Neither was it embarrassment for being the only woman on the day-coach decked out in complete ball-gown regalia. It was Ransom's blatant indifference as he tossed a coin to the train butch for a copy of the daily edition of the *Argus* that nearly unstrung India.

With a polite "Pardon ma'am," he pushed his long legs past her skirt, which filled the space between the seats and overflowed into the aisle, and took his seat and began reading the paper as if nothing out of ordinary had happened. That he could read was small comfort to India. His mangy dog jumped up on the seat beside him and watched her from cunning canine eyes while his master ignored her. The seconds ticked by. The three sat, newspaper dividing them, as silent as congregants at Sunday meeting.

India bit back her indignation while her mind ran in a hundred directions at once. How could he just pick her up and throw her on the train without notice? Whatever had possessed William Noble to think Ransom was a suitable escort?

"Mr. Ransom, don't you think you acted a bit hastily?" She might have taken a bite of lemon for the look upon her face, but since the paper blocked the view between them, Gat could not see.

"You're still breathing ain't you?" His voice floated up from behind the newspaper.

"Of course I'm still breathing. And had you not interfered, I would have found a peaceable means to settle the problem."

"Throwin' you on the train was peaceable. I'd say you're beholden to me. I've done you a favor." He turned a page. "Next time, mind your own business."

"But it was my business!" defended India. "His wife asked for my help, I gave it!"

"Out here a man values his possessions. Sometimes his woman is pretty high on the list."

"That medieval thinking is exactly the problem."

Gat put down the paper. He loosened his black string tie and unfastened the top buttons of his shirt, exposing the hollow of his throat. "What medieval thinking?"

"That a woman is a possession!" spouted India, quickly raising her eyes from his throat to his face, then to his hat. "If you believe that, you think behind the times. It might be a revelation to you, but we women have souls . . . and spirit!" The conductor coming through collecting tickets precluded Gat's answering her.

"Just me and the lady," he said to the conductor.

"If the dog sits on a seat you pay for it, cowboy." The conductor pushed back his cap and motioned to Coyote sitting next to Gat.

"All right," Gat said.

"How far?"

"Green River."

The conductor took Gat's money and fumbled in his money belt for change. "Next time buy yer tickets at the depot," he recommended.

"I second that!" murmured India as if she already had the vote. "It would be nice to have advance notice."

"You knew we were leaving tomorrow. What's a day earlier?"

46

"Mr. Ransom, I have no clothing other than what I am wearing." Luckily, she still had her handbag and a money reserve in the secret pocket in her pantalettes, or she would have been completely dependent upon Ransom.

"Out here we travel with what we can carry. I'd say you're wearing about all you can carry." With that sarcastic remark he put his nose back into the paper.

She glared at him for a moment, then despite her temper, India thought about his words and she began to consider her precarious position. To return to Cheyenne would put her speaking tour behind schedule. Yet she balked at the thought of staying with Ransom. There had to be a way out of her dilemma. While Ransom read the paper an idea popped into her mind as her eyes fell across the back page of the *Argus*. She bent nearer, her nose close to touching the page while she studied the Union Pacific train schedule in the lower left corner.

"Hell! What does Will think he's doing?" Ransom muttered from behind the paper. "He'll have every relative of Bitterman's in the territory after me, not to mention every hot drunk crony." He yanked the paper to his lap discovering India's face directly in front of him.

Suddenly finding herself nose to nose with Ransom, India jerked back. "Something bothering you about the journalistic quality of the *Argus*, Mr. Ransom?"

"Sure as hell is!" He shook the crease out of the paper and began to read aloud. " 'It was a close call for Governor Campbell but for the steady gun-hand of notorious body-guard and crack shot Gatlin Ransom in a recent showdown at Platte Waystation. Cut-Off Bitterman met his match when he dared to pull out his guns and point them at the governor. Ransom coolly stepped in, aimed for the heart and shot the black-hearted Bitterman dead.' "

"Isn't that what happened?"

"It sounds like a dime novel. It ain't like Will to lay it on thick at someone else's expense," said Ransom thoughtfully.

India cleared her throat uncomfortably. "William didn't write that piece. I did."

"You!" Ransom cast her a disgusted glance, tossed the paper aside and rose to his feet. India's cheeks colored from the obvious error she had committed.

When Ransom stepped into the aisle his spur caught on her dress. He bent down to untangle it, muttering under his breath all the while. "Listen, ma'am. There's plenty of space in Wyoming for foofaraw like this but it sure as hell ain't inside this train."

"Did I ask to be thrown on this train?" she retorted. Around them people turned to gawk. "Did I?" she said again in a tightly whispered challenge. He gave her dress a separating yank and ignored her question. He strode down the aisle. The dog looked at her a moment as if he had something insightful to add, but thinking better of it, he too jumped off the seat to follow Gat out of the car. Through the glass window of the door she could see Gat speaking with the conductor.

Humph! she thought. Well, whatever his business is had nothing to do with her. She had her own worries to attend to, starting with how to extricate herself from his company. She picked up the discarded paper and looked again at the train schedules. Her mind churned.

Suppose she got off the train at Laramie and just followed the engagements on the list William had given her? She toyed with the notion. Reaching her hand into her black-beaded silk handbag, which hung about her wrist, she took out the list. Green River, South Pass . . . well, she could ask for directions. She looked out the window into darkening twilight, tracing her lower lip thoughtfully with her forefinger.

"Lady, you want to buy a guidebook of Wyoming, only ten cents?" The blue-eyed, red-haired train butch, his pockets and person laden with sundry objects of sale, paused beside her seat. She reproachfully eyed his scuffed and muddied boots resting on the edge of her skirts. He stepped back and in anticipation of her refusal he launched into a passage recitation from the slim volume he held in his hand. "You are approaching Sherman Summit, the most elevated station on the Union Pacific and the highest in the world. 'Now, Sherman on the Rocky Mountain range, Eight thousand feet is raised toward the sky, Indian, Chinese, and many people strange, Are met or passed as o'er the earth you fly.' "

He gave her a disarming, wide, boyish grin. "Now, if you had this guide book you would know all the highlights of your railroad journey. Why, you could show all your folks at home where you'd been."

Convinced for reasons other than impressing the folks at home, India reached into her silk handbag and gave the boy ten cents.

"Thank you, ma'am," he said, and moved down the aisle hawking his wares to other travelers.

The train lugged and clanked as it came to a halt to take on water at the Sherman water tank. The conductor invited the passengers to stretch their legs, inhale the rarefied air, and enjoy the view before crossing Dale Creek bridge and heading down the mountains into Laramie.

India felt the draught of icy air when some of the passengers accepted his invitation to leave the railway car. She stayed put, wishing she still had her shawl to cover her bare shoulders. The end of her nose was numb with cold and she looked at the tiny black stove at the far end of the aisle, wondering when someone had last fueled its waning fire. Out the window, the last rays of sunset glistened over snow-capped peaks and granite-faced mountains. A shiver—from cold or the thought of being marooned in such a wilderness—swept over India's body. Where were the trees and the cultivated fields? She didn't like the openness of the West. It made her feel exposed and vulnerable.

A commotion broke out in the vestibule by the door when a suited man rushed inside holding a white handkerchief to his bleeding nose. His affliction, caused by the altitude, was taken calmly as the porter and other considerate passengers helped him to his seat. At their heels came Gatlin Ransom. India quickly turned her head with an abrupt dismissal.

He sat down and dropped a woolen blanket in her lap. "Why . . . " she faltered for polite words, but they seemed to stick in her throat. His gesture momentarily broke her resolution to be as indifferent to him as possible. She forced a tight smile, and he answered with that insolent gaze, the one that intimidated her and capsized her peace of mind. "Thank you." Begrudging his unexpected show of courtesy, she draped the warming blanket around her.

Nothing else was said between them. He tipped his hat over his eyes, settled back and made to take a nap. Coyote curled up on the seat beside him and did the same.

For want of any other pastime she watched him sway gently back and forth with the motion of the train as it clambered down the mountainside. His long legs in tight-fitting trousers looked strong and tireless—though his height was another thing she found intimidating about him. Nevertheless, she was determined to meet him on equal terms, even though the scar running down the left side of his face marked him as a man who would be taken on his own terms or no terms at all. The strong lines of his face seemed to be a signature attesting that he had discovered how to live with himself. His hot liquid eyes held a peculiar intensity of experience which with a single glance seemed to expose her completely.

His nose was nobly straight, his lips were sensually formed, even hedonistic, and in her opinion his long blue-black hair gave him the look of a renegade Indian. Admittedly, what she knew about men couldn't fill a thimble, but perhaps it was time she studied the habits of the Oppressor. In Ransom she saw it firsthand: muscled and bone-hard, broad-chested and all male arrogance. Undeniably, his masculine power fascinated her, but while this power was exciting, she could see how a man could use it to break a woman's will. It made her afraid—not of him, but of her thoughts when she was around him.

It would be disastrous for her to stay with him, better to follow her plan of slipping away from him at the Laramie depot, using a plea to attend the lady's convenience or some such other ploy. Now that she had a guide book, she could travel on her own. She would wire William Noble. He would have to be told, for she had promised him installment articles for the paper detailing her speaking tour.

The porter came through the car with a little stepladder in one hand and a match in the other and climbed up to light the lamps in their reflectors. "We are crossing Dale Creek bridge. Next stop, Laramie." He said mechanically as he exited the car.

Ransom still dozed. India felt the change of vibration as the train clipped over the matchstick-like trestle of the bridge. She was glad it wasn't daylight, for she knew she would suffer an attack of vertigo if she dared to look down the hundred-thirty-foot drop. The description in her newly acquired guide book was view enough for her. A trifle anxious, she tapped her long nails on the book's binding and kept glancing over at Ransom, wondering how much longer he would sleep. Across the aisle a golden-braided immigrant child clutched a leashed tabby cat tightly on her lap while her mother nursed a baby. The father, dressed in a black wool cap, embroidered shirt and sheepskin vest, sharpened his knife on a whetstone. He looked young to India, perhaps eighteen. His wife appeared even younger. India caught the eye of the little girl and smiled. In return she received a wide-eyed stare.

Sometime later, the train's whistle announced its approach to Laramie, nudging India to alertness. Ransom still dozed. Deciding to make her move quickly, India cautiously slipped the blanket from her shoulders, gathered up her skirts and moved past the sleeping Ransom down the aisle. She ducked inside the curtained convenience in the vestibule by the rear door. Nearly losing her balance when the train shifted to a lumbering halt, India grabbed the curtains to steady herself. With a furtive peek between the curtains, she slipped out and touched her hand to the door handle, hastily making her departure.

Suddenly, when she went to move down the iron steps of the rear platform, a long arm reached out of the darkness and barred her way.

"Ma'am, this ain't our stop," Ransom said, as courteous as the conductor himself.

"Mr. Ransom, it is *my* stop," she stated firmly. "If you're through intimidating me with your show of manly strength, kindly step aside."

Their eyes held.

Deep inside India's body, tremors began shaking her resolve. It wasn't easy to stare down a man more than a foot taller than yourself; a man with a Colt revolver slung on his hip and censure simmering in his black eyes. But the real threat came the instant his eyes shifted to her lips and his expression changed, slashing the bastion of her zeal. Her chest rose and fell in an uneasy rhythm and in an unruly act of betrayal her own eyes riveted to his lips. Twin scimitars curled the edges of his mouth in that slow insolent grin. He dropped his arm and stepped back.

"I suppose you're planning to take your little tour without my company?" His voice was casual, though he was fully aware of what he'd just done to her.

"Yes, I am." She swallowed, not encouraged by her small victory, for it was a case of winning the battle yet losing the war. Though it was a cool night, she felt like fanning herself. "I have no need of a guide." She raised the guidebook in her hand to his view and began fanning. "I will rely on this for my information."

"Well, you seem to be a know-it-all. I won't force you—not ever."

India ignored his impudent remark about being a know-it-all, but the "not ever" was another threat. Damn his arrogance! She took a confident step forward, though inside she was all mush and bluff.

"The ticket agent here is a friend of mine," began Gat. "Maybe he'd suggest a decent hotel for you to stay in tonight. I'll walk inside with you and introduce you. I'm aimin' to take the train on down the line, now I've lost my job." Gat fell in beside her as she lifted her skirts and moved to the depot building.

As India realized she had taken his job away, she felt a little guilty. "I hope you understand, sir."

"No ma'am, I don't understand. It just ain't good horse sense to take off on your own in country like this. Sure, ladies do it, but not often. Male protection might sound a bit *medieval*— he rolled the word a bit mockingly across his lips "—to a modern female like yourself, but a stroll out here is a sight more dangerous than in the genteel park of Boston Common."

"I agree," she parried, "and especially as long as you cowboys use 'horse sense' to make your judgments, I expect it will remain dangerous."

Sassy! He'd never met a woman so smart and sassy, Gat thought with aggravation. He opened the door for her and they walked inside the depot.

"Tommy," he called out to a black-capped and vested man behind the ticket desk. The man looked up from his paper work and gave a nod of recognition.

"Gat Ransom. You old bull-thrower," Tommy said, smiling as he stamped a ticket and pushed it into a waiting man's hand. "What brings you through Laramie?"

Gat pushed back his hat and looked over at India. "I'm not staying, but let me introduce you to—"

"India Simms" interjected India. She offered Tommy her hand. Tommy grinned like a half moon and instead of shaking her hand, he kissed it.

Gat cleared his throat. "Miss Simms, meet Tommy Cahoon. Tommy here is quite the legend in these parts."

"Whatever for?" India had pulled her hand back. To her thinking, hand-kissing was a form of condescension. But she couldn't condemn Tommy for his sorry attempt at gallantry, since she knew her own inappropriate dress had provoked it.

"I've got the durndest haircut in the territory, that's why, ma'am. A few months back I was fishing up on Cheyenne Creek, only three miles from here. Some Injuns pounced on me and took a scalp lock from my head. Shot me full of arrows. I crawled back to town."

India gave Tommy an amazed look.

He laughed, "If you ain't believin' me, just take a gander at this, purdy lady, and let it be a lesson to ya." He doffed his hat, showing India an oval depression seven inches long in the back part of his skull.

India swallowed hard and turned her eyes back to Ransom nervously. "That happened within three miles of town?"

"Yes, ma'am!" Tommy returned from behind the counter.

The tale had a marked effect on India. Outside, the train was building up steam. She heard the conductor's "all aboard" call.

"I've got to catch the train, Tommy. Would you see that Miss Simms finds a good hotel for the night?" To India, he almost sounded eager to unload her on Tommy.

"I sure will. You take care, Gat. Next time stay for a drink."

Gat turned away and took long strides to the door, then he hesitated as if he'd forgotten something. "Ah, Miss Simms, you still have that derringer I lent you a few nights ago?"

India shook her head slowly. "Why no, I don't. I'm sorry if you wanted it back but—"

"Oh I didn't want it back for me. I just thought, since you were going to be on your own now, you might need it." He put his hand on the door. "Good evening and good luck ma'am."

India tugged on her earring and watched him disappear through the doorway. She looked over at Tommy Cahoon, then back to the door. In her mind a small voice cautioned, *Aren't you being hasty? What if something did happen to you? Your voice on behalf of suffrage might never be heard.*

Yes, she thought, what good could she accomplish if she

were dead in some ravine, shot by Indians or outlaws? Her attraction for Ransom shouldn't impede an important thing like women's suffrage. She should have suspected something when Ransom backed off and brought her inside the depot. But he made his point. As for the other consideration, she was determined to handle Ransom.

She lifted up her skirts. "Mr. Cahoon, I think I'll continue with Mr. Ransom on the train, after all." She fled out the door, barely making the jump to the iron steps of the slow-moving rear platform of the car.

Gat merely touched the tip of his hat when India returned to her seat. She arranged her flounces around her the best she could and wrapped the blanket about her shoulders. Settled in, she felt obliged to explain her return to Ransom. However, the smug look on his face caused her explanations to die before they crossed her lips. Why state the obvious to someone who apparently knew all the answers, she thought with irritation. Nothing in the arrangement warranted congeniality. And by his manner, Ransom didn't relish his escort job anymore than she liked being escorted. In cool dismissal her eyes went to the window to gaze out on the moonlit endless sweep of sagebrush and greasewood of the Wyoming desert landscape.

After a time Ransom pulled out a tobacco pouch from his pocket, bit off a piece and began chewing. India counted tobacco chewing the height of crudity and felt inwardly revolted. To further dampen the fire of ardor flaming within her breast, she decided to pass the time by taking a mental inventory of Ransom's vices. Tobacco chewing, insolence, arrogance, guile—yes, that little episode back at the Laramie depot was certainly conjured up by someone with guile.

He turned his head to spit into a nearby cuspidor.

India frowned in censure. "Would your mother approve of such a habit?"

"I couldn't say. She died when I was ten."

"Oh," said India softly. Well, she thought, perhaps misfortune could explain his ill-bred characteristics—but not all of them.

"Let me take a look at that book that almost cost me my job." Gat reached out his hand. India fetched it from the folds of her skirt. Ransom's fingers brushed hers as he took it, purposely she thought.

The moments passed. Ransom read through the slim volume. Every so often, he chuckled and shook his head. Finally he turned his eyes on India. "I don't think the fellow who wrote this guidebook has ever been in Wyoming." He snapped it shut and returned it with a laugh.

Talk about know-it-alls! India mentally put another black check beside arrogance in her mental inventory of his shortcomings and snatched back the book.

The peaceful atmosphere of the railway car had changed with the boarding of passengers in Laramie. Clouds of tobacco smoke rose to the ceiling of the coach as a group of grisly looking men, revolvers stuck in their belts, huddled together in a game of three-card monte. In their midst sat a fat, red-nosed gambler resplendent in his knee-length, black broadcloth coat and ruffled white shirt. His card-shuffling fingers sported sparkling gold and diamond rings. His style, or lack of it, was fascinating to India. Her eyes went from the seasoned face of a long-booted miner to the unshaven innocence of the immigrant father who had joined their midst.

The slick-voiced gambler spoke loudly to the group of spectators congregated around him. "Here you are, gentlemen; this ace of hearts is the winning card. Watch it closely. Follow it with your eyes as I shuffle." His agile fingers deftly manipulated three cards in and around on the shiny wood lapboard until one could go cross-eyed watching. "Here it is, and now here, now here, and now—where? It is my trade, gentlemen, to move my hands quicker than your eyes. I have two chances to your one." He pointed to the card in the middle of the trio. "The ace of hearts. If your sight is quick enough, you beat me and I pay; if not, I take your money. Who will bet?"

"I'll go 'er," said a shaggy-haired slouch dressed in buckskin.

The gambler shuffled and laid out the three cards. "Choose the baby, friend."

The man pointed and a rumble of surprise filtered through the group for he had chosen right.

The gambler seemed angry. "Luck only, my friend. Fifty says you can't do it again."

"Yer on, mister."

The gambler shuffled and with sleight of hand reshuffled the cards.

The miner's hand hovered over the three cards and then pointed to the one on his right.

"Right again," the gambler said, frowning and reshuffling his cards.

India stretched her neck to see better.

"If you're thinkin' of joinin' in, there's a one-eyed man in the game. He and the gambler are in cahoots," said Ransom.

India pulled back as if embarrassed to be caught watching. "I'm quite aware of the evils of gambling, sir."

"The only ones who'll win tonight are the gambler and his partner," said Ransom.

For some time they watched and listened to the gamblers. The young immigrant consistently bet and lost. India couldn't help but see an anxious look on the face of his wife. Apparently out of money, he finally came back and sat beside her. Between them passed a flow of unintelligible words. India averted her eyes when she saw tears begin to fall over the wife's cheeks. She wondered how much he had lost. Perhaps all the money they had. Not much by the gambler's standards, but the money could mean the difference between survival and destitution for the young family. India looked at the little girl and the baby sleeping in its mother's arms, then back to the hard-eyed gambler.

Suddenly she swept up her skirts and came to her feet. With a reserved curiosity she moved the few steps up the

aisle, a ready smile upon her lips as she excused herself past the outer spectators and moved into the center of the action.

"May I play?" she asked shyly. Gat sat forward on his seat's edge and rolled his eyes heavenward in disbelief.

"Why ma'am," warned a voice from the group. "You're no match for these card sharks."

India flashed a brilliant smile. "The saying goes that you can't tell how far a frog can jump by looking at him." Everyone, except Ransom, laughed. "Gentlemen?" she tilted her head slightly and fluttered her lashes over her sparkling sapphire eyes, waiting for one to offer her his seat. Three jumped up at once, bumping into one another for the opportunity. "I have but two requests of all of you," her smiling eyes roved over their gawking faces as she seated herself across from the gambler. "For the moment be so kind as to refrain from swearing and spitting." Here she raised a fine winged brow and shot Ransom a pointed side-long glance. He met her hint with an insolent turn of the head and a sideways spit into the nearby spittoon. He seemed intent on annoying her.

"Ready to try your luck, ma'am?" The gambler's invitation took her attention. He smiled avariciously, revealing a row of gold front teeth. He might just let her win once. It would be good for business.

"Oh, yes. But I haven't much money. Might I begin with a five-dollar stake instead of twenty?" She reached into her black silk handbag and drew out her money as if it were a widow's mite.

"Well, just for you, ma'am." He lowered his gaze to three cards, two sixes and an ace of hearts. "Just follow the baby with your eyes and when I'm finished shuffling, you point to it." He began shuffling so slowly that even a child could pick out the ace of hearts in the end.

A few snickers from the background told India she was being indulged, a fact of which she was already aware.

"Make your choice, ma'am." The gambler put a hand on each side of the three-card fan in front of him.

"You mean, pick my poison," India replied glibly, much

to the amusement of the surrounding spectators. She knew which card was the ace, as did every other person watching who sported at least one eye. When she pointed to the card on her left, groans sounded even before the gambler turned up the card to prove the error of her choice.

"Sorry, ma'am," consoled the gambler, probably wondering how she could be so dumb not to see the obvious. "Another round?" he asked, having no twinge of conscience whatsoever.

"Why, I . . ." she looked hesitantly at the last five dollars in her purse. "I . . ." she lingered on the word, keeping the men in suspense. "Yes, I will!" She put her money on the table with enthusiasm.

The gambler shuffled his cards, this time not so slowly, but slow enough for the experienced eye to keep track of the ace. "Ma'am, you pick."

India nibbled her red lips thoughtfully, pointing to one, then the other.

A man leaned over her shoulder. "That ain't the one," he advised, and pointed to a different card.

India turned her head to him. "Sir, I make the bets with my money. You make them with yours." Everyone broke out in whoops of laughter at the little lady's spunk.

Finally she made her choice. The right choice. The group, naturally on her side, gave a disorganized cheer. "I think I'll try again," she announced, putting down the ten dollars she had won.

"Ma'am, you bet," agreed the gambler, shuffling his cards once again with practiced sleight of hand. India's eyes followed. She hesitated, then she made her winning choice.

"Twice in a row," she beamed. "It must be beginner's luck."

As the moments passed she won each game and doubled her bets each time until she had won nearly two hundred dollars from the gambler. It appeared to India that his earlier cordiality had vanished when he realized she was no novice at three-card monte. He caught the eye of his partner and gave a narrowing wink of his own. India did not miss the

signal between the men. She knew that this time the man would use a holdout card from up his sleeve or some such trick.

"I think this time I'll bet it all. How do you say it? Double or nothing?" The reddish nose of the gambler seemed to brighten at this announcement. India stacked all her bills neatly before her. As the gambler began his shuffle, her eyes took in every detail of his swiftly shuffling fingers.

A breathless silence pervaded the railway car. India pondered over her choice. Over her shoulder men watched intently as her delicate fingers moved first to one card then to another. At last in a swift movement she turned over the two cards on either side exposing two sixes. "You, sir, cannot deny I have won again for the turned down card in the middle must be the ace of hearts."

The gambler paled, knowing the women had bested him. He could not turn over the card to show the face of another six. Instead he quickly picked up his cards and shuffled them back into his deck. Needing the bracing influence of liquor, he took a whiskey-filled silver flagon out of his coat pocket. "Another round, ma'am?" This offer wasn't enthusiastic.

Before India could answer, Gat Ransom had moved to her side and had taken her arm in his. "I'm sorry, but the lady's stop is comin' up. If you'll excuse us, gentlemen." He pulled her to her feet and navigated her through the admiring faces and down the aisle as the train slowed.

"Mr. Ransom, I was not quite finished with the game," she protested quietly while he guided her along.

"Take my advice. Quit while you're ahead. Besides, your beginner's luck was bound to run out."

"Beginner's luck had nothing to do with it." She stopped short with indignant air. "No matter what you may think. I am a college-educated woman and I am not as naive as you think."

Ransom muttered under his breath. "Thank heaven for small mercies. Come on, ma'am. Let's get off before that gambler and his partner decide they want their money back."

"One moment, sir." India picked up her guidebook. She split the roll of bills in her hand and put half in her handbag and looked over her shoulder at the immigrant family. Her eyes met the young woman's and she reached an admiring hand to touch the baby's face and deftly tucked the roll of money in the swaddling shawl. "Good luck." She smiled, kissed the apple-red cheek of the golden-haired child and turned to follow Ransom out the railway car.

Chapter 6

*T*he whistle echoed and the Union Pacific journeyed westward into the night. Bathed in moonlight, the towering sandstone buttes surrounding Green River station looked like battle-eroded ruins of ancient fortresses. Above the crumbling peaks, from one horizon to the next, stars spread out in a tapestry of constellations. India stood on the platform in what was no doubt a lawless railway town. Here they were, in the middle of the night, without bed or board. A fine escort he is! she thought mutinously. Barring Indians and outlaws, she would have done better on her own after all.

Feeling abandoned in a wild, eerie land, she shivered against the nip of the night air, and looked at Ransom reproachfully. Maybe he read the message of reproach in her eyes, maybe he didn't. Shaking out the blanket he took the liberty of wrapping it around India and in a gesture of gentle consolation, as if to say, "everything will be fine," his large hands briefly rested on the curve of her shoulders. A shiver of a different sort trembled through her, and despite her own ill humor, India no longer felt abandoned. In truth, her regard for him rose a notch and she began to understand why Will Noble chose this recalcitrant but self-reliant man to escort her.

In an agreeable voice he broke the silence. "I guess we'll need a place to bed down."

Losing some of her combativeness India said, "I should confess at the beginning that I will not suffer filth. I would sooner not sleep than lie in a bug-infested bed."

Gat pushed his hat back and scratched his temple as if he would be hard pressed to find a place clean enough to meet her high standards. "Well, the cleanest place in town is a"—Gat cleared his throat slightly—"a ladies' boardinghouse. This late at night we'll have to walk, but it isn't far."

"You lead, me follow, O scout-of-many-trails," India replied, too exhausted to be anything but obedient. Gat gave a half laugh and shook his head. In the darkness, wrapped in the red-and-black-striped wool blanket, she might have been mistaken for an Indian if it weren't for that ungainly puff of bustle and skirts around her hips.

"Where did you pick up that line?" he asked as he put his hand on her elbow to help her down off the rail depot platform to the street.

"A dime novel," she replied. "All the young ladies at finishing school read them."

"I'm not surprised. But let me tell you now, Miss India Simms, life out here is a lot different than in dime novels."

"I already know that."

"Let's hope you do, ma'am," he replied rather doubtfully. He gave Coyote a whistled command to follow them down the street. "I'll try and make our travels together as easy on you as possible. We'll stay here in Green River tonight and then set out for South Pass in the morning. I'll get supplies at the mercantile. You can put anything you need on a list for me. I'm trusting you to be sensible about it. We won't have much room, unless you want to take along an extra pack animal for that damn ball dress."

India drew up defensively, "Might I point out, Mr. Ransom, it isn't my fault I'm out in the wilds of Wyoming in a ball gown."

Ignoring her remark, he asked, "I suppose you can sit a horse?"

She prickled at his tone. "We have horses in the East too." She omitted telling him she'd never ridden one. Now, she knew out of necessity she would have to learn. She was confident that after a few days in the saddle, if she put her mind to it, she would be an expert.

The lamps along the street were few and far between. India felt uneasy walking past saloons still bright with late night activity. Plenty of loungers hung around the doorways. Glittering-eyed Mexicans, savage-looking miners, high-booted and shaggy-haired roughs, and an occasional boy in blue from nearby Fort Bridger—all watched them narrowly as they walked by. India wondered why the boardinghouse was not more convenient to the center of town.

Once, Ransom lifted her into his arms and carried her over a mud hole spanning the width of the street. She had no choice but to wrap her arms about his shoulders. She thanked him politely, but he returned with a curt, "It's my job, ma'am."

His reply bothered her almost as much as his nearness. She didn't want him to look upon her as a burden. If he showed her a courtesy she hoped he was doing it out of genuine respect, not because he was being paid for it. Maybe she was expecting too much. Their arrangement had gotten off on the wrong foot and now she wanted to make amends. If they were to be traveling companions, she wanted their relationship to be amicable, not strained.

When at last they arrived at the boardinghouse, India was surprised at its stylish appearance. A gingerbread-trim veranda circled the front of a twin-turreted frame building. Across the porch hung a neatly scrolled sign, *Contessa's Boardinghouse For Young Ladies*. As they moved up the stairs, India thought it a bit odd that all the windows radiated lamplight so late at night, and that so many horses were tied to the hitching posts outside. When Gat pulled the door ringer—a gadget she hadn't seen since leaving home— a white-aproned, black-smocked, almond-eyed Oriental girl opened the door. India's attention quickly shifted to the entryway within.

"You come in, please," bowed the girl. Her eyes did not lower with the bow, but rested on India curiously.

"Will you tell Contessa Gat Ransom would like to see her?" Ransom took off his hat and hung it on the nearby hat rack. India noted it was filled with a variety of other hats, all men's.

The little maid glided over to one of the sets of sliding wood-paneled doors that exited off the entryway, and slipped through. A whiff of tobacco smoke drifted past India's nose and she heard male voices filter out from the room. Waiting silently, she curiously studied a relief of painted cattails on the wall in front of her and marveled at the thickness of an oriental rug covering the polished wood floor. Her eyes went up the narrow, walnut-banistered staircase which led to the second level. Just as she turned to remark to Ransom on the quality of the furnishings, a handsome, curvaceous woman opened a paneled door and stepped into the entryway.

"Why, Gatlin," she began with a soft-lipped grin. "I've never had anyone bring a young lady of their own before!" She picked up the train of an elegant, mauve silk dress and moved over to give Ransom a warm embrace.

At that very moment the picture cleared for India and she realized this was a young ladies' boardinghouse of sorts, but not the sort she wanted to stay in. How dare he bring her to a place like this! She felt exhausted, rumpled and dirty, and the only thing that was holding her together was her corset, and it dug into her left hipbone.

"Contessa, I'd like to present Miss Simms," Gat began, ignoring India's wide-eyed glare. "We've come in on the late train and I wondered if you could put us up for the night."

Contessa gave India the once over. "Well, she certainly is dressed for it." India realized with chagrin that her own dress was more brazen than the high-necked, laced-inset silk of Contessa's. She was of India's own height and hair coloring and her movements were marked by grace and refinement.

Flustered, India remained silent. She didn't trust herself

to speak, for whatever could she say that wouldn't border on rudeness?

"I'm escorting Miss Simms through the territory. She is on a speaking tour for woman suffrage," Gat said.

"A suffragette. My goodness, Gatlin, you are certainly improving the company you keep." She moved toward India and slipped her arm inside India's. "Come along, you will be my honored guest. I'm a firm supporter of the vote for women. In fact, the motto of your Victoria Woodhull is my own: 'women must be free to vote, free to work and free to love.'"

The "free to love" unnerved India. Of course, the radical Victoria Woodhull's philosophy advocating free love was not her own. Despite this, India remained in awe at finding a woman who knew something about suffrage. Distracted by this she slowly relaxed her moral indignation and warmed to Contessa's animated welcome.

"In the morning, after business hours, I'll have you address my girls. Now, I'll show you where you can wash up and sleep." She turned to Ransom. A warm invitation glowed from her brown eyes. "Gatlin, please feel welcome in the dining room."

"Thank you, ma'am."

India saw he needed no direction to the door which led into the dining room. Her own curiosity caused her to crane her neck through the opening, but she saw only a sideboard filled with silver warming pans and a long, linen-spread dining table. The scenes of depravity which she expected to discover inside such a house were nowhere evident.

"Tell me, Miss Simms, what has prompted you to undertake the crusade of women's suffrage in Wyoming of all places?" She led India through a door and up a back stairway.

"Ah . . . a . . ." A rare occasion, but India was momentarily at a loss for words. "It seems there are some who feel if women had the vote, the territory would attract more settlement." She heard the clank of pans and dishes coming from the kitchen.

They passed down a hall and Contessa paused in front of a closed door, took out a ring of keys from her pocket and unlocked it. "I'd like you to use my own private room."

"Oh, but you are too kind," India began to protest. "I really don't want to cause any inconvenience."

"Don't worry. You're my guest. It is rare to find a woman of my own philosophies. I suppose that's why Gatlin brought you here. He knew we would get along famously."

India followed her through the door and into an extravagantly decorated bedchamber. She had never seen anything quite like it in the West. A canopied bed draped with handworked lace curtains and covered with a soft, rose, silken spread was the room's focal point. India quickly averted her eyes from the bed and looked at the rose-papered walls. Paintings, not of scantily draped women in lewd poses but of pastoral scenes of sheep grazing in green valleys and wild fowl in flight at sunset, hung tastefully on the walls. A nickel-plated parlor stove stood in one corner, filling the room with radiating warmth.

"Feel free to use anything you need." Contessa went to a carved pine wardrobe, opened it, took out a lace-beribboned dressing gown of the same rosy hues of the room, and laid it upon a brocade love seat. "I'll send one of the girls up with hot water if you'd like to wash."

"Thank you so much, Contessa." The name felt awkward on her lips. And, as if a scarlet letter would suddenly emblazon itself on Contessa's bosom, India watched her sweep up the lace train and leave the room.

"Until the morning," she smiled, and closed the door behind her, the scent of expensive perfume hovering in the room.

Continuing to avoid looking at the bed, India turned in a slow circle and inspected the room more closely. A beautiful, glass-orbed, brass lamp sat upon a nightstand, illuminating the room with a soft, glowing light. Hand-painted bouquets of roses fanned the panels of a dressing screen, the room's one concession to privacy. A large rolltop desk, filled with ledgers and neatly stacked papers, sat against one wall next to a floor-to-ceiling bookcase. She stepped closer to examine the books, finding Gibbons's *Decline and Fall of the Roman Empire* and Plutarch's *Lives*. How curious to make such discoveries in a Wyoming brothel! Indeed, she and Contessa had more in common than she might imagine.

She turned away, remembering the list of necessities Ransom had asked her for. At the desk, she took the pen from the inkwell, and on a sheet of paper began to make her list: traveling dress and bonnet, soap, hairbrush. She assumed Ransom would provide the food and other supplies. Her personal needs were few. Lastly, she wrote down "one ledger with ink and pen." She intended on circulating a petition wherever she went, and presenting its signatures to the governor at the conclusion of her tour.

She returned the pen to the inkwell, noting the neatness of the desk and the accounting ledgers. Contessa apparently was a good woman of business. Certainly the furnished elegance of her "boardinghouse" attested to this fact. Putting prejudices aside, India admitted there were few legitimate businesses in which a woman could become successful and self-supporting. Perhaps if women had the vote and the right to own property they would not be forced into such occupations. Eventually, many left the profession through marriage, but unfortunately, too many others left by morphine overdose. What woman would choose a life of prostitution if she had other options?

A knock at the door drew India's attention. "Please come in," she called. The door opened and a youthful blond girl carried a large cast-iron kettle of hot water. She crossed the room and sat it on top of the parlor stove.

"Contessa asked me to bring you some hot water. I'm Lady Jane." She offered a friendly smile, and then promptly sneezed. "Oh, excuse me, I—" She sneezed again. "I have a fearsome cold. I've been excused from work for the evening."

"I'm glad to meet you, Lady Jane. I'm India Simms." She smiled with unease to the bathrobed girl.

"Contessa said I was to help you with anything you needed." She blew her nose into a cotton hankie.

"How very kind of you, but I think I can manage," India returned.

"You sure I can't help undo your lacings or something?" The girl's voice had the ring of cockney English.

"Why, if you'd like," agreed India, warming to the girl. "I could use help with my gown."

"Oh, it's a pretty one." Lady Jane stepped behind India and began unlacing. Soon India stepped out of the hoop and petticoats.

"Are you from England, Lady Jane?" With hands on her hips, India steadied herself while the girl's fingers worked at the tedious lacings of her corset.

"How did you guess?" Lady Jane laughed. "I was born there, but me and me mother emigrated. You see, me father was a wealthy lord of the realm, and me mother was a housemaid. So you see, I have a claim to gentry. Me and Contessa." She laughed again.

"Well, I think the name 'Lady Jane' is lovely." India slipped out of her corset with a deep sigh of release, glad to be free of it. She stood in her camisole and cream silk pantalettes.

"Well, it's good for business. Before I came to Contessa's, I called meself Red Stockings. She suggested I change me name to Lady Jane. The men are more polite when they think I'm a genteel lady come on hard times. I guess if I marry I'll have to change me name again."

"Not necessarily," replied India. "By keeping your own name you have some measure of independence from your husband. It's very popular in the East among high-minded women to add their husband's name onto their own."

Lady Jane began to giggle. "I'd never find a man who'd marry me if I held such a notion. 'Folks,' he'd have to say, 'meet me wife, Lady Jane Red Stockings.' " India had to laugh herself.

"Well, perhaps you are right," India yielded.

While they spoke, Lady Jane's fingers traveled over the

intricate tatting and satin-flowered embroidery of India's dress. "You and I are about the same measure. Could I try on your dress?"

"Why, of course you may," India declared when she saw how Lady Jane admired it. "You know, it's direct from Paris." In a reciprocal gesture, India helped her on with the dress and began tightening the lacings. All the while her curiosity was piqued over Lady Jane's occupation. "Have you been here at Contessa's very long?"

"Oh, not too long."

"Have you ever thought of doing something else?" India wondered what sorry circumstance had brought the young girl into such a life.

"Yes, all the time. Me mother did laundry but I don't much care for that."

"Perhaps you could go to school. A bright girl like you could become a teacher."

"Oh, I left school. After the schoolmaster jumped me in the cloakroom I figured I'd learned more than I needed to know." She giggled and twirled around in the center of the room, all the while keeping an eye on her reflection in the full-length, brass-encased looking glass.

India was taken aback, and sympathy filled her heart for the young girl. How truly sheltered her own life had been. She realized that circumstance rather than weakness of character could lead a woman into a life of immorality. "Lady Jane, aren't you afraid you'll . . ." she hesitated to say it.

"Get in a family way?" Lady Jane supplied easily. "Oh, Miss Simms! You having a dress from Paris must surely know about the 'French Secret.' "

"The 'French Secret,' " she echoed uncertainly, then seeing that Lady Jane was looking at her oddly, she realized the girl would think she was naive. "Oh, yes. I'd forgotten about the 'French Secret.' "

"I guess you not being in my line of work you wouldn't be concerned about such things anyway. Why, sometimes a cowboy comes along I can really like and then it can be just as much pleasurin' for me as him.''

India disguised her shock by hanging up a petticoat in the wardrobe. The very idea was unthinkable, though she wouldn't deny that Gat Ransom's strong hands touching her shoulders as he'd wrapped the blanket around her at the train depot and the warmth that had sparked through her then had been pleasurable. When he'd carried her in his arms across the muddy street she'd felt a tingling of sensation from being next to him, held close in his arms. Was that the pleasure Lady Jane was talking about? The same mysterious pleasures that her companions at school giggled over and poets wrote odes to?

"You don't know how it really is, do you?" Lady Jane said. India lowered her eyes self-consciously, for in truth she didn't know how it really was. Lady Jane smiled. "I could tell you a few things about pleasuring a man that might come in handy when you set your cap for one.''

India cleared her throat with a nervous cough. "I'm sure you could. If that day ever comes I'll be obliged.''

"If you came here with Gat Ransom, the day might come sooner than you think.'' Her eye held a mischievous twinkle. "He doesn't show up very often, but when he does, Contessa favors him. You know,'' she took her eyes off her own reflection and gazed at India, "you and Contessa have the same coloring about you. Though between you and me, I think you're much prettier.'' She gave a thoughtful sigh and began, with India's help, to slip out of the gown.

"Well, Lady Jane, just between you and me, Mr. Ransom is the last man, not only in the territory but the whole of these United States, that I would set my cap for.''

Lady Jane looked at India with surprise. "Why, how could you say that? All the girls eye him, he's that kind of man.''

"He isn't my kind of man.'' India lied, hoping if she said it enough it would be true. "First, I never intend to marry. I've chosen to dedicate my life to work on behalf of all women. And secondly, I don't intend to spend my life being a mirror for a peacock cowboy.'' India bent to gather up the dress and neatly arranged it in one corner out of the way. Lady Jane put her robe back on. India wouldn't attempt to explain further. Poor Lady Jane. Most women were "Poor Janes."

Lady Jane shrugged, as if India was beyond her understanding. "I do love your dress, miss. Not even Contessa has one as fancy." She suddenly was seized with a fit of sneezes. India quickly fetched her handkerchief and gave it to her.

"Are you all right?"

"Yes. I think I'll get cook to give me an oil of camphor rubdown, and then I'll go to bed." She sniffed.

"Oh, there's one thing more you could do for me." India hurried over to the desk and snatched up her supply list. "Give this paper to Mr. Ransom. He should be in the dining room."

"I'd be glad to. Good night then." She stepped out the door, leaving it slightly ajar.

"Good night, Lady Jane," India returned. She liked the girl immensely. Her youth and innocence. Yes, *innocence*, though because of her profession some would never think it. As India hefted the kettle and poured the hot water into the porcelain wash bowl on the wash stand, her mind mulled over their conversation.

She couldn't help but wonder about the pleasuring things a girl like Lady Jane did with the men that visited her. She remembered her girlhood friend, Annie Ryan. Annie's father was a notorious miser where his household and family were concerned, but it was common knowledge that he kept a mistress in fine style. Thinking about it, India saw no reason why Annie's mother shouldn't have known how to pleasure her husband as easily as the mistress while at the same time enjoying equal pleasure—as well as equal rights—herself. Lady Jane said the pleasuring worked both ways, and India was inclined to believe her. If so, she would never understand why marriageable girls were instructed to fear those mysteries and schooled to believe that only bad women participated in them.

While she waited for the water to cool enough for a sponge bath, she took off her camisole and silk pantalettes. She reached for Contessa's silken robe, shrugged her arms into the flowing sleeves, immediately feeling the cool smooth texture against her bare skin encircling her body like caressing hands. A thrill of pleasure shivered through her, and when she turned and caught her reflection in the mirror she was momentarily startled, then embarrassed. The robe clung to the curves of her body, and the opened spaces of the lace insets revealed the whiteness of her skin.

She thought to look inside the wardrobe for something more modest, but instead quickly worked to fasten the ties down the front opening. After a moment her fingers began to slow and she became intrigued by how much the risque robe changed her outward appearance as well as inner feelings. There was a fine line between decency and indecency, ladylike and unladylike. The robe was definitely indecent and un-ladylike, but the latent sensuality it triggered within her was an awakening revelation. She pulled the combs out of her hair and threaded loose her plaits until her hair fell in a shining web over her shoulders and down to her waist. Another woman now stood inside the oval of the full-length looking glass—a woman ripe for love, a woman wanton.

If you give men what they want they won't respect you. The thought reared up in India's memory like a guilty thief. *Only wild women allow men to touch them "down there."* These warnings from her mother had been the heart of India's education on the matters of men and women. Early on, India was never quite sure what her mother had meant by "down there." And when she had asked, she was assured that her future husband would initiate her into those mysteries. And somehow it seemed to her mother India's ignorance of her body made her more virtuous, while the knowledge in her brothers, who were in constant competition in their amorous conquests, merely improved their reputation.

It wasn't fair. Men were thought to be wiser and more responsible and so without losing respect were privy to the mysteries of love. But not women! A bride must lie trembling in ignorance on her wedding night waiting for her man to make all the advances. Well, thought India, everyone else might think it's all right for a woman to be "taken" and overwhelmed by a man. But not me! If I'm to be overwhelmed I'd expect to have some say in it. And the more India thought about it the more unfair it seemed, especially since she never intended to marry.

Except for coming West, everything India had done in life was reasonably prudent and proper, but no matter how often she tried to ignore it, she was a woman—a woman of passions. She refused to feel guilty about the feelings stirring within her. Though sometimes she found it completely disheartening being a woman in a man's world, tonight she found it oddly extraordinary. Brush in hand, she began slowly stroking her auburn tresses to a soft shine, wholly absorbed in her own changeling reflection.

Gat Ransom pushed his chair back from the dining hall table and put the linen napkin aside. Maybe he shouldn't have brought India to Contessa's, but then again, she was the one who said she wouldn't tolerate bedbugs. That was one thing Contessa's boasted on not having: bedbugs. Anyhow, Contessa had seemed to settle her in all right. But Gat admitted to himself that India Simms was a different breed of woman altogether—she was a hard one to figure out. If she'd been plain or downright ugly he could understand why she'd go on a crusade like this rather than marry and raise a family. But a more comely woman had not crossed his path. There must be more to it than he could reckon.

His eyes settled on the gilt-framed painting above the sideboard. A nude reclined on a red velvet sofa, lace draped across her nipples, tempting the eye with just the round of breast. Her lips seemed to come alive, shimmering and dancing invitingly in the room's flickering lamplight. For a moment her face wavered and her features became those of India Simms, and that image filled Gat with fierce needs. What would she be like, he wondered? As passionate and loving as she was aloof? He'd like to find that streak of fire

74

in her that could let loose her passions. He knew for a woman like her, lovemaking would be instinctual—he could see it in the line of her lips and the occasional seductive flash of eye. Despite her genteel ideas, how easy it would be to play the different forces of her primness against her own innate sensuality. How easy it would be to keep her off balance.

But after exploring the possibilities, his own sense of responsibility took over and he dismissed the idea. A woman like her would never fit into his life!

Now, a woman like Contessa suited him fine. Without wearing a man's pants, she could be good company and she knew when to let go.

It was late and he was tired. He stood up and strode out of the room and up the stairway. Passing by Contessa's room he heard humming, he knocked softly on the door and thought he heard "come in." She continued humming as he walked in and spied her bent over the porcelain wash bowl, her hair falling down about her waist. Funny, he hadn't remembered it being that long, but he did remember the soft feel of her skin next to his own. Not being a man to greatly resist temptation, an unleashed desire and fiery warmth flooded through him. He nudged open the door and walked across the thick, twining rose carpet. He leaned over, parted her hair and touched the nape of her neck with his lips. Such delicate softness he'd never tasted and the rapid response within him was inherent in the nature of his masculinity. He felt her warm body sway under his kiss. Wrapping his arms around her he caressed her breasts in his hands and gently swiveled his hips against the softness of her own.

"It's been a long time," he whispered. But at his words she tensed, instead of yielding further as he expected. He felt her intake of breath.

She swirled around and—too late, he saw the porcelain wash bowl rise up and tip, drenching him thoroughly. He leaped back with a curse. "Damn!" The water dripped from the ends of his dark hair down over his shoulders.

"And, Mr. Ransom, it's going to be a lot longer!" gasped India.

Gat swore under his breath, still disbelieving that the nymph before him was truly Miss India Simms. But one look at the flash of India's flaming eyes immediately told him his mistake. With unrestrained menace she moved towards him like a she-wolf ready to pounce.

"How dare you! How dare you bring me here and expect me to fall into your arms like some . . . some *woman!* You . . . you lecherous—"

"Not just *some* woman! I mistook you for someone else!" roared back Ransom, not missing that the splashing water caused the robe to cling against her breasts and hips. She waved a lethal fist at him and moved forward. She was so tiny, but her straight back, and the proud carriage of her head gave him the feeling they were eye to eye. He stood his ground, though he knew that once he touched her there'd be no letting go and then he'd only confirm her misbegotten idea that all men were brutes.

"Should I be offended or flattered?" she spat indignantly. Their eyes held, hers becoming sapphire heavens of swirling contradiction. And then he saw the give-away tremor of her lower lip and realized her indignation was a bluff. She wasn't afraid of him. She was afraid of herself.

He didn't answer for a long moment as he debated with his own lust and the vision of tasting her sweet lips, touching her soft skin and moving between her silken thighs. Her lambent eyes and the moistness of her trembling lips were betraying cues to her own vulnerability to desire. Sure as sunrise he could lower his head and taste her mouth, she'd give in . . . a spinster woman with love on her mind. How could she not help it? The room was designed for love, the air thick with desire, and she, stripped down to lace and bare skin, was ripe for passion. Sure he could weaken her will, seduce her, compromise her. But no, he wouldn't. It was crazy, but maybe he wanted her respect . . . or maybe . . . he just wanted her too much.

He simply turned and walked out, leaving them both

changed, unfamiliar to themselves and not knowing any longer.

The lamp flame extinguished, India climbed into Contessa's bed and luxuriated in the satin sheets. The bed was comfortable, the pillows soft and the sheets clean, but the thought of Gat Ransom kept her in a fever of wakefulness.

"Not just some woman," he'd said. Well, she ruminated, he might have meant several women all at once. On the other hand he might have just meant her . . . or as it turned out, anyone but her.

A woman's voice sounded from the next room. Thin walls appeared to be another hallmark of the West, thought India, as she heard an answering low masculine laugh. Had Ransom found "some woman" after all? The idea nudged her over the edge.

"A little higher," the woman next door coached. Her voice so clear that India might as well be in the same room.

"You're delicious," the voice was a lusty whisper. India swallowed hard and slapped the pillow over her ears. Unfortunately, pushing out the sounds did not stop the visions and after a time she was suffocating underneath the pillow and covers in the overheated room.

She lifted the pillow slightly and threw off the top blanket. Through paper thin walls the couple's breathing had grown more urgent and India's own body reacted as her cheeks flamed hot and her heart beat with embarrassment.

"Yes, oh yes . . . yes . . . ," she heard the woman sigh. India turned over on her stomach, and then, feeling shocked at the sudden warmth firing in her own body, flipped over to her back.

The woman was moaning now, "ummmm, ummm . . . ," and the pitch of her voice deepened.

India heard a throaty male groan amid more mumblings and whispers. She flattened the pillow back over her head, forcing away the visions, the concocted images, all the while ruing Ransom's unannounced visit to her room and her own reaction. Had she hesitated too long before turning on him, before demanding he leave? Or should she have allowed him to speak in defense of his actions? And what of her own defense? His kiss on the nape of the neck had sent the most mesmerizing sensations of pleasure down her spine.

Next door things became stormier and whispers weren't whispers anymore. The sounds drifted through the walls, leaving India blushing with mortification. Her stomach twisted as the moans deepened, becoming more urgent. The bed thumped in rhythm against the wall while the woman's wanton panting fairly stopped India's own breath. At last, an ecstatic cry joined by a low sigh of release left the late night heavy with stillness.

India let her breath out, completely dissolved by her own dual nature. The image of the couple bathed in slick perspiration, raw feelings satiated, stirred her with an intensity that left her annihilated. Like most women she'd thought about sexual things, but until tonight she'd only thought about them. Now, vicariously, she'd experienced them. She was a respectable woman who was tempted to break all the teachings of her background and ideologies to be with a man, a man she hardly knew, yet a man she was irresistibly attracted to. Acknowledging her response further threatened her chosen course of self-denial.

That Ransom wasn't attracted to her became the most comical aspect of it all—though she wouldn't die laughing over it. He was experienced with women and she wondered if tonight he'd somehow seen in her eyes that she wanted him. Is that why he'd walked out? Would he choose a harlot over her because he had no desire for a woman who demanded the vote, a woman who wanted to be a man? And on that hinged India's salvation and her despair. She hadn't cried herself to sleep since she was a child, but tonight India felt desolate, isolated and terribly alone.

In the morning a knock at the door woke India. "Come in," she called, and warily peered around the draped lace curtains of the canopied bed. She'd not forgotten the strange events of the night before. Rays of sunlight filtered through the slits of the velvet-curtained window as Contessa walked in, her arms filled with string-tied brown paper parcels.

"Good morning," Contessa smiled and set the parcels on the brocade loveseat. "Gatlin sent these. He hopes you'll be ready to travel as soon as possible. However, I told him you must speak to my girls first about the vote." She was still dressed in the same mauve silk, and her voice held a note of fatigue. India wondered if Contessa had been the one next door? No, she would have recognized her voice.

Climbing out of the bed, she went over to inspect the packages. "I must officially begin my crusade somewhere, and it might as well be your boardinghouse."

"Excellent. You know I am counting on you to convince the territory. It would be history in the making."

India looked at her, realizing what a farseeing woman she was. "May I ask you why you have chosen to live out here? What attraction does life on the frontier hold for a woman like yourself?"

"Freedom. On God's earth there is no freer place for women than the West. But, I believe what you really want to ask is," her brown eyes filled with wry amusement, "what am I doing running a cat house?"

India flushed at Contessa's straightforwardness. Perhaps that was her question after all.

"I ask myself the same thing, occasionally. Perhaps it is one of the few ways I can control my own life and make a living besides. I am too strong-willed to bend under the ruling hand of a husband—I've had three. Like yourself, I attended finishing school. Unlike my classmates, I opened the books on the shelves and learned that life was more than curtsying, cooking and cleaning. I have traveled the European continent, visited its museums and vaults of history. Ask me anything about the Crusades, and I can answer you. I know as much or more of military strategies as any commander at Fort Bridger. Yet I am a woman. Nor would I change that. I like being a woman and I like the company of men, for they speak of things other than removing blackberry stains from white linen." She laughed. "Have I answered you?"

India sighed, "Of course you have, and more."

"And now, you must get dressed and come down to the dining room. The girls will all be together eating breakfast." With that, she lifted her skirts and swished out the door.

India untied the string of a hastily tied parcel, finding a hairbrush, a bar of soap, ink, ink pen and ledger. She took a moment to write out the declaration of petition: "We, the undersigned, residents of the Wyoming Territory, do hereby sign our names in support of enfranchisement for all women of the Wyoming Territory."

She sat back and admired her handiwork, anticipating that one day soon the ledger would be filled with signatures. Setting the ledger aside, she opened the larger package, which she thought would contain the traveling dress. Her brows crinkled with confusion when she shook out a fringed buckskin jacket, common attire for trappers and scouts. The packages must have been mixed up at the mercantile.

But on second look inside, she found a doeskin dress with ornamented fringe. The row of colorful beadwork around the sleeves and hem told her it was Indian-made. What fast-talking trader managed to palm this off on Mr. Ransom? Her fingers untied another parcel and her discovery of a pair of knee-high buckskin, moccasins added to the puzzle. She cast them aside and opened the last parcel, her disgust rising.

It didn't lessen when she discovered a broad-brimmed plainsman hat. She took it out and plopped it on top of her head. Utterly ridiculous! Could Ransom be serious in selecting such an outfit for her? He didn't see her as a woman but rather as something in between. If she wore these clothes she would be a laughingstock. How would anyone take her seriously?

As she snatched off the plainsman hat, she saw two dime novels inside the parcel wrapping. She picked them up and suddenly the mystery was solved. On the cover of one novel, entitled *The Heroine of Whoop-Up,* was a daring maiden dressed in much the same costume as what lay before India.

Inside on the first page she read, "Nell could drink whiskey, shute, play keerds, or sw'ar, ef et comes ter et."

The cover of the second novel showed its heroine, *Mountain Kate*, taking on a grizzly bear single-handedly. Suddenly India burst into laughter. Well, Mr. Ransom had his joke, so she would have hers, too. She would show Mr. Ransom. She wondered how he would like escorting his own *Heroine of Whoop-Up* around the territory. Indeed, the costume might provoke much-needed publicity and she knew many suffragists favored dress reform. Years earlier, Amelia Bloomer had found the courage to wear the bloomer fashion for the first time. Perhaps now was the time for India Simms to follow in the Bloomer tradition. Certainly, the ungainly hoop and skirts of her gown had proven impractical.

She slipped out of the silk shift and into her camisole and ankle-length pantalettes. Out of habit, she reached for her corset and then stopped. The corset looked like some contrivance of imprisonment; it shortened the waist and was cut high in the front and low at the back. As she'd embraced the notion of dress reform, it now occurred to her the daily lacing up of her stays was an arduous ritual of self-imprisonment and that someone who wore stays wouldn't be going far, at least not very comfortably. Yes, but dare a woman give up the restraints of her corset? Too much freedom could be heady, and she wouldn't always be in the West. Dare she?

Before years of custom could sway her and before caution could overtake her first impulse, she ignored the corset and lifted the doeskin dress over her head, letting its softness fall loosely over her hips and to her ankles. She pulled the moccasin boots on, surprised at the snug fit and comfort of the soft fur lining. All the while she envied men. How foolish women were to bind themselves in the torture rack of fashion. She took a moment to brush her hair, to braid it into a figure eight atop her head, and to wash her face.

Before Contessa's full-length looking glass she put on the buckskin jacket, the plainsman hat and the Votes For

Women sash. She held up the dime novel and made a brief comparison of herself to Hurricane Nell, and she decided she looked much better than wild-haired Nell. Taking a moment to put her soap, hairbrush, guidebook and purse into a traveling packet, she took one last wistful gaze at her Paris gown squatting in the corner like a lifeless puppet. She opened the door and strode down the hallway, feeling like a different woman. In fact, like one Miss India Simms, suffragette.

Pushing open the doors leading into the dining room, she entered with theatric flair. Conversation stopped immediately, utensils froze in mid-air. Every eye turned to India. Ransom, coffee cup in hand, straightened up from his lounging pose against the wall. Still smarting from the night before, India wouldn't look at him, but in a sweeping gesture, she took off her hat and bowed gallantly. The girls whispered among themselves.

"Well, well, ladies, let me have the honor of presenting Miss India Simms," Contessa's eyes beamed. "She has consented to speak to us this morning on woman suffrage."

A soft applause rippled through the room. India stepped to the head of the dining table and looked into the girls' faces. In her breast an unexpected raw nerve of jealousy stirred like an awakening vixen. Had one of them been with Ransom last night? Her eyes passed from one rouged face to the next while her overactive imagination wallowed in the shabbiness of it all.

"Go ahead," Contessa prompted.

India, wholly disconcerted, cleared her throat, telling herself, *You must forget last night ever happened and you must cut off any romantic*—the word fairly shriveled in her mind—*inclinations for Ransom.*

"Ladies, I would request that each of you who favor the vote for women in Wyoming consider signing this petition I hold in my hands." She raised the ledger up for all to see, and then offered it to Contessa, along with inkwell and pen.

A timid hand lifted in question. "Miss Simms, do you wish us to sign our given name or professional name?"

"I think your given names will do fine." India looked to Contessa for affirmation.

"Yes, of course," Contessa agreed.

Another hand raised and India recognized Lady Jane's face. "Miss, should we write down our occupation?" She was greeted with a ripple of self-conscious laughter.

"Now, Lady Jane, behave yourself," Contessa scolded.

"I'm sure Green River, Wyoming, is adequate," returned India with an indulgent smile. "In beginning my words to you, I should like to explain my unusual mode of dress. To be truthful it isn't the latest from *Godey's Lady's Book.*" Again laughter echoed through the room. "Like many suffragists, I favor dress reform for women, especially for those who must endure the rigorous life of the frontier."

Here India meticulously avoided looking at Mr. Ransom.

"My costume is a practical necessity. We all should favor dress reform for women, because the current fashions of long skirts are a hindrance. They make women weak, helpless and passive. How can we settle the West if we must worry that our hems will catch fire when we pass too near the campfire? And what of doorways? Oft times they are so narrow we can hardly pass through and we are obliged to wait outside. I hope, ladies, you will sympathize with me in this reform, and more important, with women's enfranchisement in Wyoming."

While the minutes passed, she outlined her arguments for suffrage simply, but vehemently. She did not miss the opportunity to point out that a mistress often held more sway over a man's opinions than his wife. "Hopefully, ladies, you would keep this in mind and spread the message of suffrage to your clients." With this conclusion, applause rang out.

"Time to ride," Ransom said as he strode by.

"Gatlin," interjected Contessa, "don't be in such a hurry. I must thank her for the fine lecture. It isn't often we have an opportunity to discuss such high pursuits."

"Thank you, Contessa," returned India. "I've never had such a receptive audience." She leaned near Contessa and whispered, "Since we are traveling on horseback it would be unwelcome baggage, especially by Mr. Ransom," she added, with a narrow look in his direction. "I'd like Lady Jane to have the dress. Will you see she gets it after I leave?"

Contessa gave an understanding nod. "She will have it."

"Ma'am," Ransom called to India as he paced impatiently in the hallway.

"That man!" Contessa muttered to India. "He'd rush the dead. You best take your petition and be on your way. Good luck to you." Contessa walked with her to the front door. "Good-bye, Gatlin." She repeated the warm embrace of last evening.

"Good-bye, Tess." His eyes were warm upon her, and for a second time in twenty-four hours India felt the flush of jealousy.

Chapter 7

*R*ansom, his spurs ringing, crossed the veranda and stepped down to the two saddled horses tied to the hitching post. He checked the saddle cinch and put India's parcel and ledger in one of the saddle bags of a dappled white-and-brown paint pony. He nodded to India.

"I couldn't find a lady's sidesaddle. You'll have to ride astride. I've cut a slit in this buffalo skin and fit it over the saddle horn. It should be comfortable. It's about a three-day ride to South Pass City, maybe four. When you tire, speak up and we'll stop for a leg stretch. Any questions?"

For the first time that morning India looked him in the eye and what she saw there was an attitude of rugged sternness. It seemed as far as he was concerned last night never happened. But it happened and today she was all nerve endings because of it.

"I haven't any questions now, but it doesn't mean I never will," she answered, eyeing the buffalo skin draped over the saddle and then looking into the horses's soft eyes, searching for assurance of gentleness. She watched Ransom mount his horse by grabbing hold of the reins and saddle horn, hefting himself up and swinging his long leg over the saddle. It looked simple enough.

Well, here goes, she thought. She doubted she could swing herself up into the saddle without ending up head first in the dirt on the other side, but she would try. She put her right foot in the stirrup and in a mighty effort she attempted to climb on to the horse. But the horse had no mind to let her on. It pranced and danced nervously and during the scuffle India ended up bottom side down on the ground.

"You're trying to mount on the wrong side," Ransom said, swinging down off his horse to quickly come to her aid. "I thought you said you could ride."

India put up a hand to halt his assistance and mustering as much poise as possible she regained her feet. "No, I only said we have horses in the East, not that I could ride one." With her hat she whipped the dust off her clothes. "The truth is, my father only let my brothers learn to ride."

He was staring at her askance. Yesterday she wouldn't have cared if he thought she was a fool, but today it mattered. She licked her lips for courage and moved around to the left side of the horse before taking the reins. He followed her and before she'd realized it he'd put his large hands around her small waist and hefted her up on the saddle. For a brief second his body was pressed against her back and she could feel his muscles straining as he lifted her into the saddle. Unfamiliar sensations leapt up in her, and where his hands touched her waist a warmth encircled her.

She clutched the saddle horn nervously, her heart quickening even more when the horse shook its head with a nostril-clearing snort. Enviously she watched Ransom. He easily swung his lean body up into his saddle, gave his horse a nudge with his spurs and pulled the reins to the right.

"I looked all over town for that little cayuse mare. She's sugar-trained and lady-broke. All you have to do is lean forward an' press your legs against her sides, an' away she'll go."

Astutely, India mimicked his actions. It was a queer feeling to have her legs straddling a horse's back. Being a young lady she had always been taught to keep her knees together and her ankles crossed. With the rocking motion of the horse, the cushioning buffalo skin rubbed against the insides of her thighs, making her more aware of a particular part of her body she had never really contemplated until last night. Her doeskin skirt hitched up a bit and exposed the upper part of her moccasin boot. She tugged it down again in an attempt at modesty.

In her outlandish dress, riding through town astride and without her corset, she felt like Lady Godiva riding through the streets of Coventry. Miners and soldiers gave her more than a casual glance as she rode along. Ransom appeared indifferent to their stares. Second thoughts crept into her mind about wearing such an outfit in public. She wondered if she had the courage to face the ridicule which would surely come along her way.

India debated this question until the last shack and lean-to of Green River melted out of sight. Alongside Ransom, she rode into a wilderness of hills stretching northward. Their trail kept the river in view while making various detours around sloping hills and running by the face of tall white cliffs. Distant clouds tinted by sunrise sailed above rocky passes and jagged summits. Ahead, projecting up from the barren river bank, India saw a wooden cross grave marker. She knew they were common on the western trails and she wondered if it marked the grave of man, woman or child. She drew up her horse when she came abreast of the nameless marker.

"That's Bill Rose's grave," Ransom volunteered. "He was killed at the end of last summer."

India shook her head sadly and nudged her horse onward. "Were you acquainted with him?"

"No, ma'am," Ransom replied. The trail had widened and he moved to ride beside India. "But everybody in the territory knows what happened. He was killed by Indians."

"Was he scalped like Tommy Cahoon?" India could not hold back her curiosity.

"No," Ransom gave a humorless laugh. "He was bald, so for a trophy the Indians cut off one ear. Then they cut the sinews out of his arms. They like to use sinew for tying the steel heads onto their arrows. They cut out the sinews of his back for bowstrings. In fact, not much of poor Bill was wasted."

India's eyes narrowed and a wave of nausea rolled over her. "Is that anything to tell a lady?" she chastened.

He gave her a surly glance. "If the lady didn't want to be told, she shouldn't have asked. Ma'am." He touched his hat brim and spurred his horse ahead of her.

She prodded her own horse forward not wanting to be left too far behind. Her eyes moved furtively left and right to the surrounding bluffs. All this time she'd been worrying about her clothes when she should have been worried about her skin.

A hot, dusty wind blew through the morning hours. India's empty stomach began to gnaw upon itself when the sun stood mid-sky. Ransom had not allowed her time for breakfast, and she wondered if she should ask him for something to eat or at least when they would stop for noon meal. But before India dared speak up, the trail descended toward the river and Ransom had pulled up his horse in a grassy spot and slipped off.

"You might like to stretch your legs," he said, as he dismounted and came over to help her off her horse. His hands encircled her waist and India, though slightly disquieted again, accepted his help. This time she was glad for his support, for when her feet touched ground her knees buckled. She shifted her weight against the horses's flank, not wanting to lean on Ransom.

"Walk around," he directed. "If you need some privacy," he began, his dark eyes scanned a nearby hill, "take the opportunity now." With this he strode off, leaving India fully aware of his errand. Putting one shaky leg in front of the other, she set off in the opposite direction on the same errand.

Without the encumbrance of petticoats and skirts she found her stroll into the shrubbery simplified. She disturbed a brown-speckled bird sitting upon its nest in the brush. Despite her intrusion, the hen sat stone still. India took a moment to study and admire it before she returned to Ransom. Hurrying back to the horses, she found him sitting on a flat rock slicing strips of jerky with his knife. She was thirsty and spied a tin cup of water balanced between the V of his legs. He caught her looking.

"We'll have to share the cup." His surliness was now replaced with a hint of tease. "But then you're all for equality."

Running her tongue over dry lips she hesitated reaching for it.

"You first," he said, parting his legs a little wider.

She reached for the cup, careful not to touch him. The warmth of his thighs lingered on the cup as she put it to her mouth.

He offered her a piece of jerky, which she eyed disappointedly, before she took it and began eating with ladylike nibbles.

"We'll eat something more filling when we camp tonight." India just hoped she'd survive that long.

He helped her back into the saddle and they started on their way once more. As they rode along, she noticed that his fingers went inside his saddlebag to a paper sack. "Ma'am?" He leaned over the side of his horse and offered the open sack to her. "I'm all out of tobacco but try a horehound candy. It helps wash the dust out of your mouth."

Cheered by the news he was out of tobacco, she said, "Thank you," and took a piece of candy. He put the sack back inside the saddlebag.

"I brought it along in case we meet Indians. Sometimes a bite of sweets is enough to keep them peaceful."

"Really," she said doubtfully. "I think you enjoy teasing me with your exaggerated Indian stories. But I'm not like Milicent Templeton who swoons at the very thought." She pursed her lips, sucking the sweetness of the candy. Perhaps showing a confident air would abate her own apprehensions and keep Ransom from dwelling on the more dangerous aspects of their trip.

"Let's hope not," he returned, "though I thought an enlightened woman like yourself would like to know the risks involved. But if it's more than your gentle sensibilities can handle, I'll keep quiet."

India cast him an injured glance. "Of course I can handle it. I would despise being left in ignorance because of the accident of being born a woman."

Ransom stared straight ahead. "Accident or not, I'd say you'd better accept it."

He meant to provoke her. But her horse stumbled at that precise moment and deterred her from straightening him out on that particular idea. All of her energy went to guiding her horse, for the trail roughened as it turned from the river and went into the hills.

As the hot sun filled hours of the afternoon, she was grateful for the protection of the broadbrimmed plainsman hat. After the wearying toil of riding over the hills for hours on end she felt she had come to her limit of endurance, but pride kept her from speaking up. Her admiration for those who spent their lives in and out of the saddle was ever-increasing. She yearned to leap off and walk the distance to evening camp, but she would persevere, if for no other reason than to spite Ransom.

More than ever she realized it was her misfortune that her parents had sheltered her. A child delicate of health, she'd been cossetted by her family for many years, yet she'd inherited a vital tenacity for life and an elasticity of nerve that finally triumphed over her mother's desire to invalid her. Maids had done her bidding since infancy, and in retrospect her only applicable skill was her education, which her father had objected to. The less a woman knew the better for her and her future husband, was his philosophy. If he had said it once, he had said it to her a hundred times, "God intended for woman to marry and to educate a girl would be to undermine the institution of marriage." Though she never dared tell her father, India concluded that men supposed marriage to hold so little attraction for women who, if wiser, would give it up altogether.

Well, as it happened, he was right, but now she was giving up more than just marriage. How shocked her father and sweet mother would be to discover that their daughter was riding astride a horse, corsetless, over Indian-infested mountains in the sole company of a hired gunman. And that was the best of it! Perhaps she had more in common with the dime novel *Heroine of Whoop-Up* than clothing.

After unsaddling the horses and rubbing them down, Gat hobbled the pair and left them to graze. He gathered an armload of greasewood and knelt down to start a fire.

"Ma'am, if you'll break out the supplies, you can start fixing supper." Within seconds he had the campfire blazing, and giving India a quick look, he set off to find more wood. She hadn't complained, he'd give her that. But it was only the first day out and he could tell she'd be stiff as a stick in the morning. Tomorrow he'd find out if she was the whiny sort. Roughing it had a way of bringing out the worst in some folks. But if he'd read her right, he figured she was just stubborn enough to come through it fine.

When he returned to the campfire he saw she had the coffee pot on. He dropped the wood and bent down to add a few sticks to the fire. "We covered over thirty miles today. If we keep it up we'll be in South Pass day after tomorrow."

He saw she'd unpacked the saddle bags containing supplies and that she'd made a row of little piles on the ground in front of her.

"I wasn't sure what was what," she began. "I . . . I wondered if you had a particular menu in mind for each meal. I've found the flour and soda powder, but I must confess I've never cooked over an open campfire before. Most of my excursions into the country have consisted of afternoon picnics already packed."

"I guess you're due for a lesson, then. My specialty is biscuits and bacon." Gat's voice probably sounded more cheerful than he felt. "How about making some dough and we'll have biscuits and bacon. I'll show you the fine art of baking on a stick."

He watched her pick up the tin bowl and pour in a cup of boiling water and then a sprinkle of soda. Her method was contrary to his own, but she being a woman, he supposed she was stirring up some special recipe. He began to wonder when she dumped in a cup of flour and the batter looked more like lumpy gravy than dough. She stirred it and then she gave him a slightly puzzled look.

"Do you think I should add more flour? I'm not much of a cook. You see, we had servants do the cooking. Perhaps you might explain what I should do next," she smiled demurely.

It did beat all, a woman who couldn't cook! He bit back a sarcastic reply and gave a rueful laugh at his misfortune to be hooked up with her. "Well, ma'am, since I had no mother, I did most of the cooking for my three brothers and twin sisters."

"It must have been difficult for you."

He took the bowl from her and dumped it out behind a rock. He smiled. "Not for me as much as my brothers and sisters. My mother died in childbirth. I was the eldest so I tended house and nursemaided the little ones, until my father remarried. Things weren't too bad after that. Pay attention now," he measured in the soda, picked up the tin cup and filled it with cold water from the canteen, and mixed it together in a smooth batter. "Hot water will make it lumpy, lukewarm is about right. Let it sit a few minutes. Work in more flour until it feels sticky, then put a gob on the end of a stick and roast it over the fire or cook it in a fry pan. Out here a man can't survive unless he knows how to cook biscuits."

"A woman too," India added.

"Yes, ma'am, a woman too," he echoed patiently. "If you'll pardon my saying so, you sure are single-minded on the subject of women."

"I'll not deny it. But to my mind it's injustice I battle. You're a man so you can't see it."

"Try me," Gat said, as he began whittling the end of a long stick to a point. He noted the way India's eyes lit up at the opportunity. He figured he was bound to get preached at so he might as well get it over with.

"You know, it might have been better if I'd never been taught to read. Even in my early childhood, reading the Bible became a dangerous thing. One day, while I was reading, I came upon the words, 'Thy desire shall be to thy husband and he shall rule over thee.' Well, since it was the Bible I knew it must be true, but if it were true, what kind of world had I been born into and born a girl under the curse of Eve? Do you believe that Eve placed a curse on every woman?" she asked him earnestly.

Gat hesitated before he answered, thinking that if beauty had been Eve's curse, India Simms had received more than her share of cursing. But he knew better than to say so. "I'm not one to argue with the preachers, but it does seem Adam found it easy to lay the blame of a certain affair, in which he played a large part, on Eve. I agree with you on that, it doesn't seem fair Eve should get all the blame."

Upon hearing this, her eyes widened as if she was astonished he agreed with her. "Yes, my very own opinion exactly! Believe me, it's not easy to be a woman when, over and over, the Bible affirms the lowliness of the female sex. When I hear from the pulpit, 'Wives submit yourselves to your husbands, as it is fit in the Lord,' why, I must grip the pew to keep myself from jumping up and choking the preacher." She paused thoughtfully. "Mr. Ransom, do you believe that half the human race is born to rule and half to be ruled?"

Gat hesitated, making sure he chose his words carefully. He didn't relish a death by choking. "Well, ma'am, depending on which half I was on, it might be easy to believe." She bristled and he knew he had discredited himself, but he intended to get back into her good graces. "Maybe, ma'am, it might just be a matter of interpretation."

Her mouth opened with surprise. "You're a man of rare insight. I wouldn't have thought . . ." She stopped herself from insulting him. "Of course, it *is* a matter of interpretation. Perhaps the biblical translators, who were after all men, had biased the text. And that's why I set about getting an education. I made up my mind to learn Hebrew, Latin and Greek, so I might read the holy words in the original. My father refused to contribute a cent to such folly. So I sold my silk dresses to pay for my schooling at Oberlin College, one of the few schools that admits women."

"You have my admiration," Gat said truthfully, thinking maybe she had a point, though he didn't think she had a chance in hell of changing anything. "Now, watch closely. All you do is take a gob of dough and punch the stick through and turn it over the fire." He demonstrated with practiced skill, then gave her the stick.

"Thank you." She turned the stick steadily and the biscuit began to brown.

He sat back, impressed by her single-minded devotion to her cause. He watched her hands, small lady's hands, and he became captivated. She wanted no special treatment because she was a woman. The devil! Even if she did, there was no way he could ignore the fact of her femininity. Nor could he ignore his own desire to press his lips against the softness of her palms; to cup her dainty hand within his own. To touch her. If a fetching woman like her realized the power she held over a man, she'd never concern herself with something as one-horse as the vote.

He decided to egg her on. "Tell me, how did you come to think women should get the vote?"

She gave a self-satisfied smile. "At Oberlin I learned more than Latin and Greek. My blinders were lifted, and the truth did make me free, perhaps a little too free in many people's minds." She smiled to herself reflectively. "It began in the Congregational Church on the day I raised a hand to vote on a member's excommunication. My vote was ignored. The young man counting the votes protested to the minister, and the minister—I will never forget him—stood at the pulpit with all the powers of heaven resting on his dark, cloaked shoulders and said, 'A daughter of Eve is not a voting member!' It was the first time I had ever looked straight into the face of discrimination, and it wasn't the last."

"You've chosen a rough road." Gat nodded his head sympathetically, yet cursing the unwitting minister for planting the seed of women's suffrage in Miss Simms's breast.

"I know," she sighed. "But I am no different than you. We all choose our paths. You've chosen the rough life of the frontier."

"Yep, I suppose. I came out after the war, liked it and stayed." Gat remembered how he'd wanted a clear view and a deep breath of air that hadn't already been breathed by somebody else.

"But what could you possibly like? It is such a godforsaken place."

"That might be just the reason I like it," he said with a laugh. "But I guess it depends on what you're lookin' for."

"And what are you looking for?"

His dark eyes reflected the campfire's light. "Not much. Peace and quiet. I suppose what most folks look for."

"Well, it's certainly quiet out here." She looked around with a shiver and rubbed her hands over her shoulders. "All this peace and quiet gives me the fidgets, especially when I think of the poor, dismembered Bill Rose back by the river. I could never live out here. In fact, as soon as I can, I'm returning to New England. I'm afraid I haven't the pioneer spirit. When Horace Greeley said, 'Go west young man,' I took special notice that he said young *man*, not young *woman*."

"Yep, but here you are." Ransom found himself enjoying their conversation.

"Well, I've always been one to do the opposite of what I'm told. But I'm not here permanently. That is, not permanently unless a visit from Indians determines otherwise." She gave a bleak smile.

"Well, don't fret. I'll keep your scalp intact. That's what I'm paid for."

"Let's hope so." She looked at her biscuit on the stick. "Do you think it's ready?"

"Appears to be." He took his own out of the fire. "I'll cook up the bacon." He gave her an occasional glance as she roasted more biscuits. His eyes seemed to wander in her direction more often than not. Maybe it was the way the doeskin dress hugged her body, outlining shapely hips usually hidden in bustled skirts, or maybe he'd just seen a side of her he liked. If he were a woman, maybe he'd be crusading for the same cause. As the minutes passed, she'd roasted up a small pile of burned-brown biscuits.

"How's that?" She'd put them in the tin bowl, offering it to him. "I think I could be a real cook if I just set my mind to it."

"Well, set your mind to it. I don't plan to be a ladies' maid on this trip." He reached for a biscuit, pulled it open and stuffed a burned bacon strip inside.

"No one asked you to," she replied defensively, misunderstanding his jest. "I'll learn to cook as well as learn anything else I need to know. I'm not too dainty to lend a hand when I need to, sir."

Gat shook his head despairingly and began to eat. She was so damned touchy. He wanted to tell her to get down off her high horse and quit being so uppity. "I'm glad to hear it. And another thing, I wish you'd call me Gat." Nobody had ever called him "Mr." but her. " 'Mr. Ransom' and 'sir' both sound a little stilted for these parts. I understand your reasoning for keeping a polite distance between us, but I don't intend to repeat my performance of last night. It was a case of mistaken identity. I had no intention of taking advantage of you, and I apologize if it appeared so."

He saw her tense and knew again he'd stepped on touchy ground.

"Do you always apologize to your 'soiled doves'?" The depths of her blue eyes sparkled again with that crusading light. He felt a tirade coming and was sorry he had brought it up.

"I wouldn't consider you a 'soiled dove.' " He continued

to eat, noticing she was now more interested in making another moral point than in eating.

"Why not? I'm no different from those women at Contessa's boardinghouse. Only circumstance divides us. My experience with men has been limited"—he could second that—"which makes me morally acceptable in society. Yet those women are outcasts. Don't you ever ask yourself why they are outcasts, while men like you who visit them regularly are not?"

"No, I haven't asked myself that particular question," Gat hedged between bites. She'd picked up a biscuit stick and was pointing it at him.

"Well, it's time you did! A woman turns to prostitution out of economic necessity, not because she is depraved. If you ask me it's her clientele who are depraved."

Gat shifted defensively, thinking she didn't know much about men's needs.

"It bears out the significant double standards of our society. To further extend my argument, let us pretend for a moment that we are courting."

Gat swallowed back a laugh of disbelief. "If you say so, though I don't intend to get into double harness."

"Again we seem to share more than one idea. I, too, have vowed never to marry." Gat had heard women say that before, but this was the first time he believed it. "For a woman, marriage is a form of slavery, but then that is a topic we can discuss another time."

"I can hardly wait," Gat said, deadpan.

"Now," she began to warm up, "suppose we've not known each other long, but you are assured of my spotless reputation and moral character. The moment is ripe for you to ask my hand in marriage. Go ahead, ask," she prodded.

He put down his tin coffee cup, leaned forward on bent knee and reached for her hand, biscuit and all. He schooled his chiseled features with smoldering intensity and looked her in the eye. A jolt of desire streaked through him and what had started as a jest became more. And he saw the power of attraction was no less for her as her eyes went as flighty as a cliff swallow.

"What are you doing?" she yanked back her hand.

"Askin' you to marry me." His gaze was like hot ash.

"Well, I didn't mean for you to be so theatrical about it. Just ask me."

"No, ma'am, I won't ask unless you give me your hand." Now he gave her that slow grin, the one he knew infuriated her.

Her blue eyes narrowed warily, then grudgingly she let him take her hand. "Now ask."

Rotating his thumb slowly over the nest of her palm he made the most of holding her hand while giving the first and last proposal of his life. "Don't yew want to throw in with me? I think I kin scrap up 'nough grub to eat on fer a while."

"What?"

Gat laughed. "That's a frontier proposal. But I reckon you want all the frills." Lifting his free hand, he swept off his hat gallantly, "With your permission, dear lady, I ask you to be my adoring, faithful, obedient, always cheerful, ever beautiful wife." The imp inside him rose and he lowered his head and kissed her hand. She jerked her hand away as if it had been burned, and Gat found himself holding empty air while his lips tingled from the taste of her palm.

"Aren't you overdoing it a bit? Only a simpleton would agree to such a proposal."

He sat back on his heels and picked up his cup again, wondering if she knew the kind of fire she was playing with. "Maybe, but I'm inclined to think this whole discussion is a bit simple. Now, get on with your point."

"Well, suppose I then asked you if you were chaste. What would you answer?"

"You already know. I don't need to answer."

"Correct. But then what if I replied. 'I cannot marry you, sir, for I had hoped to wed a virtuous man.' "

Gat was sullen. "Then prepare to be an old maid, because it isn't too likely you'll find one."

"But don't you see?" India concluded. "Men expect to

marry a virgin, and yet women aren't availed that same consideration.''

"Well, if it's any consolation, you've made your point." Gat yawned and reached for another biscuit. "But it's too late for me. My seed is already sown in the true biblical sense. All I can offer a woman now is my regard and protection.''

"I do not mean to discredit you, Mr. Ransom—''

"Now we are back where we began," his eyes held hers, not without an unsettling effect. "I'd like you to call me Gat. After all, I've proposed to you, that should put us on friendlier terms.''

"I am sorry, but I would feel very uncomfortable. I fear it might be misleading and improper to do so.''

Gat wondered how a woman who had enough gumption not to wear a corset—he'd spotted it right off—and who traveled around the territory preaching something as radical as woman suffrage could quibble over the etiquette of calling him by his given name.

He stood up and swallowed the last of his coffee. "I'll check on the horses and get the bed rolls laid out. I suppose now you can cook, you know how to clean up after yourself.''

"Have no fear, Mr. Ransom.'' She gave him a warm smile.

He didn't smile back, wishing she'd never brought up the subject of soiled doves and lost virginity. Quiet nights by a campfire had a way of making a man's mind wander.

Later, settling back against his saddle, he took his penny whistle out of his vest pocket and began to pipe the mating call of the western willet into the prairie darkness. Though it wasn't much solace, a nightbird cooed an answering refrain. His eyes strayed to the form sleeping by the fire and he regretted the rare attack of conscience he'd had at Contessa's. Last night he'd bedded down with his horse, though he hadn't easily forgotten the sheen of India's lily white skin peeking through her silk robe, and the weight of her full breasts in his palms. It had been a damnable oversight to give a woman a body like that if she never intended to use it. And now, body and all, she was his responsibility. He had to protect her, not ravish her, and a man shouldn't have to endure such a temptation. The thought of spending the next months with her struck him as mighty trying. It might be more than trying: it'd be downright hell!

Chapter 8

*I*ndia jerked awake. She lay in her buffalo skin cocoon and considered remaining there until the sun was fully up. But she saw that Ransom had his horse saddled already and was leading her own little paint pony over.

"Good morning," he greeted pleasantly. "Coffee's on the fire."

Feeling a little self-conscious about how she might look, she stroked back the loose strands of hair veiling her face and managed to sit upright. Stiffness riddled her body, and when she moved to stand up, her sudden intake of breath caused Ransom to turn his eyes in her direction.

Each movement required her full concentration, and for the moment, she could only stand statuelike. To stoop for the coffee pot was out of the question.

"Time to saddle up," Gat prompted. He covered the pony's back with an Indian blanket. "You want to do it yourself?"

"Oh, yes, well . . ." She was fast tiring of the charade she had bluffed herself into. Saddling a horse was the last thing she felt able to do. Just walking to the horse would be a major accomplishment.

"A little stiff this morning?" he asked.

"A little," she returned, attempting to take a step forward.

"Come over here and I'll show you how to saddle up."

From the solicitude in his voice she knew he'd be patient. Step by step, with gritted teeth, she walked over to the horse. Gat hefted the saddle onto the horse's back. She watched closely, memorizing his every move. She vowed to saddle the horse on her own the next day, that is, if she were still alive.

While she took time to drink a cup of coffee and eat a burned biscuit, Gat doused the fire and packed the supplies into the saddlebags.

Afterwards, she brushed out her braided hair and used a piece of parcel twine to tie her hair back into a loose fall. She turned around to find Ransom had been watching her. Caught in his observation he averted his eyes and kicked dirt on the campfire. She had second thoughts—second thoughts about not wearing a corset and now, about letting her hair fall free. Perhaps he was goading her. Last night his touch on her hand had begun it all again, even though she thought he'd been mocking her.

She hobbled to the pony, gathering up the wherewithal to mount. She felt as if she'd been stretched on a torture rack, and the thought of getting back up on the horse was daunting.

"Ma'am," Ransom said. Again she felt his strong hands about her waist, and miraculously she was hoisted up into her saddle. "The stiffness will work itself out after a few days," he assured her with an understanding smile. His encouragement didn't make her feel better.

"I hope so. I would almost prefer to walk the remaining distance to South Pass," she said with a forlorn sigh.

"I wouldn't recommend it. We've got a long, dry ride ahead of us." He swung up on his own horse and led off. She nudged her mount to follow, resolving to bear her suffering in silence.

The morning sun slowly rose in the sky. They rode across a series of desolate plateaus of whitish, clay soil covered with sage brush. A chirping ground squirrel or a scudding rabbit here and there were the only living things to be seen.

Towards noon the monotony was broken by a rise of rounded sandstone mounds like huge anthills. Around their base the ground was baked and polished into a hard, burnished clay. Northward, beyond the sandstone hills, sat a line of high, rocky cliffs, and farther on rose a high, blue, shadowy range of snow-capped mountains. It all seemed to India like a great lonely wasteland.

When they stopped to eat the noon meal, Gat pointed out the Wind River Range. "Beyond them is the Yellowstone. On God's earth there is no greater country than the Yellowstone."

But India had her doubts, especially when they forded the first crossing of the Big Sandy and she saw the charred ruins of an old stage station which Ransom said had been burnt by the Indians.

In the afternoon, he shot a jackrabbit right before India's eyes. He gutted it and then hung the limp thing on his saddlebag, remarking on how tender it would be and what a good stew they would have for supper. Her stomach rolled while she watched the lifeless thing bounce against the horse's flank as they rode along.

Soon after, Ransom quickened their pace when clouds swirled in threatening gray masses on the horizon. Before sunset it was as if a lid had shut down over the heavens, leaving not a gleam of light. Suddenly, rain began to fall, thunder growled and lightning flashed above the black silhouetted mountaintops.

India quickly realized they could not stop for shelter because there was none—scrub brush and ravine was all nature offered. Lashing them with cold rain, the storm broke full force and their path became indiscernible. India's horse suddenly took fright, rearing as if ten thousand furies were after it. Desperately, she clung to the saddle horn. The horse jumped into a frantic gallop and she lost the reins. She hung on to its flying mane and prayed its next jump wouldn't be a leap to its death down a cutbank or coulee as torrents of rain and flashing lightning blurred her vision. Her terrified horse bounded past Ransom and into a water-streaming ravine and plunged forward through the murky blackness.

Suddenly, a streak of lightning wrapped the landscape in a fiery glow. *"Oh, lord!"* she muttered, and she shut her eyes in dread and when she opened them again the hard-following crack of thunder shook her.

Hearing Ransom shouting her name her eyes searched all directions. Then, she saw him riding up and he lassoed her horse around the neck and pulled it up. After tying the lead to his own saddle horn he lifted her across and solicitously positioned her in front of him. Holding the reins in his right hand, he cradled her in the bend of his left arm. India felt as safe as a babe wrapped in bunting. Her hand clutched his lapel and she looked up at him feeling assured that she was out of harm's way for the moment.

His face was a shadow beneath the rain-soaked brim of his hat. His lips were a narrow line, his black hair was plastered in thick locks down his neck and shoulders. He peered down at her and the tilting of his head brought a stream of water into her face. She sputtered. He smiled. His hand tucked her head against his chest, a proper shelter from the deluge. Her ear against his chest she listened to the steady beat of his heart and felt his muscles hard and warm through his sodden shirt. She was shivering and his embrace closed protectively around her, his fingers caressing her shoulders. His touch became the one stable thing she could cling to in the tempest around them. Chills shuddered through her body. He slowed the horse, put the reins between his teeth and rummaged with his free hand in the saddlebag.

He thrust a silver flask into her hand. "Drink this."

"What is it?"

"Wild mare's milk. It'll warm you."

She was wary, but at that moment anything that would warm her, she'd drink. Lifting the flask to her lips, she sipped. Her throat constricted and she choked as liquid fire seared her insides. After a few deep breaths she forced herself to take another drink, and as promised the warmth began to pervade her chest and spread out to her cold-numbed limbs. She sipped more as they rode on.

"I'll have a swig." Gat reached for the flask and put it to his mouth. "It's empty. You weren't supposed to drink it all!" He swore one of those picturesque phrases only cowboys have the ability to conjure and shoved the empty flask back into his saddlebag.

Well, she thought, now they were even, he'd used all her bath salts and she'd drunk all his wild mare's milk.

The rain cascaded down, the lightning flashed, and the thunder rumbled through the hills. Despite all this, India was feeling better all the time. In fact she felt quite conversational.

"Your wild mare's milk appears to be the remedy. I hardly feel a chill now."

"That so, ma'am."

"I'm surprised I haven't heard of the remedy before. It must be difficult to catch a wild mare and milk her." She snuggled her cheek against the warmth of his chest.

"Yep." He smiled to himself. The whiskey was taking the starch out of her.

"But anything is possible for a man like yourself."

"Pardon ma'am?" Gat decided the last clap of thunder had afflicted his hearing. She'd never given him a compliment before.

"I'll admit it."

"Admit what?" he returned.

"Admit I admire you. Why I'd even go so far as to acknowledge you saved my life back there."

"You'd go that far?" The whiskey had her.

"Even farther . . . but I might embarrass you."

"No need to worry on that account." Humored, he looked down at her. Water soaked her clothes, dripped over the brim of her hat and off her nose and chin in miniature torrents, but she seemed content enough. The pressure of her head against his chest, the weight of her body in his arms was more warming to him than a whole pint of wild mare's milk. With her loosened up, he was seeing another woman, one that wasn't as chilly as he had supposed.

At last he drew up their horses, helped her down and led her into the shelter of a wind-hollowed sandstone overhang. He went back to the horses and was gone for some time. She huddled inside, peering out at the rainstorm. When Ransom returned, his arms were filled with bedrolls.

"We won't be able to build a fire until morning. You're soaked. You better get out of those wet clothes." He shook out the woolen blanket bedrolls, which were protected by duck cloth wrap, and gave her one.

"But I don't have anything dry to change into," India complained.

"Who said you had to change into anything? Wrap up in the blanket," he said flatly.

The thought of taking all her clothes off in front of him seemed shocking, but not so shocking as it might have before she drank the wild mare's milk. Upon analysis her thoughts were muddled and her nose dripped while she deliberated. Finally she concluded she was soaked thoroughly from her doeskin dress to the draw string of her silk pantalettes.

"But I need some privacy," she announced to Gat.

"Listen, it's dark as hell out and the sun isn't likely to come out until morning. I don't plan to stand out in that cloudburst while you take off your wet clothes." He sounded out of patience.

India began to giggle. He did have a point, but oddly it struck her as immensely funny—him gallantly standing out in the rain while she undressed. She didn't like his being cross, so she attempted to smooth things out. Her voice took on an absurdly moralistic tone and her head tilted a high-nosed turn. "Mr. Ransom, we hold the mutual responsibility of keeping our travels on the highest plane of propriety. We owe it to the . . . sss"—she couldn't quite get through the word—"ssupporters of the . . . ssuffrage cause to ward off any hint of sscandal while we are traveling together."

He gave a half-laugh. "I've apologized for the other night. I don't intend to compromise you again."

Now, India laughed outright, for he seemed such a stuffed shirt all of a sudden. But good breeding was a habit with her, and she replied in a slightly slurred but ladylike voice, "I only require your respect sssir."

"Ma'am, you have it."

"Thank you." She hiccuped, and keeping both eyes on Ransom's silhouette, she proceeded to disrobe, only to find it difficult to hold the blanket as a shield of modesty and manipulate her clothes at the same time. Reasoning that if she couldn't see him in the darkness, he couldn't see her, she let the blanket drop from her teeth and squirreled out of every last stitch of clothing, even the silk pantalettes.

Naked as Botticelli's *Venus,* India hadn't counted on the sudden flash of lightning which illuminated the sky from horizon to horizon. She gasped with embarrassment and scrambled to wrap the blanket around her, then she began to giggle like a girl in grammar school mainly because the sensation of having nothing on beneath the blanket was so new to her. On the one hand it felt liberating, but on the other confusing.

Huddled under the blanket her concern turned to Ransom. "Mr. Ransom, aren't your clothes wet?"

"Yep."

"Why haven't you taken them off?"

"Huh?" Gat sounded equally confused.

"Because I'm a woman do you think I'm more susceptible to chill than yourself?" Droplets of water from the ends of her wet hair trickled between her breasts.

"Ma'am, you're the weaker vessel."

"So you seem intent on reminding me, but I would debate that. I think if I take cold it will be because I followed your advice and foolishly took off my clothes, not because I'm the weaker vessel. All things being equal, Mr. Ransom, you should take off your clothes, too."

Ransom was tired, he was hungry, he was as strung out as a team of desert canaries after a hundred-mile haul, but he wasn't a fool and he wasn't one to argue with a lady. "Ma'am, on the slim point of all things being equal, this one time I'll throw in with you." He began unbuttoning his shirt.

"Indeed, equality for all, that's my platform!" She hiccuped again.

About that time she smelled wet dog and Coyote nosed next to her. Without intending to she fell against Ransom, now stripped down to his pants. His arm went around her in support and goose bumps spread over her skin. "Forgive me, I . . . I didn't intend . . ."

"You're cold," he said. She might be whiskey-warm inside but she was corpse-cold outside. He hefted her onto his lap and held her close, half-expecting her to cry out in moral outrage. But she didn't resist; rather, she nuzzled her cheek against the pillow of his chest. He pulled her closer and encircled her in the warmth of his arms and body. Again all she did was sigh deeply and snuggle against his chest. "You will be discreet about this, won't you?"

"Discreet?" he echoed, grinning so wide his flash of white teeth momentarily lit the darkness. "Yep, I can be discreet."

"Thank you. I will hold you to your word." She relaxed further with this assurance.

It began innocently with Gat's hands rubbing warmth back into her small feet, and he was circumspect enough to keep the blanket buffer between his hands and her bare skin. He kept telling himself he wasn't about seduction but his hands in an unbidden way moved upward to her slim ankles. He knew had she been sober she'd be too ticklish for his ministerings, but her guard was down and she became receptive, pliant and slumberous. Forcing himself to go slower, he deliberately moved to the silken hills of her calves to the velvet hollows behind her knees, smoothing back and forth. A huge constricting knot of tenderness and desire tightened Gat's throat and his heart began to pound like a bridle-wise bronco.

India's mind drifted lazily. She was feeling wholly content now that she was warmer, and the fact that she was wearing nothing under the blanket didn't seem to matter. Her bare thighs felt warm and smooth against each other. She felt languorous and supple and feminine through and through. Gat's touch was a glowing cordial to her body and his nearness flowed into her, lapped her and enfolded her.

"What a beautiful, beautiful night," she purred, her breath hot on his bare chest.

A faint smile touched Gat's mouth but was dissolved by the intensity of his desire. Switching from warming massage to sensual stroking he traced the long line of her thighs, molding his hands over her hips and curving his fingers to the soft hollow of her womanhood. The blanket was no barrier to his imagination and daringly he followed a path over her ribs to the firm mound of her breasts, feeling their unfathomable softness through the blanket. He yearned to nuzzle her neck, kiss her eyes, her lips.

She turned. Her hands pushed out from under the blanket and tangled in the hair that dusted his shoulders. She drew him close to her breast and he felt her softness against his chest. He swallowed hard, then swore softly. She was drunk and he wouldn't take advantage of her. But he couldn't let go of her, not yet while she buried her face against him and feathered her long nails across the muscles of his shoulders. Tremors rumbled through him making him as explosive as a chute-crazy cayuse.

For India, all was right with the world and in her hazy state of mind she sought to decipher the man holding her. Heavy-lidded, her eyes were useless in the pitch darkness. So reaching out she found and traced with her hand every rise and hollow of his face, the ridge of cheekbone and the rise of nose; the skin-grain of beard, the furrow of thick lash and mound of lip. She sensed every ripple of movement in the hands and arms that enclosed her. She could more than imagine the man whose chest and shoulders sheltered her, whose heart she could feel throbbing against her breast.

Was he too feeling the thrill down the spine and the melting of will, or was she the only one this moment who had these feelings? Regardless, he was so experienced she suspected every woman had felt so in his arms. And what splendid arms were his. What fingers, strong, long, with such a touch of strength and yet tenderness. And she would tell him, but her tongue felt like lead between her lips and how deliciously sleepy she felt. In a way she felt guilty using his strength to pursue her own ends . . . She was slipping . . . slipping into the sweet oblivion of sleep. She lay in his protective embrace, her head rested beneath his chin . . .

Her breath was coming softly and he knew she'd fallen asleep. He held her as tight as he'd hold a royal flush in a final round of poker while he contemplated—*battled with* his desire to ravish her. But common sense and his own whipsaw code of honor won out. He stroked her curly mane of rain-soaked hair, cradled her against him and touched his mouth to her forehead, all the while aching to capture her whiskey-sweetened lips.

He tried to keep his mind fixed on other thoughts, but somehow he could only feel her silky skin against his own. Coyote shifted. Gat shifted and she shifted, snuggling contentedly in his arms while he tried to ignore the fire of desire that went through him as her body moved against his. Feeling as frustrated as a boomerang stallion, he shifted again, leaning into the sandstone wall at his back.

Hell! It was going to be a long night.

When morning came India opened her eyes to a cloudless sky, a crackling fire and the smell of food. The jackrabbit was skewered on a stick, roasting over the fire. Last night she'd been so hungry she might have eaten it raw. But this morning the memory of seeing it swing lifelessly back and forth the day before turned her stomach.

Then she sat up, and the world rolled along with her stomach over the edge of the overhang, and in her mouth the sour taste of whiskey puckered her lips. In daylight, her wits about her, she knew she'd been indiscreet. But the full slap of realization and remorse came when she looked down her naked body beneath the blanket. The shock brought her eyes wide open. But they winced closed with the recollection of Gat's hands moving intimately over her body. How could she have allowed it? Becoming even more aware of her predicament, she saw Ransom stripped to the waist, his shirt, vest and her silk pantalettes draped over bushes by the fire. *It was no dream, it happened!* prompted her small voice of moral conscience. *Oh, lord, it happened!* Amidst this, she was suddenly beset with a series of head-jerking sneezes.

Ransom looked over. He was whistling. She wasn't sure how much he had to whistle about. She remembered his hands . . . the warmth. "Oh, lordy," she muttered, borrowing Heddy's favorite phrase.

Meanwhile, Gat had gotten up off his haunches and come over with a cat-in-the-cream smile on his face. "Mornin'."

India was never her best in the morning and most days her first reaction was to throw the blanket over her head and go back to sleep. But this morning she couldn't do that mainly because there wasn't enough blanket to cover her head and naked body at the same time.

His eyes glittering with amusement at her predicament, he said, "You'd better get dressed."

"And what do you propose I wear?" she said in a shrewish note. Hungover and miserable, she shrunk away from him and clutched the flimsy blanket to her like a shield of virtue. But she knew this was akin to closing the barn door after the cows had gotten out.

Beside her, Gat began rummaging through his saddlebag. Her eyes held on his back, she remembered the texture of his vibrant skin beneath her hands, the rise and fall of muscle. He pulled something out and handed it to her.

She paused a moment before taking it. Clutching the blanket around her shoulders, she shook the bundle out and discovered it was a blue calico dress. It was dry. The question was on the tip of her tongue, but he spoke before she could say anything.

"I thought you might need a dress." He stood with hands on hips, the muscles of his bare chest taut.

She finally said, "But why didn't you give it to me last night?" He was suddenly suspect.

"It slipped my mind."

"It slipped your mind?" she challenged. "You have placed me in the most compromising position of my life! I have been willing to overlook things since our journey began, particularly our visit to Contessa's boardinghouse. But this . . . this," she shook the dress at him, "this is unforgivable!"

"I've told you, I don't intend to compromise you!"

"Humph!" she sniffed, cutting him off with total disbelief. Yes, it was high time she stood toe to toe with him and had it out. "I should have parted company with you at the Laramie depot as I planned. You . . . you—"

"Goatherd!" Ransom supplied. His jaw clamped in a hard line.

Her head throbbed painfully but she refused to be outdone. "No! You sidewinding snake!"

"Well, hell! If I'm such a snake then you can just get on your horse and ride out of here. You're so all-fired damn self-sufficient. I should have let Bramshill shoot you and I should have let your horse throw you into some flooded ravine during the storm. And as for the boardinghouse— shit! I won't say what I should have done there!"

"How dare you!" she gasped, her cheeks flushing a deep rose. "If you don't clean up your language, I'll . . . I'll have to plug my ears," her eyes widened and her nostrils flared, knowing but at the same time hating that she was dependent on him.

"Ma'am, I *have* cleaned up my language!" He gave her a challenging dark-eyed gaze.

Before she could level him with a hazing retort, another fit of sneezing overtook her. With dress in hand and her blanket of virtue secured toga-fashion around her, she hobbled past him. She snatched her pantalettes and camisole from the bushes, picked up her parcel of personal belongings, and looked around for the seclusion of a rock or bush. Nothing, however, was suitably private.

"Please be considerate enough to turn your back, sir." Her tone was high-nosed.

He glowered, but in the end, he turned his back.

The rest of the morning went little better. They ate the jackrabbit in hostile silence. Inwardly, India was heaping all her miseries, including her case of adolescent infatuation, at his feet. Last night she'd been ripe for seduction. She marveled how she could have been attracted to him—could have let him touch her—yet this morning she could barely tolerate his company a second longer. By his own avowal he had no interest in her as a woman, and she, by her own declaration, should have no interest in him as a man.

Later, after a pitifully drawn-out process, she did manage to saddle her own horse. She knew that, out of spite, Ransom would have let her ride bareback if she hadn't.

Around noon they rode up to a ravine-turned-river. She watched him get off his horse and walk up and down the bank to find the best place to cross. Actually she'd been watching him all morning, and no matter how detached she tried to be, she wasn't immune to him physically. Since he'd never bothered to put on a shirt, she'd eyed the muscles of his broad back and shoulders when she rode behind him, unable to forget his strength.

He remained a wall of surly silence, apparently just as aggravated with her as she was with him. When he began to remove his boots and his socks she watched, knowing he expected her to follow his lead. She had a fleeting wish that he would sweep her into his arms and carry her across, but then she was the one who'd asked for no special treatment. He left his pants on but everything else he tied up in the duck-cloth wrap of his bedroll and put it on his horse. He led the horse into the water and the pair swam across.

Resignedly, India climbed down off her horse, took off her moccasin boots. Then she paused and studied the river of muddy water. She'd have to take off her clothes for she knew the river sand would never wash out of her silk pantalettes and dress. If she were a man she could wear mud-caked pants into town, but she was a woman caught in a double bind of modesty and cleanliness. But how could she in clear conscience strip with Ransom watching her? *Never do anything that will lose a man's respect for you.*

Her mother's words were so loud in her mind she almost looked over her shoulder to see if her mother was standing there. Now she realized she had crossed the line of propriety the day she set out unchaperoned for the West. She was an adventuress, no matter how inexperienced, and she'd just have to bluff her way through it. She unfastened her own bedroll, and using her horse as a screen she stripped down. Hastily, she gathered everything into the duck cloth and efficiently secured it up on the saddle. She reined her horse toward the water's edge all the while telling herself there wasn't a soul within fifty miles . . . except for Gat Ransom.

Without a word of guidance, Gat watched her. It was an easy crossing and he wanted to give her all the lead she could handle. But he hadn't figured she'd strip. There was no accounting for a woman's vanity, but then again he was as fond of those silk pantalettes as she was. He'd hate to see them ruined. She'd been hell with the hide off all day, but now seeing the natural beauty of her, his breath caught and he forgave her temper.

She tossed her head self-consciously and guided the horse up out of the water. Gat's eyes went to her breasts, the shapely hips, the shadowed mound of her womanhood, then away, then back again, admiring. He resented the effect she had on him and her constant denial of her own passion—that core of fire deep within her that drove her to fanaticism in her cause. Why couldn't she be like other women? But then if she were like other women, he wouldn't be captivated by her. He tossed her his own dry shirt to wipe off with and turned to other business, because he owed her privacy while she dressed. He took the tin cup and jerky from the provisions and laid out lunch on a rock.

Though they didn't share conversation, they did share the cup and she made an exaggerated point of turning the cup each time, so as not to allow her lips to drink from the same side of the rim as his. Her primness amused him as well as perturbed him. He'd seen her naked beauty, he'd held her in his arms all night, and now she was attempting to cut back into the crowding pen, but he didn't aim to let her. While he ate he thought about her and himself, and then he took an opportunity to nap in the warm afternoon sun.

When Gat closed his eyes India knew she could look at him without his knowing, so she did. He had looked at her boldly enough when she crossed the river, so now she would repay the favor. She wanted to touch his back, the way she wanted to touch his thigh when she'd reached for the tin cup of water. Last night she had touched him, running her fingers through the hair on his chest, drawing her nails across his shoulders and tracing the lines of his face. Last night. India's eyes stopped at the top button of his pants.

When she lifted her eyes she met his smoldering gaze head on. She straightened to her feet and put her hands on her hips as if daring him to accuse her of immoral thoughts. But inside she felt as knotted as a china shawl. She wished she hadn't lain in his arms last night—even worse, she wished she hadn't enjoyed it so much.

Without breaking their gaze he came to his feet, his face inches from hers. He was done playing games, holding back. It was time to put all the cards on the table.

"I'm going to kiss you," he said bluntly.

India didn't move; her eyes narrowed imperceptibly as if to dare him to try.

"I've been kissed before," she taunted, ever bluffing. Never mind that it was only by uncles and aunts, grateful old ladies and doting parents. Survival was her forte, even if it involved stretching the truth.

"Not by me," he muttered, not losing the moment.

Her hands were still on her hips, still daring him. His hands slipped through the loop of her own, encircled her and drew her near. His lips touched hers with fierce tenderness while his hands pressed gently on the hollow of her back. Lost in a river of pure sensation his lips molded to hers, his mouth moving persuasively, yet unbidden. He wouldn't take advantage when she was confused with whiskey, but now . . .

She intended to be as distant as a happenstance onlooker, but sensation seared through her. She fitted her mouth to his as his hands moved slowly down her spine, again igniting a glowing warmth within her. Slowly, her hands moved from the absurd defiant pose on her hips to circle his neck. She'd been wanting to touch him all day, that's what had triggered her temper. Their legs, thighs, and hips pressed together, moving instinctively in the age-old rhythm of love. Desire exploded between them and the kiss deepened.

Her lips parted for breath and his tongue circled hers in an erotic tracery, coaxing them to part wider for him, then slipping between them, tasting the silky, moist hollow of her mouth, then gently, with a teasing challenge his tongue retreated, daring hers to follow. Accepting the dare hers threaded after. She kissed him endearingly, endlessly, a long wildly exciting kiss that sent deep tremors to the very core of his being. He thought she said her experiences with men had been limited. If this was limited . . . His arms tightened around her demanding more.

"I want to make you a woman," he cajoled, forgetting his promise not to compromise her.

Suddenly, she pulled away.

Her eyes widened with apprehension and his first thought was that she was in over her head and was spooked. He loosened his hold.

She stepped back, her auburn hair a wild halo in the sunlight. Her nostrils flared and the temper lines touched her kiss-swollen lips and he suddenly realized he'd misjudged her mood.

She gave him a haughty look to end all haughty looks. "I'm already a woman, thank you!"

She turned away and began throwing the tin cup, food and all, into the saddlebag. Gat watched, the jaw muscles on his cheek ticking.

Still stuffing the saddlebag, she turned back. He saw the glint of tears push at the corners of her eyes. Her voice was barely controlled. "Make me a woman! What you want is to make me a swooning Nelly. You want to break me like you break those wild-eyed mustangs, but I won't fall for it. I won't be detoured."

She picked up the saddlebag and flung it on her horse with such force that the animal danced. Her breast was heaving as she attempted to settle down the horse as well as herself. Gat caught the horse's bridle and gave her the reins.

Subdued, India ran her fingers through her hair and raised her blue eyes to his. Her voice was resolute. "Because I am a woman I won't deny I'm attracted to you. My heart beats faster, by face gets red, I feel a rush of weakness in my thighs when you come close, but I also know when I want to be touched and when I want to left alone." She grasped the reins with finality. "Leave me alone, Mr. Ransom."

Watching her climb up on her horse Gat simmered with the pent-up potency of his manhood. She might demand the vote, she might throw off her corset and swim naked as Eve across the river, but she was one of the few woman he'd ever known who knew what she wanted. Fire and ice. Spur and spirit. Who in hell's half acre would want a woman like her? He did.

At sundown Gat finally spoke, after riding all day in silence, "South Pass is over the next rise."

In reply, she blew her nose for the hundredth time into a red bandanna handkerchief he'd given her. She spurred her horse forward. "I hope they're ready for me."

"I hope so too," said Ransom, deadpan. He contemplated the straight-backed form of the woman in front of him, then looked to the setting sun for a dose of fortitude before he urged his horse down the steep incline to South Pass City.

Chapter 9

*M*orning sun speckled the brightly colored fans of the patchwork quilt spread across India's bed. She reached to the bedside table for a lace-edged hanky, blew her nose, and snuggled deeper beneath the warmth of the feather tick.

"Good morning," Esther Morris greeted cheerfully. She came into the bedroom with tray in hand. "I've made you some tea, and there's hot bread fresh from the oven, with strawberry preserves."

India sat up. Esther set the tray, including china teapot and cups, onto the bedside table. The sight of the graying-haired, nearly six-foot-tall woman in her neat white apron and calico dress, radiating a smile as bright as sunflowers, seemed to take the edge off India's misery.

"I'll never be able to repay your kindness. I've been in bed for two days with this miserable cold and you've waited on me as if I were royalty. I'm determined to get up and about this very afternoon and quit making a nuisance of myself."

"You aren't a nuisance," Esther protested, pouring a cup of tea for India. "It's a pleasure to have your company. I seldom have the opportunity to visit with a bona fide suffragette. Of course the church ladies meet weekly to quilt, or hold discussion on household affairs, but nothing as truly invigorating as women's enfranchisement. I've attempted to spur them on to this matter, but until recently few were interested, and of course the pastor is dead set against women having the vote. I've been hard put to arrange a time when he would allow you to speak in the church. Yesterday, he finally agreed when I suggested we could collect an attendance fee."

"I'm grateful to you." India sneezed, and prayed she'd be recovered in time. "Have you settled upon a day?"

"Yes, Saturday night. Every Saturday the pastor's wife, Emily, plays an organ recital. You see, the pastor made quite a sacrifice to bring the organ all the way from St. Louis, and Emily is a very talented organist. It's our good fortune he finally consented. The recitals are very popular and I foresee a full meeting house."

India bit into the warm bread oozing with sweet strawberry preserves. "This is delicious. It's going to be difficult to leave South Pass and your cooking. I'm envious."

"No need to be, a child could do as well. Not to boast but my true skill is sewing. Before I married Mr. Morris, I'm proud to say, I carried on a thriving millinery business in New York state. It was hard for me to give it up and come West with my husband, but a woman must do these things, you know, whether she is inclined to or not. I'm settled now and accustomed to Wyoming, but how I pined during those first months."

India sighed with empathy. "I think I know exactly how you must have felt. I intend to return to my home in Boston after my speaking tour. Unlike you, I doubt I could ever become accustomed to the West. Although I admire women who come out here, it is an uncommonly hard life."

"We frontier women take the bad with the good. Because the West doesn't have the restricted conventions of the East there are rewards, and hopefully women's enfranchisement will be one of them." She paused to sip her tea. "I've written the candidates to the territorial legislature and asked them that if they're elected, to work for the passage of the right of suffrage. I received a note back from Colonel Bright and he's given his pledge to do so. I feel his young wife must be sympathetic to the cause and has influenced him in our favor." Esther put down her cup and gave India a penetrating look. "You should stay in Wyoming. We need women like yourself to make this a model territory."

India laughed. "I'm afraid my recent experiences have convinced me beyond doubt that I don't belong out here. I'm sure even Mr. Ransom is of the same opinion."

"And are you privy to Mr. Ransom's opinions?" came his deep drawl from the doorway. He removed his hat and ducked through the doorway. He sauntered across the room with his customary loose-limbed stride. "Esther. Miss Simms," he greeted politely. I just dropped by to see how our gal was doing." His smile lifted in a quirk of amusement.

India had a mind to roll over, put a pillow over her head and feign sleep, but instead she sunk under the bed covers, remembering with renewed anger their quarrel and . . . *the kiss*. How could she forget it? Even now her pulse quickened at the sight of him, but a civil greeting stuck like a piece of burned biscuit in her prideful throat.

"Why, Gat," said Esther, beaming and getting up from her chair and hastening to pull him up another. "I'll get you some coffee and you can help yourself to bread, warm from the oven." She scurried out of the bedroom.

Gat pulled the chair closer to the bed than India thought courteous and sat down. He leaned forward elbows on knees, turning the brim of his hat in his hands. After two days away from him the impact of his presence was a shock, but despite her inward nervousness she tightened her lips to a snobbish pout, waiting for him to speak.

The silent seconds were punctuated by the ticking pendulum of the shelf clock. He said nothing, aggravating her with his arrogance. The same male conceit which had caused him to declare he would "make her a woman." India fought back the bitter sting of guilt. A *fallen* woman was more like it!

If you give a man what he wants he won't respect you. It was too late to follow her mother's admonition now. She'd already lost Ransom's respect twice over; once when she'd slept naked in his arms all night and once when she stripped to cross the river. Why else had he so boldly kissed her? A man would never kiss a lady he respected like he had kissed her. Losing his respect mattered a great deal to India, for a woman had nothing if she didn't have male respect. It was all such a double bind, a woman just couldn't win in a man's world. The arousal she'd experienced from that single kiss had been so intense it had frightened her, and she feared if she allowed anything like it to happen again she might lose control. Respectable ladies didn't have feelings like that and the torment lay in the realization that she wanted it to happen again; she wanted to be in his arms, kissing his lips.

The pendulum marked the passing minutes, as India refused to meet his black eyes. She felt his gaze as tangible as wind and smoke upon her. Could he be aware of the turmoil going on inside of her? Thinking anything was better than the silent tension between them, she finally asked, "Did you come to gloat?"

"No, ma'am," he said directly.

She wished Esther would hurry and bring his coffee. "I suppose you think my illness is proper retribution for my contrary conduct."

"No, ma'am," he repeated, seeing her nose had started to drip. He pursed his lips so as not to grin. She looked like a pail-fed calf, a fragile, bewitching maverick. The china blue of her eyes glistened with misery and aloofness. He'd intended to apologize for his behavior on the trail, but doubted she was in the mood to accept it.

She snatched up the hankie and blew. "Well, thank you just the same," she sputtered between blows. "If you didn't come to gloat, then why did you come?"

He balanced his hat on his knee and cleared his throat. "I came to a—"

Just then Esther came in with a tray loaded with bread, cheese and preserves. "—For my homemade bread," Esther set the coffee and bread down in front of him. "Help yourself."

Gat shifted, a little upset Esther had taken the slack out of his rope. He'd just have to speak to India another time when she wasn't sulky, but the way things were going between them that moment might never come.

"Eat up, cowboy," Esther said, spreading his bread with butter and strawberry jam.

Gat fixed his attention on eating, allowing that the two ladies had him beat; one by her goodwill and the other by her hostility. "You're too good to me, Esther."

"I quite agree," India said. "Esther, I do believe Mr. Ransom is capable of buttering his own bread." What was it about Ransom that made very woman so anxious to please him? He had passable manners, but then so did most men. He was handsome, but not dashing, and besides, Esther wouldn't be interested in him romantically, she being twice his age and already married. Maybe he needed mothering, but then again, he was one of the most independent souls she'd ever met. No, he didn't need a mother. Whatever his charm, India was exhausted from making the effort to withstand it.

"How's your brother James doing up at the digs?" Esther asked.

"They keep him busy surveying new sites. I sometimes think he's the only one making any money up there," Gat replied.

"You must meet James, India. He's about your age, and if I had a daughter, he's just the one I'd match her up with. He sang at the Friday recital a month ago and I've never heard a man sing like he did. Not even on the stage in New York. I really think James should join the opera. Such a talent is wasted here in the gold fields."

India couldn't hide her surprise.

"You never mentioned you had a brother here in South Pass," she said to Gat. "I'd like to meet him."

"I can arrange that," Esther said enthusiastically. "He always comes into town for the recitals."

"Do you sing, too?" India questioned Gat.

"No, ma'am," he said between mouthfuls.

"Don't be modest, Gat. He can stir up a pretty good evening's entertainment," Esther told India.

"I'm certain he can!" India remarked, remembering the brothel.

He lifted his eyes to hers, not missing the sarcasm. The air in the room sparked between them. But Esther, oblivious, chatted on. "Perhaps you could spread the word up at the mines that Saturday night's recital will include a speech on suffrage."

"I think the word will spread itself, Esther. But I'll do my best to let everyone know." He wiped his lips on a linen napkin and came to his feet. His towering presence made the room confining. "I'll be up at Miner's Delight till the end of the week. I'll bring James back down with me Saturday." He put on his hat and turned to India. "I hope you recover, ma'am," The intensity gone, a hidden half smile played at his lips.

She lifted her chin imperiously, eyes shining. "I am sure I will. I hope you don't count it as your misfortune if I do."

"No, ma'am." His face was serious again. "I'd be out of a job, then, wouldn't I?"

Esther followed him out and India heard the ring of his spurs as he stepped onto the porch. Why was it so difficult to speak a civil word to him, she wondered? She stared out the small glass window and attempted to analyze her feelings rationally. She didn't like depending on him, but there was more to it. He threatened her, he intimidated her, but worse, he changed her.

Her eyes fell to an incomplete letter on the bed stand. It would not be amiss to write her family. But how could she ever tell her family the truth of her travels? Her father would either disown her or catch the next train West and demand she return with him. Nevertheless, she owed the truth to her sister, the one person she trusted. Picking up the pen and paper, India mentally plotted the method of sending a letter to Sissy in care of their Aunt Elinor, who at her great age was unable to see well enough to read. Sissy spent one afternoon a week reading and writing Aunt Elinor's correspondence. Surely the letter would fall safely into Sissy's hands.

Dearest Sissy,

Since I wrote last much has happened to me. Indeed, were I to detail out my adventures in this letter you would be reminded of that old satanic tempter of our youth, novel reading. Though I have not suffered the horrid fate of seduction and consequent madness of the hapless heroine Charlotte Temple, my experiences are worth retelling, but not repeating, especially to our dear parents.

Firstly, I have learned to ride a horse! Imagine me on a horse, Sissy. It was you who always slipped behind father's back and begged a ride with our brothers. In truth, it is not so easy or as comfortable as it looks. But I intend to master the equestrian art as well as the specialty of campfire biscuit making. My trail guide, whom I will write more of later, is adept at frontier cookery. Along with biscuit making I have tried my hand at gambling. Yes, don't be too shocked, but it was only out of moral obligation to right a wrong that I became involved in a game of cards on the train. Truthfully, Sissy, I found it extremely occupying. The West affords many experiences to ladies which are taboo elsewhere.

I have had one close call, perhaps two. The most siginificant was while traveling from the railroad town of Green River to South Pass City. Without warning a storm broke. Oh, what a storm it was! The lightning jumped across the mountains and seemed at times to fall in forks everywhere. The thunder crashed and roared, and down came a deluge of rain. My pony became skittish and bolted off the trail. It was so dark I could not distinguish the surroundings. It was truly harrowing. After a wild ride I was able to rein in my exhausted pony and take shelter. Now, as a result, I lay in bed with a cold. But I do not despair, for it is a bed with clean white sheets and not some rocky spot in the wilderness.

I am recuperating in the home of a suffrage supporter

named Esther Morris. She has arranged for me to speak in the town church on Saturday night. A lady speaking in public might be considered a trifle vulgar in the East, but I am finding that here in the Wyoming such an occasion is very popular, so popular that the locals willingly pay an attendance fee. Wouldn't father be surprised to know that people are actually paying to hear me speak!

I cannot say where I will speak next for I am dependent upon my guide, a Mr. Ransom. He is an aging gentleman and I believe at one point in his life he had the inclination to take up the ministry. But various circumstances, the war included, led him along another path. Well, Sissy, that is all for now. I must begin preparing my Saturday night speech. God bless you all at Rosemount House.

Love,
India

India felt a slight prick of conscience as she folded and addressed the letter to Sissy. She had wanted to confess her feelings for Ransom to her sister, yet though she hadn't exactly lied, the less she said about him the better. She would lose all credibility with her eastern supporters if they knew she was traveling unchaperoned with a man the likes of Gat Ransom—the likes of whom she was falling in love.

Little heads bobbed underneath the pieced quilt stretched on frames in the center of Esther's parlor, while mothers busily stitched above. The soft giggles of the little girls floated up while they and their rag dolls played out magical fantasies beneath the seclusion of the quilt tent.

India, thimble on finger, leaned over the quilt frames and neatly stitched along the chalk-marked lines.

"I think we should rename the pattern the 'Wyoming Star,' in respect for our new territory," suggested Hanner White. With an approving nod, India looked across the bursting star design to the old, white-haired grandmother.

"And when women achieve the vote in Wyoming, each of us should embroider our name on the star points to mark the celebration," added Esther with a covert wink to India.

"Do you really think such an ideal will ever be achieved, Miss Simms?" one woman asked doubtfully.

"Of course," assured India. "But women must want it first. Each of us must see the merit of equality for ourselves, and then men will join us hand in hand to bring it about. There's not so much opposition as you think, especially here in the West where women are allowed more initiative."

"Oh, my Rob is against such notions. He refused to allow me to attend the Saturday recital once he heard a suffragette was speakin'," chimed in one young mother. "He said, she'd be a 'poisonin' my mind."

"I'll not poison your mind," laughed India. "But encourage your husband to come and listen without you, and perhaps I can soften his views. It would be to his benefit in the long run. Point out to him that your vote along with his own would give him a stronger voice in government."

"I'll try, but my Rob listens to his own counsel in most things."

India's own father was such a man, and she knew too well the young mother's plight. "Be patient with him," she encouraged, although she doubted the outcome.

"Well, I think it's time to roll the quilt," Esther said. She rose to her feet. "Another afternoon's work and it will be ready for binding."

"One moment," piped up old Hanner. She picked up a pair of brass scissors, adjusted her spectacles and proceeded to circle the quilt, scrutinizing the stitching for flaws. She took particular pause beside India.

For a moment, India feared she would ask her to unpick and restitch. Esther had warned her that it wasn't unheard of for a quilter's unsatisfactory stitches to be unpicked and restitched after everyone had gone home. India saw that Hanner was a perfectionist, and decided not to be offended if she chose to pick out her stitches.

"You know, Hanner, I must confess that when I was a girl

I hated sewing. My sister and I traded tasks. She would finish my samplers if I would figure her sums," India said, awaiting Hanner's judgement. The giggles of the other ladies told India that they, too, thought Hanner a bit extreme in her quest for the perfect stitch.

Hanner clicked her false teeth and looked over her spectacles. "Humph!" she muttered and then smiled slyly. "I hope you figure sums as well as you stitch." She moved on around the quilt, and India put her hand over her heart in exaggerated relief.

"India, why don't you bring the tea and cake while we roll the quilt," Esther directed. She unclamped the quilt frames and shooed the children out from underneath.

India hurried into the kitchen, picked up the tray of tin cups, sugar water and cake, and called the children to the outside sun porch for their own small party. Returning to the kitchen she poured the boiling water into Esther's flowered china teapot, and began to carry trays of cake and cups into the parlor. While the tea steeped, the ladies rolled and put aside the quilt.

They helped themselves to the pound cake and India went about pouring the tea.

"Delicious cake as usual, Esther" complimented one woman. "I'll have to have the recipe."

Esther looked over at India and smiled. "You'll have to ask Miss Simms for it, Elizabeth. She used that old recipe book of Mrs. Clawson's. You know the one we found in her cabin after she died last fall."

"Why, wasn't that the one written in some foreign language? I'm surprised you kept it," replied Elizabeth, sipping from her teacup.

"I'm glad I did. It was written in French and Miss Simms reads French. I've given the book to her. She says she has need of a recipe book."

"I am not a cook," India added, as she refilled Elizabeth's cup, "But French cuisine is known to be excellent. Especially the cakes. Unfortunately for the cake, some ingredients must be substituted. I'll gladly copy down the recipe for whomever would like it."

When the last lady left with pound cake recipe in hand, India was beaming. The recipe book must have been heaven-sent, because now, with a minimum of experimentation and a little advice from someone who could cook, she would be able to "stir up the grub," as Mr. Ransom put it. Clearing away the teacups, she thought about Mrs. Bow, the family cook back home whose recipes were all memorized, for she had never learned to read. Well, thought India, I can read, and certainly nothing could remain a mystery for long if you could read!

The small church was crowded to suffocation. Mostly men streamed in, but an occasional bonneted head bobbed in the audience. Butterflies swarmed in India's stomach as she sat on the stand and gazed out at the strange faces. She looked anxiously at Mr. Wright, the pastor, who was at the organ giving his wife, Emily, last minute program instructions. India turned her eyes back to the audience, wondering if Ransom and his brother would show up as promised.

"Miss Simms, I think everything is in order," assured Pastor Wright when he came and sat down beside India. "I'll give a few introductory words and then Emily will play the organ, after which you may address the audience. I do believe this is the largest crowd ever to fill the church, and to think they are paying to do it!" The pastor situated his middle-aged girth comfortably in his chair and began thumbing through his notes. India wondered how he would introduce her, for he had asked nothing about her personally.

He came to his feet and moved to the wooden podium. "Friends, it is time to begin our meeting. In opening, I will give a word of prayer."

Just as India bowed her head she caught a glimpse of Gat standing against the wall toward the back of the hall. During the prayer, she peeked through one eye, deciding the younger man beside him must be his brother, James. Their coloring was the same, though James appeared to have a more civilized demeanor. His hair was neatly cut and he wore a Prince Edward suit-coat.

At the prayer's conclusion, the pastor settled his notes on the podium and looked penetratingly into faces of his audience.

"If one greater evil or curse could befall American people than any other, in my judgment it would be to confer upon the women of America the right of suffrage." India sat up in her seat and nudged Esther, wondering if she heard correctly.

In punctuation to the pastor's words, a stick-thin old man stood up in the front row and shouted with amazing vigor an enthusiastic "Amen." A rumble of joining amens filled the room.

"Woman is intended to be delicate," Pastor Wright continued, warming to his subject. "She is intended to soften the asperities and roughness of the male. She is intended to comfort him in the days of his trials, and not to participate herself actively in the contest, either in the forum, in the council chambers, or in the battlefield!"

The old man shouted "Amen" once more, and India wondered how much the pastor was paying him for his support. The pastor's trick irritated her, but she could not deny the audience their right to hear both sides of the argument. She would sit in polite silence until her turn.

The pastor wiped his brow with his handkerchief in a dramatized gesture and sputtered onward, "The great God created all the races and in every race gave to man, woman. He never intended that woman should take part in national government among any people. Men assume the direction of government and war; women the domestic and family affairs and the care and training of the child. To keep her in this condition of purity, it is necessary that she should be separated from the exercise of suffrage and from all those stern, contaminating and demoralizing duties that are commissioned upon the hardier sex, man."

The popinjay! India smoldered and nudged Esther with every sentence. How could he be so biased? So closed minded? How could liberty and the right to vote be contaminating? The clergyman, determined to prohibit something, had turned to the prohibition of woman suffrage.

"Giving woman the vote would be a great step in the line of mischief and evil, and it would lead to other and equally fatal steps—in the same direction."

India inwardly questioned what those equally fatal steps were. Could enlightenment be a fatal step?

"In the depths and silence of the night when I send up my secret orations to my maker, my most fervent prayer is that the women of my country should be saved and sheltered by man from this great contamination. The ballot is God-given to man, not woman. From Bluestocking, Bloomerism and strong-minded she-males," he thundered, "God deliver us!"

The old man rose to his feet with a precarious sway and shouted "Amen" once again, and a commotion of applause resounded.

India could have wept. But at least she would have the last word! The pastor gave the signal to his wife who began to play. As the organ music rang out, India mentally inventoried her arguments and felt herself on solid ground. The final notes of the song came to a resounding halt.

India made to stand, but just as she did, the pastor put a cautioning hand on her arm and signaled to his wife once more. This time the organ burst into the more popular refrain of "Annie Laurie." Followed by "God Save the King" and "Praise God from Whom All Blessings Flow."

The evening wore on and India realized the pastor had no intention of allowing her to speak. Each time she started to rise, she was forced back to her seat as the organ burst into song. The audience was getting restless.

At last there came a short lull as Emily, exhausting her memorized repertoire, paused to open up a page to the hymnal.

Sudden inspiration seized India, and she arose, raised her hand, closed her eyes and said, in a loud but reverent voice, "Let us pray. O Father who art in Heaven, I ask that the spirit of harmony might abide among us, bringing us protection from the bigotry and tyranny of the pulpit. Father, absolve us from all vainglory, animosity and self-righteousness. In all things may our human judgment be tempered with mercy, that press, people and pulpit might alike be inspired and led to understand that absolute freedom for the mother-sex is the fundamental need of our slowly awakening country.

"Let the hand of love, not violence, rule every home, enabling mothers everywhere to do better work than raising and releasing to the world a progeny addicted to drunkenness, vice and crime.

"We pray the preachers of morality might be led by the Christian spirit of love into the ways of righteousness and peace, never prohibiting the spirit of liberty; and especially, as a means to this end, that the mothers of this race might be freed from the servitude without wages, and the slight of taxation without representation.

"Father, let us each know within our hearts that the ballot belongs not to the white man, not to the black man, not to the woman, not to the pastor or merchant, but to the citizen. We pray for the ballot for woman, not for woman's sake, but for man's! Amen."

When India ceased her prayer and opened her eyes, she beheld a silent, astonished audience. The poor pastor sat, elbows on knees, his open hands clasping his jaws, his eyes staring vacantly. The crowd slowly rose and began surging forward to clasp India's hands.

Suddenly the organ burst into an enthusiastic rendition of "The Battle Hymn of the Republic." The pastor jumped to his feet and rushed to the organ and attempted, without success, to silence his wife who was now caught up in the moment.

"Why, ma'am, ain't you the best lady prayer this side of the Mississippi," complimented one grizzly-bearded miner, as he pumped India's hand in greeting. Esther came, and the quilting ladies, while men starved for the sight of a comely woman waited patiently to shake India's hand.

"The petition, Esther. Are they signing it?" India was suddenly anxious that no one leave without signing.

"Don't worry, it's on the table by the door," Esther called in return.

When at last the crowd emptied from the church and the pastor had managed to restrain his wife, India collapsed in a pew and slowly perused the numerous signatures on her petition.

"Well, ma'am," she heard a deep voice from behind. "I believe you gave them their nickel's worth."

India turned to face Mr. Ransom, anxious to be polite for once. "I hope I gave them more than that!"

"I warrant you certainly did!" smiled Gat's young companion.

"Miss Simms, I'd like you to meet my brother, James."

India stretched out her hand to James and smiled. "I am happy to make your acquaintance, Mr. Ransom."

"My brother has told me about you. I am in sympathy with your cause and wish you success, though I am sure you'll succeed if tonight's prayer, ah, speech was an example."

"You are very kind, sir," India returned with a modest smile.

"Well, since you two are fast becoming friends," Ransom gave India a chafing gaze, "I'll leave you to escort Miss Simms home, James. Ma'am, be ready first thing in the morning, we're moving on."

"So soon?" India didn't relish the thought of climbing back up on a horse.

"Yes, ma'am." Ransom turned away and strode out of the church.

India's eyes followed his departure, a bit disappointed that he did not stay and share the company.

The kitchen of Esther Morris's home seemed to be the favorite spot for conversation when Esther, India and James came in the door. Esther called to her husband, Hayward, who sat rocking back and forth in front of the woodstove reading. When he saw them, he gave a welcoming nod.

"Good evening to you, Hayward," greeted James. He took off his hat and pulled out a chair for India. His manners were beyond reproach, his speech educated, and his refinement obvious.

Lamplight illuminated the spacious kitchen where the copper teapot on the stove hissed in readiness. Esther shook out a tablecloth and spread it over the pinewood trestle table. She retrieved cups and saucers from the cupboard.

"How was the meeting?" Hayward asked.

"A great success! Why I do believe Miss Simms beat the preacher at his own game." Esther laughed. "Though I declare my side is black and blue from India's nudges and pokes as she listened to his speech."

India flushed. "I apologize, Esther. I was riled to the extreme."

"But I thought it was Miss Simms who was invited to speak," said Hayward.

"It seems the pastor had his own idea about that," said James. "I hope all Miss Simms's lectures are not thwarted in a like manner."

India nodded an agreement. "I pray there is only one Pastor Wright in Wyoming, or my speaking tour will be a short one."

"Gat says he hopes to have you back in Cheyenne by the end of July," began James. Esther poured him a cup of tea.

"I think he's in a hurry to be done with it," India replied. "I can't blame him for preferring the company of cattle to escorting me." Nevertheless, it upset India to think Gat was counting the days till he was rid of her—*a woman for whom he'd lost respect*. She lowered her eyes self-consciously, dreading that Gat might have disclosed her indiscretions to his brother, who in turn might pass it on, until every man, woman and child in the territory knew of the suffrage lady's wild ways.

James laughed. "My brother does have his preferences,

that's for sure, but not even he would choose the company of cattle to that of a beautiful, genteel lady.''

India lifted her eyes with relief at his compliment. Suddenly, she was confident that Gat had kept his own counsel and her reputation was still intact. But then she wanted to know why Gat hadn't accompanied them back to Esther's after the lecture. Of course, it should make no difference to her whether or not Ransom found her companionship enjoyable, but it did. When the choice was his, he always chose to go somewhere else. The saloon seemed to be his usual habitat. The thought piqued India's curiosity about the brothers. She was sure James would never patronize an establishment like Contessa's, would never chew tobacco, or hire out his gun, or for that matter even carry one.

In their brief discussion on the walk from the church, James had quoted Plato and Aristotle and confessed that John Stuart Mill had swayed his own philosophies in favor of women's rights. Imagine, she thought, a man acquainted with Mill in South Pass City!

"You and your brother seem to have little in common," India said, offering him a berry tart, another of her baking experiments.

When he raised a querulous dark eye, so much like his brother's, India almost retracted her words. "Why do you say that?" he said.

"Oh, it's just that . . ." she fumbled for the right word afraid of insulting the Ransoms, "he has little interest or education in philosophy. I gather he has no use for the cause of suffrage. He merely escorts me about for payment."

"Gat is not an easy man to get to know," returned James. "He keeps his own counsel, but don't underestimate him. He is better versed than I in most philosophies. After our mother died Gat, being the eldest, was the one who reared us until our father remarried. As our schoolmaster he taught us to read and write, a skill he learned from our late mother."

James paused thoughtfully. "You know, when he went off to the war, it nearly broke my heart. The day he came back alive was the happiest of my life. But he'd changed. He walked up to me and pulled out a roll of greenbacks and put it in my hand.''

James's voice was reflective. "He said, 'Jamie, take this money and use it for the university. You won't ever be a soldier if I can help it.' I took the money and used it for an education in engineering. So, ma'am, don't judge my brother too harshly. The war roughened him around the edges, but he is no different from me inside.''

"Any mother would be proud of you boys," said Esther, patting James's arm affectionately. Snoring from the vicinity of Hayward Morris caused Esther to look over at her dozing husband and shake her head. "I believe that man could sleep through an earthquake.''

"It's late," James said. He picked up his teacup and carried it over to the dry sink. It was a task India had never seen a man bother with before. "It's been a pleasure, Miss Simms. I hope we meet again.''

It wouldn't be likely, but India smiled and offered her hand to him as a parting gesture. "Thank you so much for escorting me home. It seems now I am indebted to both of the Ransom brothers.''

"And might I speak for both of us in expressing that it is an honor to make your acquaintance. Good night, Esther.'' He put on his hat and stepped out into the night, leaving India to ponder over the inaccessible Gat Ransom.

Chapter 10

I think I've struck it!'' hollered India. Gat saw her running along the river with a goldpan in hand. He set aside his fishing pole and squinted up into the late afternoon sun while she tilted her pan for him to inspect. "You see, it's sparkling," she ran her finger over the dregs.

"I suppose you think you've found El Dorado," he grinned. Picking up his pole, he cast the line back into the stream. He had thought it a good joke when James had given her that goldpan the day they left South Pass, but the novelty had worn thin after four days of standing by while she sifted half the banks of the Sweetwater every time they stopped for camp. "I think you've got gold fever."

"I have more sense than that!" she said defensively, following the line of his eyes to her exposed legs. With a self-conscious show of modesty she unhitched her skirts. He frowned but wasn't thwarted in his observations.

He likened her to a child let loose in a mud hole, running barefoot over the banks, hitching her skirts knee high as she waded along. The turn of a shapely ankle and flash of a bare leg had been entertaining, but for him, it wasn't child's play anymore. He'd realized it that night in South Pass after he'd introduced India to James. When a man becomes jealous of his own brother it's time to face up to a few things. James was everything he wasn't and more suited to a lady of refinement and education like India, maybe it was a little of the "dog in the manger" in Gat, but that's why he'd made the decision to move on so soon.

"The only gold you'll find around here is the speckles on the trout. Now why don't you take the fish I've caught and fix some grub?"

"I don't know how to cook fish," she said, brushing the sand from her legs.

"Well, look it up in your fancy cookbook." He'd been glad to find the week at Esther's had broadened her cooking skills. Since then, the times she'd decided to cook over the campfire had resulted in food that was more than passable.

"I did."

"And?" She could be stubborn. Willful and stubborn, he decided. She was always looking for an argument.

"It said to rub the innards with garlic and juice of lemon; pepper and salt to flavor and braise in fresh-churned butter."

"Well, what are you waiting for?"

"We don't have any of those ingredients."

"We got salt, ain't we?"

"Yes . . . but . . ."

"Maybe you'd rather stand here and catch the fish and gut them?"

"No thank you. You win, I'll cook. But when supper's over I'm going to pan for gold. And if I strike it rich, won't you be surprised."

He gave a scoffing laugh. "There's only one thing that would surprise me more."

"And what would that be?"

"Women gettin' the vote!"

"You might be a born pessimist, Mr. Ransom, but I'm your match, because I'm a born optimist!" She flashed him a parting smile, drew the string of trout out of the water and with her arm stretched to an exaggerated length carried them up to camp.

Gat cast his line into the river and settled back to wait for a bite, he watched the light little figure with the defiant tilt of head disappear up the riverbank. He had to admit she could do about anything she put her mind to. The only problem was getting her to put her mind to it. There was something of the she-fox in her nature.

He'd known what was happening to them both and he was pretty certain she knew too, but he'd be the last to let her know he'd fallen for her. What would she say if she knew? Would she be shocked? Or would she laugh in his face and spout something about matrimony being slavery? To hold her a man would have to be twice as strong, and twice as determined. Willful, altruistic and wholly female: no, she wasn't for him.

Even so he liked her—her hard, bright intelligence, her lack of affectation. She was a woman who used her brain and was proud of it—even though most of the time her philosophies bordered on the eccentric, but he attributed that to her naivete, or what he supposed was her naivete. She hadn't seemed so inexperienced that day he'd kissed her on the trail. He still thought of that kiss. He thought about other things too.

His dark eyes rested on the shimmering river and he recalled a forest in the Colorado Rockies he'd wandered into a few summers before. It was a place a man didn't forget; a rare spot on earth within the depth of wood and canyon. Because of the hot spring the Indians called it "the place of good medicine." Overhead tips of pine and aspen nodded in the breeze, shafts of sunlight, flecked with dust motes, dappled the soft forest floor while wisps of steam rose from the clear pool partly formed by lichen etched rock. The dream haze lifted slowly and India was there beside the pool waiting for him. She walked toward him skyclad, an earth goddess, unconcealed, with the undulating motion of wind on water. Like the aspen leaves in the trees surrounding him Gat trembled with anticipation. All this time she'd excited him with expectation and yet denied him satisfaction. Now, she took his hand and they walked barefoot over the moss to the pool and he waded into his longings.

The water was warm compared to the mountain air and warmer still was the taste of her lips against his own. Like the sun breaking through the mist she kissed him deeply and a rapid pulse burst to his extremities as she unfurled herself to him like leaves to spring. Her hair, the auburn of willow catkins, swirled in the crystalline water and her earth musk fragrance was pungent in the heavy air. He drew her close, running his hands through her hair's silkiness and sliding his fingers down over hips that held the innocence of earth. The mist, a seductive breath, enveloped them and their lovemaking became a dream of wildness, wild and strange and inexhaustible. He could never have enough of her . . .

Suddenly, Gat heard screams, India's screams! His daydream vanished as quickly as the rustle of the breeze. Coyote growled and ran up the bank. Gat dropped the fishing pole, pulled his gun and scrambled up after the dog. Her cries were overridden by a blood curdling Sioux war cry. By damn! thought Gat, Indians!

Belly down, he crawled through the brush to the camp's edge. He spied only one, but others could be lurking nearby in the willow. The brave held her by the hair and he was bending over the fire, snatching at the broiling fish.

"White woman steal Bear Claw's fish. Bear Claw not happy." She struggled under his hold.

With wagging tail, Coyote ran and sniffed the Indian's heels. A slow smile of relief crept over Gat's face when he recognized the voice and then the profile. Tom Skinner! That old devil. He could pass for an Indian even among Indians.

"Bear Claw take white woman to tepee, make good cook." Skinner's words didn't seem to intimidate India.

"White woman go nowhere with Bear Claw." She shook her head with finality. "White woman cook poison for Bear Claw. Give him big stomachache." Gat chuckled under his breath.

Skinner gave a merciless yank on her hair, then pulled out his knife and waved it threateningly. India returned his stare, without a hint of fear. Now, Gat was impressed.

But about that time, he decided he'd better make a grandstand play and come to her rescue. No use letting her get too confident or he'd be out of a job.

He rose to his feet and raised his hands in a sign of peace. He said, "White woman big trouble. Bear Claw take woman. I give Bear Claw woman." The look of shock on India's face was well worth the charade. Gat had never thought to see her dumbfounded.

Tom Skinner looked to the face of his friend and gave a conspiratory wink. He tightened his hold on India's hair and squatted down beside her. Nose to nose he leered ferociously. "Your man give you to me. You my squaw now."

"I no man's squaw!" she sneered. "Better trade for Bear Claw to take white man's scalp than lazy squaw."

Skinner could not contain himself. He jumped back and let out a guffaw. He held his belly and hooted. "Ransom, where'd you find this gal? I never knowed a lady so plucky. Why, she'd out-grit a bear. Yer scalp ain't much use to her."

Gat walked forward, wondering himself. "It appears not." He gave Skinner a hefty pat on the back. India looked from his face to Skinner's in confusion. Then, Gat saw the truth begin to dawn on her face like sunrise in morning. "Miss Simms, this is Tom Skinner, 'Mountain Tom' to his friends."

She got up off the ground, shook the dirt from her leather skirt, and gave him an outraged stare. Gat was still chuckling, but his amusement subsided quickly. The fury in her eyes simmered like the sulfur pools of Yellowstone. They'd gone too far.

Gat cleared his throat. "Tom, sit down, have some supper. We've got plenty. I left a mess of fish and my pole down by the river. You had me goin' too, I'll say that for you."

India said nothing.

Gat kept looking over at her, a little uneasy about his part in the joke. Then, with lips clenched, she turned without a word and went over the bank and down to the river to fetch the fish—he hoped. He knew she had put on a brave act and he admired her for it. Suddenly, he realized she was probably fairly unsettled. Perhaps an apology was in order. That would make a second one he owed her.

When she finally returned with the fish, Gat attempted to

draw her into their conversation, but all he received was a contemptuous glare.

Tom was not averse to talk, however, and after supper he propped his feet up on a stone by the fire, lit a pipe and gazed at the summer sun still high in the sky. His hair was waist long, straight and black, against a face browned by years in the sun and wind; his eyes were clear and keen as a hawk's. Indians, miners and soldiers became his subjects of discourse. He talked about various occurrences during his many years of trapping and living in the West. Gat listened attentively, as youth listens to experience.

"I suppose with the railroad done there'll be more pilgrims. Maybe if we're lucky they'll ride on through to Californy." Tom took a long draw on his pipe. "I'm sorry a white man ever saw these valleys. Mind you, I ain't no Indian lover, but when I traveled these valleys twenty years ago there was no trouble with the Indians. I've been through all their camps—Blackfeet, Sioux, Crow—and they treated me with the best they had in those days. Now the same Indians would shoot me if I got near 'em." Gat nodded in genuine agreement.

"It's the damned government's two-tongue talkin' that has riled 'em up," said Tom with a forlorn sigh. "Times is changin'. You know it's a fun'un you should try and give me this here woman for a trade." Skinner looked over at India who was spooning more coffee into the pot. She gave him a baleful glare in return. "I've been thinkin' on takin' a wife."

India's eyes riveted to Gat's as if warning him not to suggest her as a candidate.

"Sounds like you're gettin' civilized to me, Tom," Gat said. "But I'm sure you can find a woman who could be prevailed upon to undertake that honor." He gave India a sidelong glance. "I hear tell there's an overabundance of heart-and-hand females in the East just hankerin' for male companionship."

India's eyes narrowed.

"Yes sir, most likely, but the devil of it is, could a man

find the right kind? Better be without them at all than get one of the wrong kind."

"Well," remarked Gat, "you'd have to take your chances like the rest of us."

"Maybe," Tom mused. "I expect if it turned out bad, I could drop her like I did my squaws. There's no divorce in this country."

"Suppose she got tired and wanted to drop you first?" interjected India, much to Gat's enjoyment.

Tom looked over at Gat incredulously. "Where'd you find this heifer?" Gat only grinned. "She reminds me of a little Snake squaw I bought for a pistol and bullet about twelve year back. She was purty skeered at first and run away, but I caught her and whipped her good. Clipped a little slice out of her ear, then she stayed close by."

"Mr. Skinner," India began with a politeness Gat knew she didn't feel, "it might pay you to visit civilization now and again. Times may be changing, but believe me, it is for the better. Perhaps you would care to sign a petition in support of giving women the right to vote?" She went to her saddlebag and pulled out her parcel. "We no longer live in the dark ages, and if you intend to keep a wife by slicing her ear, do the female population a favor by remaining a bachelor."

Tom took a puff of his pipe and gave Gat a sly wink. "Maybe you are right, Miss Simms. In this country it's better to take a squaw than marry a white woman. They are more profitable. They ain't got expensive luxuries, and they can dress in skins and catch yer horse if it has a mind to run away. Why, they can do all kinds of work. And most mainly, their powers of conversation is limited." He laughed heartily at his own joke.

Gat looked over to India, wondering if Tom Skinner knew how close he was coming to a death by choking.

Her eyes narrowed and she gave a tight smile of toleration, then with an exaggerated "humph," as if to say she was done casting pearls before swine, she turned her back on them. Gat supposed she was at the end of her tether. He watched in mock gravity while she opened the parcel and took out the petition ledger, set it aside, and picked up one of the dime novels. She sat down and settled back against the support of her saddle and began to read silently to herself.

"What you readin', Miss Simms?" Skinner asked. He bent to pour himself another cup of coffee.

"A ten-cent novel entitled *The Heroine of Whoop-Up*." She continued reading.

"You mind readin' aloud, Missy? I have a particular enjoyment of such stories."

Gat thought she perked up to the request.

"I don't mind, Mr. Skinner, but I am not sure you or Mr. Ransom would enjoy this adventure, for the heroine is quite outspoken. At one point in the story she says to the hero, 'Oh! sir, but you are venturing into peril on my account. Pray do not do that. I would rather accompany you and thus share the risk.' And then the hero replies, 'Lady, you are wrong. You are not one to brave peril when I, whose very life is made up of peril and adventure, am able to act in your behalf.'"

"Well, he's certainly right in keepin' her out o' trouble," agreed Skinner. He put down his cup and rummaged through a beaded leather pocket attached to his legging.

"But don't you think her assistance might be useful in a tight situation? Women can shoot and ride as well as men," India proposed. Gat wondered if she ever got down off her soapbox.

"Maybe, but from my experience they just get in the way. Here Missy, this here's the story to read." He displayed his own dime novel.

"A few years back this writer feller came to Fort Laramie and set by my campfire one night. I told him some o' my adventures, and a year later when I was down to the fort again, this package was waitin' thar fer me and this ten-cent novel were in it. Mountain Tom. That's me." He pointed proudly to the buckskin clad man on the cover. "It ain't of'en I come across someone that kin read. I kin't myself.

Course I know it by heart but it would pleasure me to have you read it aloud.''

"I will gladly," India relented. "It isn't often one can meet a genuine hero in person." Gat could see in her eyes Tom had been forgiven as she carefully opened the pages of the wellworn novel. He just wished his turn would come.

" 'The Far West!' " she began. " 'Magnificent and un-known region—with its boundless oceans of verdure, its endless prairies, its stupendous mountains, its enormous rivers, its fierce animals, and fiercer men!

" 'Our story opens on a certain afternoon, about three of the clock, many years ago.

" 'A single horseman sits upon his beast and surveys the territory about him. The rider is a trapper, one of that sturdy race of frontiersmen which is fast fading away before the advancing strides of civilization. His eyes are decidedly black, with a grim sort of humor in their depths—the play-fulness of a tiger, perhaps. His shoulders are broad, and the development of his chest and limbs is enormous; there is no superfluous flesh, but his muscles stand out like whipcords. His body is too long and his legs too short to be symmetrical; he is, in fact, a vast amount of rude strength, compactly put into a very small compass. He sits astride his steed like one who feels fully and perfectly at home there.' "

Before continuing, India looked over at Tom critically. The color of the eyes matched at least. She continued.

" 'This man is a trapper, and let it suffice for the present to say that his name, according to the parish register of a little town in North Carolina, where he was born and chris-tened, is Thomas Skinner. He is known by his hunting acquaintances, however, by the more familiar cognomen of ''Mountain Tom''.' "

"I didn't know you were born in North Carolina, Tom," interjected Gat.

"Sure was. That writer feller got it all down purty good. I reckon I'll become a legend in ma own time." They laughed.

India cleared her throat for their attention and began to read once more. " 'Mountain Tom was evidently a trifle out of humor about something. His face wore an expression of doubt, not unaccompanied by anxiety.' "

"Excuse me, Missy," Tom interrupted. "I wonder ef'n you could tell me what that word . . . *anxiety* means? I never knowed it."

"Yes, it means to worry," India replied.

"To worry? Humph!" Skinner seemed to discredit the thought.

India continued, " 'Mountain Tom raised himself in the stirrups and was looking intently to the right, among the hills, beyond which flowed the waters of the North Platte.

" ' "Claw my hair!" he ejaculated, in a heavy, substantial tone, indicative of ill humor and also good lungs. "Ef them ain't Injins, then thar's no use of a feller havin' either eyes or nose. Them ain't deer, nor buffler, nor coyotes. Them's beyond doubt pesky Injins—Snakes, like's not, an' they'll lift ma scalp fer me."

" 'The trapper was correct. A party of some twelve or fifteen Snake Indians appeared out of the hills to the east. They were mounted, and seemed to be moving toward the hunter. Then, with a yell, they darted forward.' "

The sun lowered in the sky as India read of Tom's heroic scrapes with Indians, grizzly bears and wolves. Every so often she would stop and ask him to verify a particular happening, which he did without hesitation. At last, when sunset gave way to twilight, she set down the book and rubbed her tired eyes. "You've lived quite a life, Mr. Skinner, if this ten-cent novel is to be believed."

"Why, Missy, that ain't the half of it. Thar's one gut-twistin' story I never dared tell that thar writer feller, but if you ain't the faintin' sort, I'll gladly relate it to ya now."

"Indeed yes, Mr. Skinner, I would like to hear your story," India prompted with sincere interest.

"It's purty scary, but I swear it's true. Ya might not want ter sleep alone after ya hear it." He looked over at Gat and winked on the sly.

"Don't worry about me. I'll be quite content to sleep alone, Mr. Skinner," India assured him as she snuggled into her woolen blanket cocoon to ward off the cool night air. She made a marked effort to avoid Ransom's dark-eyed glance, pushing away the unsettling image Skinner's words had sparked.

Since South Pass, she and Gat seemed to collide much more than usual when they moved around their camps, and his hands held her a little too long when he helped her off her horse. Occasionally, as they walked side by side, the backs of their hands touched, and she'd quickly steal a glance at him, but he'd continue looking straight ahead, unaware. It was as if something threatened to explode inside her, and some nights she'd go to bed with her body so tense she found it difficult to fall asleep.

The embers in the fire burned low, and the coyotes called across the silhouetted hills. Tom produced a rough carved pipe from his leg pouch and prepared to smoke. He began to tell his curious story in a soft, slow voice. Gat and India leaned forward to catch his words.

"Some years back I had this here partner, a Frenchman called Defago. Defago wanted me to ride into the Yellowstone to find new trappin' grounds. Well, he talked me into it, agin my better judgment, mind you. Oh, it weren't just Indians made me hesitate, it were the strange goin's on up in that country." Tom paused and his eyes seemed to glow like the hot coals of the fire. "Queer things like the devil's work," he finally breathed in a chilling voice.

India looked slowly left and right into the darkness and inched a little nearer the fire.

"We camped in snow by a lake. Fer three days we set traps but never ketched nothin'. On the fourth night a wind storm came up. Funny thing though, the trees was standin' perfectly still, nary a branch or leaf moved. We could hear the wind howlin' but just couldn't see it. And as we listened, it sounded as if it were callin' Defago's name. 'Da-faaaaaaaaay-go!' it'd call. 'Da-faaaaaaaaay-go!' until we thought we was losin' our minds.

"Well, my partner started to get skeered and he buried his head in his arms. 'What's goin' on?' I asked, but he wouldn't say nothin'. The wind kept callin' to him, 'Da-faaaaaaaaay-go!' " Skinner wailed out the name and stared steadily into India's face. He paused, and a deep hush fell around the trio. A shiver rippled down India's spine as the strange and scary imps of her childhood imagination crept into her mind.

"Da-faaaaaaaaay-go!" Skinner suddenly jumped toward India. The unexpectedness of it brought a yelp to her lips and she jumped toward Ransom for protection. His arm went around her shoulders and a slow smile touched the corners of his mouth. He had to hand it to Tom for being a real matchmaker. "Now Tom, you'd better not scare her. I think she's had enough of your teasin' for one day."

"I ain't teasin'. No, I just wanted her to feel how skeered I was m'self."

A little embarrassed, India attempted a smile, and moved from beneath Ransom's arm, not a great distance but enough for propriety's sake. Then she prompted, "Go on, Mr. Skinner."

"It finally got to ma partner, and suddenly he jumped to his feet and went runnin' off into the trees. I chased him an' tried to wrestle him to the ground. He broke free o' me. The wind kept callin'. He was screamin' as he went. Again and again he cried, 'Oh ma fiery feet, ma burnin' feet o' fire.' After a spell, his voice faded away and the wind died down.

"At daybreak, I followed his tracks in the snow. Lordy, they got longer and longer like no man could have made 'em. Then they just disappeared. It made no sense. While I stood thar wonderin' what had happened, the wind picked up again. It were howling like the night before. Then I heered Defago's voice. It were comin' from above, and he were a screamin', 'Ma fiery feet, ma burning feet'. I couldn't see nothin'.

"Well, I decided I needed a change o' scenery real quick. I went back to camp, packed up, left some food for Defago and started south." Skinner took a long draw on his pipe and shook his head thoughtfully. "It were surely queer."

"Did you see Defago again and discover what had happened?" India's curiosity got the best of her.

"No, ma'am."

"But what could have happened to him?" she puzzled.

"Well, I kin't say fer sure but I believe it were the *Wendigo*."

"The *Wendigo*?" India looked over to Ransom doubtfully. But he seemed to take Tom's disclosure with gravity.

"Yes, ma'am," said Skinner. "The Indians believe the *Wendigo* is a female spirit what calls her victims to her. She carries them away so fast that thar feet ketches fire."

"So you think that is what happened to your partner, Defago?"

"With nary a doubt," returned Skinner. He tapped out his pipe and yawned. "Well, I'm ready to rest ma bones. How about you, Ransom?"

"It's about that time of night. I'll check on the horses before turning in." He stood and walked off into the darkness.

Ransom's absence made India uncomfortable. In the flickering light of the campfire Tom Skinner's wild appearance became odious, and she hadn't forgiven him for the prank he had played on her earlier. Adjusting her bedding, she situated herself close to the fire and made sure Ransom's bedding was between her and Skinner. As she drifted off to sleep her thoughts pondered over the missing Defago, and she decided it was just another attempt of Skinner's to tease her. Yes, she'd almost fallen for it.

Later, India sat upright in the darkness and probed underneath her bedding for a stone that jabbed her back. The fire burned low and both Ransom and Skinner were sleeping soundly. The wind picked up, whipping the limbs of the trees and bushes along the riverbank. India tossed the stone over her shoulder and lay back, only to find another, more pointed than the last. She sat up once more.

Skinner had begun to snore. She supposed she wouldn't get much sleep that night. The wind pulled at her hair and suddenly an idea sneaked into her thoughts. Skinner seemed almost too peaceful, snoring away. Perhaps he deserved a turnabout. India smiled mischievously.

Stealthily, she crept out of her bedding and picked up her horse blanket. Using the blanket, she carefully picked up one of the hot rocks circling the fire and carried it over to Skinner. His large stockingless feet protruded from under his blanket. She set down the rock, putting the warmest face near Skinner's feet. After another noiseless trip to the fire circle she put a second rock next to his other foot. Then she secluded herself behind some scrubby bushes off to the side.

"Skinnnnnn-ner," she wailed. The blowing wind carried her voice. "Skinnnnnn-ner, Skinnnnnnnnn-ner." She called more loudly, raising her voice to a harpylike shriek. "Skinnnnnnnnn-ner!"

She noticed Ransom was stirring and so she cried out again. "Skinnnnnnnnnnnnnnn-ner!" Tom sat up suddenly. She called out his name in a shrill eerie note.

"Lordy! Deliver me!" yelled Tom, still half asleep. He grabbed at his feet and jumped up. India kept calling his name. "Ma feet's afire. Lordy!" he shouted, as he danced around. "The *Wendigo* has got me!"

By now Ransom was awake. Seeing India's absence from her bed and watching Tom dance around, he figured out pretty quick what was going on. "Run to the river, Tom. Cool off your feet," Gat shouted.

Tom didn't need any encouragement. Off he ran, through the brush and into the river. India kept calling until Gat routed her out of her hiding place.

"Haven't you got better things to do than scare the breeches off that poor soul?" he chastened her, but with a grin.

"I couldn't sleep, and besides, I don't think he is so poor. He frightened me more than I could ever frighten him. Skinnnnnnnnn-ner!" she called out toward the river just for good measure.

"Well," Gat gave a half laugh. "come on, we better catch him before he drowns."

When they got down to the river they could hear Tom swearing.

India tried not to laugh outright. It wouldn't be polite to gloat.

He was wringing out his pantlegs and shaking his head. "I have to admit that woman of yers bested me this time. Whar'd you find her? I declare she's got more guts than you can hang on a fence. I've never been caught by ma own stories until now. Lordy!" He began to chuckle.

So did India, at first softly, then she forgot courtesy and her lips broke into a gloating grin.

In the morning they broke camp, and just before they went their separate ways, Skinner came over to India. "Missy, I reckon I'll put my scratch on yer petition fer the vote."

India turned to him with surprise. "Why, Mr. Skinner, I'd be honored to have you sign."

"I got to thinkin' 'bout what you said 'bout changin' with the times. You know, that's how I survived all these years, by movin' with the weather of things. I ain't never voted m'self, but I sure hope a gritty lady like yerself gets a chance ter, ef 'n she wants ter."

Happily India flipped open the petition ledger, dipped the pen into the inkwell and handed it to Skinner. He slowly scrawled his name across the line. "Excellent," she said at its completion.

He walked over and offered his hand to Gat in farewell, and then climbed up on his horse.

"Keep that scalp of yours on your head," cautioned Gat, with a final wave of good-bye.

"I intend to!" he called back. Skinner let out his famous war whoop and rode off.

Chapter 11

*A*fter Tom Skinner, the miners in the goldfields seemed tame to India. Often when she rode into a camp the men stopped work and respectfully listened to her speak, and many signed her petition. When she stayed the night, someone was always ready to offer her their bachelor quarters to sleep in. This hospitality was sometimes double-edged, for India often couldn't abide the filth of the shacks. Some nights, after the lights went out, vermin drove her to sleep in a chair or to curl up on a tabletop. Preferring mosquitoes or even snakes to the creeping critters of the miner's huts, more often she chose to make her bed outside near Ransom, though in some ways this was even more discomforting.

It again became the question of who would protect a woman from her protector. Ransom might not be overt in his desire for her, yet the potency of his masculine presence was a constant threat. He watched her. It seemed as if he never took his eyes off of her; he never left her alone except when she needed personal privacy. In mining camps he might attend to the horses, sit off to the side and play tunes on his penny whistle, but the spot he chose to situate himself always had clear view of the camp and India. His dark-eyed gaze became an unbidden but connective thread between them. Sometimes she had experienced a prickliness at the nape of her neck only to turn to meet his intense gaze.

One particularly warm day she yearned to retreat from those watching eyes and succumbed to the luxury of a tub bath within the privacy of a miner's tent. She'd asked a willing miner to fill a pine tub with hot water, and after he left she proceeded to lift the doeskin dress over her head, unfasten the camisole top, and slip out of her silk pantalettes. Unfortunately, there was no soap to be had, so India made do with sprinkling the water with wild mint leaves. She spent a leisurely hour of self-indulgence, soaking off the trail grime and imagining what it would be like to be really clean again. While humming a lilting refrain, her skin and hair fragrant with mint, she dressed and sauntered out of the tent to dry her hair in the sun. At the tent's threshold her humming as well as her heart stopped. Gat stood, pistols drawn, holding every miner in the camp at bay. She was mortified.

"Collect together your things, ma'am. It's time we moved on," Gat said quietly.

India lost no time in getting on her horse. He never took his eyes or his guns off the miners as he climbed up on his own horse. They rode out of the mining camp in silence. India dared not look back.

Later, when they were out of danger, Gat spoke. "Your first mistake was in asking that damn Swede to carry in the tub. Some of those men haven't seen a woman in six months. He spread the word fast."

"I just never thought . . ." India began.

"It's time you did!" Irritation filled his voice. "Besides voting, there are other things a woman doesn't do and one of them is flaunt herself in front of men."

India flushed with indignation. "I was not flaunting myself! Why is it I'm to be blamed?"

"You don't drag fresh meat past starving wolves."

"That is no comparison. Are you a man or animal?"

"It's hard to say. When the dinner bell rings I can get down on all fours and run with the best of them." His black eyes locked to her own and she saw the smoldering heat of his lust; the core of his masculine power and its undeniable threat to her own independence. Goosebumps tingled across her skin and a cloying lump rose to her throat at the undisguised carnality of his nature which in a glance could unleash her own.

Her retort was swift, sharp, penetrating. "By God I wish you were a woman! A woman escorted and chaperoned everywhere she went because the male population of the earth lacks willpower? Yes, I'd like to see you imprisoned from head to toe in skirts of calico and being ever reminded that beneath all that yardage you are the tempter's tool!"

Gat muttered under his breath, "Lord, deliver me from temptation."

Overhearing, India said hotly, "Have no fear, at least *I* have willpower!"

"Ma'am, that might be your misfortune."

India's eyes narrowed at his insolence. "You are my misfortune, Mr. Ransom, and every man like you!" Her red lips tightened stubbornly and she spurred her horse ahead.

Gat swore and drew up short. His own anger snapped like a whipcord. Day and night had required all his control to keep himself on leash, let alone an entire mining camp. Just the thought of her naked, white, slender body soaking in the pine tub made him want to drink rot gut and start a barroom brawl out of pure frustration. He wanted her in every possible way a man could want a woman. Every time she moved or spoke, or even looked at him, he'd wanted her. Clenching and unclenching his fist he fought to regain reason, all the while regretting he'd lost his temper with her.

The storm had been gathering all afternoon, and once it broke, the heavens burst like a hundred rivers. India and Gat spurred their horses into a dashing gallop, across a ridge and down into a valley toward a homestead cabin. Ransom pounded on the door of the cabin, leaving India to face the occupants, while he returned to retrieve their gear and supplies from the horses.

A black-bearded patriarch of a man opened the door to India and he immediately grasped their situation. He motioned India inside, and then ran out to assist Ransom. Inside, a fire blazed in a rock hearth and a row of golden heads lined the benches of a long table. They eyed India curiously but said nothing. Water dripped in pools around her feet. A woman, sitting in the corner nursing a baby beneath the screen of a shawl, gave India a faint smile. She was fair-skinned, her hair the color of tallow and her eyes pale gray. She seemed but a wisp, as delicate and fragile as the child she nursed.

"We were caught in the storm," India explained. Her eyes rested on two older boys whose hair and eyes were marked by the light coloring of their mother. The door opened behind her and in came Ransom and their father. India took a step toward the fireplace, conscious of trailing water with each step.

"My wife and I are grateful for your hospitality," Gat said, as he put down an armload of saddlebags and gear. India looked at him aghast. She opened her mouth to make a denial, but Gat quickly put his arm around her, his fingers squeezing her shoulder in a signal of caution. Her lesson at the mining camp caused her to hold her tongue temporarily, but she was completely unable to halt the tingling sensation his touch sent through her shoulder and down her spine. "We're on our way to Hedemen Ranch."

"Hedemen's?" quizzed the man, apparently unfamiliar with the name. "I expect you'll have to stay the night here. I'm Silas Beadle. My sons," he motioned to the three older boys still seated at the table, "Matthew, Mark and Luke." A pause followed as they waited for him to introduce the woman and other children, but Silas Beadle appeared to be done with introductions.

"I'm Gat Ransom, and this is my wife, India." Gat's hand roamed over the curve of her shoulder possessively. India lowered her eyes and swallowed back the havoc his touch was creating with her senses. Most likely he was right to be cautious: a man and woman traveling together could be suspected by some in circumstances like these unless they were married. But he was playing his part too well.

Beadle offered Gat his hand, "Sit down, Ransom, and have a bite to eat. We were just finishing. Children . . ." All the little girls scuttled off the bench and left the table to their older brothers, the guests, and their father. "Mary, fetch a plate for Mr. Ransom."

India looked around in confusion, for it appeared that the invitation to eat at the table had not been extended to her. She stepped awkwardly nearer the fire, feeling her doeskin dress stiffening as it began to dry against her body. She looked toward a muslin-curtained alcove at the far side of the room and thought to ask permission to change into her dry calico dress.

The woman put down the baby, which began to cry almost immediately, went to a cupboard and got out a cup and plate.

"Shut up that baby!" commanded Silas. One of the little girls ran over and picked it up, but had little success. The infant's supper had been interrupted and it was none too pleased.

"Let me. You finish feeding your baby." India moved beside the woman and took the plate and cup from her. Without a word Mary went back to the baby, unfastened her bodice, and sat down to finish nursing.

"Mary can do that, Mrs. Ransom," said Beadle. "Mary."

"I don't mind, Mr. Beadle." India began ladling some turnip stew from a pot simmering over the fire onto the plate.

"Mary!" Beadle said sharply.

Still mute as a doll, Mary put down the infant, refastened her bodice and moved to her husband's direction. This time India picked up the child and rocked it into temporary silence while Mary poured a round of coffee in the men's cups. That accomplished, she stood at her husband's elbow, awaiting his beck and call. The little girls had already begun to clear their plates from the table, and one who looked about three sat at a bucket washing the utensils.

"Have you been in Wyoming long?" Gat asked, taking a bite of his stew.

"We came in last fall. We've lived on buffalo meat and

wild game all winter. Mary planted the turnips you're eating in early spring. They've been a nice change from game. I expect we'll do all right. How about you?"

"I've been wrangling for Hedemen's outfit off and on. My wife and I are just married."

Beadle studied India appraisingly. His pimple-faced sons exchanged equally lascivious glances, and she decided she was content to be Ransom's wife for the night. The baby had dropped into a doze, so she carefully put it in the cradle and took the opening in conversation. "I wondered if I could change into my dry clothes, Mrs. Beadle?"

The woman looked immediately to her husband and waited for his response.

"Go ahead behind the curtain. Mary, help the lady." At his command, Mary quickly left his side and India bent to rummage through her saddlebag for her dress and hairbrush. Dress in hand, she followed Mary behind the curtain, where she saw a rope bed with straw mattress and quilt. Mary put the lamp on a wooden crate, showed her a cracked pitcher of cold water, and slipped mouse-like back through the muslin curtain.

"This is mighty tasty turnip stew, ma'am," Gat complimented when Mary returned. "I'd appreciate it if you would give the recipe to my own wife." He said this loud enough for India to hear and made to reach for the coffeepot.

Beadle stopped his hand. "Mary, pour a cup of coffee for Mr. Ransom." Mary dropped the task at hand and hurried across the room, picked up the coffeepot and poured Gat a cupful. She set it down, then looked to her husband like a faithful dog looks to its master. "Fetch the Bible and I'll read a few verses to our guests." She moved to the fireplace like a shadow and lifted the leather-bound Bible from the hearth's ledge.

Gat noticed the boys shift uncomfortably on the bench. The corners of their mouths turned downward in disappointed frowns. It looked to Gat like scripture reading didn't seem to be too popular with them.

"Put your whittlin' away, Luke," his father said, opening

156

the Bible. Begrudgingly, the boy did as he was told. "One of the reasons I brought my family West, Mr. Ransom, was to counteract the evil influences of society. My sons and daughters were being corrupted by the ungodly ways of our neighbors. Drink, tobacco and gambling ran rampant, not to speak of the unmentionable temptations of scarlet women. The school in our town took to teachin' unholy philosophies of men. They came to my door and demanded I send my daughters to school. It's my belief that writin' and readin' ain't for women."

While their father ranted, Gat noticed the bored gaze had left the boys' faces and they seemed to be staring at something behind him. They nudged one another with elbows. Gat turned his head slightly, hoping to discover what was so interesting, and quickly saw the spectacle they were devoting their full attention to.

The lamplight behind the muslin curtain silhouetted India's dressing form against the curtain. He was tempted himself to enjoy the show, but knew where his duty lay.

Clearing his throat, he came to his feet. "I think I'll stretch my legs a bit, Beadle, while you read aloud." With that he stood up, and much to the dismay of the onlookers, his large frame soon blocked their view. Soon after, India came out from behind the curtain, though modestly dressed, apparently a pleasurable sight not only to Gat, but to the greedy eyes of the boys as well. Now that the men had eaten, she dared to take a seat at the far end of the table and, on the order of Silas, was served some turnip stew by faithful Mary.

Silas thumbed through his Bible selectively. "With you being newly married, I think I should read to you from Paul concerning your duties as head of your family. He cleared his throat and began. 'For the man is not of the woman; but the woman of the man. Neither was man created for the woman; but the woman for the man.' "

He flipped the pages and continued speaking, particularly in India's direction. " 'Let your women keep silence: for it is not permitted unto them to speak; but they are commanded to be under obedience, as also saith the law. And if they will learn any thing, let them ask their husbands.' "

Gat heard what he knew to be a rebellious cough from India's end of the table. He hoped she could manage to contain herself. Beadle seemed to be adept at dropping a word here, and adding a word there, to substantiate his interpretations.

Beadle droned on. " 'Wives submit yourselves unto your own husbands, as the Lord. For the husband is the head of the wife . . .' " Gat looked uneasily at India. She'd quit eating and he could see her lips twitch. He knew instinctively Beadle wasn't a man to abide what she might have to say.

"I like the one two verses down, in particular," Gat interjected quickly. " 'Husbands, love your wives, even as Christ also loved the church and gave himself for it.' Or the one in Corinthians: 'Let the husbands render unto the wife due benevolence.' " Both India and Beadle looked over at him, one in outright surprise and the other in admiration.

"Well, you're a man who can quote the Good Book, Mr. Ransom." Though Beadle seemed to be taken aback at the words Gat had quoted.

"Yes," came India's voice from the end of the table. "Before the war Mr. Ransom planned to enter the ministry." She gazed in Gat's direction in mock loving adoration.

It was Gat's turn to cough. "I think the rain's let up some. I better go see to my horses." He put on his overcoat and hat and walked toward the door.

"Wait up, Ransom, I'll go with you," said Beadle. "Boys you come on and do the evening chores." The boys gladly shoved themselves away from the table and followed the two men outside.

But for the crackling fire, the room was quiet. No sooner had the door shut securely than the little girls began to chatter among themselves. India was still recuperating from the shock that Ransom could quote the Bible when Mary Beadle came over to India and sat down across from her at the table.

"Mrs. Ransom, you're the first woman I've seen since we

came out here." Mary announced timidly. "I've been awful lonely. If you and your husband settle nearby, please come a callin'," she requested softly.

"I'm sorry, but I don't think we'll be settling here. But I'll be sure to tell any other women I meet in these parts to stop by."

"Silas won't allow me to visit."

"You better give me your turnip stew recipe. It seems Mr. Ransom . . . ah . . . my husband favors it." India smiled, taking mischief in the idea of Gat being her husband. It would be the only time in her life she could make such a claim. "Let me fetch my recipe book and pen." India left the table and got her parcel from the saddlebag.

She opened it to a blank page in the back and dipped her pen in the ink. "All right, tell me what you do, step by step."

"You can write?" Mary was staring at the book and pen.

"Of course, this is a French recipe book. I can write your stew recipe in it and not worry about forgetting it."

Mary seemed quite amazed. "Have you a recipe to tell me?"

"Well," India fanned the pages. "Do you want a dessert or a main course?"

"Both!" Mary at last smiled.

"How about a pound cake with lots of butter and eggs and then a . . . a"—her eyes scanned the pages for something practical—"a red beet pie?"

"Oh yes, we have chickens and a milk cow and I have planted beets in the garden."

So the ladies bent their heads together and exchanged recipes while the little girls crowded around them, fascinated by India's pen-and-ink writing. She took a page from her petition ledger and showed each one how to write her name. Then she tore the page into tiny slips so each could keep a copy.

"Now you keep those hid from your father," Mary cautioned the girls as she looked nervously at the door. "You better put away your books before my husband comes back," she continued. Then she reached over and clasped India's hand and lowered her voice. "You seem to have experience in most things, Mrs. Ransom. I have no right to ask you this, but I am near desperate. It's that French cookbook of yours that brought me around to thinkin' on it. I've heard tell"—she looked at the door again and then back to India—"I've heard there is a way some women know how to keep from getting in the family way. I've heard it called the 'French Secret.' Can you tell me that secret? Maybe being just married you don't understand why I would ask, but . . ."

"I understand, don't worry." India's heart went out to the poor woman. "But I don't know what it is myself. Just like you, I've heard about it, but not the particulars. I'm sorry." At that moment they heard the thump of boots and low conversation of the returning men. India quickly swept up her books and pen. With the lift of the door latch the little girls again fell silent and Mary rose to her feet and went to tend the fire.

The one-room cabin and loft were hardly spacious enough for the Beadle family, let alone visitors. India and Gat lay like a pair of spoons on a straw tick before the stone fireplace. India gazed at the dancing flames, while around her she listened to the settling sounds of the children. Gat had made a gentleman's effort to keep the proper amount of space between them, and India, in an odd way, was disappointed. His knee was very close to hers, but not touching; his arm, as he shifted to comfortability, brushed her back but never touched.

Suddenly, something cold and writhing fell across India's face. She screamed. Ransom jumped up, grabbed it.

"What is it?" gasped India.

"Everything all right?" called Beadle from behind the muslin curtain.

"It's nothing. Just a blow snake fell through the rafters," said Gat matter-of-factly. He stepped over sleeping children, opened the door and threw it out.

India, still trembling, rubbed the cold clammy feel of the creature from her skin.

Gat returned beside her. "Lie back down. It's over."

"I can't." She sat upright, her eyes roving over the roof above.

"Don't worry. It happens all the time. They're drawn by the warmth. Most folks put sheeting up to catch the critters." He picked up his blanket. "Put my blanket over you if you think that will help."

"But what will you use?"

"I'll be fine," he assured her.

"You'll be cold," India took his blanket. "We could share."

"I figure I'll take the lesser of the two evils and be cold."

"Well, I'm not worried. If you came too close, Beadle would read you a few verses of moral scripture," she whispered.

"The tempter's voice must be whispering a lot more to you than he is to me. Tonight, I haven't got anything on my mind but sleep. Goodnight." Gat stretched out beside her.

He had misunderstood her offer. India burned with humiliation with this added insult. Along with the kiss, the events at the mining camp apparently only clinched his idea that she was a woman of easy virtue. How could a man who apparently had his pick of respectable and unrespectable women in the territory have the audacity to think she was the one to have a lecture on morals?

The man infuriated her to no end. It wasn't as if she was all withered inside, though she'd spent half of her life repressing her carnal nature. He did have a way of making her terribly aware she was a flesh-and-blood woman, and she knew her very denial of marriage and her dedication to her cause added to her vulnerability. It just wasn't fair!

The stillness seemed to magnify small movements, and a tension flowed between their unconnected bodies. As the hearth fire died down he moved closer to her. His body curved with the bends and hollows of her own, very close, but not touching. She sensed him rather than touched him.

161

Slowly, a pulse and heat gathered force inside her and she suddenly turned, shifted and rearranged. So did Gat. The current between them was undeniable now. It became a silent flirtation of breath and movement. Curled in the half-moon circle of his body she paced the rise and fall of his chest with the warmth of his breath on her neck. The warmth traveled down her spine like massaging fingers, caressing her secret places. He flowed into her without touching, and the warmth grew between her legs, a little ticking throb started up, which was irrefutably linked with the rhythm of his breathing.

She wanted him closer: she willed him to touch her. And in the hazy half-sleep of her dreaming, he did.

She was at Contessa's again, only this time she was in the main parlor playing the piano for the girls and their gentlemen. A hundred seed pearl buttons bastioned her high-neck snow-white dress, which cascaded in chaste lacy folds around her. The other girls were lounging in various states of dishabille, but not India. But for a red stocking toe which peeked from beneath her dress pressing on the piano pedal, she was pristine, purehearted and unblemished. Her graceful hands danced over the ivory keys and her glass-blue eyes watched the room's reflection in the gilt-framed mirror above the piano.

Suddenly, the doors into the parlor opened and Gat Ransom stepped inside. In desperado stance, he slowly surveyed the room with a dark penetrating gaze. Contessa moved forward, but his interest focused past Contessa's welcome. India glanced down at the keyboard with a soft-lipped smile of satisfaction, all the while feeling a wild excitement move through her body. Tonight he had come for her and her alone.

She continued playing, outwardly oblivious to the tall cowboy who now stood behind her. But inwardly she simmered beneath the heat of his black-eyed gaze which ignited a pulsing fire of ripe expectancy within her. She would ignore him for a while, pretending indifference, after all she was the virginal pianist of the establishment.

Then, with a pretended inconsequential glance she lifted her eyes to the mirror and met the smoldering reflection of his own. Her fingers stumbled over the keys and then halted. He would not be ignored. His dark head lowered and lips warm as Jamaican rum brushed the nape of her neck and then moved to the hollow of her ear with a deeply whispered, "I want to make you a woman."

The words no longer affronted her, but filled her with a feathery expectancy, and at last, deep within in the chamber of her hidden secrets, she conceded she wanted him, she had always wanted him. With a demure smile she willingly submitted when he swept her into his arms, and shivers of anticipation coursed through her as he carried her from the parlor and up to Contessa's room.

Upon entering, the rose patterns of the bed curtains bloomed to brilliance in the soft lamplight while the room's atmosphere radiated the sultry sheen of a faceted ruby. Gat's arms loosed around her as he placed her beside the bed and with the alacrity of a magician his adept fingers had quickly cast off his own shirt. The resulting sight of his sun-bronzed torso mesmerized her. Seeing this, he smiled a hunter's smile when a long-stalked quarry has been captured. His fingers caressed her throat and slowly moving downward, miraculously unfastened the hundred seed pearl buttons of her spotlessly white dress. The gown fell about her ankles unveiling her splendorous breasts enshrined in the vigilant constraints of an alabaster corset. Another pass of his hand and the corset fell, releasing her breasts to the soft folds of a red-lace camisole. He became her liberator, each touch of his hand untying, unbinding, unshackling, over her hips down her long sylphine legs to the ivory garters of her red silk stockings. At last, he stepped back letting out a slow breath as his eyes drank in her unbound beauty, then he fell to his knees in homage before her, saying abjectly, "I am unworthy of you."

"No, no . . ." India mumbled herself awake to the stillness of night and the dying embers of the fire. Inwardly, she struggled to linger in the dream and hold the warmth of anticipated fulfillment. Fighting back the disappointment, reluctantly, her eyelids flicked open and she found herself facing Ransom. That his face was inches from her own was shocking but not so shocking as the flashing images of her dream. Her breath caught in her throat and she feared he might be awake, but from the steady ebb and flow of his breathing it was apparent he still slept deeply.

By firelight she watched him in sleep, studied the rough texture of his jawline compared to the swelling softness of his lips. Without touching him she lifted her fingers and let them hover above his black-thatched brows over to the long scar running down his cheek. If she touched him he would wake, and so instead, savoring the sensations of her dream, from the depths of her heart, she entreated, *Why did you stop?* Moisture gathered at the corners of her eyes. He was *not* her misfortune. She loved him.

The commotion of a child's crying and the shout of loud voices brought India rudely awake.

"You and your woman are about the devil's business, I'll not have it in my house!" yelled Silas Beadle. He'd snatched Ransom's gun and pointed it at him. "I have ways of taking care of your sort. Matthew, go build a fire under the tar pot."

India looked about in confusion. Beadle's other two sons leaped forward to hold Ransom.

"Outside, you devil." They pushed Gat out the door.

"What's happening?" India turned in confusion to Mary. "What is wrong?" Mary held her youngest daughter, who sobbed hysterically.

"Oh, something awful! Rachel here sneaked into your pen and books this morning while we were all sleeping, and Silas discovered her. Oh, he'll whip her good, and he's got something awful mean in store for you and your man."

"But why should he be so angry about a child playing with a pen and paper?"

"It wasn't that so much as something he read on the paper." She rocked back and forth in distress.

India hurried over to her saddlebags and gathered up her parcel. "The petition. He must have read the petition." There probably wasn't a greater sacrilege than women voting, as far as Beadle was concerned. "Mary, what is he going to do?"

"You heard him, he's going to heat up the tar and he's going to tar and feather you and your man. Oh, I'm mighty sorry, Mrs. Ransom, but I can't stop him. He's done it before to folks when he gets riled."

India ran to the door and barred it, then she peered out the window. They'd tied Gat to a fence post while one of the boys stirred the tar. Silas had torn off Gat's shirt. India's mind whirled. What could she do? "Mary, is there another gun in the house?"

"Oh, I couldn't be part of that." Mary shook her head and clutched the little girl closer to her, but then her eyes moved slowly and rested on a battered traveling trunk in the corner.

India ran over to the trunk, fell to her knees and pulled open the lid. Inside she discovered a shotgun. It didn't matter to her if it was loaded or not. She'd just have to bluff her way through. A quick glance out the window told her there was no time to spare. The Beadles had already begun their foul work. Gat's chest was a mass of sticky tar and feathers. She unbarred the door and with gun in hand, rushed out of the cabin.

Beadle still held the gun, but less guardedly. "Mr. Beadle, drop your gun!" India commanded with as much bravado as she could muster.

Though taken by surprise, he didn't drop his gun, but Gat's reflexes saved the moment. The second India distracted Beadle he lifted his foot and kicked the gun from Beadle's hand.

"Hold it right there, Mr. Beadle." India moved forward, still holding the shotgun. She stooped for the gun. "Now untie Mr. Ransom."

The boys looked to their father and he gave a slight nod. Once untied, Gat left India to hold the Beadles at bay and went inside the barn and brought out their horses. He hastily saddled them and then, to India's relief, finally took the guns from her. He herded the Beadles inside the barn and barred the doors.

"Go get your things from the house and give the shotgun to his wife. Tell her not to let them out for at least an hour. I doubt they'll follow us." Ransom had taken his shirt and was attempting to scrape off the tar and feathers. India ached for him, for it looked painful. Quickly she rushed inside the cabin.

"I'm sorry, Mary, but we had to do it. Please give us a head start before you let them out of the barn." She laid the gun on the table and gathered up her belongings. "Goodbye," she said sadly, then she moved quickly to Mary's side, gave her a warm embrace and ran out the door.

Mary Beadle followed India, her head turning to the demanding calls of her husband and sons from inside the barn. Then her eyes moved to India as if to say it was a relief to have them locked up.

"I'll tend to my chores first," she said and stepped back inside the cabin and closed the door. Riding off, India felt a sharp pang of remorse, for she knew that later Mary would pay dearly for their freedom.

Chapter 12

*B*y the time India and Gat saw the corrals and barns of the
Hedemen ranch, shadows had fallen and the sunset cast a
golden glow across the tops of the great bare buttes. They
spurred their horses forward on the last stretch of a long
day's ride.

Barking dogs and a passel of excited children ran out to
greet them. The children squealed, giggled, pushed and
jostled one another to surround Gat—an obvious favorite
among them—as he swung down off his horse. He came
prepared, quickly searching through his saddlebags for the
sack of horehound candy. On his command the children
lined up with outstretched hands and he filled their open
palms, not forgetting the two hiding in their mother's skirts
in the cabin doorway.

"Eugenie, how you doing?" he asked their smiling, preg-
nant mother.

She pushed back a loose strand of black hair and sighed.
"If you want to know the truth, I feel as bloated as a month-
dead carcass. I'm due anytime now." She patted her large
belly affectionately. "Russ will be glad to see you." Her
sparkling green eyes settled in a friendly welcome on India.
"Who's this you've brought with you?"

"Well, I'll let her introduce herself," Gat said.

India, still up on her horse, gave Eugenie a smile. "I'm India Simms."

Eugenie stepped from the doorway. "I'm glad to meet you, India. I suppose I should introduce my brood here to you while they're all standin' still. Elizabeth, the eldest, Emma, Cora, Jacob, Samuel, Florence and Sarah here, the youngest."

"Happy to meet you, children," India greeted, more concerned about Gat's condition than introductions.

"Eugenie, I could use lye soap and some mineral spirits if you could see your way clear to provide them. We had a little run-in with some of your new neighbors." Gat began unbuttoning his shirt, and all the children's eyes opened wide as he revealed his tarred-and-feathered chest.

"Good heavens, Gat! What happened to you? You standing there like as nothing is wrong! You'll be blistered and sore for a week," gasped Eugenie. "Come in. You need more than lye soap and mineral spirits. Elizabeth, see to their horses," she ordered, hustling Gat inside the cabin.

India slipped down off her horse and began helping the young girl unstrap the gear and unsaddle the horses. She wanted to follow Gat inside to ensure that Eugenie would take proper care of him, but she didn't want to appear overattentive. On the trail he had declined her offers of help, saying he'd be fine. The man was impossible.

"Elizabeth, how old are you?" she asked the girl.

"Fourteen, ma'am." She took a moment to tuck a loose lock of sun-streaked hair beneath her faded yellow bonnet. "Pa said if Mama wasn't expectin', he would have let me ride roundup this spring, but now I'm needed here."

"Roundup? What's roundup?" India questioned.

"It's when we round up and brand all the cattle on our range, ma'am.

India was surprised. "A young girl like you can do that?" She took off her horse's saddle and led the horse into the corral.

"Yes, ma'am. Everybody rides roundup. Even Mama when she can. The Anderson sisters, us and all the other ranchers runnin' cattle on this range meet together for roundup. We're always shorthanded, I guess that's why Gat's come."

India raised a contemplative brow. She had suspected they were making a diversion and now she knew why. Gat had intended to make the roundup. Well, he was not getting paid to chase cows but to escort her. She'd speak with him about this roundup business.

She left Elizabeth and walked across the yard to the log cabin and went inside. Gat sat stiff in his chair beside a long wooden table while Eugenie meticulously picked off the tar, gob by gob.

She stepped inside. Her eyes went around the room, taking in a fancy wood-burning cook stove, a great walker spinning wheel, a patchwork-quilt-draped bed in one corner, bright gingham curtains hung over twin glass windows, and the most eye catching off all, a pump organ.

The cabin was tidy. Bottled preserves and various stores of legumes and spices lined makeshift shelves. The furniture was mostly handmade from saplings and pine. Buffalo skins lined the dirt floor and muslin the ceiling. She wouldn't have to worry about snakes falling from the rafters. A ladder led to a half-loft above, where two blue-eyed girls—Emma and Corra she thought—peered over the edge.

"I'm afraid I'm the one responsible for his condition," India admitted.

Eugenie gave her a sidelong glance. "Gat has told me about your adventure and your errand in this part of the territory. I'm sorry you met with some opposition, though it don't surprise me much." She stood up and nodded to a gray crock of lard on the table. "Since you're the one responsible, Miss Simms, I'll let you finish the job. I'm afraid there'll be nary a hair left on your chest, Gat. You'll be as smooth as a baby." Eugenie hurried over to the cook stove to tend to a pot of boiling potatoes. "Rub that on his chest to work the last of the tar off," she said over her shoulder to India, who stood immobile.

India stared at Gat's hairless bare chest. His exposure

seemed to become a recurring event between them. Gat looked back as if to say, Well, lady, hurry up. Finally, drawing up her small frame and assuming an air of take-charge, she walked over to Ransom and sat down on the stool directly in front of him, which Eugenie had vacated. When she leaned forward his long legs seemed to surround her and her own knees fit snugly within the V of his thighs. She swallowed back the anxious feeling his nearness always provoked in her and dabbed her dainty fingers in the lard. Her hand was shaking.

An odd tingle rippled through her as her fingertips touched his skin. "Tell me if it hurts," she said, rubbing tentative circles on the mound of his broad chest.

"It doesn't hurt."

She let her eyes travel only as high as his mouth to see the stoic curve of his lips. Knowing her discomfort, he most likely was taking a perverted pleasure out of all this, even though she could see by the redness of his skin he should be in pain. Gently, she worked the tar from the furred matte of his chest, ever aware of the soreness he might be experiencing whether he'd admit it or not.

Once she relaxed, she enjoyed ministering to him. In a way it was like having a small taste of being the real Mrs. Ransom. Mrs. Ransom would like attending to her husband, feeling the softness of his skin and the hardness of his muscle. Sun freckles spread over his shoulders to fade in the hollow of his throat and with her eyes level on that spot, India could not help imagine brushing a light kiss against his skin. Another place Mrs. Ransom might touch a healing kiss would be the discolored taper of scar on the righthand side of his chest, just above the nipple. She clicked her tongue and her concerned eyes swept over his bare arms and chest, taking toll of past wounds. So many scars—too many she thought.

"What are you cluckin' your tongue about?" Gat asked.

India lifted a winged brow and said, "How is it you're alive? You've more scars than a tattooed man has tattoos."

"The war, ma'am," he said curtly. Perhaps it was rude,

but her eyes were drawn to the long scar running down his face. He turned his head then, putting that side of his face to the shadow. Something chafed against her heart and she lowered her eyes. He had done that often enough before, turned his good side to view, but until now she hadn't realized why. No man liked wearing his past on his face.

"Well, I think I've done all I can for now." She wiped her hands on a rag.

Eugenie had been mixing up another remedy and came with a small milk glass jar of ointment in her hands. "Rub this on a couple of times a day. It works good for inflamed udders, so it ought to work for you."

"Eugenie, my udders ain't inflamed," Gat said, pushing the ointment aside with a sniff. "And skunk grease smells better. I'll manage fine, thanks the same." He came to his feet.

"Cowboy, I swear, you're numb to pain. Your hide must be as tough as a fifty-year-old buffalo. And since when did you start worrying about how you smelled?" Her eyes rested on India with speculation. "Well, suit yourself, I'll try and get the tar off your shirt."

India opened her mouth to add her support to Eugenie, but the clink of spurs outside announced an arrival. The door opened and Russ Hedemen ducked inside, accompanied by his daughter Elizabeth. He was tall and lean like his counterpart, Ransom. The hours on horseback in harsh weather told on his face.

"Why, howdy, Gat." He stepped across the floor and reached out a welcoming hand. The men were two of a breed, rough cut for a rough life. "I've been down on the river with a two-year-old heifer who was debatin' motherhood. She finally gave in and pushed out a healthy, bawlin' calf."

"She accept it?" asked Gat.

"Sure did. After I cleaned it up for 'er and showed 'er what to do with it. You know there ain't nothin' dumber than a two-year-old heifer—exceptin' two of 'em." The men laughed.

Behind Russ, India stood unobtrusively in the corner. When Gat moved across the room to fetch another shirt from the saddlebag she'd brought in, Russ turned and noticed her for the first time. "Why Gat, you bounder! I saw two horses in the corral but I never thought . . ."

"Well, no use to start thinkin' now," interjected Eugenie, who had moved to the stove and, with hot pad in hand, pulled a pan of biscuits from the oven. "This is *Miss* Simms. Gat's escorting her through the territory. She's a suffragette."

"A suffragette? Why, I thought you ladies usually rallied in the East." His eyes traveled over her measuringly. "But it's still my pleasure, ma'am."

India liked his manner and extended her hand. "Glad to know you, Mr. Hedemen."

He shook her hand hardily. "All my friends call me Russ," he said in a voice touched with a down-South drawl.

"Yes, well . . ." India looked at Ransom. She could hardly call him Russ when she couldn't call Ransom Gat.

"Let's eat, darlin'," announced Russ. He called out the door to the children. "Come on, everybody, supper time."

He went over to the wash bowl and splashed water over his hands and face. Soon after, India followed his example. Eugenie and the girls busied themselves setting the table with biscuits, beef stew and turnips.

After her experience of the night before, India hesitated to seat herself and made an offer to help serve the table, an offer quickly rejected by Eugenie. Russ motioned her to take a seat on his left, opposite Gat, and he stood a moment waiting for Eugenie to take a seat opposite him at the far end of the table. India noted that none of the children took their places until their mother sat down. Grace was brief, and then the next moments were filled with clanking utensils and "pass-me-pleases."

"Gat, I was beginning to think you wouldn't show up for roundup. We're mighty shorthanded," Russ said. He poured himself a cup of coffee and, as a courtesy, topped off India's cup. The gesture provoked images from the previous evening at the Beadles', and she stared at Russ oddly. "You did want more coffee, didn't you?" he asked.

"Oh yes," she stumbled. "Thank you."

Across the table a mocking smile touched the corners of Gat's lips and humor lit his eyes, as if to say, "Not all men were like Beadle." India shifted in her place, accidentally nudging Gat's long leg with her knee beneath the table. He nudged her back, a playful tease in his black eyes. After a few moments, he nudged her again. She attempted to ignore his impertinence, though she liked the feel of his knee against hers.

"Well, I'm not sure if I'll be able to stay too long. Miss Simms here has her own business to attend to, and I don't think roundup was on her list," replied Gat.

"Miss Simms, why don't you consider staying over? You're welcome, and Eugenie is so near her time I'd feel better if another woman were around to help her out. The closest midwife is in South Pass," said Russ.

"Now why not be honest with her, Russ," Eugenie said. "You know you've delivered most of our babies yourself and that you're as experienced as any midwife in birthing, whether it be a beast or a woman. Tell her the truth, Russ. You need her and Gat on the roundup."

"Now, Eugenie," began Russ.

"Don't 'Eugenie' me, Russ Hedemen!" The two rows of bright faces between turned in unison each time one of their parents spoke.

"To be honest, my wife is partly right. But," he looked down the table in her direction, "I am concerned about you. I'm not so self-serving."

India felt a nudge under the table as if to say, "Now here's a man who loves his wife."

She nudged back, and instead of Gat reacting, Russ Hedemen suddenly looked at her. She stammered an embarrassed, "Excuse me," shooting a sharp-eyed glare in Gat's direction, suspecting he had lured her into nudging Russ all the while.

"Ma'am, I wish you'd stay and lend a hand. I'll give you a good horse," coaxed Russ.

Feeling all eyes on her, India began doubtfully, "You want me to ride roundup? I don't know anything—"

"Anyone who wants to vote like a man should learn to muster cattle like one," challenged Gat, his eyes holding hers.

India met his gaze, his eyes daring her to rise to the challenge. Well, she thought, if Eugenie and young Elizabeth had ridden roundup, so could she. Gat would find she was as good as the next man, or woman. "I must warn you, I know nothing about cattle."

"You'll do fine," Russ said.

With that decided, the dinner went on in a light-minded chatter. Later, Gat and Russ exchanged news and chewing tobacco, while Eugenie enlightened India as much as possible on frontier life. When the children were sent to bed, the discussion on sleeping arrangements broke out.

Russ slapped Gat's knee and said, "It's out in the barn for you and me."

India looked to the only bed in the cabin and spoke up, "I have no intention of putting Mr. Hedemen out of his bed," and then added too hastily, "I'm used to sleeping with Ransom."

Russ coughed and his hand covered his mouth in disguised thoughtfulness. Eugenie gave an uneasy look up to the children peeking over the edge of the loft.

Gat's eyes twinkled with amusement, but his words became a stern reproof. "You better say that one over, Miss Simms. I think Russ and Eugenie might get the wrong idea."

India's cheeks blossomed a deep red and she stuttered, "I . . . no . . . we . . . I'm sorry. It's the out of doors I'm used to sleeping in . . . not Mr.—"

"No need to be sorry." Eugenie cut in and she nudged Russ to his feet while she collected a blanket and pillow. "During roundup the women always take the cabin. The Anderson sisters will take the loft and you and I will share the feather bed." She patted India's arm reassuringly.

Gat had picked up his bedroll and along with Russ he walked out the door. When the door shut India heard the two men's deep laughter from the porch. She was ready to crawl under the bed, not in it.

The next day, India began settling in at the Hedemens'. She learned firsthand how to cook on a woodstove and how to churn butter. In fact, in the afternoon, Eugenie suggested India lie down for a while.

"You are the one who should lie down," responded India.

"Me lie down?" Eugenie replied with amusement. "Why, you know I couldn't do that." She stood in the doorway a moment and looked out. "The milk cow and the mare get turned out to pasture a month before they birth, but me, I keep workin' right up to the last.

India laughed, but inwardly she vowed to make these last days of Eugenie's a bit more leisurely by taking on more work herself. The following days India became adept at laundering and scrubbing. When Eugenie told her it was the right phase of the moon to make soap, she gathered up all the grease and fat trimmings and under Eugenie's direction made a batch of lye soap.

In the evenings the children carded wool and Eugenie spun it on the great walker. India attempted to learn, but being a beginner she never could get the spider-web-fine thread that Eugenie could spin. Instead, India read nightly installments of her dime novels while others carded and spun.

During more relaxed moments the children showed her how to braid strands of straw and then sew them together into a sun hat. In return, she lent them her prospector's pan, and they all spent an unprofitable but nevertheless happy afternoon down by the river's edge panning for gold.

In the way friends sometimes do, Eugenie and India became thick as molasses, spending all their time together with heads bent in talk. Beside Eugenie, India worked untiringly preparing stews and biscuits, plucking chickens and baking pies and cakes for the traditional roundup supper. The next days, beginning with Ty Pierre, Heddy's son, cowhands began by twos and threes to ride into the Hedemen ranch, sometimes carrying a sack of flour or cornmeal, a side of beef or antelope, setting it by the cabin door as their contribution to the food reserves for the weeks ahead. As the pile grew, India could only sigh, knowing she and Eugenie would be the ones fixing all of it for the work-honed appetites.

One afternoon India took a rest from cooking and climbed up on the corral fence to watch the cowhands break in the rough string. She watched Gat ease himself onto the back of an apron-faced mare while Ty held her.

"Let 'er loose!" he called, gripping the buckstrap to keep his balance. The boys pulled the blindfold off the horse's eyes and she walked as sedately as an old woman crossing the street, then suddenly her eyes rolled white and wild and she lowered her head and lunged with her back arched. She bucked like she had a bellyful of bedsprings, but Gat held on, his chaps flapping against her sides like bird wings. India chewed her lip and tugged her ear anxiously, sure he was going to end up in the dust with his neck broke.

The hands hollered and heckled. "Chin the moon, cowboy!" "Hop for mamma."

A straightaway bucker, the mare jumped high and then, started down, kicking with her hindquarters. The cantle of the saddle hit the seat of Gat's pants and he flew high and hard, kicking free from the stirrups and going limp, he hit the ground rolling. India gasped and nearly leaped into the corral to his side, but he stood up, picked up his hat and dusted himself off. He looked up at her grinning. "Keep your seat Miss Simms. It's only the first go-round."

In no time, the mare was lunging around the corral again with Gat on her back and this time she was high-tuned to dance, jackknifing and pitching from the outset. Every so often India clamped her eyes shut just sure Gat was being thrown, but when she opened them again he was still in the saddle.

"Don't spoil her! Waltz with the lady!" hollered the hands in encouragement.

Suddenly, the mare, with an unexpected tactic, gave a throw back pitch toward the fence. "Fall back!" shouted a cowhand sitting over from India. But the warning came too late. As the mare careened into the corral fence, Gat jumped free pulling India with him over the rail. Together they tumbled head over heels onto the ground, and India found herself on top of Gat, his arms protectively around her and his body cushioning her fall.

"You all right, ma'am?" Gat asked. India pushed her hands against his broad chest, her cheeks flamed from shock and embarrassment, for he seemed reluctant to let her go. The cowhands had already begun calling out good-natured jibes.

"Once you release me, Mr. Ransom, I'll be just fine!"

He let her go and she scrambled to her feet and strode off toward the cabin. He came to his feet, taking his time to make sure his bones were still in the right place, but allowing his eye to follow the sashay of her hips. She's one gal who's never been curried above her knees, he thought, and she'll need more gentling than the whole rough string put together.

Later in the afternoon, a buckboard with rider alongside rattled into the ranch, setting up a commotion of whoops and hollers from the cowboys milling around by the corral. "That must be the Anderson sisters," Eugenie said. She waddled out the door. India followed with a pan of creamed hominy to set on the long wooden table that had been moved out of doors to accommodate everyone. She watched as the wagon pulled up beside the cabin. Down jumped two brown-eyed, brown-haired women dressed in ankle-length wool skirts and muslin blouses. They wore plainsman hats, too, like India's own.

Eugenie embraced each woman in turn and acknowledged their hired cowhand, Boots Hansen, with a friendly "Howdy, Boots." His homely-handsome face smiled back a wordless greeting.

"I am sorry we're late, but Pa lost his pipe and he

wouldn't come without it," said Clarett. She hurried around to assist the elderly man from the wagon. She gave him a crutch when he finally managed to climb down. One leg and arm hung limp as he pulled himself along.

Russ and Gat had come over to shake hands and India took particular notice that the taller of the two sisters, whom she had heard Eugenie call Bess, looped her arm through Gat's and sauntered with him over to the corral without even a "howdy do" in India's direction. Right off she didn't warm to Bess.

"India, this is Clarett Anderson and her father, Lars," introduced Eugenie. "No doubt Bess will introduce herself to you later. She's a little preoccupied right now." Eugenie and Clarett exchanged knowing smiles, which stirred not only India's curiosity but another emotion, jealousy. Evidently Bess and Gat were more than friends. At the thought, something plunged to the bottom of her stomach. Maybe it was her heart.

Forgetting her manners for a moment, India stared at Gat and Bess standing by the corral. Along with the other cowhands, they watched Ty Pierre expertly ride a bucking horse from the unbroken remuda.

She pulled her eyes away. "Glad to meet you, Clarett, Mr. Anderson." Her voice was flat.

Anderson nodded absently, his own focus on the activity in the corral. Clarett helped him over to a chair with a clear view. She came to stand beside India.

"Pa fell off his horse last fall. He hasn't been the same since," Clarett said to India in explanation. "I've brought some apple pies and fresh-baked bread. I'll put them out on the table."

At first glance India judged the sisters to be nearing their twenties, perhaps only a year apart in age. Their coloring was similar, but Bess appeared to be a little more flamboyant in her manner—a flirt, in fact. Well, India thought with a touch of aggravation as she ducked back inside the cabin, the least Bess Anderson could do was renew her acquaintance with Gat after she'd lent a hand getting the meal on the table.

India called the children inside, lined them up and filled their arms with plates, bowls and pots filled with food to pile on the table.

"I'll call everyone to come and eat. Looks like the last couple of hands are riding up now," called Eugenie through the doorway.

India gave a nod and began rolling out one last batch of biscuits, then she cut the dollar-size circles for the baking sheet. Putting the batch in the oven she picked up butter and a coffeepot and started out the door. It was oddly still outside as she plopped the butter dish and coffeepot on the table. Everyone seemed so stiff, as if they were posing for a group photograph. Her own eyes followed the direction of everyone's attention.

Gat and a stranger stood facing each other, hands poised above their holstered guns. She could see how tense Ransom's shoulders were and by his very stance she knew there was trouble. The two men eyed each other threateningly.

Suddenly, little Florence ran around the corner of the cabin and toddled into the space between the men. India leaped forward and bent to pick up the child.

"Ma'am, step out of the way. You might get hurt," warned the man facing Ransom.

India was in no mood to be intimidated. She stood her ground between the two, facing the stranger. "I guess I'll have to get hurt, then, Mr. . . . ?"

The man gave her a black look for her interfering.

"India," Ransom called her name in a quiet, but deadly plea. She ignored him.

"My name's Bitterman and Ransom here killed my brother."

India felt sick. Her article in the newspaper had prompted this showdown. Ransom had anticipated as much. She was at least partly responsible.

"Have you ever thought that your brother needed killing?" she began bravely. "You knew he tried to kill the territorial governor, didn't you? Mr. Ransom was only protecting the governor when he shot your brother. I believe you folks call that *provocation*."

The weathered lines of Bitterman's face pinched into a sneer.

India straightened up confidently. "Now, why not put your gun away?" She turned to Ransom. "You too, Mr. Ransom." I've spent two days cooking this supper, and I'm not going to have everybody lose their appetite because two men decided to shoot each other in front of us all." She took a step closer, little Florence wiggled in her arms.

Bitterman looked around warily like a cornered coyote. His hand relaxed on his gun handle.

"If Ransom wants to hide behind a meddlesome woman's petticoats, that's his choice, but I aim to get my revenge one way or the other." His lips pursed into a deep frown, but his gun hand went slack to his side.

"Thank you, Mr. Bitterman." She turned to Gat. "Mr. Ransom?"

He gave her a short nod, but disapproval was clearly marked on his face.

"I don't expect you two to shake hands, but I swear, if either of you starts trouble I'll shoot you both myself." She put the child down and walked toward the cabin. Ransom and Bitterman left in opposite directions.

Someone gave a half-nervous laugh. Russ took advantage of the quiet to step forward with a word of grace over the food. He included a passage about the importance of loving thy enemy.

India stood within the shadows of the cabin and leaned against the wall for support. Her knees were buckling, and her heart was pounding as loudly as summer rain on a tin roof.

Chapter 13

*G*et up and hear the birds sing," Russ Hedemen's voice sounded at the open cabin door. India was positive no birds were awake this early. She controlled the urge to put the pillow over her head and go back to sleep by concentrating on the smell of hot coffee brewing on the woodstove.

Through a waking fog she heard the chink of spurs across the wooden floor. "Time to earn your grub, Miss Simms. All hands need to be up and at it. We've got no use for layabouts." Gat's voice, so early in the morning, was an unnerving tonic to India's ears.

She found her voice and managed to open one eye. "I'm not a layabout. The sun's not even up yet!"

"Gat, it's her first roundup. Let her wake up before you saddle her on a horse," Eugenie advised, standing with Bess and Clarett Anderson in the doorway.

The sight of Bess up and dressed brought India fully awake. She brushed a tangle of auburn hair away from her face. "I'll be ready in five minutes."

Gat smiled and poured himself a cup of coffee. "Your little mare has a swollen foreleg. We'll cut out a cayuse from the remuda for you."

This news disturbed India, for she'd learned the value of a good horse. Her little mare had become quite a pet. She'd named her Bluestocking because she was very sensible and intelligent. The mare seemed to have the feet of a cat, and the way she climbed up and down hillsides and around obstacles was truly wonderful. During their travels they'd become great companions. Everyone was amused by the way Bluestocking walked after her, teasing for sugar and affection.

Reluctantly, India climbed out of bed. Behind a patch quilt curtain she quickly pulled on her doeskin dress and boots, then she headed out into the dawn for the outhouse. A few minutes later she spied Eugenie giving Russ last-minute instructions while he and Gat were saddling the horses by the corral.

She walked over to join them. "I need a horse," India said, eyeing the skittish horses. Most didn't have the look or temperament of having been ridden regularly. The past days she'd watched Ransom and the other hands break horses to the saddle that had roamed free all winter.

"I'll try and pick a gentle one, but they are all fit and rarin' to go," Russ said.

"What do you think about givin' her Smart Charlie?" Gat suggested.

"Well, he's a good cow pony, but he's kinda high-strung."

"Don't put her on something that'll kill her," admonished Eugenie.

"Ah," Gat said, "if the lady's gonna do a man's work, she needs a man's horse."

India bore his folksy comparison with grace, but inwardly she wanted to gag him with his own handkerchief.

"Bring out Smart Charlie," Russ yelled to a hand.

Soon after, India was being handed Charlie's reins. She didn't like the spooky way his eyes rolled back and showed the whites when his head jerked at the bit, but he looked healthy enough. "You sure he's been broke?"

"Yesterday. I rode him myself," Gat assured her.

India took a deep breath and hefted herself up into the saddle.

"Now all you have to do is lean forward and press your legs against his sides and away he'll go," Russ instructed.

"I've learned that part already," she said, and that's just what she did and away she went. With every lunge of the horse, India feared she would fall off. Around and around the corral Charlie galloped. India held on. Then suddenly, Charlie stopped short where they had started and India slid forward and slipped off over his lowered head.

She picked herself up off the ground. A blush of embarrassment tinged her cheeks. She was not hurt, and when she looked around to assure everyone of that fact, she realized they were all more than entertained by the incident. A smirk covered Bess Anderson's face, but beside her Eugenie was giving Russ hell. And Ransom . . . the light of his dark eyes was the heart of laughter itself.

"We didn't know what was goin' to happen," Russ said.

"Of course," Eugenie returned. "You and Gat don't know nothin', because both of you are crazy and shouldn't be allowed to mingle with civilized people!"

"Eugenie, I'm all right," India said, tying her hat back on her head.

"Sorry." Gat walked over to India. "Charlie has his tricks." He climbed up on the fence and called to one of the hands. "Cut out that little mare with the foal at her heels. Miss Simms can ride her.

Meanwhile, Ty Pierre had walked up beside her. His nut-brown face radiated honest concern. "Pardon me for saying so, ma'am, but Charlie's a trick horse. That's why they call him Smart Charlie. You make friends with him and he be a regular lady's horse. Don't let them cowpokes best you."

India looked over at Russ and Gat. The looks on their faces were serious, but she didn't miss the underlying amusement they were sharing. Well, no one liked looking foolish, especially her. If she was to prove herself, it was now or never. She fished in her pocket for two lumps of sugar and rubbed Charlie's neck for a moment, speaking softly, for she believed animals instinctively recognized kindness. Charlie nosed her hand and sampled the sugar.

"Mr. Ransom," she called out. "I'm satisfied with Charlie. No need to put yourself out saddling another horse for me." She winked at Ty and climbed back up on Charlie. Still talking softly, she walked him through a few paces and discovered him to be responsive to her control. Hopefully they'd reached an understanding.

"Are you sure?" Russ Hedemen asked.

"I've no intention of flying over the moon with another of Mr. Ransom's choices. At least I know what Charlie is up to. Now we've had our fun, perhaps we should begin the roundup."

"Let's go get 'em," Russ shouted in agreement.

The fifteen or so cowhands let loose with whoops and hollers. Soon everyone was saddled up and ready to go. Charlie danced with excitement, but India held him in as the cowboys rode past her.

Ty called over to her. "Ma'am, jist give Charlie his head and he do all the work."

Bess Anderson, with Gat riding beside her, rode past. "Tally ho, Miss Simms!" She spurred her horse forward. Admittedly, India was envious of her. Bess was confident in the saddle and in every other aspect of frontier life. It was obvious to India that Bess Anderson had everyone's respect—including Ransom's.

Ransom hung back. "I hope you're none the worse. The boys admire someone who can take a joke."

"No harm was done." With this tight reply and an air of independence, she spurred Charlie forward, leaving Gat in her dust. She was miffed at him and it would be some time before she would forget the incident.

It was a ride of about ten miles—two hours over rugged landscape—before the main herd of cattle was found feeding in a valley. The leaders of the herd scented the approaching riders and began to move in the wrong direction. India thought they showed the habits of wild animals rather than the domestic cattle she was familiar with.

Russ, riding point, yelled, "Head 'em off, boys!" India didn't know what to do, but her quandary was soon solved by Charlie. She couldn't hold him in. Downhill, uphill, leaping over rocks and bushes, Charlie galloped. Dogs, horses and riders dashed on at racing speed, passing and repassing each other.

Suddenly, Chic Bitterman swerved toward India, and with a wicked leer, took his quirt and whipped Charlie maliciously. Charlie leaped forward and India hung on for dear life. The wild ride prompted India to pray and to rue her decision to leave Ransom's side. The terror of being thrown and then trampled by the moving herd gave India the strength to keep her seat. Dizzied and breathless, she saw Ransom riding ahead with the others. They were turning the surge of bellowing cattle into themselves. At last, Charlie began to slow with the swirling cattle. This was not reassuring to India, because of the proximity of their huge, widespread horns and wild eyes. The cows with calves at their sides seemed to charge at anything.

Frightened, India wanted to turn Charlie around and ride back to the safety of the Hedemen ranch. She was frazzled before the roundup had even begun, but the sight of Bess Anderson, collected and tall in the saddle, renewed India's resolve. Ransom had said it: If she wanted to vote like a man, then she must muster cattle like a man. Turning tail and riding back to the ranch would prove nothing. She must see it through no matter how grueling.

After a time the real business of driving the cattle started, and Charlie began to break India in as he doubled back and forth like a fox after a hare. Still shaken from the episode with Bitterman, India chose to ride partner with Gat and together they rode up hollows and canyons hunting for strays to drive back to the herd. He showed her how to drive them as gently as possible so as not to frighten or excite them, riding first on one side, then on the other. When they deliberately went in the wrong direction, Charlie galloped in front of them to head them off. The great trial was when one would break away from the herd and run up and down the hills. Charlie took the challenge in a sporting way, galloping over and among the rocks and bushes, doubling when the cow doubled, heading it off till it went back into the herd.

One cow gave India infinite trouble by standing at bay. It

tossed a dog three times, and resisted all efforts to move. Gat rode over and suggested that since the cow had a yearling calf with her, and seemed very attached to it, that India should herd the calf instead. Accepting his guidance, she began herding the calf in the right direction. Soon the mother followed. The high point of India's day came when she and Gat herded more than a hundred cows out of a canyon.

"You're catchin' on," he praised her.

After that hard-won compliment she took a break to eat. Everyone carried lunch in a pouch slung on the saddle. Ty advised her to eat her lunch with her reins knotted over the saddle horn and both eyes open. This she did, but her eyes were on Chic Bitterman, not the cattle. She realized she'd made an enemy of him. Now she took the precaution of keeping out of his way.

As the day wore on, India became exhausted, but she was determined to brave it out. Once Ransom rode past with the shouted order of, "Don't get off your horse, it ain't safe." By his look, India thought he was thoroughly enjoying her tribulation. Like the other hands she'd tied a neckerchief over the lower half of her face. But her eyes still suffered from the combined effects of dust and sun glare. And then there were the buffalo flies, horrid pests that crept into everything—into her hair, down her collar, up her sleeves—and bit, driving her nearly crazy.

By late afternoon, India had begun to get the knack of herding cattle. She found the bulls were easily routed, but the cows with calves, old or young, were troublesome. By accident she rode between one cow and her calf in a narrow gully. The cow rushed her with slicing horns, but Charlie reared and spun agilely aside. India found Charlie so well trained that he kept perfectly cool at any threat, always jumping aside at the right moment without any direction on her part.

One rolling-eyed red cow seemed determined to protect her large yearling calf from all fancied dangers. A young dog foolishly barked at her until she was infuriated. India counted her turning at bay at least forty times. She rushed at India several times with mad rage, and when India attempted to herd her and her calf across a stream she doubled back again and again. Tearing up the ground with her horns, she finally tossed the dog viciously. Letting her be, India left her to more experienced hands, and though she'd been warned not to get off her horse, she guided Charlie toward a grove of trees where the wounded dog had dragged itself.

Climbing down, she inspected the dog as it lay dying. There was nothing she could do. She hadn't witnessed many such things, and looking into its anxious eyes she pet the dog until it took its last breath. Afterward, she walked behind some bushes for privacy's sake and then started back to her horse. Suddenly, out of nowhere, the red cow appeared. She snorted threateningly and swept the earth with her long horns. India knew better than to run. She stood stone-still, praying the cow would back off. Bellowing, the cow charged her.

A shot rang out. The cow's head and horns caught India's skirt and knocked her to the ground. Momentarily stunned, she heard another shot and the cow's legs buckled underneath it, only to struggle to stand and then collapse.

"Damn it! I said stay on your horse!" Ransom shouted. Despite his angry words he was kneeling beside her, taking her tenderly into his arms. "You're safe now." His voice was filled with concern.

Shaking, India sought the security of his nearness, his strength and his protection. Involuntarily, her arms went around him, she put her cheek against the leather of his vest and clung to him for a long moment. Then she drew back and slowly opened her eyes, meeting the dark intensity of his own. His lips hovered over hers and the moment became more tense than her collision with the cow.

She wanted him to kiss her. Every nerve and fiber of her body ached for his lips to cover hers. But the stark realization of the consequences, fired by the look of no return she saw in his eyes, sent her struggling to her feet.

She turned away, arranging her hat and dusting off her

skirt. She went swiftly to remount her horse, but all the time she was aware of Ransom staring at her back.

Nearby the orphaned calf lamented piteously.

Without another word Gat mounted his horse and with the help of Coyote, he successfully moved the yearling calf towards the main herd.

All the while he felt like he'd swallowed a bull snake that wouldn't keep still. He'd take her on any terms and he'd seen the look of desire in her eyes. Not even the blind, deaf and dumb could miss the lightning that was striking between them. He'd almost kissed her then; only some innate sense of self-preservation had kept him from it. It was something neither of them wanted to happen—but it would happen.

The rest of the afternoon while he herded cattle back toward the ranch Gat kept his distance from her, but she never left his sight or his mind. They'd both been bit, just how deep he couldn't reckon.

It was after sunset by the time the herd was bunched up and settled on the outskirts of the Hedemen ranch. Gat shadowed India, amazed she could still sit upright in the saddle. He was dog tired himself and even Bess had ridden in hours before. He watched her pull up Charlie by the corral and slide off. Her legs seemed to buckle when she hit the ground, but she held onto the saddle a moment and through sheer determination began to uncinch the girth strap. A cowboy offered her his help, but in a barely audible voice she politely refused the offer.

Meanwhile Gat unsaddled his own horse while still keeping an eye on India. She uncinched her saddle and then collapsed under its weight when it slid off. He bit back a grin. He should have helped her, but he knew she had just enough spirit left in her not to accept his help. Breathing deeply a few times, she managed to get back on her feet to drag the saddle over to the corral fence. Around her, cowboys easily hefted their saddles up on the fence. Stubbornly struggling amid offers of help, she finally got her saddle up. She led Charlie into the corral and slipped off his bridle. Gat was surprised to see Charlie follow her to the gate; then he understood when she gave him a lump of sugar. Each cowboy forked a load of hay from the haystack into the corral for the horses and India followed in turn.

A few minutes later, when Gat lined up with the hands for supper, Eugenie called to him.

"Where's India? You boys did bring her back with you, didn't you?"

Gat looked around a little puzzled. "She came back all right. She was over by the corral last I saw her." He eyed the outhouse, the door opened and a cowhand stepped out. He set down his plate and headed for the corral. Nobody there had seen her. Perplexed, he scanned the darkness, then he walked around the haystack. There she was, collapsed and sound asleep in the hay.

Gat smiled to himself. This was no place to leave a lady, especially a lady who could do a man's work. He picked her up in his arms. She snuggled comfortably against his chest and mumbled an incoherent phrase.

He carried her inside the cabin and laid her gently on the bed where little Sarah was curled up in sleep. To his mind beauty and innocence lay side by side. For a long moment he studied her face, holding back the desire to touch the dust caked, tangled, auburn hair and taste her sun-chapped lips. Letting out a low whistled breath, he rubbed his neck with his hand. He'd been bit all right, and if he didn't stop the venom from spreading, the woman would turn him as crazy as a coyote yodeling at the moon.

Chapter 14

When branding finally began, over a thousand head of cattle milled around the outskirts of the Hedemen ranch. India readily volunteered to help Eugenie and Clarett with the cooking, for branding calves was where she drew the line in doing men's work. To India's mind cowboys weren't human, but a separate species. They prided themselves on not making things comfortable, so as to enhance the "roughing it." After four days of riding in the four directions rounding up cattle, she'd had her fill of cattle, men and men's work. During the days she had chased bellowing critters, and in her dreams at night they had chased her. There were other things in her dreams: a face that haunted her in daylight and sensations that left her blushing in the dawn.

Her dreams came often and always stopped at the same place, where Gat fell to his knees before her and confessed his unworthiness. India thought about it as she gazed across the dooryard, spying Gat at work in the branding corral. More comfortable in the saddle than in a cushioned chair, he went about his work of heeling and branding calves like a schoolmistress writes the ABCs. He possessed a rugged arrogance which could never be misconstrued as conceit. She knew he would never get on his knees to anyone, especially her. So why did the dream always end that way, leaving him impotent and her hanging on the edge, wanting more? The limits of her experience became the only answer and her own ignorance of the mysteries of love always brought the dreams to a halt. Lady Jane had offered to enlighten her on the subject and now India was deeply sorry she had passed up the opportunity. If by never marrying she was going to miss something, at least she wanted to know what she would be missing.

"We'd better get started," Clarett called from inside the cabin.

India turned back inside and walked over and sat down in the pine rocker.

"Give Miss Simms the slate board, Elizabeth, and she can write it all down," Clarett said, kneading bread on the table, while Eugenie, peeling apples, acted as counsel.

"They'll soon be hungry as crickets at harvest time," Eugenie said. "We need to figure how many loaves of bread, corn cakes and biscuits, how many chickens, prairie hens and quail, how much beef, boiled, fried and stewed, we'll need to feed the hands twice a day."

"I don't think I can throw another plucked chicken in the pot," Clarett said, sighing.

Young Elizabeth leaned dejectedly against the loft stepladder. "And I don't think I could pluck another chicken. I'd rather help with the brandin'."

"That's men's work, young lady," Eugenie pronounced.

"Then how come Bess gets to help?" complained Elizabeth.

"Because she's a good hand at it." Eugenie straightened up with a long intake of breath.

"Then if a woman is a good hand at it, it must be women's work too," said Elizabeth.

Eugenie started to answer, but her voice broke in midsentence.

"Are you all right, Eugenie?" India asked suspiciously.

"Well, for the time being, but I think it's beginning. Elizabeth, you'll have to help Clarett bake. Send Jacob to gather eggs, and tell Samuel to fetch water. Emma, Cora," she called through the door.

The pair came scampering inside. "Yes, Mama," they chimed in unison.

"I want you girls to kill three chickens and pluck them for the stew pot."

"Oh Mama, do we have to? You know how we hate that," whined Cora.

"Listen, you do it, we can't ask Miss Simms. She wasn't bred to farm life."

India didn't want special treatment. "I can help the children." She stood up and followed them out the cabin door to the chicken coop by the barn. She opened the gate and without any warning a rooster, talons arched, flew at her. India ran. The rooster chased her around the barnyard in vindictive pursuit.

"Hit 'im with a stick! Hit 'im with a stick," cried Emma and Cora, jumping up and down.

India didn't have a stick, but she discovered she had an audience. The cowhands were lined up on the corral fence watching as if it were a Sunday cockfight. Soon they would be placing bets.

Emma came running with a hatchet. At the sight of the hatchet the rooster seemed to become even more infuriated. Dust and feathers flew. Like a gladiator, India swung the hatchet through the air, missing wildly at first, then on the odd swing she knocked the chicken out. Whoops and whistles sounded from the corral fence.

Feeling triumphant, India turned and took a bow. "You don't think I'd be run off the place by a chicken, do you?" The cowhands hooted with laughter.

"Chop off its head, quick!" cried Cora.

India swallowed. She might be able to knock it out, but she knew she'd never be able to chop off its head. The rooster twitched.

"Hurry, hurry, he's comin' 'round," declared Emma.

India's eyes swept the faces of the onlooking cowboys, then stopped short on Gat's. His glinting black-eyed gaze aggravated her predicament. He had an infuriating "I dare you, lady" grin on his face.

She could just hear him: *If you want to vote like a man, you have to chop chicken like a man.* That did it! Gritting her teeth, India picked up the rooster and carried it over to the chopping stump. She lifted up the hatchet, took aim, pinched her eyes shut and swung. Upon opening her eyes, she nearly collapsed on the spot.

The headless rooster flopped and wing-flapped off the chopping block and across the barnyard. India leaped back from the spattering blood and swallowed back rising nausea. But her tribulation wasn't over, for Emma and Cora had caught two more squawking chickens which they held by the feet near the execution stump.

If she didn't do it quickly she would never do it. "Emma, Cora, put the chickens on the block one after the other."

She brushed a feather from her face, clamped her lips tight and swung. She missed! Rowdy advice sounded from the cowboys. Again she drew up and swung the hatchet. The chicken's head flew off as its body in turn flopped like the rooster's. Cora quickly laid the other chicken on the block, and India, more experienced now, lopped off its head first try. She was no longer able to stomach the spectacle of headless, flopping chickens, and with the pretext of putting the hatchet away she left the yard and went into the barn. Here she let loose her revulsion and vomited in the straw. She doubted she'd ever be able to eat chicken again. If chicken killing was left to her, everyone would eat bread and milk.

After gathering her composure she walked back into the yard. Luckily the cowhands had returned to their work. Emma and Cora were dipping the chickens in boiling water so the feathers would come out easier. That task completed, the three sat down to pluck feathers.

Before they could finish, Elizabeth came out of the cabin. "Mama says things are goin' faster than she thought. I'm ridin' out to fetch Pa." She leaped up on a saddleless horse and galloped off with skirts and hair a-flying.

India set aside the chicken and hurried into the cabin. Clarett was putting a kettle of boiling water on the stove. "I think we're going to have us a baby today." She smiled.

"What should I do to help?" India asked.

"Just convince her to stay down. She thinks she has to help get things ready," Clarett said, on her way out to the water pump.

"Oh, Eugenie," India hurried over to the bed. "Now's no time to work. You need to rest."

"If it's rest I need, I'm sure livin' in the wrong place." She gave a half-laugh and then sobered. "I sure miss my mother at times like this."

India fluffed the tick feather pillow and put it behind Eugenie's back. She sat down on the edge of the bed and took Eugenie's hand in her own. "I just don't understand how you could leave your family and come out west? Hasn't it been hard?"

"Oh yes, it's been hard. The day we left Kentucky I wept hankies full over leaving my family and friends for the wild and woolly West, and I've cried an ocean of tears since."

"Why is it the woman who must follow the man? If you didn't want to come West, you shouldn't have had to. You should have a say in the matter," said India.

"Oh, I had a choice. I've always had a choice. When I married Russ, I already had ideas of my own about the husband being the head of the family. I took the precaution to sound him on "obey" in the marriage pact. Approval or no-approval, that word "obey" would have to be left out, I said to him.

"I'd served my time of tutelage to my parents as all children are supposed to. I was a woman and capable of being the other half of the head of the family. His word and my word were to have equal strength. Still, I would have walked barefoot behind the wagon if he had told me I couldn't come with him. Russ was what I wanted, not a fancy house in Kentucky. So I came and I'm not sorry."

Eugenie's breath quickened with the onset of a labor contraction, and then with its passing her breathing became even again. "Can I help you?" India asked, distressed at the obvious travail Eugenie was going through.

"No, when you get this far along, there's not much anyone can do. The pain will come and go and I'll just have to ride it out."

India moved so she could massage Eugenie's shoulders and back. "Eugenie, would you stop having children if you could?" She couldn't forget Mary Beadle's plight.

Eugenie laughed, humorlessly. "Don't ever ask a woman in childbirth if she'd stop having children. Of course she'll say yes. But then after it's all over and the pain is forgotten, you see the little darlings and think it's well worth it."

"I've heard there are ways to keep from having children. Someone I met . . . ," India hesitated slightly, "who said . . ."

"I suppose she told you about the 'French Secret,'" said Eugenie.

"Yes, she did, but she didn't tell me what it was."

"Well, I know about the French Secret. Some of my children are French Secrets," Eugenie chuckled. "It isn't too dependable, but on occasion it serves its purpose."

"But . . . but what is it?" India asked, still thinking of Mary Beadle, for whom such knowledge would probably do little good because her husband would construe it as a wicked notion.

"The French Secret is a silk hankie," said Eugenie with a grin.

"A silk hankie?" India's curiosity overrode her embarrassment. "I still don't understand."

"I guess a woman has to be married to understand," said Eugenie.

"Since I don't intend to marry, at least tell me what I'm missing. We trade recipes for pound cake and remedies for laundry stains, but no one says anything about what goes on between a man and a woman. What is it like to love a man, Eugenie?"

Despite her discomfort Eugenie released a soft knowing laugh, and then she said thoughtfully, "It's like being thirst-parched on a devilish hot day and then finding all the cool water you can drink."

"That's all? Won't you tell me anymore?"

Eugenie's green eyes narrowed suspiciously. "Has Gat Ransom touched you?"

India shifted uncomfortably. She looked at her hands, then up at the pine log ceiling. "I don't think he respects me. I . . . some things have happened on the trail." Her eyes began to cloud. She swallowed and blinked back her emotion. "I had to strip down to cross a river and . . . there was a storm and I got soaked . . . at a mining camp . . ." As she confessed to Eugenie all the events that had happened between her and Gat, she felt wretched. "Believe me, Eugenie, I didn't mean to compromise myself."

"Has he touched you?" Eugenie's question was more insistent.

"No . . . yes . . . well, at the river he kissed me. He said . . . well, never mind what he said. We had a fight. Now he's polite, but distant. That's what I want, but he's lost his respect for me, and then the dreams keep coming."

Eugenie swore under her breath. At first India thought she was having a labor pain, but then she realized Eugenie was still intent on their conversation. Suddenly, India regretted saying anything. She would never have dared tell even Sissy the whole of it.

With a slow sigh, Eugenie pursed her lips and then patted India's hand. "I won't say nothin' against Gat, only he's a loner and a heartbreaker. He's the best and worst kind of man to fall for. For your own sake I'll tell you what you want to know, but not now." She clutched the bed quilt tightly and began breathing deeply. "I've got my own bread to bake."

After the contraction had passed she said, "Where is that man? Just because he takes his own sweet time with cows and horses doesn't mean he can with me. We ain't the same!"

She asked India for a drink of water. Clarett had returned

and so, after fetching the water, India went outside and looked toward the hills hoping to catch sight of Russ.

Gat had seen Elizabeth ride out for Russ minutes before and when he looked up again from his work he saw India outside watching the horizon. He thrust the branding iron back into the fire, pulled off his gloves, climbed the corral fence and walked toward her. Ever since that day in the mountains during roundup she'd avoided him. When he went in the cabin she left, when he left she went in. Around the corrals she'd visit with the boys, but if he walked over she'd find an excuse to leave. Let her deal her cards, he'd concluded. They'd come back to her threefold.

"How's Eugenie?" he asked.

"Doing her best. But she would feel better if Russ showed up." She turned to go back inside the cabin.

He caught her hand and led her around the corner of the cabin, out of sight of the corrals and barnyard. A look of misgiving crossed her face, but she leaned up against the split logs where he braced his hands in a relaxed stance on either side of her. His face hovered above hers, the fragrance of wild mint touched his nose and he saw a tiny bouquet clipped in the upsweep of her hair. He felt a tightening in the groin and resented the power her nearness wielded over his body.

"Have you something to say or are we just taking in the sun?" she said, feeling weak in the knees. Everything about him exuded masculinity. His broad shoulders and muscled chest strained beneath the leather of his vest and woolen shirt, while his unwavering black eyes gave her no quarter.

His lips curved into a slow smile that eventually touched his eyes. "I wanted to talk to you in private." He paused, prolonging the moment. There was a tranquillity about her he'd missed and now, looking into the serenity of her sapphire eyes was like coming home. "I wanted to thank you."

"For what?" Her eyes danced with puzzlement.

"For putting your speaking tour on the back burner till roundup was over. And for helping Eugenie like you have." She let loose a slow breath and the pink tip of her tongue slid across her lower lip with relief. He dropped his hands and stepped back, aware he smelled like dirt, cow and sweat. He touched his hat. "Ma'am." And strode off.

Back in the cabin India was humming as she poured hot water into the tin washbowl and began washing her hands. Afterwards she helped Clarett spread out a linen sheet on the bed, and then they sponged Eugenie's body with cool water.

"It won't be long now," remarked Eugenie, who was certainly the expert of the three. She became less talkative, intent on pacing her breathing and reserving her strength. India clasped her hands and kept looking out the door.

The children had been told to stay outside.

When the chink of spurs sounded on the porch, India rushed out to meet Russ. "She says it won't be long," India said anxiously as he hurried inside. He made a brief inquiry to Eugenie who only moaned an answer, and then he quickly took off his dusty shirt and washed his upper arms and body.

"Clarett, you'll need to put some of those linen sheets on the stove shelf to warm them. The baby needs to be kept warm at first," he directed. Leaning over Eugenie, he felt her pelvic area. Then he stuffed pillows and blankets behind her back to bring her into a comfortable sitting position. "You've got to start pushing, darlin'. Don't tucker out on me. The head is down and a-comin'."

India could not help but stare in fascination and admiration at the amazing event unfolding before her eyes. The closest she had ever come to witnessing a birth was the mother cat back home, and for some reason that sly old tabby always had the kittens at night or in some secret place that India never found till afterwards.

The shelf clock ticked away the minutes. Eugenie's dark hair now hung in wet strands about her flushed face, and sweat beaded across her forehead and moistened the hollows of her eyes. She groaned, gasped and panted until India could hardly bear to watch.

"Push, now. You know how," Russ coaxed, the lines of his face reflecting the intensity of his concern. "I see it. I love you, darlin'. You can do it. Just once more and we'll have it in our arms." Eugenie gave a body-shaking push, and with the effort of it her cathartic yell cut the air. Seconds after, the wriggling baby slipped into Russ's waiting hands and he let out a loud whoop.

"It must be a boy! He only whoops like that when it's a boy," breathed Eugenie, whose face held the radiance of the Madonna.

"Now darlin'," Russ said, lifting the baby for Eugenie to see, "I always whoop no matter what. But he's a fine little buckaroo. He's got all his fingers and toes, and listen, he's a-fussin' already."

Russ wrapped the infant in the warmed linen swaddling and with a triumphant smile he laid it in the crook of Eugenie's arm. The look of love exchanged between Russ and his wife left India amazed, envious and feeling like a lonely outsider. They radiated with the vibrancy of love, hope and new life. Until now, India had never really understood what she would be giving up by never marrying.

The little thing let loose a loud wail. "Well, now we know that works," giggled Eugenie, and from the doorway her humor was echoed by her children. "Come on in, then," she beckoned to them. "See your new little brother." From Elizabeth on down, they crowded around the bed with oohs and aahs, some reaching timidly to touch a tiny, fisted hand.

Russ crossed the room and yelled out the doorway. "I've got me a little buckaroo!" Rejoining whoops and cheers rang from outside. "Come on in, Gat. Don't stand out there. You bachelors need to see what you're missin'."

Gat stepped inside the cabin with hat in hand. India felt the need to turn her back and make herself busy at the woodstove.

Gat walked over to the bed. "Eugenie, mind if I hold him?" Gat asked.

At this request India stole a glance over her shoulder.

"You go right ahead, Gat," invited Eugenie.

He put down his hat and readily picked up the baby, as readily as if he were a wet nurse. He cradled it in his arms and then gently laid it against his shoulder. "I'd say he's a nine-pounder, at least. How about you, Miss Simms?" he asked, catching her eyeing him.

All India could do was drop her mouth open in surprise. The truth was, she'd never, ever held a baby. How was she to know? "Why, I haven't held him, I'd be no judge," was her flustered reply.

As if Gat read her mind, he said with penetrating sagacity, "Take a turn. Considering your philosophies and all, it might be your only chance. There's nothin' like it."

Chin out, she stepped forward. "To clarify the issue, sir, I have nothing against babies. It's their fathers who concern me." She gladly took the proffered bundle into her arms. Her agitation melted instantly as she gazed upon the beautiful child. A lump swelled in her throat and tears glistened in her eyes, partly from the wonder of it all and partly because she would never experience such a joy with children of her own.

Little Sarah turned to her father and pulled on his shirt sleeve, "But Pa, you haven't named him yet. What are we going to call him?"

"Well, it's your mother's turn to name, and she hasn't even told me. What's it going to be, Eugenie?"

A sparkle lit Eugenie's eyes and a smile turned up the corners of her mouth. "Well, we named Jacob after your father and Samuel after mine. I think that since you were here to catch him—just barely, mind you—I think I'm naming this one Russell."

"Are you sure, darlin'?" He turned his head with exaggerated caution. "You won't be gettin' mad at me later on and want to change his name, will you?"

"Oh, go on. I'm not ever going to get that mad at you."

"Russell Hedemen the second it is!" confirmed Russ, and with that he took the child, slapped Gat on the back and together they strode out the door to show off the baby to those waiting outside.

"Do you think it's all right for them to take him outside?" India asked Clarett.

Clarett shook her head with a laugh. "Of course I don't, but what are we to do?"

For the rest of the afternoon, while Eugenie slept and India and Clarett fixed the supper, Russ sat in the pine rocker and tended the new baby. India never expected to see such a demonstration. A man, in whose occupation the wonder of birth was common, sitting and doting over a baby! She guessed Russ was an unusual man, a man with his heart where it should be. Yes, he might be gruff and rough of manner on the outside, but he was gentleness at the core.

Chapter 15

*G*at leaned against the corral fence and stared at the glorious tamarisk-gold and purple Wyoming sunset. It was the time of day he found most peaceful, and after a long day's roping and riding, it was time to relax. Coyote attested to that by curling up at Gat's feet with his nose resting on his boot toe. Gat listened to the lowing of the cattle roll over the hills and watched night hawks dive into dusk. He'd been searching for something all of his life and at moments like this he was sure he'd found it.

But deep within he felt incomplete, and no amount of beautiful scenery could still a longing he couldn't put into words. Maybe what he'd found here in the West wasn't what he was looking for. He'd always worked for somebody else, not taking much for himself, and he'd liked not being tied down. Since the war he'd wandered around, mostly just drifting, trying somehow to remake the past and resolve old conflicts. Now maybe it was time to take a new direction. Some direction was better than none.

Take Russ for instance. He'd nearly doubled his herd since last spring, and Gat thought if the winters didn't get too mean, Russ could do all right running cattle along the Sweetwater. With three government forts nearby to buy the beef and the railway completed, he foresaw real opportunity in ranching for Russ and maybe himself, too. He had in mind the place to start, just over the territorial line in northern Colorado. Not as much Indian trouble down that way. Maybe it was time to be done with drifting, time to carve out a niche for himself.

"Evening, Gat." Bess Anderson brushed up against him with an inviting smile. "They're going to bring out the organ and have a little dancin'. Eugenie says she's up to playin', and I'm up to dancin' if you'll take me as partner."

"I'll be happy to, Bess, but I don't think I can keep you to myself every dance. All the boys like to have a turn," he answered with a touch of standoffishness.

"So . . . ," she smiled coquettishly, "I can choose who I want and I choose you."

Gat smiled back. Bess was young but she knew what she wanted, and he knew she wanted him. There had been some talk and speculation concerning them, and each time he came to the Hedemens', he and Bess had been thrown together as a matter of matchmaking. If he were the marrying kind, she'd be the woman he'd need, because her temperament was right and she'd been bred on the frontier. She could ride and rope as well as any man, and she had slim ankles to boot.

Luckily, he'd always had the good sense to ride out and leave the petticoats and "I do's" to the other fools. His eyes wandered past Bess to the uppity pack of goods standing in the cabin doorway directing four cowhands out the door with Eugenie's pump organ. Now, Lady Liberty was a filly of another color. A woman like India Simms could cause a man's resolve to disappear as fast as water in the badlands. Why did he take to a woman like her, all flare and explosion? He wasn't some goosey kid who tossed his rope before building a loop. He knew women, and this one was a maverick. She had something against men, and even if he had a mind to, she'd never take to brandin'.

"Come on then," urged Bess, as she looped her arm through his. "Ty's brought out his fiddle and Eugenie's set herself down at the organ."

Gat and Bess strolled over, arm in arm, and joined the

group gathering around the organ. Eugenie pulled out a few stops and gave a push on the foot pedal, but was rewarded with a dull thump.

"What's wrong?" India asked.

"I can't get the foot pedal going. Russ, do you want to look and see if you can figure it out? I haven't played it for a month. Maybe . . ."

Russ bent down and took off the front panel. A moment passed before he gave a chuckle of discovery. "Well, I'd say here's the problem: a music lovin' blow snake. Look at the size of this critter." The ladies gasped as he drew out, tail first, a four-foot snake. He stepped back and twirled it around his head and let it fly into the brush. "Now, we can get started. Ty, you ready?"

"Let's get movin'." He began tapping his foot and bowing his fiddle. Eugenie followed his lead on the pump organ.

"Everyone join hands in a circle," instructed Russ.

All the cowhands, including the Hedemens' four oldest daughters, India, and the Anderson sisters, clasped hands to form a circle. Of course there was a woman shortage, but that was remedied by Jacob, Samuel and some other young cowhands, who much to the amusement of the others, had donned aprons.

> "Ladies in the center, gents 'round 'em run:
> Swing your rope, cowboy, and get you one!"

When Chic Bitterman partnered India, a sour taste rose in Gat's mouth. Bitterman was as sly as a hungry coyote, and Gat knew he had only one use for a woman. Two nights before, around the campfire, Bitterman began to tell stories of whoring down on the border, which Gat hadn't found entertaining. He said as much, and added to the bad blood between them by walking off.

Gat kept an eye on India and Bitterman as they danced around the circle. Bitterman was adept at putting his hands a little too low or a little too high on her. When everyone changed partners again, Gat lost Bess and ended up with young Samuel.

Russ sang out:

> "Swing the other gal, swing her sweet!
> Paw dirt, doggies, stomp your feet.
> Swing an' march, first couple lead,
> Clear 'round the circle an' then stampede!"

There was an outbreak of whoops and hollers and the music picked up pace as everybody kicked up the dust.

The dancing progressed. Gat and India circled toward each other in different directions while Gat's dark eyes raked over the sway of India's hips and the flip of her head as she sashayed around the circle. Then, just when his reaching hand went to clasp hers, the music stopped. The set broke up. Bess was back at Gat's side and India turned to the attentions of an adoring young cowhand.

Clarett Anderson sat down at the organ to spell off Eugenie, and Ty called Gat over to accompany a song or two on his penny whistle. Bess reluctantly let Gat go, but made it clear she expected to dance with him again. From beneath hooded lids Gat watched the cowhands line up to dance with India, and he felt as territorial as a high-desert wolf. His jaw tightened in a slow burn and he had a mind not to play at all, but Ty looked over at him with a go-ahead nod and Gat picked up the tune.

He'd never seen India so friendly. And the more he watched, the more it rankled him. From where he stood, she looked like she was "countin' coup." He was a man whose slow, smoldering anger was neither easily nor quickly aroused, but as he watched India's genial ways his possessiveness simmered and gathered strength, shaking him to his granite-firm foundations. She had penetrated the secret place no one else had ever quite reached—his heart.

Finding no end to partners as the music played, India enjoyed round after round of polkas and waltzes. But it was

Gat Ransom she danced for and deep inside she knew it was only him she wanted to dance with. On every waltzing turn she looked toward him, where he leaned against the pump organ piping away.

After a time he took a break from playing, but instead of asking her to dance, as she hoped he would, he asked Bess. India was jealous. Whether she wanted him or not, she didn't want anyone else to have him.

The moon rose to mid-sky and the wild things in the hills began to call to each other, and he still hadn't asked her to dance. Sparring glances crossed between them and his taunting began to grate on her. When he wasn't dancing with Bess, he pulled his hat over his eyes and leaned against the fence. India should have retired for the evening, but she couldn't make herself leave. Though she dreaded his scrutiny, perversely she wanted him to look at her and so she smiled broader and laughed louder as if she was having the time of her life, which she wasn't.

After sullenly watching Gat and Bess dance again, she made up her mind to turn him down if he did ask her to dance. Why I was just planning to sit this one out, Mister Ransom, she would say. Unfortunately, the opportunity to refuse him never came, and after a while she was so smitten with jealousy she excused herself from the dancing and slipped off into the shadows to sort things out.

She leaned against the cabin and stared at the prairie moon, realizing there had been no moment when she'd thought, *I will love this man.* It had just happened. She had not wanted to love him—or had she? A great swelling ache washed through her and she knew that even in the beginning it had been an orbiting attraction between them, like moon to earth or earth to sun. She had not intended for it to go this far.

No answers came

She took a few deep breaths, striving for some semblance of emotional calm. But that calm was short-lived when Chic Bitterman came out of the shadows and thrust his unshaven face inches from hers.

"I'd like a dance! You've been avoidin' me," he sneered. "That ain't good manners, *ma'am.*"

India's heart quickened. Bitterman's presence made her uneasy. She knew firsthand that he was brutal and cowardly, besides being devoid of manners and good feelings.

"You're wrong. We'll have more opportunities to dance before the evening's over." Lifting her skirt she stepped forward to leave but he positioned himself directly in front of her.

"Well, now's yer opportunity." He put his arms around her and held her like a rabbit in a steel trap and began to sway to the music. His touch was repugnant, but she was afraid to speak up.

When the song ended he pressed her up against the cabin wall and with a grotesque smile said, "Give me a kiss."

Revulsion filled India. Turning her face away she said, "Let's go back with the others."

A burst of rotten breath hit her nostrils. "I don't want to dance anymore. I just want a kiss."

She would sooner kiss Coyote and was on the verge of saying so. "I won't kiss you."

"If you won't kiss me, I'll just do it my way." He pressed a wet tongue inside the hollow of her ear. Shivers of disgust rippled down her neck. His action seemed to be the vilest of insult and disrespect.

"Please, I . . ." Mustering her courage, India pulled away, but he caught her back. His hands cradled her hips and pressured them to his own.

"What's wrong, ain't Ransom ever done that to ya?" A growling chuckle rose from his throat.

"No! Nor would any gentleman behave so toward a lady." She faced him again and met his eyes with indignation.

He guffawed in her face. "You don't know nothin' 'bout how gentlemen behave toward ladies. Why, I bet yer *Mr.* Ransom has kissed more tit than you could count. I oughta slide between yer legs, girlie, and let you sample a *real* man."

Bitterman's obscene suggestions disgusted her. "Let me go, or I'll call out," she threatened between clenched teeth.

"Go ahead, call out. Maybe *Mr.* Ransom will save ya," he mocked. Not easily put off, his mouth came down on hers and he forced her lips apart with his teeth. Pinning her body against the wall he held her face in his hands and thrust his hips against hers.

"Let go!" she gasped.

"Not until you kiss back. Come on, kiss me back. I ain't sure you're a woman." He was a strong man and India knew that no amount of good manners would waylay his intentions. Something snapped. Her eyes widened with fury and she bit him. It cost her more than she'd anticipated. Bitterman's arms clamped her in a painful hold and he rammed his mouth onto hers, thrusting his tongue between her teeth so violently that it could never be misconstrued as a kiss. "You'll be sorry, woman!" he muttered.

"Pardon me," came a low, deadly voice.

Chic's gaze ricocheted past her face. India turned to see Ransom coming toward them.

"Ty's about to put away his fiddle. I'd like a waltz with the lady." His voice was slow, soft and lazy. He looked directly at Chic and then at her.

Chic had loosened his hold, but hadn't completely relinquished her hand. His whole demeanor shifted in the face of Ransom. His brutish attentions softened to outward flirtation.

"The lady and I were just sharing a kiss." His voice swelled with challenge.

Suddenly, India realized Chic had used her to inflame his vendetta against Ransom, and fear for Gat's safety, as well as shame for her own part, flooded through her. She attempted to ease her jangling nerves by tidying loose strands of hair.

Gat's dark eyes watched her speculatively, awaiting her answer. Nausea crept up her throat, for she read in his cold gaze a heart-raking reproach. Again she'd confirmed she was woman not worth his respect. *Don't look at me like that,* she wanted to plead, but instead she said, "Yes, Mr. Ransom, I would like to dance."

"Maybe she'll give you a kiss like she did me," said Bitterman with a smirk.

India's eyes darted to Gat. He stood motionless, his whole body relaxed into a deceptive hair-trigger readiness. A tremor of stark apprehension went through her and she was stunned to see the bold, dangerous riptide of pure hatred Gat's eyes riveted on Bitterman. Kissing a woman wasn't enough provocation to kill a man, but just now it might be.

Thankfully their guns had been hung up before the evening's dancing. She swallowed back her sickening dread and stepped toward Gat with a false smile quivering on her lips.

In silence, she and Gat walked toward the yard while the air of controlled violence radiating from him became a tangible curtain between them.

The sweet strains of a familiar waltz began and he wordlessly extended his hand to her. Humiliated and yearning to explain, she didn't feel like dancing anymore as her own shaking hand reached out to him to maintain her balance. She took his hand, clasped it and held fast to his long fingers, strong and warm.

Nothing in her life had prepared her for the jolt of senses when he pulled her into his arms. She felt his strength spread through her like a breath of immortality. He held her as close as Bitterman had, yet nothing at all was the same. Gat Ransom was a veritable mountain of dependability, courage, patience and determination, and in his arms a treacherous warmth was seeping through her. Her mind forgot Bitterman, forgot women's rights and other high-minded resolutions, and focused on the feel of Ransom's body next to hers and the dizzying scent of his masculinity.

The waltz went on and on and she never wanted to leave his arms. She floated in an airy mist, flying free like a mountain bluebird, rising, swooping on a whim or breeze but soaring expertly, catching the sunlight between clouds and reflecting it off turquoise wing. Content in his embrace, she didn't hear the music end and when he released her she wondered why.

Their eyes met and neither of them spoke.

Finally she said in a sweet, clear voice, "Mr. Ransom, thank you for the waltz."

The intensity in his eyes deepened as they held hers. He pursed his lips consideringly. "For someone who doesn't intend to marry, you sure are a flirt. If you want my continued protection, you'd better keep your eyes lowered and your hips still." He touched the brim of his hat. "Evenin', ma'am."

India stared at him unbelievingly as he walked away. Her nostrils flared, pulling fresh air into her tight lungs. Tears stung her eyes. If she'd tripped and fallen flat on her face, it wouldn't have smarted as much.

Chapter 16

*T*he next morning began with a cuss and a snort, and Gat's mood traveled downhill, making him as nettlesome as a cornered porcupine. With only a swallow of black coffee he went to work. A raw brush horse bucked him off and a cow kicked him in the thigh. Even a warm smile from Bess left him mute and surly, although with impeccable teamwork and timing they paired off cows and calves, cutting them out of the herd for branding. Without the usual camaraderie they worked together through the morning, and when the others broke to eat, Gat kept working.

A glance over at the chow line brought a contemptuous curl to his lip. India had brought out her petition and had asked the hands lined up in front of the cabin to sign it. Then, with the help of the Hedemen children, she was dishing out beans, cornbread and rib eye steaks. Today Gat was content to go hungry. He'd had enough of what that lady could dish out.

Later, India came over and climbed up on the corral lodge pole fence. Still paired up with Gat, Bess made an overhand toss for a calf's head and pulled the loop tight around its neck. Gat rode up behind, made a heel catch on the animal's hind legs and together they toppled it. He dismounted, leaving his rope tied to the saddle horn while his horse leaned back to hold the rope taut.

"How about a cup of coffee and some dinner, Mr. Ransom? The food is about to be cleared away," India called, watching as he downed the calf and reached for a hot branding iron. "Doesn't that hurt?" she asked, sounding like any greenhorn.

"Yep!" he replied, without looking at her. "Sit your bare bottom on a hot stove and you've got a good idea how the calf feels about now."

Up on her horse, Bess giggled. India seemed to shift slightly at the impropriety of his allusion. He touched the branding iron to the calf. Hair and flesh smoldered, all the while the calf bellowed and bawled. Then, he pulled out his pocket knife and knelt down to castrate it.

"Hasn't it gone through enough? What are you doing?" India protested.

Under his breath, Gat swore at her ignorance and deftly cut the calf's scrotum, let loose the ropes holding its legs and sent it off bawling. He nudged the brim of his hat up and looked her straight in the eye. "Ma'am, I've just done what you and your lady fanatics would like to do to the whole male population of Wyoming!"

She glared back at him. Suddenly her eyes widened as the meaning of his words dawned on her. He'd seen the same shock-eyed look on a stallion he'd lassoed in a box canyon once. A devilish pleasure touched him on knowing he'd hit right on target.

Her jaw clenched and for a second he thought she'd fly off the handle, tossing all her good manners and fine breeding to the four winds. Then, she shifted like a summer storm and her anger melted into determination. Good Lord! A speech was comin' on.

"I don't want to unman you, nor do I want to be a man myself. I like being a woman!" Her eyes flashed with fervency. "When I open my mouth I want to sing like a lark, not a bullfrog, and I don't want to pound my chest with bravado or be tough as rawhide. I've no desire to possess, brand or subjugate you. Just like you, I want freedom, not subjection, equality not servitude. And if, because of my gentler nature, I'm to be ruled, at least allow me a vote in choosing my ruler!" Her silvery voice never wavered. "Tell me, how can you be unmanned if I walk beside you instead of behind?"

The other cowhands standing around the branding fire had stopped working, for nobody with eyes and ears could miss the fire between Gat and India. They were all entertained by the exchange, as Gat shot back with, "Ma'am, I don't give a damn where you walk! Just watch out for buffalo chips and keep out of my way!" A supporting volley of whistles and whoops sounded from the cowboys.

India's cheeks reddened with humiliation. She'd laid bare her noblest ideals and he'd made a joke of them. She'd expected more from him.

The laughter, the smell of burnt hair, the dust and smoke, the endless bellowing of cattle became too much for her. She climbed down off the fence, removed her apron, and walked to the cabin where she resolutely hung it on a wooden peg. Then, without a parting explanation, she saddled up Bluestocking and rode off for the solace of open spaces.

She spurred her horse into a gallop, heading in no particular direction. She just wanted to get far away from the noise of the cattle herd, the smell of burning flesh and the branding iron of male oppression. She rode for some time, and then in a grassy meadow specked with wildflowers and salt sage, she climbed down off her horse and sat on a flat rock while Bluestocking shook her head with a snort, content to graze on the green shoots of prairie grass.

Letting out a godforsaken sigh, India listened to the trilling of a lark as she stared off vacantly. For the first time during all her debates, lectures and travels she'd hit head-on the bastion of male prerogative in the flesh-and-blood embodiment of Gat Ransom. Suddenly, her efforts on behalf of woman suffrage seemed absurdly futile. What a fool she was to think she could hope to change centuries, even millennia, of reasoning that men held the divine right to command, rule, and reign, when she couldn't even change the man she loved? She looked up into the snapping blue Wyoming sky and doubted God's justice. Were the heavens womanless?

She stood outside the citadel of power while the knights lined up shoulder to shoulder on the battlements, intent on keeping her from the Peacock throne of mastery. Couldn't they see usurping power was not her arena? Power could never be the highest good. Her aim was justice, equality, and fairness. A wheel of despair churned inside her. It might be better if she were ignorant, invisible and swaddled from head to toe in the veiling purdah of the women of Islam. Eve, the outsider, hopelessly gazing into the promised land.

As time passed, curious little heads peeked from the nearby burrows of a prairie dog town. Soon, more daring, the golden-furred creatures sat up on hind legs and chattered like gossiping busybodies. A refreshing breeze rippled the grass as India's mind wrestled with discouragement and the ever-intruding image of Gat Ransom.

The man and the country weren't for her. She'd made one mistake by traveling with Ransom, and now another by falling in love with him. Besides, she thought as she wallowed in self-pity, he preferred Bess Anderson. She was suited to the life Ransom intended to lead. Bess would bear him ten children in a mud-chinked log cabin, cook his food and rope his cattle.

India licked the dust from her lips. It couldn't be denied that the land had a wild, untamed beauty unyielding and ever-innocent. She could see what held Ransom here as her eyes swept the far-off mountains and the rolling prairie grass. Despite badlands, weather and Indians, he was part of this land. Ironically, even she had left the strictures of civilization to find justice here.

But in ways, though everything was different, everything was the same. She bent to pick a wild buttercup and marveled at its sun color, thinking it no less lovely than the cultivated rose. A spring dooryard of buttercups outside a cabin could be somewhat redeeming, but she immediately pushed the vision from her mind.

India caught a glimpse of movement and the slither of

brown black scales through the grass, and her breathing stopped. Even the prairie dog matrons paused in their gossip, ears and heads cocked cannily at the rattlesnake's passing. Behind her, India heard the crack of twig and the uneasy snort of Bluestocking. The setting sun hovered on the horizon and she knew it was time she should ride back.

At dusk India finally resigned herself to being lost. She should have reached the ranch by now or even crossed the fringes of the cattle herd. But around her she heard only the call of night birds and coyotes. Bluestocking's gait slowed. India climbed down off her and examined her foreleg. The swelling hadn't returned, but to be on the safe side India unsaddled her and prepared to stop for the night. Anxiousness teased the edges of her mind, for she'd grown used to the security of Ransom's company and she felt alone and vulnerable.

India concluded the most sensible thing to do was to sit it out till morning, and turned her immediate attention to her horse. After hobbling Bluestocking, India laid out the saddle blanket and curled up against the shelter of a sagebrush. Looking up at the stars she thought of her family, and forgetting thirst and hunger, homesickness became her major malady. In her next letter to Sissy she would paint her night alone on the frontier as a great adventure. But it was an adventure she could have lived without. By counting stars, she attempted to push out of her mind the stories Ransom had told her of Indian spirit bands that rode the prairie darkness. Nevertheless, wild visions crept in and out of her thoughts while she awaited the night light of moonrise.

Gat sat staring a hole through the bottom of his coffeecup. He was unaware when Ty, balancing a supper plate filled high sat down beside him. Nor did he answer Ty's friendly comments on the fine quality of the food and the chances of finding more work after the roundup was over. It was Russ Hedemen that broke Gat's reverie by asking if any of the hands had seen Miss Simms.

"I saw her ridin' out this afternoon," Ty said. He took off

his hat, pulled a red handkerchief from inside and wiped his mouth.

Gat stopped staring at his cup and looked up. "She rode out?"

With a disapproving tone, Ty said, "Yep, right after you showed her how to deball a calf."

Gat's dark brows knitted together, his eyes narrowed and he cursed himself under his breath. He'd had no call to be so rude to her and now she'd gone off like a wounded pup to sulk.

"Eugenie's worried about her," said Russ. "Seems nobody's seen her since then.

"Which direction did she ride off in?" Gat asked, rising to his feet.

"Not sure. Maybe west," Ty said.

Gat put down his cup. Without another word, he walked over to the corral, saddled up a horse and rode west into the rose light of sunset.

India's thirst was dizzying. She'd been moving since sunrise, now leading Bluestocking rather than riding. Everything looked the same—salt sage, jackrabbits, flies, alkaline dust and dry wash. She couldn't tell where she was going or where she'd been as she watched storm clouds gather in gray masses on the horizon. Things always seemed to happen fast in this country. One minute you'd be sweltering and parched to the bone, the next you'd be drowning in a cloudburst. By now she had sense enough to keep to high ground and hopefully dodge the lightning.

By late afternoon she came across a baldface bull marked by the Hedemen shooting star brand. She followed him until he joined up with a harem of heifers and calves, and not long after the rising wind carried the faint lowing of the main herd.

Silhouetted in the distance, she spied a horse and rider. A vivid flash followed by a peal of thunder prompted her to climb up on Bluestocking and ride toward the far-off figure. Soon the rider spotted her and loped his horse towards her.

A shiver ran down her spine the moment she recognized the features of Chic Bitterman. She'd rather meet with a passing rattlesnake than him, but she was dying for water.

"Well, ma'am, ain't it a pleasure. Everybody's been wonderin' about ya." He leaned over his saddle horn and pushed back his hat with a sinister smile.

"I'm fine. But I could do with some water." She didn't smile back.

"So happens yer in luck." He climbed down off his horse and unhooked his canteen from the saddle horn. "Come and get it."

Thunder rumbled through the hills and Bluestocking fidgeted while India paused nervously. Her thirst finally won out and she climbed down and walked over to Bitterman. He stepped around to face her, his hand dangled the canteen of water. Her hand moved toward it. He jerked it out of reach.

"You'll have to come a little closer." The coldness in his eyes ruined his face more than a deformity.

India's gut instinct was to leap back on Bluestocking and ride off, but instead she swallowed back her nervousness and backed away to put distance between them. He plunged forward and caught her in a relentless grip.

"Let me go!" India tried to pull away from him, but he tightened his hold and leered in her face.

"If you want water, you've got to feel this." He gripped her hands in his and forced them to his swelling erection.

"Forget your notions of women's rights. This here's all you got a right to."

Horrified, she broke away from his hold, ran for her horse and leaped on. Off she rode, bounding across the prairie, but within seconds Bitterman, a more experienced rider, closed in. Hair and skirt flying in the wind, India leaned into Bluestocking while her eyes frantically scanned the horizon, looking for a familiar landmark, anything to set her direction to the Hedemen ranch.

Bitterman closed the gap, and suddenly she heard the whizz of his lasso above her head, and then with a head-wrenching snap she was yanked to the ground where she lay stunned. Bitterman, with a bull-dogger's expertise, was upon her, tying her feet, arms and hands.

"Let me go!" she moaned in a soft voice. Her heart pounded wildly.

"You ain't goin' nowhere. You and your notions about women. You need to be kept in your place!" He stood above her, unbuckled his holster, dropped it aside and then unfastened his pants, exposing himself.

She clamped her eyes shut, turned her head away hoping to block out this nightmare. Like most women, she'd never been free of the fear of ravishment. For every woman it was something to be feared and prayed against like fire and lightning. Now, by attempting to cross traditional roles and boundaries, had she invited it?

Standing above her, Bitterman became the embodiment of male power and its misuse. Behind him shadows lined up in more subtle disguises as lawmakers, clergy and patriarchs, all offering him a hand to subjugate womankind.

Anger and the instinct of self-preservation seized India. Heaven help her but she wouldn't lay and accept his violence as her just punishment! When he snatched at her skirts and his weight came down on her she screamed and kept screaming, until the point of his knife pressed her throat.

"Girlie, Ransom ain't gonna want ya when I'm done!" He swore abhorrent things, things that twisted in her stomach as sharp as the knife he held at her throat.

A shot rang out.

Bitterman groaned. He'd been hit. With his hideous body slumping on top of her, India writhed to break free as she felt the warmth of his blood spread over her stomach and chest. Then, the wet nose of Coyote, licking and sniffing her face, assured her help had arrived.

Gat pulled up his horse, leaped down and rolled Bitterman off India. He drew out his knife and cut the ropes binding her. Their eyes met, his overflowing with unspoken apology, hers with unsaid relief. The lightning flashed with skeletal vividness across the sky and the subsequent crack of thunder returned them to the moment.

Gat shouted over the storm. "Stampede. I need your help!" He was putting her up on her horse when she fully understood. The herd was spooked and ready to stampede. Another crack of thunder and they'd break. He was up on his own horse now, galloping off. Coyote yapped after him. She dared a look at Bitterman's still body on the ground. Putting peril and hesitation aside, India spurred her horse after them. By now it was so dark she could barely distinguish the herd ahead, though their nervous bellowing roared between the rips of thunder.

Suddenly, the herd leaders broke and ran like racers. The surging wave of wild-eyed long-horned cattle was a terrifying sight to India, and she realized that without help, she and Gat would have to corkscrew them into themselves. Gat hooted and yelled as he rode forward. India almost quailed, but Bluestocking plunged ahead. Choking and blinded with dust India galloped alongside the herd, serving as a circling sentinel.

The black clouds burst and rain poured down, and with the cooling deluge the herd seemed to lose its frenzy. What seemed like hours was only minutes by the time she and Gat had turned the bovine wave into itself.

Exhaustion seared through India like a lightning bolt and with water streaming down her face, she used her last threads of strength to whoop with relief when she saw other cowhands riding up.

"You all right, Miss Simms?" Gat yelled through the pouring rain.

"No, Mr. Ransom," she called with honesty as thirst and exhaustion took its price. She felt herself slipping, her grip loosening and the world spinning.

When India regained consciousness the next morning, Elizabeth Hedemen was sitting beside her. The girl's eyes widened and she jumped from her chair and ran to the cabin door hollering, "She's awake, Ma. She's awake."

The first thing on India's mind was water. A crockery water pitcher sat on the table and India made to rise, but weakness halted her progress. "Elizabeth," she rasped softly, "please bring me some water."

Elizabeth quickly turned back to her patient, bringing the water pitcher with a cup. Her thirst was so great that India almost drank straight from the pitcher, but running her tongue over her parched lips, she waited for Elizabeth to pour a cupful.

Eugenie, followed by Russ and Gat, hurried in. "Thank God. You've slept like the dead," Eugenie announced. "Gat's told us what happened."

India's eyes lowered. She wished the whole affair could be hidden under a cloak of silence.

"I thank you for saving my herd," Russ said.

"I did what anyone else would have done," she replied modestly. "Mr. Ransom deserves the credit for anticipating the stampede."

"Unfortunately, there was a casualty. Chic Bitterman must have fallen from his horse. He was trampled by the stampede," Russ said.

India's eyes met Ransom's in a soul-searching exchange. He gave a self-conscious cough. India realized he hadn't told them what really happened. Was he protecting himself or her reputation?

"It's done with now, no need to dwell on it," Eugenie said. "We've been real worried about you. Going off and getting yourself lost."

India was reviving. "I wasn't lost, I just didn't know where I was for a few hours."

"We've heard that before," Russ said, laughing. He'd gone over to the pine cradle and picked up the awakening baby.

"I told her not to get off her horse," Gat said with mock seriousness.

"I didn't get off, I fell off," she replied defensively.

"Well, ma'am, you were as good as a man!" Gat said.

India smiled, just barely. For this praise was of little consequence to her. "No, Mr. Ransom, I was as good as a woman." He smiled. He always looked so intense until he smiled.

Then everyone laughed, especially young Elizabeth.

Gat had stepped over to the bed. A glint of admiration seemed to sparkle in his black eyes. Well, any way you look at it, you have my thanks."

India held his dark gaze with her own for a long moment. Something had happened out there between them. The rivalry was gone. She supposed to Ransom's thinking she'd proven herself. She'd participated in the mysterious male ritual that turned boys into men, and in her case, a woman into a man. No matter, she still didn't want to be a man. But she did want something for her trial.

"Mr. Ransom, I want more than your thanks. I want your friendship."

Gat's lips broke into a calculating grin. "Why sure, ma'am. But then you'll have to call me Gat. All my friends do."

Now India grinned. "Well, Mr. Ransom, I guess it will be Gat from here on.

In the late afternoon, India awoke from napping to stillness. She looked around curiously, for it was unusual to be able to hear the mantel clock ticking and the teapot whistling amid the constant activity of the Hedemen household. The creak of the pine rocker drew her attention and Eugenie met her gaze with a soft smile.

"Nice, isn't it." Sun filtered across her shoulder from the window and illuminated the angelic face of the sleeping baby in her arms. "It sometimes happens, but not often. Everyone's out by the corral watching Ty Pierre trick ride. I suppose it's as good a time as any to speak with you—now you and Gat have become friends."

India flushed and turned in the bed. "I . . . I don't know if it's for the better or not."

"Believe me it ain't for the better. Friendship leads to other things." She lowered her eyes thoughtfully. "I know from experience because there's more to the story of why

Russ and I came west than I told you, and maybe my telling you will save you the grief I've had." She looked past India for a moment as if to decide how best to begin. "You see, Russ and I came west because . . . because my family disowned me. Well, we weren't married and I got in the family way. I thought I knew about those things, but I hadn't expected how uncontrollable passion could be." She gnawed her lower lip. "Not that I don't love Russ. I surely do. But marrying a man because you have to is different from marrying because you want to, and it's the same with him, maybe worse. A man hates to be cornered, and too, with a woman there's always a niggling doubt he married her out of duty, not love. Oh, sure, I thought a girl needed a man to take care of her, but I've learned that a woman ends up taking care of herself, no matter how strong the man is. Marry for love, not convenience, I always say."

Fascinated by the depth of Eugenie's insights, India drew up her knees beneath the quilt and rested her chin on her arms. "But can't love grow between a man and woman after a time?"

"Sometimes. I love Russ more now than I ever have, but it's different from when we were young. Oh, we still have our moments. We have a grassy spot down by the river and sometimes we let the older children take care of the young ones and we spend a little time together, alone—no interruptions." Eugenie didn't miss the sudden show of interest on India's face. A sly smile touched Eugenie's lips. "And I suppose that's what I promised to tell you . . . what goes on between a man and a woman when there are no interruptions."

"Yes, I want to know. Men shouldn't be the only ones to know it all."

Eugenie began to laugh and shake her head. "My soul, men don't know nothin', only what pleases themselves. A woman has to teach her man how to please her. Why, by the time a man's spent himself, it's just beginning for a woman."

India smiled self-consciously, wondering if she was indeed ready to hear what Eugenie was about to tell her, but curiosity was ever her forte. She settled back and directed her undivided attention to Eugenie.

The shelf clock ticked away an hour of enlightenment, and for India the whole story of creation seemed to be put back in an orderly fashion. Yes, in that single hour what Eugenie revealed to her about the reciprocal nature of love between a man and a woman made better sense than anything she'd ever heard in vulgar slang, puritan prudery, or softly whispered innuendo.

But Eugenie's last confidence became a disquieting caution. "Remember, India, it's up to you to pull in the reins if it goes farther than you want. It's always the woman who has the most to lose."

Well, India thought, *I've already lost my heart—what more is there?*

Three days later, their leave-taking at the Hedemen ranch became a sorrowful parting, especially for India, because she knew she'd never return. The children lined up beside Eugenie and Russ in front of the corral and India reluctantly gave up the new baby to its mother's arms, and with a teary sniff, moved down the row of children, giving each a kiss and a hug.

"You come back soon, now," reminded Eugenie. She gave India a one-armed squeeze and a kiss. "You'll always be welcome, and hopefully someday I can repay you for all the help you've been to us."

"Yep, I add my thanks to Eugenie's. I'll sure miss that Frenchy cookin' you stir up, ma'am," Russ said, grinning.

Eugenie threw him a look of mock disgust. "Well, if you don't like my plain cookin', Russ Hedemen, you can fix supper yourself."

"Now I didn't—" he began.

"Ah, Eugenie. Russ likes your cookin'. He told me that's why he married you, for your biscuits," Gat threw in.

"And I suppose that's all," Eugenie grumbled with a sideways wink at India. "I guess I'll leave home one of these days and take up the cause like India here. I might get a lot more than the vote for women. I might get some genuine appreciation after I'm gone and all of you have to do your own fetchin' and slavin'.''

"Well," India said with a smile, "saddle up a horse and come with us. You should take a holiday. Gat's a pretty good campfire cook and we might have a fine time of it."

"Now, now," Russ spoke up. "Don't go putting such temptations in front of my wife. Why, last time she got a wild notion, I had to bring that fancy pump organ all the way from St. Louis to keep her here."

"And if ever a woman deserved it, Eugenie did," Gat said. "She has my standing proposal that if she ever gets tired of an old cowpoke of a husband, I'm ready and waiting."

"Is there any female in the territory who wouldn't want your standing proposal, Gat?" asked Eugenie with a mischievous eye.

Gat shifted. "Yep, there's one." His eyes moved to India. She'd turned suddenly and got up on her horse. "Some heifers spook mighty easy." Eugenie and Gat exchanged smiles and he climbed up on his horse. "We'll be seein' you folks."

India waved a final farewell, not trusting herself to say another word without breaking into a flood of tears. They rode out of the Hedemen ranch toward the river, pausing a moment by Bitterman's newly turned grave.

She looked over at Gat. "Why didn't you tell them?"

"It's done," he said.

"Do you think I invited it?"

He pursed his lips thoughtfully, remembering his sharp words the night of the dance with regret. "No woman invites that, and besides he was using you to get at me."

Swallowing back the memory she said, "he didn't . . ." Then her voice trailed off.

He cleared his throat. "Don't think about it. Just don't judge all men by Bitterman."

Momentarily her eyes held his in an assessing gaze and then she nudged Bluestocking on.

Gat followed beside her. After a while he said, "The Hedemens are fine folks. That Eugenie, I'd say, was strained through a silk hankie."

India looked over at him with puzzlement. "What?"

"I said, the Hedemens are fine folks."

"No, the other part."

He grinned. "I said, that Eugenie was strained through a silk hankie. You've heard the saying?"

India began to giggle, then she broke into full-hearted laughter. "No I haven't, but I understand," thinking of Eugenie's explanation of the French Secret. "You cowboys have such a way of saying things. 'Strained through a silk hankie,' " she repeated between fits of laughter.

Gat caught her eye and suddenly joined in. "I'd say your laugh is about the most pleasant sound I've heard in some time." And for a moment their shared gaze became an embrace of eyes.

Chapter 17

*A*fter riding two days and encountering only one home-stead and a single cavalry detachment on patrol, India won-dered why everybody in Wyoming had such an aversion to living next to one another. Nowadays, most people traveled by train—only the poor, the adventuresome and the eccen-tric did otherwise. The eccentric, she thought, looking over at Gat. That would describe him. In fact, that would describe everyone willing to settle in the territory. Her eyes ached from gazing at an endless blue sky and her mouth throbbed for a cool drink of water. She spied a grove of trees in the distance and prodded Bluestocking to a quicker pace.

When she rode into the trees she cocked an ear. Was it a baby's cry or a mockingbird? Maybe she'd been out in the sun too long, for she was hearing babies crying in the wilderness. Next she'd be seeing mirages. Bluestocking moved through the high brush into an opening under the cottonwood canopy where India saw the smoke of a camp-fire. Caution caused her to draw up her horse and wait for Gat, who was not far behind. Then she heard a faint whimper again and knew this time it wasn't a bird, but the cry of an infant.

"Hallo, is someone here?" she called, deciding if there was a child, whoever was there couldn't be too dangerous. A rustle sounded in the bushes close to the stream, and then a hatless, red-thatched head popped up and slowly looked around. A youth hesitantly stepped out of the brush with a bundle in his arms. A tiny clenched fist batted the air and a red face squealed a long bawl which sounded as anguished as a calf at the Hedemen ranch on branding day. India slipped down off her horse and walked over to the boy. "My goodness, what have you got here?" She extended her arms and the boy gave up the child easily.

Gat rode up. The boy looked to him when he spoke. "I'm mighty glad someone's finally come. I've prayed night an' day fer help. My wife's died of the fever an' the babe is hunger'un fer somethin' to eat," he blurted out sorrowfully.

India exchanged a puzzled glance with Ransom. She wouldn't count the stranger in front of her more than a boy, freckled face and lean, at that. But apparently he was man enough to have a child on his hands and now, a dead wife.

"Where's your wife, son?" Gat asked, climbing down off his horse and walking over to the lad.

"Her body's in the tent by the handcart in those trees. She birthed a day ago and just kept gettin' sicker and sicker." He shook his head. "I couldn't help 'er. They all said not to come an' we didn't pay no heed." He began to sob.

Gat put a comforting hand on his shoulder. India thought she had never seen such a tragedy. The baby sucked ravenously on her finger tip, and finding no satisfaction, howled anew.

"Have you given anything to the baby?" Gat asked.

"Nothin'. Ain't but flour and meal, an' a baby kin't eat thet."

"India," said Gat. "Maybe you'd better find a piece of cloth, twist it into a teat and soak it in water. I'll go bury his wife."

Gat left them and went inside the tent. When he came out he was carrying the woman's body wrapped in a blanket. He called to the young man and together they found a gravesite. While they took turns digging he told them his wife's name

227

had been Hope, and his own was Jobias Smythe. They'd been on the way to the gold fields at South Pass.

The water calmed the baby until evening, but then as Gat cooked up burned-bacon dumplings on the fire, the infant awoke and started howling once more. "You can't blame the little thing," India sighed, giving it more water. "What are we going to do?" she whispered aside to Gat.

Gat shook his head, and then an idea seemed to take hold. He reached for the slab of bacon, cut off a thick strip of fat and put it in the baby's mouth. To India's amazement the baby began to gum the rind contentedly.

"It isn't enough nourishment, but if we keep giving her the water, she can survive till we reach the next settlement."

"How far is it?" India asked.

"Too far," Gat said.

Into the dark hours of the night India rocked and fretted over the bawling baby. Gat woke to spell her but Jobias slept deeply, impervious to the situation.

A long time after midnight Gat nudged India awake. In his arms the baby was crying full force. "She won't take the water or bacon fat."

"What can we do?" India sat up.

Gat cleared his throat. "Give her your breast."

India was slightly dazed with sleep. "What?"

"Let her suckle on your breast. It should calm her."

"But I've never . . . I don't have any milk."

Starlight twinkled in his eyes and an assuring smile touched his lips. "Believe me, it don't matter."

From her talk with Eugenie she was aware of the underlying message of his remark, but night sometimes makes people more forgiving, and as India watched the baby's struggle she was willing to do as Gat asked. Mumbling to herself she unfastened the leather lacings of her doeskin dress. Gat draped a blanket over the edge of her shoulder for privacy.

"I'm not sure I know what to do," she said. An embarrassed shiver crept through her as she bared her breast to the night air. The baby rooted instinctively but had no luck capturing the flat swell of India's nipple. "She can't catch hold. I think one has to be a genuine mother to execute these things."

Why she agreed to it at all was beyond her understanding and became just another of the extraordinary predicaments she'd experienced in Gat Ransom's company. The baby nuzzled the fleshy mound and whimpered, then caught the upthrust peak in its mouth. Absurdly self-conscious, she avoided Ransom's eyes and wondered how long the baby would be content to suckle an empty breast.

In the awkwardness of it all, the blanket slipped off her shoulder and exposed her breast to Gat's view. For a moment Gat did not move, did not breathe. Then with a dutiful politeness he adjusted the blanket back on her shoulder, took a seat by the fire, and in some part attempted to remove himself from the intensity of feelings he'd just experienced. He'd never wanted a woman as much as he wanted India, but tonight he wanted her in a different way. He studied her circumspectly, and admiration for her self-sacrifice swelled through him. Her head was bent over the baby and in the silhouette of firelight he no longer saw her as a desirable calamity but the wellspring of hope itself. In her he saw the chance to remake his past; with her he might have one more chance. Yet he knew to love her would be full of risk, but also full of real promise.

"I think it's working," she whispered across the fire.

He watched the baby settle into sleep and smiled inwardly. The mantle of motherhood suited her, though he knew her nipple would be as sore as hell in the morning.

With sunrise, she poked Gat awake with her foot, handed him the baby and walked off down by the river. Careful not to lose her balance and fall headfirst into the river, she knelt down, unlaced her dress, dipped a hankie in the water and pressed it's coolness to her tender nipple. She was tempted to ask Gat if he still had Eugenie's ointment for inflamed udders, for she hadn't expected mothering would be so uncomfortable.

Off in the distance, a voice called to her from upriver. The stranger waved and moved along the shore toward her, approaching with a wide smile.

"I saw you preparin' to wash up and I thought I'd better warn you that a pair of gents was camped up the way." He preened his fuzzy salt-and-pepper beard. India's face warmed and she clutched together her unfastened dress and rose to her feet.

"That was polite of you to warn me, sir." She looked past him but couldn't see his partner. "I'm camped here with my . . . my husband and a young man. You and your partner wouldn't have a tin of milk with you, or something to nourish an infant? The young man's wife has died in childbirth, and we've nothing to feed the baby."

The man pulled his beard and shook his head. "We've got a little whiskey," he chuckled, but India remained straight-faced, thinking his jest in poor taste. "No, ma'am, I don't reckon we have much fer babes. My partner and I are drivin' a mule team to South Pass City with some minin' equipment. Ain't no baby feed in the wagon. Tell you what, ma partner is hitchin' up the wagon now, and we'll pass by your camp in a while. Maybe we can think of somethin'." He walked off and India returned to camp.

Jobias seemed the most interested in the news of the mule drivers camped up the river. After he drank a quick cup of coffee, he asked India the direction and went on his own up to find them.

Soon India and Gat saw the wagon, led by ten mules, wheeling down the trail. Jobias was riding in the back. The man India had met earlier and his partner were in front. They introduced themselves to Gat as the Badger Brothers, freight line owners, and took a moment to exchange trail talk, since both had been where the other was going. The brothers spoke of seeing a few Sioux braves.

On hearing this, India set about clearing up the camp. She was anxious to be on their way, not only because the proximity of Indians made her nervous but the sooner they left, the better for the baby's sake.

The great surprise came when the Badgers climbed back

up on the wagon and Jobias expressed his intentions of going with the brothers.

"But you can't take that baby with you. You'll have to come with us. We're closer to a settlement this way," protested India.

Jobias looked over at Gat and then down to his boots, "I kin't raise a baby, a girl'un." You take 'er, ma'am."

"But Jobias, I . . . I . . ." she wanted to say she wasn't even married, but then she'd told the Badger brother she was, and he was looking on with interest. "What about your family? Would they take the child? You could come back with us and arrange a home for the child with your relatives, then return to the gold fields."

"No, ma'am. Ain't no one goin' take it, I know." He had gathered his pitiful belongings and bundled them up moments before. "The Badgers is waitin' on me. You take the baby to one o' them foundlin' homes. I kin't take 'er," he turned to heft himself up on the wagon.

"Gat?" India pleaded in his direction.

He stepped forward and rubbed his neck with dilemma. "I think we better take her. The boy's right. The child has a better chance with us." He walked over to India's saddlebag and pulled out her petition ledger, uncorked the ink bottle and scribbled something on the last page with the pen. "Here, Jobias, you sign this. It gives me guardianship over the baby."

Jobias hesitated, and India thought he might have a flickering of parental responsibility. "I kin't write," he finally admitted.

"Just your name, Jobias," prompted Gat. "Here, I'll guide your hand if you'd like."

Agreeing, Jobias climbed down off the wagon. He stepped next to Gat and in a long moment, the pair managed to scrawl out his signature. Then he climbed back up on the wagon. The Badger brother pulled off the brake, and with a simple jerk of the line, backed by a powerful voice and the crack of his whip, the wagon creaked forward.

"Oh, ma'am, one thing," called Jobias. "Call 'er Hope, after her ma."

The wagon rolled down the trail, and India looked over at Gat with an uncertain shake of the head. "Now what?"

He shrugged back, "Who knows. We'll have to *hope* she's a fighter."

Chapter 18

*W*hen five Sioux Indians rode across the river, India reined her horse to a standstill and swallowed hard. She hadn't forgotten meeting Tommy Cahoon or seeing the grave of the dismembered Bill Rose. Not taking her eyes off the approaching Indians, she muttered aside to Gat, "I hope you still have some horehound candy."

"I think they want more than candy." Gat raised his hand to the graves, *"A'hou!"* he saluted. Each brave saluted back.

Hands tight on her reins, India studied their movements and dress. One wore a buffalo skin over a linen shirt; the other one a woolen blanket and a jacket of deerskin ornamented with fringes much like India's own doeskin dress. The object that caught her eyes was the decoration of scalps hanging from the deerskin jacket, the mere sight causing her stomach to feel like a butterfly migration. The braves circled them. All the while, Gat was talking to them in a combination of sign language and Indian tongue, incomprehensible to her.

"They are going to take us to their encampment farther up the river to meet Chief Red Cloud," Gat said at last.

"Red Cloud!" echoed India. "Why, isn't he the one—"

"He's the one," interrupted Gat. then more softly he

cautioned. "Watch what you say. Some of them speak tolerable English."

India worriedly glanced at the baby, still asleep in its saddlebag cradle, and guided her horse close to Gat's. Two braves rode ahead, three followed behind.

After riding an anxious two hours, India saw the tepees of the Indian encampment across the river. Their entrance into the encampment caused a great commotion, as everyone stopped their tasks and crowded around the riders. A dog fight erupted between Coyote and two uncongenial dogs, but it was curtailed when Gat whistled Coyote back to his side.

There was no mistaking Chief Red Cloud, hooded-eyed and hawk-nosed, sitting beside a smoldering buffalo-chip campfire at the central tepee. He was a man who needed no braid or brass to signify rank, and around him his braves were an imposing sight, strong and stately with the appearance of intelligence and independence.

India had typeset an article in the *Argus* regarding Red Cloud's reputation for arrogance and stubbornness in negotiating with the government. In past years he'd led hostile raids against the U.S. military and Indian tribes alike.

She looked over at Gat, and though she saw no more of his face than his indecipherable profile, she could sense the tension moving through him by the line of his broad shoulders. Following his lead she climbed down off her horse and they were led to the fire.

The brave with the scalps on his jacket acted as interpreter, though India suspected Red Cloud probably understood English as well as she did. Gat pointed to the baby in the saddlebag and seemed to be explaining their problem. Red Cloud motioned Gat to sit down within the circle. Gat turned his head to India and she glimpsed the assuring glint in his eye. He pointed to a spot adjacent him in the council circle and India obediently sat there. Then he turned his full attention to Red Cloud.

"Red Cloud wishes to speak," said the interpreter. A murmur rippled through the group and more and more Indians collected around the council circle.

Red Cloud began speaking, and after a moment the interpreter echoed the long flow of words. "Red Cloud is not much impressed with the white man's world."

The wind changed direction and India's eyes began to tear from the campfire smoke blowing in her face. The baby, still tucked in the saddlebag, woke up and started crying. A woman was summoned, and much to India's satisfaction, she sat down by her and proceeded to bare her breast to baby Hope. She nursed like a greedy kitten and soon fell asleep with the nipple still in her mouth.

The sun moved lower in the sky and Red Cloud spoke on. A gourd of water was passed through the circle, and India drank thirstily, thinking a long-winded clergyman had nothing over Red Cloud.

"I have met many councils with the white chiefs at the forts. It would have been better for me to spend my time hunting buffalo than to visit the white chiefs," continued the interpreter. "The white chiefs seduced my ears with pleasant words and soft promises which they will never keep. They made sport of me by saying I should dig the earth and raise animals. I, who am always with the buffalo and love them. From my birth I am strong and I lift my tepee when necessary and go across the prairie according to my pleasure. I know the Great Spirit has made us all, but he made the red man in the center with the others all about. You have come to Red Cloud and I treat you fairly, but does the white man only take from Red Cloud? Have you a gift for him?"

A hush fell over the circle and India looked over to Gat, knowing he didn't have enough horehound candy for everyone. What could they possibly have that Red Cloud would think worthy of his person?

"Whatever is mine, is yours, Red Cloud," returned Gat diplomatically. India squirmed, seeing a vision of herself being traded to Red Cloud.

At that point some zealous Indian took it upon himself to unstrap the saddlebags from the horses and lay them at Red Cloud's feet. Everyone crowded closer like curious children at a birthday party when the gifts were unwrapped. The interpreter tipped open the saddlebags, spilling out the contents to Red Cloud's view.

Amazingly, Red Cloud pointed to the brown sack of horehound candy, which was immediately opened. He took a piece, popped it into his mouth and passed the paper sack on. Other items were examined. Of major interest was India's black-beaded, silk-tasseled handbag. This was set aside. Luckily, it didn't contain all her money, most of it was secure in the secret pocket of her silk pantalettes. Nevertheless, if she was required to give up the money she decided it would be a cheap price for their lives. The dime novels and petition ledger came to view. Red Cloud picked up the dime novels and studied the covers a moment and then thumbed through the petition ledger with an inquisitive eye.

"Red Cloud wishes to know whose signatures are in this book," announced the interpreter.

Gat looked over at India with a twinkle in his eyes. "This woman carries a paper asking the white chiefs to give the white women a voice in the council meetings. Many who want this have put their signature to the paper."

The interpreter repeated Gat's words, and for the first time everyone, including Red Cloud, began to laugh. A short discussion transpired between Red Cloud and his interpreter. The interpreter spoke once again. "Red Cloud wishes to put his mark to this paper."

Aghast, India looked at Gat. He grinned back at her and reached for the pen and ink and gave it to Red Cloud.

"Red Cloud thinks it a great joke if the white women have a voice in the white man's council," explained the interpreter.

"Things might go better for the Indians if they did," muttered India, apparently loud enough for the interpreter to hear. He repeated her words to Red Cloud.

Red Cloud's dark eyes narrowed and for a long moment he turned and studied India as if he hadn't seen her before. He spoke again.

"A spring fawn does not shift the breath of a winter wind,

nor can a gentle voice waylay the white man's greed," said the interpreter. "The woman's desire is not without honor. Red Cloud would name this woman 'Windsinger,' one who sings against the breath of the wind."

India marveled at his perception and understood why he had such a notable reputation in the West. He dipped the pen into the ink and signed the ledger, then he smiled shrewdly at her and spoke.

"Now Red Cloud asks if you have something more for him, something equal to the value of his signature on your paper."

India cast an anxious look toward Gat. What more was there? They had nothing equal to the value of his signature. Their horses and supplies were all they had. Then Gat rose to his feet. He was tall and his physical prowess would be an equal match to these virile sons of the plains if challenged.

Slowly, he unstrapped his holster and laid it at Red Cloud's feet. Again comment moved through the encampment.

"I accept your gun as equal payment," said Red Cloud, omitting to use his interpreter. His free speech showed his pleasure in receiving the weapon. "It is worthy of a warrior. Stay in my encampment until the child gains strength." With that, he picked up the gun and two boxes of cartridges from the saddlebags. He stood, then stooped back down, for something else in the pile had caught his eye: India's Votes For Women sash. Red Cloud's craggy face broke into a grin and he took a moment to drape it over the wide shoulders of a nearby brave.

Everyone laughed and the brave strutted comically in front of the tepee. He then fell into the entourage of women and children following Red Cloud out of the encampment. Moments later, India heard gunshots in the distance as Red Cloud tried out his new gun.

India and Gat were left alone in front of the central tepee with the Indian woman who had been summoned to nurse the baby. Gat spoke to her, and after some hesitation she answered, telling him her name was Woman-Who-Killed-A-Bear and that they could stay in her tepee.

India gathered up the items the Indians had discarded and put them back in the saddlebags. Leading the horses, she and Gat followed Woman-Who-Killed-A-Bear to her tepee. India smiled to herself, thinking not even Sissy would believe this adventure. But in the back of her mind nagged the unfortunate worry that she may not ever have the chance to write and tell her.

After two days in the encampment, India decided that Gat should have given Woman-Who-Killed-A-Bear the gun instead of Red Cloud, for it was she who nursed the child faithfully and prepared food for them, not to mention all of the other tasks involved in tending to her own family.

The Indian women seemed to be the most degraded slaves on earth. It appeared to India that once married, the young girls soon lost their maidenly beauty through hardship and drudgery. The women did all the work in the encampment while the noble braves strutted about proudly, like inflated turkey cocks. Wherever the men chose to go, the women walked behind carrying the burdens.

One afternoon India watched Woman-Who-Killed-A-Bear dress a fresh buffalo hide. The procedure was most involved and laborious, and India would much sooner have the task of killing the buffalo than preserving the meat and dressing the hide. If any group of human beings would benefit from equal rights it would be these women, and India had in mind to say as much. But she was hardly in the position to speak out and rally them against their braves.

Still, an opportunity came on a windless afternoon while she sat watching a group of women sewing beadwork. Their sewing was the most beautiful she'd ever seen. Even old Hanner White would have been impressed. One woman, her thick braided hair streaked with gray, worked on a tiny pair of doeskin moccasins. They looked as if they were made of satin, so finely ornamented with colored beads.

"You like them?" asked the Indian woman, aware of

India's close perusal. India was taken aback by her clear English.

"You speak English?" India asked with surprise in her voice.

"Ya, I speak. Long time ago I trapper's woman. I learn."

India remembered Mountain Tom and quickly looked at her ear, but it wasn't cut.

"The moccasins are very pretty," said India.

"I give them to you for the *chin cha*. White man's shoes cripple tiny feet."

India smiled. "Thank you." The other women in the group all nodded at her and returned her smile, and India felt self-conscious especially when they put their heads together and whispered. She knew they spoke about her and she tried not to notice, keeping her eyes on the older woman as she finished the intricate beadwork design on the moccasins. "You are kind to make these for the baby," she said to her.

Not looking up from her sewing, the woman replied, "We feel sadness for you because you have no milk for your *chin cha*."

"Oh, the baby is not mine," corrected India. "Its mother died on the trail and its father could not keep it."

The woman relayed this news to the others. They spoke among themselves, digesting this information.

The older woman spoke to India again. "We think you and your brave have much luck to find *chin cha*."

"I have no brave," said India attempting to clear up the matter. "I am no man's woman."

At this the woman looked up from her sewing and spoke to the other women. Her words provoked such discussion among them. Summing up the general opinion of the women, she spoke to India. "We still feel sadness for you."

Their sympathy was lost on India and she decided to take the opportunity to spread her message, whether they understood it or not. "Do not feel sadness for me. It is I who feel sadness for you. You must carry the burdens of your braves and follow them as a slave follows a master. You do all the work while your men hunt and smoke the pipe. This is unfair.''

The woman gave India a wide smile and quickly proceeded to tell the others what she had said. They stopped their sewing and seemed to hang on every word of the translation. Suddenly, they all started to giggle and chatter to each other with great amusement.

Indian looked at them a little bewildered. "Why are they laughing?"

"They laugh because you have given them a great compliment," said the Indian woman.

"But I have called them slaves," India replied.

"We do not think of ourselves as slaves. It is only the white eyes who see this. The work of man and woman is different but the same. It is just as hard to hunt the buffalo as to skin it. Each task is done faithfully and well. You must see that the brave walks in front of his woman to protect her from unseen attack. Only a brave who does not value his woman would follow behind. This is the way of things with my people. The way of the white man is different. I slave to the white trapper. I do not like his ways. So I run away, back to my own people."

With inward wonder India regarded the woman beside her. She was a woman like herself, with the same spirit and feelings, yet so unlike her in life's purpose. India thought of her domestic life in Boston. It had been hedged in by conventional opinion, social duties—with every prospect of independence, liberty and activity closed more rigidly by invisible barriers than tepees by their buffalo hides. These daughters of the prairie sat at their ease without constraint or effort, without stays or the anxiety to charm. Who was she to shift the breath of the prairie wind? Her voice had no listeners here.

At sunset on the third night, a party of braves rode into the encampment and met in council in front of Red Cloud's tepee. When Gat returned to the tepee, he told India that the visitors were Sioux from the Black Hills. Apparently they'd had a run-in with some prospectors who had trespassed on Indian land looking for gold.

"Once the word spread that there's gold in the hills, nobody will rest until a full-scale war is waged and the land taken from the Indians," he said.

"But the government has a treaty with them," India protested.

"The treaty was signed before anyone knew there was gold there. The speculators will move in and stir up the Sioux, forcing them to fight for the land. They love the Black Hills country like you love your New England," Gat said. "Nobody will take it away from them without a fight. Greed changes people. It makes them forget about agreements signed and promises spoken. If white men want the Indians' land, they'll take it from them by hook or by crook, most likely by crook."

"There is little justice in the world." India shook her head sadly. She looked over at Woman-Who-Killed-A-Bear's two children wrestling on a buffalo skin. "To the Indians men say make peace and be content with what we give you, and to women they say hold your tongue and keep your place."

Gat looked over at India with genuine warmth in his black eyes, and in a soothing voice he said, "There's more justice in the world than you think. But it takes a windsinger like yourself to bring it about."

Something deep within India melted towards Gat. Here was a man who had stood beside her, supported and protected her right to speak up, and now he was giving her gentle words of encouragement. How could she not love a man like this? Tears misted in her sapphire eyes and hurriedly she wiped them away. "I don't know why . . ." The tears kept coming like unwelcome torrents of spring rain and India lowered her head into her hands, her breast heaving with a long-overdue release.

Gat swallowed hard, half-embarrassed at his own sudden rush of feeling at seeing her tears. Like most men he didn't know how to handle a crying woman, but instinctively he leaned over and put a comforting arm across her shoulders.

"No need to worry, everything will be all right. You'll see." But what he didn't see was the reason for her tears, and as he held her in his arms, the familiar scent of wild mint touched his nose and he brushed his lips to the silk of her hair. He'd never understand her, he thought, but then there was no understanding himself when he was around her.

Just then, Woman-Who-Killed-A-Bear came into the tepee. Her usually impassive countenance was marked with strain. She hurried to the sleeping baby, petted it awake and began nursing it while speaking to Gat. India had gained some semblance of control, and she looked anxiously from one to the other, impatient to know what was distressing the woman.

At last Gat turned to her, his own face marked with concern. "She says we better leave quickly. It is no longer safe for us to stay. She's sent her daughter down to the river with our horses, and we must meet the daughter there."

"Shouldn't we wait until dark?" asked India.

"It might be too late." Gat pushed her toward the tepee opening.

Woman-Who-Killed-A-Bear gave baby Hope a lingering gaze and then almost reluctantly handed her to India, motioning to the tepee's flap opening. India wanted to thank her but didn't know how. "Tell her thank you," she directed Gat as she stepped out the flap.

Chanting and drum beating vibrated through the air. Gat said a thank-you over his shoulder to Woman-Who-Killed-A-Bear and followed India. Trying to appear inconspicuous, they walked to the outskirts of the encampment. It was difficult because Coyote followed them, and wherever Coyote traveled so did half the village dogs. Scuttling down into a gully for refuge, Gat pelted them with stones until they shied off.

Gat and India lay, belly down, listening to the drum beating from the encampment. India suddenly jabbed Gat in the ribs. "I forgot the petition ledger. You've got to go back and get it from the tepee."

"I'm not going back," said Gat flatly.

India looked to Coyote, then back to Gat. "But the ledger. I won't leave it!"

"Listen, I'm no dime-novel hero. Those Indians are fired up and I'm not taking any chances."

"Well, you don't have to take any. I'll go back for it. Here, take the baby." She had thrust it into his arms and disappeared over the rise before he could grab her.

Under his breath he swore foully, regretting the day he got roped into escorting that high-nosed female farther than a lunatic asylum. Five minutes ago she was whey-faced from weeping tears, now she was ready to tomahawk a whole Indian village.

He crouched back down. The minutes inched by. At least the baby was content to keep quiet, though her eyes were open. He touched her tiny fingers and marveled at her innocence, all the while cradling her protectively in his arms.

He reached into his pocket, one-handedly pulled open his tobacco pouch and bit off a piece. As he worked it in his mouth, he thought of how he would be forced to rescue India when she didn't come back. He saw himself spread-eagle and skinned on a torture mound, and all for that damned petition.

The singing and drum beating stopped. Gat's jaw halted in mid-chew.

Miraculously, over the slope rolled India, breathing hard.

"Anyone see you?"

"If they weren't after us before, I think they are now," she gasped.

"Sh—" Gat started to swear.

"Don't say it!" India cut him off.

But he said it anyway and yanked her by the arm down into the gully. The river was about a half mile away. He was counting on the dips in the landscape to conceal them. Over his shoulder in the twilight, he saw the flare of torches on the outskirts of the encampment and someone riding in their direction. He pulled India into a wash, but a snake's rattle warned him it was already occupied.

"What's that?" whispered India.

"Don't move. something else was here first." His eyes traveled slowly, searching. He spotted the rattler curled up on a stone within striking distance of India's leg. The dry rattle of warning cut through the night air once more. Seeing the threat, India bit her lip in horror.

"Don't move," Gat hissed, then he took aim and spit. A squirt of tobacco juice arced through the air, landing smack on target. The snake turned tail and slithered off.

"Now, ma'am, what did you think of that?" whispered Gat.

Though her heart was in her throat, India managed her usual scolding retort. "I still think it's a disgusting habit!"

"Well, if we get out of this with our skins, I promise I'll quit chewin'." With that pledge he gave her a shove and together they leaped out of the wash and ran across the last open stretch to the river.

The horses were waiting, but Woman-Who-Killed-A-Bear's daughter was gone. Gat tucked the baby in the saddlebag and India climbed up on Bluestocking. He swung up on his own horse, hoping the swiftly falling darkness would cloak their escape across the river back into Wyoming Territory.

Chapter 19

Gat shook the dust off his hat, his eyes searching the horizon in a slow sweep as India reined up her horse beside him in the stirrup-high grass. She squinted against the noonday sun and absently ran a finger under the collar of her dress. Thirsty and saddle sore, she was positive that if she were to lift her skirts in front of a looking glass her legs would now have a definite bow to them.

She leaned forward and gave Bluestocking an affectionate pat on the neck. Gat had made a good choice, though in the beginning India had had qualms about climbing up on her back. The mare had proven to be a princess of ponies, gentle as a kitten despite her bronco blood.

India turned her gaze to the baby still sleeping in the saddlebag pocket. The days in the Indian village had given the tiny thing a good start, but she still worried. The baby needed milk, a commodity they did not have.

Waving away the insects from her face, India looked over at Gat. Though the July afternoon was warm, Gat's shirt sleeves were still buttoned at the cuffs and a dark ring of perspiration shadowed his underarms. Beneath his sweat-stained hat, his face was tanned and weathered from sun and wind. His brows hunched over his eyes in the constant narrowness that she had grown to recognize in western wranglers. Now, traveling along, corsetless, wearing the lightweight calico dress, her bare legs browning in the sun, she was conscious not only of her own body, but also of Ransom's. Removing herself from the thought of temptation, she nudged Bluestocking forward.

"Hold up a minute," Gat said, then took the rope from his saddle and slowly shook out a broad loop. He spurred his horse forward and India watched curiously as rider and horse seemed to target some unseen prey down along the river. Then she saw the flag tail movement of a herd of goats grazing on the bank.

Standing with heads alert, the goats eyed Gat's approach, then suddenly their gamey hindquarters leaped gazelle fashion up the embankment. Gat closed in, singling out a pendulous-uddered doe and her kid. For a moment she eluded him, then the horse closed in with an explosion of pounding hooves and flashing legs, and cornered the goat and her kid against the river. The horse feinted left, then rolled back on his hocks and broke to the right. Swiftly, smoothly, Gat cast the rope, his wrist turning downward at the moment of release with practiced skill. The loop fell softly on target. With a jerk Gat threw his weight on the rope, and it made a zipping sound as the loop tightened around the goat's neck. By now the kid and mother were calling anxiously to one another as Gat towed the doe towards India.

"Here's the little bummer's grub." Gat was grinning. "I'll tie up her back legs and you can milk her while I hold her. I don't expect her to be too willing." He cinched the rope around his saddle horn, slipped down off his horse and quickly lashed her dancing hind legs together. "Get the pot out of my saddle bag. By the show of her udder we'll get a fair milking if we can hold her still."

India found the pot but approached the tied-up goat hesitantly. Gat strained, bracing the struggling goat against his body. "Well, what are you waiting for?" he finally asked, while she stood immobile beside the goat.

"I don't know how to go about it. I've never milked before."

"Damn!" Gat swore under his breath, a habit becoming

246

more common with him as his days with India progressed. He yanked the rope to signal his horse to tighten up the slack.

"You couldn't ride, you couldn't cook, now you can't milk. Tell me, India Simms, what are you good for?"

She drew herself up to match his rough temper and said smartly. "Voting, Mr. Ransom, for voting!"

He gave a hopeless snort. "Get down off your soapbox for one minute, watch me and I'll show you how to milk this contrary critter."

After a bit of maneuvering, he tied a back leg to a bush and depended on the horse to keep the rope line taut so the goat would be unbalanced enough to keep it from bucking. In no time he had the pot foaming with milk. "Come on then, get a little nearer and I'll give you a lesson. You know it's easier for a woman to milk a goat because of the size of her hands. Come a little nearer," he encouraged, a twinkle in his eye. India knelt on one knee and peered down with sincere interest. In a sly movement Gat turned the angle of the teat and squirted her full in the face.

"Why you . . . you devil!" She squealed and shoved him back on his heels. When he tumbled over, he pulled her with him. They rolled over and over like a pair of scrapping children until his thighs straddled her legs.

"Honestly, I didn't think you'd fall for it. I couldn't help . . . ," Gat apologized with a laugh.

Gasping between fits of laughter she pushed her hands against his chest. "And I suppose you can't help that you have me wrapped up in your arms like a papoose in a cradle board, either."

Her playful push triggered a sudden awareness of the intimacy of their position, and pent-up emotions within Gat broke loose. He looked into her beautiful blue eyes, soft with humor beneath nutmeg lashes. Seconds passed. Her soft breathing evened and there was a long silence while he struggled between what he wanted to do and what he was duty-bound to do.

He remembered the kiss on the trail, the outright lust of

it, and her own desire. He knew how easy it would be at this moment to put his lips to her cheek and feel her tremble from his kisses; to unloose the masses of tight-braided auburn hair and unravel it under his caressing hand. With his lips just inches from hers, he could bring his head down to taste the words leaving her tongue and lips, and with the mere thought a rigidity touched his groin. But again self-preservation held him back, for he knew if he made the first move she might blame him later for taking advantage of her. No, she'd have to come to him on her own terms, in her own time, and with her philosophies he knew it just might be never.

Matching his gaze with genuine warmth. India could feel the tension in his muscles and she knew innately he wanted and desired her. Why did he hold back? *Kiss me!* Every part of her called out to him for he had touched off in her soul a powder keg of longings, which she feared might never be quenched. *Kiss me . . .*

All the while his dark eyes searched hers, and then between one eyeblink and the next his intensity cooled. Reaching out a finger he brushed a cottonwood puff from her hair and pulled back. "Pardon, ma'am." Reserve took over.

Wildly embarrassed at the depth of her own wanton nature and his bland rejection, India retreated behind her schoolmistress facade. "Give me a hand up," she said, tightness touched her throat. Gloved in leathery shield, he gave her his hand, and then he turned away to tend to the goats.

Far to the west the sky was on fire as daylight slowly faded away. Dusky silhouettes of ash and cottonwood marked the twisting flow of the river, and in their heights nightbirds sang out high, thin, single notes while India rocked a fussing baby Hope in her arms and listened to Gat echo the nightbirds' refrains on his penny whistle.

"She asleep yet?" whispered Gat, lowering his whistle.

"No."

"Let me take her." Gat bent down and took the baby into

his arms. "I think she's made a pig of herself on the goat's milk. She's got colic from overeating."

"How do you know so much about babies?" India handed him the baby and leaned back against her saddle.

"A cowboy's job is nursemaidin'. Most little critters are the same." He was gently patting Hope on the back and walking around the campfire. "You've got to keep moving. That's why she sleeps so good in the day when we're riding."

"Since I never intend to marry, I haven't paid much attention to such things." India shook her head and gave a laugh of afterthought. "It's odd how life plays tricks on us. Think of all the women yearning for motherhood and here I am with a baby. The one women who has no wish for babe or beau."

"You ever had a beau?"

India laughed outright. "Never! Though I did have the opportunity. When I was sixteen my parents forced me to attend the coming out ball. I was a willing wallflower the entire evening until Mr. Burnham Cooper asked me to dance. Then with unparalleled conceit he kindly informed me that I must not fall in love with him because he deigned to take pity and waltz with me. I remained polite but managed to stumble and step upon his polished patinas as much as possible." India smiled reflectively. "And you? Is there one in the long line of women you've known you would call sweetheart?"

Gat walked towards her and placed the now sleeping baby in the horse blanket cradle near India. "There hasn't been all that many women in my life." He sat down by her, stretched out his long legs comfortably and stared into the campfire. Bitterness touched his voice. "I've never had one I'd call sweetheart, but I did have one who broke my heart. I sometimes wonder what happened to Emmeline Carlisle and her banker husband," he began, as if speaking to himself.

"It did beat all, the way she honey-tongued me into enlisting during the war in place of her rich beau. I didn't know he was her beau at the time and the two hundred dollars they paid me to enlist in the cavalry made it all a little easier to swallow. But the truth was I had just enough banty rooster in my veins to show off for my gal. Emmeline had foresight, I give her that much. But after all was said and done, she and her beau probably didn't escape the war anyway. None of us did.''

The disillusionment in his words touched India's heart, and with a soft surge of empathy she wanted to reach out, to say something that would heal his wounds. Regarding him with eyes the color of a high mountain lake, she glimpsed his vulnerability and realized his strength was softness, his toughness, fragility. Her hands wanted to stroke his hair, his face, his mouth.

A vagabond tear slipped down her cheek. Gat was looking at her and he reached over with a calloused thumb and tenderly brushed it aside.

She stopped breathing.

Even with the scar and an unshaven jaw he was dazzlingly handsome, with the magnetic vitality and sun-bronzed complexion of a man bound to the earth.

Impulsively, she leaned across to him and put her hand to his own; his fingers closed warm and rough around hers. She drew his fingers to her lips. Then he leaned toward her, shadowing her face. His lips parted a little; she felt his breath and she sat so still she thought she must have turned to porcelain, and all the sound on earth had ceased. *Kiss me.* Her pent up longings became explosive. *Kiss me.* Her blue eyes blazed brightly while his smoldered.

At last Gat knew his thoughts were her thoughts, her desire his. Brief moments stretched into a one-way ride and her simple kiss on his hand blazed the trail to mutual ardent clasping.

The stubble of his beard prickled against her cheeks and he pulled back with a mumbled apology. India, trembling, swallowed back her own confusion, turned away and then turned back. Her arms opened to him and she drew him to her because she dared not let him go.

250

His fingers raised her chin and their lips met. The kiss became smooth, moist and magnificent as they settled into the genuine pleasuring of it and then their lips parted, but only long enough for breath. Now, at last Gat was secure in the knowledge India would need no gentling, for the trembling of her body and her rising desire were unmistakable. By nature Gat was sensual and deeply passionate, but his touch was as refined and as delicate as any woman could ask. He would coax the uncertainty from India even though her red lips might become swollen from his kisses, but he could not and would not rein back completely the consuming passion he'd stifled for months.

India willingly surrendered her mouth to Gat's probing tongue, yet still feeling that only loose, wild women allowed men to kiss them so intimately, so deliciously. At first she felt uneasy, embarrassed, unsure, but never sinful. Hadn't Eugenie assured her God had designed woman to delight, excite, and satisfy the man and in turn the woman was designed to be delighted, excited and satisfied as well? At this moment the coursing fire in her veins left no doubt that she was being delighted and excited as his thrusting tongue explored the soft folds of her mouth and his strong hands caressed the curves of her waist and hips.

After a time, they broke for breath and she lay her head on his chest. Against her ear his heartbeat became as dependable as the thrumming of a summer cricket. "I never knew it could be like this." She snuggled closer.

"You didn't, huh? And I took you for a know-it-all," he returned lazily.

She gave him a playful punch in the ribs. "I never claimed to be a know-it-all. It's you who seemed so all-fired sure of yourself."

"Me? Now I could have sworn you kissed me first."

India bolted upright. "Why . . . you don't think I'm as forward as all that, do you? How could you accuse me of taking advantage of you? I may want the vote, but I still have some notion of propriety."

Gat seemed to enjoy teasing her. "Well, ma'am, I haven't

any notion of propriety whatsoever." And with that he drew her near and matched his lips to hers, his tongue finding hers, and she forgot propriety as well.

Sometime later, his lips left hers and brushed her eyes and forehead. The moonlight, where it touched her hair, turned it a burnished copper, and he began to finger-comb the thick, silky curls. "India, will you give me a lock of your hair?"

"What ever for?"

"For a keepsake, I might get lonesome sometime and want to bring back the memories." He had taken out his pocket knife. His hand unloosened the silver clip that fastened her hair. Auburn tresses cascaded down, and lifting them he cut a swatch above the nape of her neck.

"I wish I could have washed my hair first. It smells like trail dust, not violets."

"Don't worry. My perfume bath at Heddy's cured me of flowery smells." He pulled the drawstring on his empty tobacco pouch, slipped the lock of hair inside and placed it in his shirt pocket. The pocket over his heart.

India gave him an endearing gaze and sought his lips time after time until she wished they might stay together forever, holding this moment of love in suspension. The old prairie moon rose high in the sky, bathing them with pearlescent light. In the distance the coyotes called a lonesome refrain, and all the while India felt the urge to sing back the elation of love that swirled within her soul.

India slept against Gat's shoulder, all spirit and spunk dissolved. He'd like to think she'd always he so pliable, but with her changeable moods and wild enthusiasms he would never assume it. He'd take his time—if she didn't push him beyond endurance with her airy notions. She flew free with the dare and swoop of a cliff swallow. Moving his head a little, he kissed the delicate curve on the outer corner of her eye.

She moved in her sleep, her arm tightening around his rib cage as if she found reassurance in the touch. He was feeling a desperate tenderness toward her, for he wanted and needed her. And he'd show it in unmistakable ways if she'd just let him. A stir of wind brought him the peppery smell of sagebrush and shifted the smoke plume of the fire. Gat grinned across the fire at Coyote who seemed content to sit on the outer edge of the campfire light and watch the proceedings.

Coyote yawned a head-shaking whine.

"Don't say nothin', partner. You ain't no smarter," Gat muttered into the prairie night.

Chapter 20

*D*istances weré long and populations small in the territory. During the next weeks they traveled cow trails or, more often, no trails at all to spread the word of suffrage. Suffrage, however, was not foremost in India's mind as she spoke in saloons, fort canteens, log cabins and beside covered wagons. Her affection for Gat and baby Hope consumed her thoughts. They seemed like a family each night as they relaxed by the campfire where Gat entertained her by echoing night birds on his penny whistle, and sometimes even reciting poetry, which in turn provoked thoughtful and enlightening conversation. They debated philosophies and sometimes sang favorite wartime melodies which often set Gat to sharing his experiences in the cavalry. Beneath his frontier-calloused exterior she discovered a true man of culture and a child of nature.

His sense of fairness and soft-heartedness became most apparent to India the day they rode into the growing settlement of travelers, traders, and soldiers around Fort Laramie. Outside a drinking establishment a group of layabout brutes were ill-treating a mangy, yellow dog. They vied with each other in concocting abuses for the poor beast. Someone had tied an old pot to its tail and had begun to pelt the pot with stones. Gat climbed down off his horse, and since the poor dog was too terrified to run, Gat was able to untie the pot.

"Come on, boys," Gat chided, "give the poor critter a square deal."

When she and Gat rode up to the Overland House, along with Coyote, the yellow dog followed faithfully.

"I think you've made a new friend," observed India.

"Yep, I seem to attract all the mavericks," he laughed, looking back at their entourage of goats and dogs.

They took rooms at the Overland House, stabling the animals out back. The rooms were clean, with white-curtained beds and carpets. India discovered that Will Noble had forwarded a letter to her from her sister, Cordelia. It was quite a treat, after the rough life, to indulge in the luxury of a bath, sit in a parlor chair and read a letter from home. Sissy's letter was full of news about family and friends, but oddly, none of it brought on the slightest hint of homesickness. In fact, just the opposite occurred.

> . . . Mother's feelings have not changed and she wishes you to return home by fall. She doesn't feel women are groaning under half so heavy a yoke of bondage as you imagine. She feels dreadful about your lecturing in public places and hopes you will return to civilized society and carry your cause from house to house.
>
> Now, dear India, you will hear what Father has to say about your public speaking. He says he would rather you marry and have twin babies every year. Luckily, he did not stipulate how many years! As for me, if you have brass enough, and can do more good by giving public lectures than in any other way, I say go to it! But, India, I miss you so. Your last letter. which I received safely, spoke of such adventures. I would join you and your old Mr. Ransom in a moment, but Father does keep me on a short leash for fear I will follow the eccentricities of my elder sister. However, twice in the past month I've sneaked out to rallies. I've been hosed with water and pelted with mud. It is a bitter struggle but one we shall someday win.

A knock sounded at India's door. She put down the letter and rose to open the door.

"Good evening, ma'am," said Gat, formally as a preacher. Beside him was a stout gray-haired woman. "I'd like you to meet Mrs. Hewitt. She's offered to tend little Hope while you lecture at the hurdy-gurdy."

India offered her hand. "I'm happy to meet you, Mrs. Hewitt."

"Likewise, Miss Simms, as I am a supporter of women's rights myself. Esther Morris has written to me about you," she said pleasantly.

"I suppose Mr. Ransom has explained to you about the baby." India looked at the sleeping baby on the bed.

"Yes, I'll take good care of her. I've raised ten of my own. Now, you'd best be off. The soldiers get awfully rowdy if their entertainment doesn't start on time."

India, dressed in the clean, cotton calico dress, felt more like her old self than she had for a long time. She followed Gat out of the room, down the stairs and onto the hotel veranda. Coyote and the yellow dog, which Gat had named Square Deal, tagged after them down the dusty street to the hurdy-gurdy house.

The hurdy-gurdy turned out to be a large tent supported by framework scantlings. Stepping inside, they found the floor to be tamped earth, and India guessed it was the frontier version of a ballroom. Around the sides were rough benches for dancers and onlookers while two or three oil lamps dimly illuminated the scene. In a corner next to the bar stood a battered upright piano, which sounded tinny and badly out of tune when the pianist played some chords. Gat explained that the customers pay the musicians as well as buy drinks and dances. By eight o'clock the dance hall had filled with clumsily booted miners, cowboys, and soldiers whose money was out and ready to buy dances and drinks. The girls were waiting, sitting demurely on their chairs; the bar was ready and the glasses washed.

The bartender called out. "Gents, tonight we've got a special attraction. A suffragette has come all the way from

Boston to speak to us on wimmin's rights." Disgruntlement sounded through the tent, for most of the customers were ready to dance and drink. "Miss Simms, give me your hand." He lifted her up onto the bar counter.

"By gol! What's a woman talking politics fer?" shouted a deep voice from the crowd.

"Is she married?" hollered another.

Suddenly, Gat was up beside her. "Now, since this little lady has come all the way from Boston, I reckon she deserves to say her piece. I don't agree with all her opinions myself, but I'll defend her right to speak them. And the first man who tries to interrupt her, I'll see outside." The room fell silent and Gat winked a go-ahead to India and jumped down off the bar.

India gave a short but valiant oration. She assured the men that if given the vote, women would not necessarily vote away beer and whiskey and she offered a free dance to any man signing her petition.

When the fiddler called out, "Gents, take your partners for a dance." India was mobbed. But with Gat's help she set up an orderly system in which she took a brief promenade with every petition signer. At the end of the allotted time, India, following the lead of the other girls, deftly steered her partner to the counter, where he could buy a drink. After the drinks had been speedily consumed, the bartender rapped the counter with his bung starter as a sign for the girls to sit down for a minute to get their steam back up. One full-figured girl lifted her skirts ankle high and displayed to India a heavy pair of miner's boots, which she wore to protect her feet from the customers' clumsiness. Fifty partners later, India yearned for a pair of boots just like them, for her own feet were battle bruised.

Toward the evening's end, when some of the men were so drunk they were discharging their six-guns at the tent ceiling to the beat of waltzes and polkas, India never let her partner lead her far from Gat. Finally, when the fiddler called out "One last dance, gentlemen," followed by "Only this one more afore the gals go home," India breathed a great sigh of relief.

"Ma'am, may I have the last waltz?"

India, dry-mouthed with exhaustion, turned and looked up into Gat's grinning face. "Did you sign the petition ledger, sir?" After all these weeks his was the one signature that had been denied her.

He kept grinning. "No, ma'am."

"Oh, you can agitate like the devil himself." But she'd had enough of politics for one night, and so she let herself fall into his arms, placing her small hand in his warm palm, reveling in the reassurance of the warmth of his grip and the heat of his gaze. When the music began it was enough to stay in one spot in his embrace and sway to the rhythm of the last waltz, and even as tired as she was, his lithe hardness made her tremble like no other man could.

For a moment Gat closed his eyes, savoring the sweet smell of wild mint that he'd come to associate with her, and his long fingers caressed hers as his other hand pressed gently against the small of her back. It had been like sitting on spurs to have to stand by and watch her dance with nearly every hyena in the territory. But she was all his now, and where her cheek rested on his chest a heat seeped through his shirt and he felt a thickening in his loins.

Within his encircling arms, pressed against his hard-muscled length, India felt the swell of his desire and her own unrestrained response. When the waltz ended he drew back and considered her a long moment. She smiled a little and drew a deep breath, trying to steady herself beneath the deep canyons of his gaze. He had never seemed so tall, so male, so much a part of her, yet so much a stranger.

"Let's go." His words came out queerly level and quiet.

Her mouth felt dry, her lips as if they belonged to someone else. "I have to get the petition ledger."

With wordless assent he caught her elbow and guided her through the crush of dancers where she picked up the ledger.

Outside, their walk back to the Overland House was slow and wordless. The night wind tugged at India's loose strands of hair, and when she and Gat finally arrived at the steps of the hotel she wet her lips and hesitated for a long moment, wishing they didn't have to part to separate rooms at all. It was an immoral notion and she lowered her eyes wretchedly to the scuffed toes of her shoes.

Suddenly, Gat sought her hand and pulled her into the shadows. He was not so wretched, nor was he as shy, though he was aware it was neither the time nor place to kiss her. But he would risk it anyway. His lips captured hers. And for some minutes he smothered any breath of protest with his mouth until he was obliged to let her breathe.

"Do you wish to have a corpse on your hands?" she gasped, pressing her graceful fingers against his chest for support. "Every—" he kissed her "—gossip—" he kissed once again "—in town—" once more his mouth swallowed her words. "Stop!" she giggled. "I'll be the first suffragette ever to be kissed to death." Trembling from the force of her own desire, she broke away from him and ran toward the hotel steps. But a last glance at him over her shoulder sent her back to his side where on tiptoe she took pity on him and pressed a sweet goodnight kiss to his grinning lips.

Gat watched her disappear into the hotel doorway, pushed his hat back on his head, and thought to himself with a wild uneasiness, *You've been lady-broke, Gat Ransom!*

They stayed three more days at Fort Laramie. India had soaked her feet in epsom salts most of those days and had lectured in the afternoons to ladies' auxiliaries. The morning of their departure India walked out on the hotel veranda with baby Hope in her arms and found Gat sitting on the steps reading the *Fort Laramie Flyer*.

"Anything interesting?" she asked, seeing he'd already saddled the horses and had the menagerie of goats and dogs assembled.

"There's a comment by the editor about you."

"Will you read it?" she asked.

He gave her a doubtful eye. "You sure?"

"Yes! If all the world is to know it, I should too."

"You asked for it." Gat began reading. " 'A mild affliction

259

has visited the Fort in the form of one Miss India Simms. She supports women's equality and representation for all. She encourages single women to refuse to marry and married women to refuse to assume their marital duties until women are given the vote. Indeed, a spinster with a pair of bosoms that look like two gingersnaps pinned onto a cottonwood shingle must be an excellent authority on such subjects.' "

Without even raising a brow, India turned and walked down the veranda steps. She comfortably secured the baby in the saddlebag and climbed up on her horse.

Gat, paper in hand, was still standing on the porch looking at her. India looked back, straight faced. "Well, do you think that was a proper description of my attributes?"

"Well, I . . ." Gat stuttered, trying hard to lend the proper gravity to his answer.

India bit the inside of her lip to keep her own manner serious. "Well, what?"

"Well, I don't know much about gingersnaps."

India burst into giggles. "You don't know much about gingersnaps! I could see you were about ready to split wide open with laughter when I came out."

He tossed the paper aside and climbed up on his own horse. "You're the damnedest woman to put a man on the hot seat!"

Still laughing she said, "Until you give us the vote, that's where all of you belong!" With a jaunty tilt of the head she gave him a flashing red-lipped smile and nudged Bluestocking down the street.

With each setting sun it became more difficult for India not to lay out her blanket beside Gat and spend the night in his arms, but to her mind propriety must be observed, boundaries of intimacy drawn. She'd put a halt to his love making more than once until he began referring to her as the vestal virgin of suffrage, and when they traveled during the days, her thoughts were not necessarily on crusading for the vote, but more frequently on the feel of Gat's arms around her and the taste of his lips.

While her feelings for Gat heightened, her puritan upbringing would not allow her to sink into the much-touted arrangement of "free love." Though Gat seemed to perceive her dilemma, he was not altogether sympathetic, and was at times, particularly in the evenings, downright testy.

Being a woman, India tried to smooth out his moodiness, but that only compounded the problem between them. One evening, he gave a casual tug on her hand and called her into his arms with the slightest of protest from her. Once he took her into his arms it always happened that her strength of will dissolved and she found herself flowering to his touch. She felt like a hypocrite.

"India," he whispered her name against her cheek. "India," he kissed into the soft hollow of her throat, nuzzling past the lacings of her doeskin dress, to press soft kisses down the warm furrow between her breasts. Each place his moist lips touched left India inwardly shaking as if she'd been burned. But oh, what a sweet burning!

All was pure sensation for India. She felt herself standing on the edge of a wondrously exquisite pool and Gat was calling her to dive in. She wanted to—by heaven, how she wanted to! His hands massaged her hips, moving slowly, then slipping beneath the doeskin dress and under her pantalettes to the silkiness of her thighs.

Suddenly, his roving hand was halted by India's own. It was probably the single greatest act of self-control of her life, but she knew she was on the brink of no return where passion was concerned, and she remembered what Eugenie had said: *You can stop it anytime you want*.

Gat swore under his breath and broke their embrace, surprising her with a reaction that wasn't very understanding. She reached for his hand, but he stood up and moved opposite the campfire.

"I think you are trying to sit two horses with one fanny."

"What do you mean?" asked India, offended that he had so abruptly left her.

His face was shadowed, but the smoldering fire seemed to

reflect the tenor of his mood. "A man can only take so much come-hither, Miss Simms."

"Miss, Simms, is it?" echoed India, on the defense for a change. The air, earlier sparked with desire, now sparked with irritability.

"Yep, Miss Simms it is! I think we've stretched the tether about as far as it will go and if you aren't willing to let hold, we better just cut it off."

"Cut it off? But I—"

"—Enjoy it?" he supplied. "Don't we all, and I'd like to enjoy it more. Kissing isn't exactly the best part."

India frowned. In the past weeks she'd felt some pretty cataclysmic things while Gat held her close. "But . . . but our philosophies are different on the matter."

Gat shifted his long legs and perched a foot on a stone by the fire. "I'd say so. You're against matrimony and your high-tone morality keeps you just out of reach. I think we better cut it off until you decide which horse you're going to ride." His manner had relaxed and his voice loosened into thoughtfulness.

"But . . ." India somehow felt they had been through this before. Oddly, the image of Tommy Cahoon and his scalped head came to mind. Gat was up to something. He had a way of herding cattle going in one direction into another without even a flick of his lasso and he was doing that to her now. If she only knew which direction he favored she would go the other, just to show him he couldn't manipulate her. "Well, maybe you are right," she raised an arrogant brow. "We'll keep the arrangement platonic."

Gat frowned, giving her a hard, contemptuous look. The baby chose that moment to cry and Gat moved to pick her up. Nothing more was said between them.

The next day the only one contented was baby Hope. Not touching Gat or being touched by him, yet being so close, became another great exercise in self-denial for India. What rankled her was Gat's stoicism in the matter, besides his being extraordinarily surly. She felt like Lucifer cut off from heaven. Worst of all, the end of her speaking tour was in sight and she would sorely miss the fire-lit nights of close companionship and endearing conversation.

Later in the afternoon a great opportunity came for reconciliation when Bluestocking threw a shoe and they had to ride double on Gat's horse. India wrapped her arms snugly around his waist and reveled in his nearness, her pulse coursing the entire distance. But Gat seemed oblivious. Once again he was her escort and nothing more. Now, India felt spurned and wondered if he'd ever really cared for her in the first place.

Chapter 21

*T*hey rode into Laramie late in the evening, trail weary and spent. With Hope in her arms, India walked inside the livery stable, sat on a barrel and watched Gat shoe Bluestocking. The livery forge smoldered crimson in the evening light. Stripped to the waist, Gat's muscled chest glistened with sweat. At first India had prudishly lowered her eyes, then realizing that he was intent on his work she looked at him without his knowing it. Soon her gaze began to devour the sleek contour of frame and form while she admired his strong powerful forearms, the shadowed curve of biceps, and the way his buttocks moved under his dust-coated pants. She wanted to touch him, run her hands through the dark hair on his chest, draw her fingertips across his shoulders. The hot night and the heat of the smithy fire flushed her face, and she felt droplets of perspiration trickle down her cleavage and sticky-wet dampness spread between her thighs. The ring of hammer against anvil shocked through her high-pitched senses until her own vulnerability to Gat's virility could stand no more. She suddenly stood and left the stable.

Later, she and Gat stepped into the sleeping room he'd arranged for her in a dingy railway hotel. It came with the usual bed, chair and vermin, while air smelling of soot and rubbish filtered through the open window.

"If you need me, I'll be sleeping out behind the livery stable."

It seemed to India he wanted to put as much distance between them as possible. How she yearned for the peaceful nights they'd shared on the prairie. It no longer mattered to her that they had to share the battered tin cup and eat strips of burned bacon stuffed into equally burned biscuits.

"I'd rather sleep behind the stable than here," she said.

"Ladies don't sleep outside in towns." He tossed the saddlebags on the straw-mattress bed.

She wanted to tell him that she didn't care, that she just wanted to be with him, but by his surly manner it was clear he didn't want to be with her.

"This is a filthy hole," she retaliated.

"It's the best I could find this time of night." One eye narrowed and the muscles of his jaw began to flick.

She regarded him with resentful eyes and snapped. "What, all the brothels full?"

Anger tensed every line of his thick shoulders and the sudden thunderous look he gave her made her sorry she'd said it.

"Ma'am, I hope not!" he shot back, striding across the wooden floor. Between one eyeblink and the next he was out the door.

India winced as the door slammed and the ring of his spurs down the hallway became a dirge. Why had she been such a shrew? It was she who should be in his arms, not some woman down the street. Could he really sleep with another woman after all that had passed between them? But then who was she to pass judgment on him? She was an adventuress who had tossed off the conventions of society, a fanatic who demanded equality for women, and for some inexplicable reason her sins seemed to be the greater. The sting of tears burned her eyes and her heart crashed to her toes while in her arms the baby fussed to be fed.

Gathering her fortitude, she moved to the bed and took from the saddlebag a feeding bottle filled with goat's milk. As she put the bottle to Hope's lips, the innocence of her angelic face caused India to pause. Perhaps her philosophies were carried to the extreme, and maybe if the laws were changed marriage wouldn't necessarily be all slavery and subjection. Babies needed both a father and mother and a family to grow up in. Sympathy filled her heart for the little child in her arms who was destined to grow up in a foundling home.

If only she and Gat could . . . She cuddled the baby closer to her. But no, she could never be happy on the frontier and he would never leave it. Even if she could live life in settlements full of flies and dirt, coarse food and coarser speech, she wouldn't make that sort of choice and betray the cause of equal rights.

A black cricket wriggled out of the straw mattress, paused and then crawled across the worn muslin sheeting. Watching, India wondered how many more bugs were living inside the bedding, though she was almost beyond caring. She yawned and gazed out the open window into the night. Below the window, freight cars were being shunted, but the noise and bedbugs weren't agitating her so much as the niggling image of Gat in the arms of a henna-haired harlot. Even so, as the poet might have written, she could not love him half so much, loved she not freedom more.

Gat strode past three saloons before he entered one. Coyote and Square Deal sat down outside, waiting like dutiful chaperons while he bought a bottle of whiskey. He then walked back outside, uncorked the bottle, took a swig or two, and headed toward the outskirts of town. Tonight he preferred solitude. He sat down on a hogback ridge, leaned back, and stared heavenward, and slipped into a stupor of soul-searching.

He was near the end of his rope where India was concerned. He didn't like the arrangement, but since it was her idea in the first place he'd gone along with it in hopes she'd come around. One minute she was as ornery as a skittish mare, and the next she was so winsome he'd come close to taking her on the spot. But to his thinking she wasn't playing by any rules and he wasn't going to be strung along in a game he couldn't win. A man had enough misfortunes. He stared into the night sky, seeing nothing, seeing everything.

It appeared to him that she still intended to go back East and despite what had happened between them in the last month, no choices had been made, no understandings reached. He knew her aversion to frontier life and he wouldn't ask her to stay where she felt she couldn't be happy. Besides, what man would propose to a woman who protested the present laws of marriage as injurious to women? They were at a stalemate, and with each passing day the strain tore them apart.

He took a long pull on the whiskey bottle and ruminated over India's ideas of equality and independence. Sure women had it tough. Sure they ought to have rights. But why was he the one to bear the brunt of a thousand years of injustice? Like a fool jackrabbit he'd been snared in a trap and now he'd have to see it out, barbs and all. The bachelor's life he'd grown accustomed to seemed as flat as the prairie now that he'd been with India and the baby. He wasn't sure if he could settle back into the loneliness of the wrangler's life. A man could take only so much lonesome.

Towards midnight the moon slowly rose with virgin shyness, and while the whiskey had eased the pain in his gut, it hadn't stopped the battle going on in his head, instead it just fired the confusion. Dejectedly, he nursed the whiskey bottle until it was empty and then tossed it down the hill. During the hours until sunrise he threw rocks at the bottle and joined Coyote in howling at the moon.

The next afternoon, beneath the willow-woven roof of Laramie's outdoor bowery, India listened sedately while her opponent in the debate made a clever speech. The lawyer's wit occasionally evoked applause and laughter in a crowd that was an odd mixture of gentility and ignobility. Men in alligator boots with wild unkempt hair and beards stood next to well-tailored merchants. Tired-looking women, strangely

267

dressed in gowns that must have been old on their grandmothers, sat beside finely frocked socialites.

India smoothed her hair and straightened her own dress, all the while conscious of Gat's insolent eyes on her from where he stood on the sidelines tending baby Hope, a task which, except for this afternoon, he'd always agreeably volunteered to do during India's lectures. Around him women waved white handkerchiefs to keep away the buzzing insects, and men took furtive nips of liquor from secreted flasks. Minutes before when she handed the baby to him she had remained aloof, avoiding his dark eyes, but remarking distastefully that the air fairly reeked with whiskey.

"And my friends," continued the lawyer relentlessly, "if women were given the right of franchise, they would correspondingly come under the obligation to bear arms. Do you want your sisters, your wives and your daughters going to war?"

The crowd, which India had held in her sway only moments before, vacillated to the lawyer. "And if women vote at all, the right should not be exercised before the age of twenty-one. And when a woman marries, her vote should be merged with her husband's. The vote of the husband must be regarded as the vote of the wife—bone of his bone, and flesh of his flesh." It particularly irritated India when her opponents quoted scripture to lend credibility to their arguments. The lawyer drew a lurid picture of women deserting husbands and children for lawyers' offices and judges' seats, leaving the deserted men to quiet the babies as best they could with rubber substitutes. Looking over at Gat, who held fussing baby Hope, and who was attempting to do that very thing, caused India to bite back a smile. Was it so horrible in the young lawyer's estimation to tend a child?

After entertaining the crowd with similar stock arguments for fifteen minutes longer, the lawyer folded his arms in dramatic fashion. "In conclusion, gentlemen, allow me to say that I have often known a hen to try to crow, but I've never known one to succeed!" He took his seat amidst a storm of laughter and applause, relinquishing the platform to India for rebuttal.

In reply, India turned to him. "It is clear my worthy opponent is a bachelor. I hope one of the young ladies present would some day be kind enough to initiate him into the mysteries of matrimony and maternity, and cure him of his present fear that women would neglect their babies if enfranchised. I beg to inform him that women would never dare neglect their babies, for if they did, we'd never have any more bachelors."

The bachelor lawyer blushed, the audience tittered and baby Hope let out a colicky yowl. Ransom cast India an agitated glance as he patted and pillowed the infant on his broad shoulder. With each head-throbbing cry from the baby, Gat regretted his all-night drunk, but most of all he regretted falling in love with the beautiful, high-spirited woman standing at the podium.

A man standing behind Gat, dressed in soldier blues and buckskin trousers, began to crow, mainly to entertain his far-from-sober companions. Gat's eyes shifted warningly toward the men and then back to India. But apparently after what she had survived the past months, she seemed hardly ruffled.

"Friends, the gentleman said he has often known a hen to try to crow, but he has never known one to succeed. Well, I am free to admit he is right. I have found the same peculiarity in hens. But once in a poultry yard I saw a rooster try to set, and he made quite a success of it!" The bowery fairly vibrated with laughter, but instead of thwarting the heckler, Gat knew she had merely fueled his fire. Even so, he couldn't help but admire her. By now, well schooled in the art of public speaking, India maintained calm in the face of insult, and parried the heckler's increasing disturbances with humor.

"It has been proposed that a woman and husband share one vote. Then I say, if a married man be entitled to one vote, the unmarried man should have one-half a vote." Applause rippled the crowd. "If women had the right of franchise would they also be forced to bear arms? No, I say. There are large classes even among men in this land who are exempt from services in our armies because of physical incapacities and reasons of conscientious scruples.

"Think of the woman who pays a large tax, and the man who drives her coach and the man who waits upon her table. They go to the polls and decide how much of her property goes to support the public good. She has no voice in the matter. She is taxed without representation."

The heckler let loose a loud holler.

"Jeers and calls are not arguments, sir," India retorted to him directly. "If you choose to bray like a mule, then please come up front and let the audience compare the better argument."

Her bold challenge settled him down momentarily, but it was apparent he had come, not out of public conscience, but to make nuisance of himself. India was nearing the conclusion of her rebuttal while Ransom was nearing the end of his patience with the fretful baby.

Somehow the heckler had made a connection between the two and leaned toward Gat and snickered loudly, "Why don't you give it yer titty. Seems yer wife is busy!" It was the wrong thing to say to Gat Ransom at that particular moment. Without even a hint of forethought, Gat swung a right fist at the man hitting him squarely in the jaw. The blow knocked him out cold.

"Hey, you can't do that," protested the heckler's companion as he drew himself up to size.

Someone of a calmer nature spoke up from behind. "Now settle down, Curly. That man's holdin' a baby. You can't hit a man holdin' a baby."

Offense flashed in Curly's narrowing eyes and it was apparent he wasn't convinced. India's concluding remarks fizzled into silence as she stared, along with everyone else.

Gat turned to a nearby woman. "Pardon, ma'am, would you hold the baby?" She took it readily. "Now, Curly," Gat challenged, "I'm not holdin' a baby."

Curly threw the first punch and the fight was on. Women

and old men scattered while the more hardy joined sides, not for Gat or the heckler, but those in favor of women's franchise and those against. It seemed the perfect afternoon for it, the perfect place, and the perfect method of settlement, fist to face and knee to groin.

Aghast, India watched her debating opponent leap from the platform and into the melee with undisguised exuberance. She called for peace, but she might as well have whistled in the wind. Suddenly, something in her head snapped and she became seething mad. How dare Gat do this to her! How dare he turn the debate into a brawl? Every paper in the territory would write up the story.

Heedless of the possibility of being hit herself, she pushed over to where Gat and Curly were still slugging it out and began shouting at Gat. "How dare you turn this into a common brawl! I'm leaving. Do you hear? I'm taking the next train out of here," she yelled. "I'm leaving and I'm taking the baby with me!"

Never minding that Curly had his hands around Gat's throat, India took Gat's silence as indifference. She pivoted on her heel, took the baby from the gaping matron who had been holding her, picked up the petition ledger, which had been knocked off the table into the dirt, and stomped off down the dusty street toward the train depot.

Moments later Gat called to her. "India!" But India didn't slow her headlong pace or turn to answer. He moved beside her and easily matched her pace, stride for stride. "I'm sorry." He took out a handkerchief and wiped the blood from the corner of his mouth.

"Humph!" India sniffed with rising wrath. "Mr. Ransom, your escorting job is finished! Do you hear? Finished! I'm done with traveling around this godforsaken territory with a . . . a womanizer and brawler." She opened the depot door and stepped inside to the ticket counter. Muttering, Gat followed.

Tommy Cahoon was at his usual spot. Recognizing Gat, he called out a friendly "Howdy." Gat didn't answer.

India, baby in arms, stepped up to the counter. "*One ticket to Cheyenne.*"

"Why, ain't you the one . . ." He looked over at Gat and seeing the black scowl on his face thought he'd better hold his tongue.

"Wait a minute," Gat took her arm and swung her around to face him. "Now, get the burr out from under your tail, woman. This fracas hasn't been any picnic for me, either." He gave a sideways spit into a nearby brass spitton.

She grimaced. "I thought you quit that disgusting habit."

"I did. That was part of my tooth." India felt a twinge of sympathy, but quickly squelched it. She started to turn back to the ticket counter but he held her tight and his touch fueled the fire.

"Must you always resort to brute force?" she challenged, glaring down at his hand on her arm. The baby had started to cry again.

Tommy Cahoon kept looking over to the baby and then curiously at Gat.

Gat knew his hold on her was hardly brute force, but he released her. "India, be reasonable. You've worked up this all-fired idea that—"

"Just bite your tongue and don't tell me my ideas. I'm capable of thinking for myself." She fished in her pocket for the ticket money. A line up had formed behind them at the ticket counter. Outside, the eastbound train was building up steam for departure.

The train whistle blew and with it went Gat's patience. "Bite my tongue? I should have held mine less and bit yours more!" he thundered.

India stared straight ahead but her chin quivered with outrage and her nostrils flared like a race horse running the quarter mile.

He opened his mouth and swore. "Lady, you can get on that damned train and ride it all the way to hell for all I care!" He turned heel and strode off.

Cahoon stamped her ticket and handed it to her. He

watched the two leave by opposite doors and rubbed the hairless patch on the back of his head.

"Friends of yers?" asked Tommy's assistant.

Tommy shook his head with puzzlement. "Yep, him and that little gal was in here not more 'an a couple months ago, the two of 'em barely acquainted. Now a baby an all. Why I hadn't taken Gat to be such a fast worker."

The day coach occupants were men, slouching barroom characters playing cards, smoking and spitting tobacco while talking in boisterous tones. India heard the conductor's final call, and the train began to move slowly forward as she took an isolated seat. Little Hope still bawled in sporadic bursts. India stared out the window vacantly watching the ill-arranged buildings and shanties of Laramie pass out of sight. A single tear, then another, fell hot against her sun-freckled cheek until she was crying uncontrollably.

Chapter 22

*I*t was hard to know who suffered more from the parting, Gat or India. India retrenched in Cheyenne, throwing herself into the cause of suffrage with fanatical zeal. Her days were spent lobbying the legislators and lecturing the populace on behalf of women. At night baby Hope became a gossamer shield against her loneliness, and her confidants were pen and paper.

One night in a letter to her sister she confessed:

> *You may find it shocking after all my letters berating the frontier, but I am adjusting to life out here. The very air I breathe seems so free that I have not the least desire to return to the constraints of eastern society. Admittedly, I am a wee bit lonely, despite little Hope's companionship. She is a dear and I do love her, and I have petitioned the foundling home for legal adoption, though I wonder if she should not have a true father and mother. At times my concern over this dilemma is enough to tempt me into marriage. Truthfully, I'm enough of the old-fashioned woman to want to love and be loved, but never to be ruled. I fear a year or two of married life would pall upon me and I should demand my freedom.*
>
> *Oh, perhaps there are better ways to achieve equality*

than by preaching about and heralding the idea abroad until everyone is tired of the subject, though I nearly tire of the topic myself. Indeed, Sissy, life is not so simple as I once thought.

Betty Bright caught the eye of her husband, Colonel Bright, and mouthed silent instructions from her seat in the gallery of the assembly hall.

"Betty, I'm sure he'll do very well on his own," India advised, her own eyes unwavering from the Colonel, who with quiet seriousness nibbled the end of his cigar.

Along with him, India studied the faces of railroad men, miners and cattlemen, the elected officials of Wyoming Territory, some of whom could not read or write. The room was hazy with smoke and smelled of sweat and tobacco as the barkeep from the saloon next door made his appearance with a tray of mugs for the thirsty legislators. India glanced at the jeweled timepiece pinned on Betty's bodice and shook her head, wondering if the debate would ever end. The Colonel's bill to grant the women of Wyoming Territory the right of suffrage and to hold office might have passed the Council, but she realized that the opposition in the House would be more formidable. They sat listening all day to the opponents bluster against the bill and she was beginning to doubt its passage altogether.

The news of Colonel Bright's "Female Suffrage Act" had spread about the territory, though most thought it was some sort of practical joke. India knew Bright himself was worried that he wouldn't be able to fulfill his campaign promise to his own wife and her good friend Esther Morris. Both of the women had worked so hard on his behalf to elect him as the representative from South Pass City, and now they were all counting on the efforts of women all over the territory who had taken the opportunity to write letters and pay personal calls on members of the legislature and even the governor. With the help of Will Noble, the *Argus* had done its share to shift public opinion.

"Gentlemen, this is a pretty important move," began

Badger Bigsby, a Union Pacific manager elected by the railroad men of the southern part of the Territory, as he took the floor.

India stifled her desire to gag the old windbag before he could do more damage. She knew Bigsby and Ben Sheeks were the leaders of the house opposition to the bill. They had taken the initiative to destroy the bill by amending it to death.

"Gentlemen," continued Bigsby, "a measure like this is kinda like a wild train on a single track, and we've got to keep our eye peeled or we'll get into the ditch. It's a new conductor making his first run. He don't know the stations yet, and he feels as if there were a spotter in every coach besides. Female suffrage changes the management of the whole line, and may put the entire outfit in the hands of a receiver in two years. We can't tell when Wyoming Territory may be sidetracked with a lot of female conductors and superintendents and a posse of giddy girls at the brakes."

A supporter of the bill stood up in protest. "Mr. Speaker, I shall pull in favor of the move. You boys should couple onto our train. I'd regard it as a promotion going from a cattle train of male politics to a train with a parlor car of ladies." India gladly noted he received a light applause.

"Mr. Chairman, or Speaker, or whatever you call yourself," spoke up Unusual Barnes, the owner of the Bar G horse ranch on the Upper Chugwater. "I agree with the chair that we want to be familiar with the range before we stampede and go wild like a lot of Texas cattle just off the trail. When we turn this maverick over to the governor to be branded we want to know that we are corralling the right animal. After we've run this bill into the chute and twisted its tail a few times, we might want to pay two or three good men to help us let it loose again."

"Give women the vote and they will want to be President of the United States and senators and want to be marshalls and sheriffs, which is supremely ridiculous," shouted Ben Sheeks out of turn.

In supreme agitation India nudged Betty with her elbow muttering, "That man is a pestilence!"

"In my opinion women officials could give this territory a boom that will make her the bonanza of all creation," yelled a bill supporter.

Bigsby jumped to his feet in an attempt to derail such sympathies. "Enough people are already entitled to vote. We need to restrict the vote privilege instead of enlarging it."

Elias Kilgore, a retired stage driver raised a calming hand and slowly got to his feet. "The member from Sweetwater County says we are to restrict the vote, does he? Well, Mr. Speaker, because God made men first, they have become mighty stuck on themselves. The fact is that God made the mud-turtle and the bedbug before he made man. He also made the jackass and the baboon. When he had all the experience he wanted in creating, then he made woman. He done a good job. She suits me fine."

The assembly let loose with reverberating laughter.

"I second Elias in that," said another representative. "The more Godlike we get, gentlemen, the more rights we will give women. The closer you get to the cannibals the more apt a woman is to do chores and get choked for her opinions."

"I believe that the mother of a statesman is better calculated to vote than a man who can't read or write," continued Elias. "I may be a little peculiar, but I think that when a woman has marched a band of hostile boys all the way up to manhood and has given 'em a good start and made good citizens out of 'em with this wicked world to buck agin all the time, she can vote all day so far as I'm concerned."

India clasped and unclasped her hands with excitement. The wind of opinion was changing in favor of the bill. She saw Bright catch the eye of Buck Slocum, his colleague in support of the bill. The time was right to call for a vote, before support could shift again.

"Mr. Chairman, I propose we take a vote on the measure," announced Slocum.

Bigsby bent over to his cohort Ben Sheeks, and after a moment's consultation, Sheeks took the floor.

"I propose to amend the suffrage bill by moving that the age requirement be changed to thirty years in place of eighteen, on the theory that no woman would vote because none would admit to being thirty." He grinned, apparently pleased with his own cleverness, but India wanted to tweak his bulbous red nose.

During more debate the age of eighteen was raised, not to thirty, but to twenty-one. However, Sheeks wasn't thwarted. He took the floor again and India and Betty exchanged worried glances.

"I again propose a change in particular in Section One of the bill. I would require the word "woman" be stricken and the phrase "All colored women and squaws," be inserted."

This proposal brought a hearty round of applause from the opposition and an unladylike hiss from India. Sheeks took his seat and another man stood up proposing that the vote on the bill be postponed until July 4, 1870—a holiday and a year when the legislature ordinarily would not be in session.

Debate was keen, but all the amendments failed except one: the change of age requirement from eighteen to twenty-one was accepted. India shifted with relief and knew they were on the downhill slide.

At last the chair called for an end to the debate. Bright gave a nod to his supporters in the house. India crossed her fingers. The final vote was taken.

Outside the *Argus* office, a cold November wind relentlessly whipped the building's signboard. Will was putting wood into the stove when the door burst open and along with a blast of cold air, India and the Brights stepped in.

"We have wonderful news," gasped India.

Betty unwrapped her woolen cape. "The Colonel's suffrage bill has passed the House. I'm so pleased! I declare my husband is a magician." She turned to the Colonel beside her and kissed him on the cheek.

"That is grand news!" Will exclaimed, rushing over to shake the Colonel's hand.

"We knew once Colonel Bright was elected in September he would see it through," India said.

"I don't deserve all the credit. It must be shared with you, India, and my wife." He looked at Betty lovingly. "Betty, it's a shame that I should be a member of the legislature and make laws for such a woman as you. You are better than I am. You know a great deal more, and you would make a better member of the Assembly than I, and you know it. I have done everything in my power to give you the ballot. Now it lays with Governor Campbell."

"I fear the governor is not sympathetic with our cause," frowned India.

"Don't be completely sure," Betty said with a twinkle in her eye. "Perhaps the Colonel can influence him as he did the Assembly. You know, when he introduced the bill people smiled. There was not much expectation that anything of that sort would be done. However, my husband is a shrewd fellow. He said to the Democrats, 'We have a Republican governor and a Democratic Assembly. Now, if we can carry this bill though the Assembly and the governor vetos it, we shall have made a point. We shall have shown our liberality and lost nothing. But keep still,' he said, 'don't say anything about it.' He went to the Republicans and used another logic. And likewise they agreed to vote for it. So when the bill came to a vote it went right through!" Betty clasped her hands together with triumph.

India smiled widely. "Imagine, Will. The members looked at each other in astonishment, for they hadn't intended to do it, *quite*. Everyone laughed and said it was a good joke, and that they had put the governor in a fix."

"They make it sound easy," said Bright. "I had my doubts while they debated in the house. Sheeks had set up a strong opposition." He pulled out a paper from underneath his overcoat. "I've brought a copy of the bill for you to print in the paper, Will."

"Esther has launched a letter-writing campaign throughout the territory," Betty said. "I think the governor has been getting a lot of mail."

Bright handed the document to Will, whose eyes lit up as he skimmed the writing. "Why, Colonel, this is a stroke of genius. You have not only given women the vote, you have given them the right to own separate property and to enjoy the fruits of their labors." He read further and shook his head with awe. " 'Property rights for wives and parity pay for male and female teachers.' I could not have dreamed for a finer bit of legislation."

"Indeed," echoed India.

"Yes, we shall see," Bright said on an optimistic note. "Betty and I had best be on our way. It looks like snow." He put his arm around her and shook Will's hand once more.

"Just think, next election we might be voting, India," Betty proclaimed, as her husband ushered her out the door. "Good afternoon."

India watched them hurry down the street, thinking that next election she wouldn't be here to vote. She had stayed four months longer in the territory than she'd intended, and now with the conclusion of all her efforts, her stay was almost at an end. Her trunk was partially packed and her train ticket purchased, and she and baby Hope would be in Boston for Christmas.

"India, after such good news, I fear I have something unfortunate to tell you," Will said, coming up behind her.

India turned, her blue eyes concerned. "What is it?"

"Mrs. Horn from the foundling home came by and said they've denied your petition to adopt baby Hope."

India's heart fell. "But why? They are begging for homes for their children."

"Ben Sheeks is against you because you are unmarried, and according to the paper the baby's father signed, Gat Ransom is the legal guardian."

"Unmarried! Why . . . why Sheeks is prejudiced against me because I'm a suffragette. How can they listen to him? And as far as Gat Ransom being the legal guardian, he's an irresponsible drifter . . . nobody has seen him . . . I've not seen him since . . ." Tears began to gather in her eyes from frustration and the memory of their Laramie parting. In a half-crazy way she'd hoped Gat would have come after her that day, but he hadn't. Months had passed and with each day she knew with more surety that she'd never see Gat Ransom again.

Will put a comforting hand on her arm, but she shrugged it away. "Thank you, Will, but I'll be all right. I'll think of a way to get around Mr. Ben Sheeks." She swung her shawl over her head and moved to the door.

"It won't be easy," cautioned Will.

She turned and opened the door. "I'll think of something. Whether the law thinks so or not, I'm the only mother the child has known and I won't desert her. Thanks for preparing me, and good afternoon, Will." She hurried out the door.

The blustering wind snatched at India's shawl and nudged her down the street. Something pelted her skirt, then she was struck on the side of her head. She looked down and saw oozing goo on her shawl. Rotten eggs! She muttered under her breath as her eyes darted to the nearby alleyway, spotting dark heads a split second late in their concealment.

India hitched up her skirts and sprinted into the alley. *I'm coming after you! This is the last time you'll plague me. I've endured your mischief long enough!*

It wasn't the first time the pair had lain in wait for her. Among the local rascals it seemed to be a mark of distinction to torment a town suffragette. She had been the target of stones and pits, mud balls and paper wads countless times. But rotten eggs! That was grounds for retaliation.

When she was almost upon them, they jumped up and ran, but determinedly she followed, jumping obstacles and taking odd turns. They had youth to their advantage, but she had anger to hers. Her breath was coming heavy when the taller of the two assailants stumbled. She leaped upon him like a coyote on a jackrabbit. He squealed for help, but his cowardly companion kept running.

"Now, I've caught you!" She used the age-old ear pinch

to hold him. "Why do you tease me? I've done nothing to you."

He was on the verge of tears, though he seemed a brave boy. "Pa says you want women to have the vote. The vote ain't for women, only men."

"Did your Pa tell you to throw rotten eggs at me?" She thought maybe she had the wrong culprit by the ear.

"No, ma'am," he said with sudden politeness.

India looked around. They were on Thirteenth Street, famous for its dance halls and saloons. The boy needed an object lesson more than a thrashing. Her eyes traveled to the steps of the Red Dog Saloon to the passed-out figure of the town drunk, Thirsty Parson. Giving the boy an unmerciful yank on his ear she pulled him along till they stood over the pitiful drunk.

"You see this man?"

"Yes, 'um," replied the boy, squirming.

"I say he's better than your mother!"

The boy's eyes squinted with insult. "No he ain't. He's a good-fer-nothin' drunk."

"He's better, because he can vote. Think about it. If a drunk can vote and your mother can't, then he must be better. Now you get on your way and next time I catch you I won't be so nice." Once she released his ear, he shot off like a bullet.

"Lordy, what's that smell?" Heddy sniffed when India came into the boardinghouse kitchen.

"It's me. Those little scoundrels waylaid me again today and threw rotten eggs. But I caught one and I think he learned his lesson," India said, taking off her shawl and heading for the bathroom under the stairs. "Good news, Heddy. Colonel Bright's bill on suffrage has passed the Assembly."

"Well, heaven be praised! First, emancipation and now the vote. We be livin' in interestin' times, we surely be." Heddy's wide mouth broke into a white-toothed grin.

"Where's Hope?"

"She nappin' still." Heddy picked up a wooden stirring spoon and began humming "The Battle Hymn of the Republic." "A letter came for you this morning. I put it there on the clock shelf."

"Heddy, I've some bad news, too." India had left the door open while she filled the pinewood bathtub. "The people at the foundling home have denied my request to adopt Hope because I'm unmarried."

Heddy stopped her work. "Oh, Miss Indy, that is bad. What we gonna do? I sure gonna cry if I lose ma baby Hope."

India began unfastening her dress. "I think we're all going to cry. But I intend to fight the decision."

On a shelf above the dry sink, the kitchen clock chimed four o'clock and Heddy threw up her hands. "Lordy, I near forgot, I have to run this basket of clean laundry down the street by four. Yee Jim gone to the railroad dining hall to help out when the eastbound train comes in." With that she picked up a basket of freshly pressed linen and hurried out the door.

After a few trips, India had filled the pinewood tub with tepid water. She undressed, stepped inside and lowered herself gently down. The water covered her stomach, just under her full breasts, so that they floated and undulated like cast away blossoms on a pond. With a sigh of relaxation, she contemplated her breasts for a self-conscious moment. When she was a young girl she'd agonized and fretted how it would all end up. Would she have large breasts or small? What size would her waist and hips be? Somehow being attractive was of tremendous importance to everyone. And a good young lady knew how to control herself as well as her gentlemen so she would not be taken advantage of.

I'm not a very good young lady anymore, she thought dejectedly, and then she settled back pondering the sensations she'd felt when Gat had kissed her, and in particular the times he'd pressed against her as if he wanted to melt into her very being. That night on the prairie he'd said kissing wasn't the best part; unfortunately she'd never know the best part, the pleasuring that Lady Jane and Eugenie had talked about. Her eyes followed the contours of her body from toe tip to hidden crevice. Where was the woman's witchcraft that preachers so readily denounced? What power did women embody that threatened men so? Talking to herself aloud she said, "You will never know, *Miss* Simms!"

Unfastening her hair, she let the strands cascade down to cover her bare shoulders and breasts. Everything, perhaps her thoughts included, would have to be washed clean. She lathered her body and hair with soap, then reaching for a porcelain pitcher of warm water, she rinsed off her hair. A door opened and closed and in the hall she heard the creak of floorboards. Heddy had returned. She splashed another pitcher full of water over her and stood to reach for a towel on the chair by the tub. Suddenly, the door left accidentally ajar, opened full swing.

"Hed—" The male voice stopped in mid-word. Gat Ransom's tall frame filled the doorway.

India stood statue-still, the moisture beading like unstrung pearls over her body. She felt his black eyes move carefully, wasting not a glimpse, from her limply wet auburn hair to her dove-white breasts and lowering to her rounded hips.

He expelled a slow breath.

The kitchen clock ticked away as embarrassment bloomed and withered. Seeing him again was like seeing him for the first time. Strong dark brows hovered over twinkling black eyes. His dark hair curled away from a sharp down-curved nose to brush the shoulders of his buckskin coat. A deep yearning swelled inside her and the grip of his eyes held her in place as solidly as shackles. In that moment, as brief as an eagle's cry, she fell into the black fire of his eyes and she felt the dulcet blood-rush of desire. Suddenly she wanted him with an intensity that clutched her bodily.

"I don't think anyone is here, Gat," came a woman's voice from the hallway.

"It appears not," Gat answered. Regret passed like a veil over his features. He took a step backward and softly closed the door.

"I hope Heddy has rooms," said the woman.

Stunned, India recognized the voice of Bess Anderson. Wrapping a towel about her wet head, she stepped out of the tub and quickly put on her robe. Her knees weakened and she sat down on the stool, her pulse pounding. She'd stayed too long. She'd been a fool not to return East months ago. Deep down, she knew she'd stayed because of Gat Ransom, and now because of him she must go. Seeing him again made it as clear as sunlight. His free indolence that attracted and charmed without the least aggressiveness would subvert her reason. They were so different, he the bachelor cowpuncher and she the maiden misogamist. Their love had been conceived in contradiction.

Chapter 23

*I*ndia burst into Ed Lee's office in a whirlwind of tumbleweed and dust. The brewing storm had blown loose strands of her chestnut hair into a scattered halo and had tugged her topknot into a lopsided horn. Upon seeing her Gat cracked a smile, for she bore the true appearance of a lovely but wild-haired fanatic. Barely two hours had passed since he'd seen her stark naked in the boardinghouse bathtub, yet he never ceased to be amazed at the constancy of her beauty.

"I received Gat's note and came as soon as I could," she gasped, attempting to straighten her disheveled hair and clothes. Gat was on his feet offering her a chair while Ed took a seat at his rolltop desk.

"I've told Ed about the problems you've had in adopting Hope," said Gat.

"Who told you?" India quizzed. As far as she could tell, the man had only been in town a couple of hours, and already he was stirring about in her business.

"Heddy," he said, not returning to the chair beside her.

Ed Lee drummed his fingers on his rolltop desk and shook his head thoughtfully. "I don't know if I can help you, Miss Simms. Gat seems to think I can, but if Ben Sheeks has convinced Mrs. Horn at the foundling home that you aren't a fit mother to baby Hope because you're unmarried, then perhaps the only thing you can do is get married."

Looking out the window, Gat watched the Red Dog Saloon's failing sign rip loose and cartwheel down the street, but at the word *married* Gat turned and stared hard at Ed as if he hadn't heard right.

India straightened up in her chair like a quill on a porcupine's back. "I have no intention of ever marrying!" affirmed India, terribly conscious of Gat's spurs clinking on the wood floor as he moved to sit in the chair beside her.

"Oh, I don't mean a conventional marriage." Lee smiled a little to himself. "I mean a marriage of convenience. Gat is already the legal guardian of the baby. You could marry him."

As Gat sat down, India shot up out of her chair. "You are being absurd, Mr. Lee. It would be a mockery for two people who don't—" she was going to say *who don't love each other,* but in truth she knew how desperately she loved Gat Ransom "—who aren't suited to matrimony to join in marriage. Can't he just sign the guardianship over to me?"

Gat who had been studying India silently now spoke up. "We tried that, but guardianship, according to Sheeks, is a male prerogative. He refused to let me sign the baby over to you."

India began pacing. The two men followed her with their eyes momentarily mesmerized by her grace and intensity. Suddenly she stopped short and stared narrowly at Gat. "Suppose I agree to marry . . . Mr. Ransom. How long would it take for an annulment afterward and still not affect the legalities of the adoption?"

"Generally, you have three days to annul the marriage, and as far as the adoption I could write up the papers immediately after the marriage. Sheeks will have no choice but to concede."

India began pacing once again. Gat rolled his eyes heavenward and then exchanged a tolerant smile with Ed.

Her pace slowed and she stared thoughtfully out the window. With a deep sigh she finally turned and said, "I'll do it!" Then she looked a little embarrassed. "Providing Mr. Ransom agrees."

Gat rubbed his chin slowly, the old devilment awakening in his eyes. "I don't know. Marriage is a pretty big step, it might take me a few days to get my courage up."

Though they had been parted for months, and India had spent much of that time idealizing him in her mind as the lovesick sometimes do, she was not so lovesick that she was blind to the mischief-loving side of his nature.

"No fence-sitting, Gat Ransom," she snapped. "By the time you get that kind of courage they'll be pounding nails in your coffin. Besides, the marriage will be over before it begins."

That's the problem. I'll miss out on the best part, Gat thought, then said, "I've never had a lady propose to me, but I suppose just this once I'll accept, Miss Simms."

Her hand clenched into a small trembling fist against her black merino wool dress, and she could have slapped him there and then for his teasing. "I *did not* propose to you, Mr. Ransom!"

As Ed Lee looked on he realized there was more going on between them than met the eye. "Now, now, you two. Let's not have the divorce before the marriage. It's getting late and we had better get started." He began pulling out papers from the desk.

India, awash with an odd sense of panic, said, "Now both of you have to promise me you won't breathe a word of this to anyone." After all she had been the woman who had stood on her soapbox from one side of the territory to the other telling women not to marry until they had the vote.

"You have my word as a gentleman, though the marriage and the annulment will be recorded in the town records," said Ed Lee.

India tugged on the small gold earring in her right ear out of nervousness. She turned to Gat, her blue eyes bright with anxiety. "And you, Mr. Ransom?"

His dark eyes held hers a moment. "Have I ever let you down?"

Quite regularly she wanted to say, but in truth, in the things that counted most, he never had let her down, and suddenly feeling repentant for her sharpness toward him, her voice filled with a soft caress and she said, "Thank you."

Gat stood then. "Well, Ed, you start writin' the marriage license. I think the parson is just across the street."

Gat was out the door before India connected with the word *parson,* and she quickly turned to Ed Lee. "But I thought it would be only we three. I . . . I didn't plan on a ceremony."

Ed was busy writing but took a moment to explain. "The license is only an application for marriage. You have to have a ceremony to make it binding. Don't worry—"

Just then the door opened and in came Gat with the parson, or "Thirsty Parson" as everyone called him. "Don't worry, the parson won't remember a thing."

Thirsty leaned precariously against Gat, who guided him to sit in an empty chair. "Now Thirsty, I'd like you to marry the little lady and me," said Gat.

"I haven't done that for sssome time," he slurred, and then attempted to tidy up by dusting off his frock coat and straightening his bib and tucker, though his stovepipe hat still sat crookedly on his head. "I seem to have lost my Bible along the way."

During one too many visits to the publicans and sinners, thought India, wholly aghast by what she'd gotten herself into.

"I have one here," Ed grabbed a leather-bound volume from his bookshelves and thrust it into Thirsty's hands. India squinted closely and read *Tom Jones* on the binding. She gave Ed an intolerant eye, but he gave a hopeless shrug.

Thirsty opened it and cleared his throat. "Forgive me if I don't ssstand, but my health isn't what it used to be. If the bride and groom will place themselves in front of me."

As the two moved together Gat looked over at India and saw that the porcelain skin of her high cheekbones was vivid rose. Under his assessing gaze her hands patted her cheeks self-consciously and she said, "My goodness, it's warm in here."

"If there was a fire in the stove it might be even warmer," he said, deadpan, not missing the opportunity to slip his hand around her waist. He felt her tense from his touch like a jerk-away colt, but he didn't drop his arm.

Thirsty licked his finger and dully thumbed through the pages. "Dearly beloved . . ." he began, his head swaying and his eyes focusing briefly on a random page. "It hath been observed by wise men or women, I forget which, that all persons are doomed to be in love once in their lives." He hiccuped, fumbled the book and then after taking a moment to find his place he continued, "As in the season of rutting—"

India's mouth dropped open with affront and Gat reached over and clapped the book shut. "Why don't you just have us put our hands on it."

"Ah . . . that might be best," agreed Thirsty.

Gat took India's small hand into the warmth of his own and rested them on the book. She didn't pull her hand away as he expected, but she did pinch her lips together and glared at him sidelong.

"Now pronounce them man and wife," prompted Ed.

"I now pronounce you man and wife," echoed Thirsty. A genuine etheric light touched his watery bloodshot eyes as he smiled on the newly united couple. "Don't forget to kiss the bride," he urged Gat.

India opened her mouth, "I don't think that is necess—"

Gat took her in his arms, lowered his head and captured her protesting lips with the kiss of reconciliation he had wanted to give her earlier at the boardinghouse. It was the kiss he had dreamed of during long days and nights herding cattle on the prairie, and if it was to be their last kiss, it would be the memory of this kiss he would savor during the skin and bones of loneliness in years to come.

Not surprisingly, India jerked back, but this time Gat used his superior strength to hold her gently but determinedly fast. And with the rich, pleasurable touch of Gat's lips India's starch soon dissolved and she relaxed into their reunion. His tongue moved inside her mouth filling the empty space as he kissed her deeply and blissfully. Her eyes closed as if she were in a deep sleep and her arms crept around his wide chest while her tongue tasted the heady nectar of his own. Between them time hung in suspension, renewing the past, holding the present and promising the future.

It was Ed Lee who finally cleared his throat. "The papers are ready to sign. I'll witness along with Thirsty."

India pulled away from Gat, her eyes lowered and her nostrils widening so she could catch enough breath to speak. Her ear tips had turned red and her faced flushed; she felt as soft as jelly and as weak as watered-down broth.

Gat just stood there considering her, hands resting low on his narrow hips, his black eyes smoldering with private thoughts, all the while knowing that from where he stood, seeing her flushed with the heat of her obvious desire, she would continue to deny him and herself the ultimate union.

Turning, he said with resignation, "Let's get this over and done with."

So he wants it done with, thought India, slightly wounded by his abrupt manner. She picked up the pen and quickly signed where Ed pointed, one paper after the next. Gat had to guide Thirsty's hand while he signed the marriage certificate to make the signature legible.

Before he completed the adoption papers Ed paused. "Ma'am, you'll have to go back and add Ransom to all your signatures. Now that you're married, you take your husband's name."

India's lips tightened stubbornly, but amazingly she said nothing and proceeded to re-sign all the papers. "Now, Mr. Lee, I'll have my annulment."

"Yes, in a minute." He shuffled through the papers. "Now," he picked up the papers one by one and stacked them neatly. "here's the marriage license application, the marriage certificate, and the legalized adoption certificate of one Baby Hope to Mr. and Mrs. Gatlin Ransom and all have my signature as territorial secretary."

"And the annulment?" she continued to press him.

Suddenly, a young boy off the street burst into the office shouting, "Fire! Fire! McDaniels' Museum's on fire!" He ran out again sounding the alarm next door.

Ed dropped his pen and jumped up.

Gat was across the room and out the door. "By hell, that's the whiskey side of town, and once it gets going in this wind it'll burn like Independence Day!"

Without a second thought to India both men were half way down the street before she could call to them about the annulment. She looked over at Thirsty, who dozed in his chair, then muttering to herself she hurried out the door and followed them down the street toward the plume of smoke swirling above the rooftops.

India and Heddy carried platters and bowls of food into the boardinghouse dining room, where guests were seated at the table. Voices filled the air and the subject of the museum fire seemed to be the main topic of conversation, but the main concern for India was whether Ed Lee had returned to his office after the fire and written up the annulment. India let her eyes stray over to baby Hope's cradle where Gat provoked the infant's delighted coos and giggles by playing peekaboo. All afternoon India had fretted and stewed over the matter, knowing she'd been completely mad to marry Gat Ransom, and until the annulment, the less that passed between them the better.

"Luckily, McDaniels had a water wagon out back or we'd never have gotten the fire under control," said Buck Slocum, who was boarding at Heddy's while the legislature met.

"Did they discover how it started?" asked Bess, who stood beside him.

"Yes," Gat spoke up. "Some drunk stuck a cigar in the stuffed grizzly's mouth." Everyone laughed.

"If yo' belly's empty, it's the time to fill it," Heddy called cordially, and those not seated sat down.

"We'll ask Mr. Slocum to offer grace," she announced, once everybody was situated. All bowed their heads for the brief prayer, and then she and India began serving.

"I'm sure hungry," declared a middle-aged railroad man who was staying in Cheyenne on Union Pacific business. "I've never had such food as you fix, Miss Heddy. It's enough to make a confirmed bachelor want to marry."

"Anyone who'd marry just to have a cook should stay a bachelor," said Gat. India looked at him in spite of herself. He looked back, the dark smoke of his eyes challenging her own. Lowering her eyes, India poured coffee into Bess's cup. She felt guilty enough for perverting the sacred vow of marriage for her own ends without his blatant condemnation.

"Thank you, India," said Bess with a pleasant smile. "I had no idea you were still in Cheyenne. Gat never mentioned it."

"I didn't know, myself," Gat spoke up. "It seems all the women I know can't wait to travel east."

"Me included," interjected Bess. "Now that my sister has married, I've decided to see the part of the world I've missed. After a few days stay in Cheyenne, I'm going to take the train east. I have a great-aunt in New York state who has invited me to come and stay the winter."

"So Clarett's married," Heddy said.

"Yes, to Boots Hansen," Bess said.

"Seems some boys are lucky," Gat began, looking sidelong at India. "The way I heard it, no one was marrying in the territory until women got the vote."

India smoldered, unable to ignore the taunt in his words.

Coffeepot in hand she passed him up and exited to the kitchen, where she slammed down the pot on the stove and began to toss dirty dishes into the wash tub with uncharacteristic disregard. *How dare he rub it in! I might be a hypocrite, but at least I have a good reason.* Still unable to get a handle on her anger she reloaded the serving tray and reluctantly returned to the dining room.

"I believe you've brought dessert instead of the biscuits," Heddy remarked in passing.

India looked down at the tray of apple pie dessert. "Oh, I'm sorry."

"That's quite all right with us if you hurry dinner along,"

interjected Bess. "Gat and I must leave. He's taking me to
see *The Circassian Girl* at the town theater tonight."

India's lips pressed into a tight line and she returned to
the kitchen for the biscuits. She should have guessed it! On
their wedding night he was stepping out with another
woman. No wonder he appeared particularly virile, dressed
in black wool trousers which outlined the heavy muscles of
his thighs above his best hand-tooled boots. His buckskin
coat stretched over his broad shoulders, giving him a flaw-
lessly masculine profile, though she did have the wild urge
to retouch the lopsided loop of his string tie.

Later, from the kitchen doorway, with the beginnings of a
headache behind her eyes, India watched Bess lean into the
circle of his strong arms as he helped her on with her cloak.
India winced with a sudden sense of despair as she saw him
and Bess leaving, arm in arm, for the theater. *You have no
one to blame but yourself if the man you love walks out the
door with another woman on his arm,* she thought miserably.
There's no denying it, you've dug the hole yourself!

In the boardinghouse kitchen baby Hope fussed in the
cradle of India's arms. It seemed as if tonight nothing would
settle the infant. By lamplight, India read the letter she'd
received form Sarah Bramshill that day. Sarah had never
made it to San Francisco. She'd gone to the gold camps of
Nevada instead.

*I have made my fortune, India, not in gold, but in
pies. I've cooked and sold pies for two dollars each to
the miners, and now after thousands of pies, I am a
woman of some means. For the time being I can support
myself, and though I've had offers for my hand in
marriage, there is not a man alive who can tempt me
into the wedded state. I am as happy as I can be. How
good it seems to have everyone treat me respectfully. I
never hear complaining, nor an unkind word, and in
these past months I feel as if I had been let out of
prison. I love my freedom. As for Huntington, I have*

learned he was wounded during gunplay in a St. Louis saloon, and died soon after.

Rocking back and forth, India put the letter aside, and her lips kneaded together with relief. After all this time she realized she'd been right to interfere in Sarah's affairs. Sarah had returned the money she'd given her, but more importantly, at a time when India needed it, Sarah's letter bolstered her spirits. For India, Sarah's new-found happiness was a reward in itself. However, the battle still raged within her own mind, for she knew not all marriages ended in misery. Many marriages flowered into great happiness, but she had placed that experience beyond her grasp. What could have been between her and Gat was a dismal prospect to face during the late-night loneliness.

Shortly after midnight India heard Gat and Bess come in. Bess's laughter filled the hallway, and her passage up the stairs interrupted India's quiet reverie.

The creak of the hallway floorboards drew India's eyes to the kitchen door. Gat stood there, the scarred side of his face turned toward her as the lamplight played across his darkly rugged features. Thinking back to their first meeting she wondered how she ever could have thought him ominous. He was modest to the point of shyness and sentimental to a fault.

He pulled his hat down into a dove-tailed dive over his eyes, folded his arms across his chest leaning his wide shoulders against the door frame. His gaze was steady on her.

She shifted the colicky baby in her arms as a steamy sensation flushed unbidden through her body. She'd never wanted someone to go away so much and at the same time stay.

"If you have something to say, say it," she murmured.

"I've missed you," he said.

There. It was out in the open. He had the knack of cutting courtesy to the bare bone. It fairly unnerved India, especially tonight while she'd been stewing over her misfortunes, all perpetrated on herself by herself.

He came into the room.

"It doesn't matter." Her voice was stone, but her heart melted into a simmering liquid.

"It does." He held her eyes in confident reproof. Then he knelt down before her and traced a finger over Hope's golden-curled forehead. "Let me take her, after all I'm her legitimate father until we sign the annulment papers."

"And when is that momentous occasion?" Her own remedies failing, India surrendered Hope to his arms.

"Ed promised to draw up the papers first thing tomorrow." He looked back to the baby, his dark eyes filled with a prideful sparkle. "She sure has grown. I figured you wouldn't be able to give her up when it came down to it."

"Just because I don't intend to have a husband doesn't mean I shouldn't have a child." There, she thought, if that doesn't keep him at bay, nothing would.

"You're still on the soapbox!" His eyes lowered in disappointment. Then he let out a slow, thoughtful sigh and raised them again to probe hers. "So, why did you stay all this time?"

"The suffrage bill. But I'm leaving day after tomorrow for Boston. I have the train ticket," she said in an attempt to verify her motives. "What brings you to town?"

"You know."

"I do?"

"Bess needed an escort and I came to collect the rest of my fee from Bright." He was slowly pacing. "I've a hunch Campbell will sign the bill. If he does, Bright owes me a little more money."

Hopelessness seeped into her rupturing armor. So he'd come because of Bess and the money.

"Did Bess enjoy the theater?" she asked, more out of jealousy than interest.

Gat smiled. "She sure did. Like a child turned loose in fairyland. She's inclined to high society. That's why she's goin' east. I think she's roped her last steer and branded her last calf."

With relief, India thought so, too. An awkward silence fell. The kitchen clock ticked like an impatient chaperon.

Gat paused before the windowpane and peered out. "The rain has turned into snow."

A brief vision of her and Gat being snowbound, alone together, flitted through India's mind. Pushing away the thought, she put the rubber-nippled bottle aside and stood. "It seems you've put her to sleep."

"Some females melt to my touch." He rested smokey eyes on India. In the kitchen chill her face flamed. "I'll carry her up," offered Gat.

"Thank you, Mr. Ransom."

"So you're back to that. It sounds a little formal for two people who just got married a few hours ago."

"We are married in name only," she reminded. "I got what I wanted from the bargain and you . . ." Her voice trailed into silence as she calculated what Gat had to gain from it all. Other than securing proper care for Hope there was nothing. Widening her eyes quizzically she looked over at him and opened her mouth to ask just exactly what he had to gain, but the question died on her lips. Every light and shadow of his rough-hewn face, from the dark knot of his brows to the intense line of his determined lips, told her the answer. And the slow, canny shift in the depths of his obsidian eyes told her he was here to collect.

A tremor, warm as gold, tumbled through her, and she drew in a slow breath and held it for a long second before letting it go. Gat's whole body remained relaxed in deceptive propriety, but he watched her and in his gaze she knew herself to be not only wanted, but passionately desired.

In the feathered silence they stood measuring each other, the banter, the sparring, the teasing gone. It became a falling of fences and a forgetting of philosophies, and there was no dilemma in her mind now whether she should or should not go to bed with him. At some point during their months together, the decision had been made for her, and she knew tonight she had no alternative, not because she had put her signature to a somewhat dubious marriage certificate, but because she loved him.

She turned away from him. Picking up the lamp, she started up the back stairs and, with babe in arms, Gat followed.

When the door to her room creaked open she gave an uneasy glance down the hallway. No respectable woman would be seen entering her bedroom with a man so late at night. But of course, this was a special circumstance, tonight the man was her lawful husband.

Inside the room the cradle was to one side of a small woodstove that bellied a glowing red fire. India set the lamp on the writing desk and straightened the cradle blankets. Pressing a kiss on the baby's wispy curls, Gat laid her down.

They stood and gazed at the baby, while outside, winging snowflakes touched the cloudy windowpane, spying, then melting into slick droplets. The silence was profound and the shadows of the lamplit room hallucinatory.

"India," his voice was low and she turned her head to catch the whisper of her name. Now, she was not looking at him with the eyes of a spinster, nor of a woman who'd sworn never to marry, but of someone in desperate need of intimacy.

She wanted him to take her into his arms and knew he was dying to, but the first move had to be hers, and after swallowing back years of prudence, with never a thought to silk hankies, she rested a trembling hand on the pine bedstead and said in a soft, silver voice, "I want to make a man of you, Gat Ransom."

The strong lines bracketing his mouth relaxed into a smile. "Hell, ma'am, I'm not easily gentled and you'll never make a swooning Nelly of me, but I'm yours heart and hand." He hung his hat on the bedpost and rewarded her with his insolent half-grin of *I dare you.*

Not a quiver of doubt touched her eyes as she stood on tiptoe, wrapped her arms around his neck and made a tentative, brushing pass on his lips. He responded by circling his large hands around her waist and lifting her in balance against the hard, muscular length of his body. He pressed his mouth upon her cool, moist lips and soon her eyes closed and she lost herself in the sweet promise of loving. Rotating, merging, blending, their lips sought to make the intangible tangible, and she had a breathless sense of being alone with him in a world where nothing had substance and reality but his touch and the sound of his breathing.

Now more than ever Gat realized there was nothing wrong with being lady-broke, especially by one so confident and loving; after all, the best kind of loving came from the heart with no price tag. When she touched his face with her gentle lips and secreted her hands beneath his buckskin coat to massage his back and shoulders, he couldn't help but kiss her full mouth, exalted, trembling. Although the lead was hers, he was discovering newfound pleasures in the naivete of the pace.

He yielded to her soft cajoling to undress. Soon he had shrugged out of his coat and was slowly taking off his shirt. She stepped back, seating herself on the edge of the bed. Next his boots came off and then his fingers stopped at the line of buttons on his pants. Unsure of what she wanted him to do, he looked over to where she sat, her elbows propped on her knees and her chin resting in her hands. Her sapphire eyes were as luminous as silvered glass and filled with more curiosity than a baby racoon. He'd lain back appreciatively and watched many a woman undress over the years, but this was the first time he'd been the one to put on the show, and again he was experiencing the other side of loving. He gave a soft smile, feeling totally vulnerable under her admiring gaze, but with innate male conceit he was confident his tall, muscled frame, which molded up to a dense rib cage and wide shoulders, was a wonder of creation.

Leaving on his pants, he sat down beside her on the bed and put his arm around her shoulders. She leaned into him and rested her cheek against the warm skin of his bare chest. Where her cheek touched him a warmth streaked along his nerves and the familiar minty scent of her hair filled him with a sense of homecoming. He picked up her small hand in his own and splayed her fingers in comparison over the large reach of his own hand. Then interlacing his fingers with hers he marveled at the delicate graceful fingers of her small woman's hand, but he also saw within her palm a strength beyond his own.

"You know you aren't the first woman I've . . ." His words were soft against her ear and tinged with regret, "I wish you were."

The husky sound of his voice sent shivers through India, and overcome by the sincerity of his words she lifted her face to the rich, dark brilliance of his eyes and kissed his lips with reassurance. Breath and scent created an enchanting elixir and her hands caressed him and pulled him closer.

They drifted back onto the feathered folds of the bed like a pair of falling angels and soon her wrapper and pantalettes rained to the floor in a shower of silk and cotton tatting. Side by side, face to face, they lay while their lips touched in random meetings. Gat's hand moved over her hips and rested on the small of her back. The warmth of his hand, its potency, its solidity released a slow radiance through her whole body. The current from his palm flowed downward like molten gold over her woman's mound, down farther, down the insides of her legs, Awakening instinctive senses. *So this is loving,* India thought. *It is like dying of thirst and then discovering all the water you can drink.*

Gat withdrew his hand, and India felt a brief emptiness, a yearning as the fiery rush subsided. But it began again as he replaced his hand, so slow, so unhesitating, between her thighs.

She dared not breathe.

His fingers circled, pressed, gently kneaded the satin softness of her flesh. Her lips found the hollow of his throat and her nails lightly laced a pattern on his smooth muscled back. By now, India's mind had shed all anxieties, worries and cares. Her responsibilities no longer mattered because her whole being was melting. She felt like liquid—no bones, no muscle, no resistance.

They clung to each other while their mouths tasted flesh, and explored, nipping, licking, sucking. Against his rising and lowering chest her breasts lost definition as did her very being. She was him and he was her, floating entwined in a boundless sphere of harmony.

India's legs caught around Gat's cool thighs opening herself to him. His hands guiding her hips, he pressed forward against the white silk of her virginity, and between them the dark steady heat pulsed. Her breath caught ever so slightly, and she curved her body around Gat and rode amidst slow undulations as lithe and fluid as the prairie breeze. Farther ... farther ...

Desire arched delicately, swirled, twisted and trembled, leaving India to soar and fall—fall so deeply into Gat's heart and spirit that when she surfaced from the ecstasy she had grasped a perfect sense of him. A fine sheen of perspiration coated her body, from the crown of her head to the tips of her toes, and then she felt the answering shudder of his flanks.

In the aftermath he was quivering, breathless and hot. He touched her hair, caught a strand and took it to his nostrils. "Sweet India," he whispered. Looking deep into his beloved eyes, she cupped the back of his dark-curled head and his mouth found the cream soft flesh of her throat.

Through the night their loving flew as if on the wings of a red-tailed hawk encircling them in ever-tightening jesses of passion. Before the dawn, in the wee hours when the moon flies golden sails across the lower sky, as he strained into her, need shuddered through them in unison.

Her breath stopped. Something utterly exquisite had happened, more so even in its fleetness.

As a great wind retreats, he withdrew and rested his dark head against her breast. Sighing, she buried her face into his curly hair and breathed deeply in its clean, handmade-soap smell, letting her tears of fulfillment trickle in single droplets into its sooty mass. At last he lifted his head, and for a long time they looked at each other without speaking. What needed to be said had been said without the utterance of a single word.

When he left her side she wanted to call him back, and she knew the feeling of abandonment that swept through her would never be erased from her memory. All that she was, all that she knew and tried to hide from herself or kept secret, he had embraced. For a few blessed hours there had been no separation between them and her heart swelled with an infinite tenderness for him. Their loving had changed the world for her.

There is no way to love without being changed, she thought. She understood now why men fear and subjugate women, and why, from the beginning, Eve became the temptress. It is not easy for men to be mastered by a need so intense it defies holy convention.

By lamplight, in the snow-shrouded silence, she watched him as he dressed; she watched him feed wood to the smoldering embers of the small potbellied stove, and with new eyes she followed his every movement across the room. He went to the window and opened it, hung his head over the snow-swept sill, and took a deep, invigorating breath.

She snuggled deeper into the quilts, rolled over on her stomach and closed her eyes. When she was seventy in her cottage filled with cats, if nothing more, she would have this memory to cherish.

She heard his footsteps cross the room, silently, loving him. He bent over her, lifted her hair and pressed his lips against the nape of her neck. His kiss became spark to tinder and she was racked with a longing for him. Turning over, her full lips sought his and their farewell became bittersweet, laced with reluctance on her part and true resolve on his. In the end, his jaw set with bronco-riding stamina, he strode out the door with a polite, "Thanks for the keepsake."

He left her hovering between heaven and hell.

Later that morning, the day of December tenth, India sat primly in the gallery inside the rented two-room Assembly hall with other women who'd vowed not to leave until the governor signed the suffrage bill.

Her mind wasn't on suffrage. It was on songbirds in December. That morning, outside her window, she'd hear Gat's penny whistle serenade of the wistful mating call of the western willet, and she felt a softness inside her at the thought of the night past.

Now, she started trembling—a sure sign Gat was in the vicinity. She scanned the many faces in the hall and watched the door. A minute passed and he strode through in the company of Ed Lee. As if she had called out to him across the hall, he turned his head and met her gaze. For one split second everything around her receded, the buzz of voices, the motion of movement and the thief of time. Her daytime mind was pulled back to the past night and the pure sensations of loving him.

Ed Lee had followed Gat's eyes and together the men began moving through the crowd toward India. She watched Ed's hand search in the breast pocket of his coat, retrieving a folded parchment paper. A shadow of dread sent last night's memories scurrying. India excused herself from the other ladies and stepped to Gat's side.

"Ma'am," Gat touched the brim of his hat. "Ed has a paper for us to sign."

"I'll need both your signatures." Lee smoothed out the paper on a nearby table and reached to dip his pen in an adjacent inkwell. Someone came up to him on legislative business and drew his attention away for the moment.

India looked over at Gat but his eyes were scanning the hall with cool indifference. *I love you,* she wanted to say.

Ed turned back and held out the pen. Neither one of them reached for it. "Who's signing first?"

"A . . . a . . . Mr. Ransom," deferred India, not wanting to sign at all.

Gat shook his head. "Not me. Ladies first."

He looked at her with *I dare you* insolence and immediately turned the affair into a Mexican standoff. A very real anger began brewing inside India as temper lines touched her lips. It was too late to swallow her pride, for it had stuck like one of Gat's burned biscuits at the back of her throat. She drew up stiffly and snatched the pen from Ed Lee, scribbled her name on the paper and without another word she stalked off.

Gat didn't miss her hesitancy to sign, and a slow, shrewd smile spread across his lips and touched his dark eyes. *Just throw a big loop and keep hold of the jerk line*, he thought, *in time she'll come callin'.*

"Well, I've other business to attend to," Ed announced impatiently. "Are you going to sign or not?"

"Nope!" Gat said.

Ed face's shifted to puzzlement. "No? If you don't sign, the annulment isn't binding."

"I aim to waltz with the lady," Gat replied.

"If there's one lady in the territory who won't be waltzing, it's her."

"Then let 'er buck." Gat turned and strode off, leaving Ed Lee shaking his head.

The hall began to quiet down when the governor entered and took his seat at the governor's table. Ed Lee, officiating as territorial secretary, held a pile of bills to be signed. Lee announced each bill in turn, handing them to the governor to read, approve and sign.

The time dragged and India's eyes and mind kept wandering to Gat Ransom across the hall. Her emotions were at such a pitch, she felt as if she were sitting on tacks.

At last Ed Lee presented the suffrage bill. Colonel Bright leaned to whisper in Governor Campbell's ear and comment rippled through the hall.

Betty, who sat next to India, reached over and clasped her hand tightly. "He must sign, he must! If he doesn't, I'll never invite him over for supper again."

"Did you tell him so beforehand? It just might make the difference," India said, her eyes still on Ransom. So much hung in the balance that when the governor picked up the pen, the room became as still as a church. Then, without hesitation or public discussion, and to the amazement of most in attendance, with a flourish he signed the act granting the women of Wyoming the right to vote, to own property, and to hold office.

He stood, gave a polite bow to the women all sitting in the gallery, and said, "Ladies, prepare your ballots."

India's eyes riveted to Gat across the hall. He touched the brim of his hat and gave her a nod of salute. Then Betty Bright was hugging her and she was hugging someone else and such a commotion followed that the Assembly had to be called to order. Ed Lee had left his seat to escort Amelia Post, the spearhead of Cheyenne's suffrage group, to the front of the hall. Amelia awaited patiently for the Assembly to settle down, all the while a bright light of triumph filled her eyes.

"Today," she began, "Wyoming is the first place on God's green earth which can claim to be the land of the free. Thank you, gentlemen of Wyoming, for a patient hearing, and for securing the ballot in our hands. May you have no cause for regret; but may this measure make us more helpful wives, more womanly women, more patriotic mothers."

Applause resounded through the hall and everyone left their seats to congratulate one another and extoll the history-making occasion. Colonel Bright came over to his wife and gave her a heartfelt embrace.

Gat walked over with Will Noble to shake Bill's hand.

As Gat approached, India wanted to throw her arms around him from pure elation at the bill's passage. The victory had catapulted her into a quicksilver state of mind. But Gat remained reserved, polite, and distant.

"Well," he said to Bill, never looking India's way, "what do you think changed his mind?"

"I have a suspicion it was India's petition ledger," offered Bright. "We presented it to him this morning. When he came across Red Cloud's signature, he fairly shook with laughter.

"He said, 'When the women of Wyoming can procure a signature that the United States Army has sought for years on a peace treaty, I think it's time we pay attention.' "

They all laughed at this, and then Bright turned to Gat. "I owe you for a job well done." And he took out his wallet.

Gat put up a halting hand. "No, I won't take it. You keep the money. When Campbell signed the bill that was payment enough for me."

India stared at Gat. Wasn't that why he'd come back, for the money?

"Are you sure?" asked Bright.

"Yep, I'm sure." He touched the brim of his hat and turned back to the ladies. "I guess I'll be ridin' out. There's still enough daylight to cover a few miles. Mrs. Bright." He turned to India, *"Miss Simms."* He turned and walked away.

Dying inside, India watched him leave. In all her strata-gems and philosophizing for women's rights she'd never taken into account the power of love. *Who or what in heaven could take his place?* He might not have always agreed with her opinions, but he had defended her right to speak them, and she'd experienced the worst and best of his nature.

"I hear he's settled down and taken up ranching," re-marked Betty.

India looked at Betty with surprise. "Who's taken up ranching?"

"Why, Gat. Didn't you know?" Betty looked at India curiously.

India stared blankly.

Then, excusing herself from the Brights, she hurried out of the building only to stumble over Coyote and Square Deal lounging by the doorway. Nearby Gat attended to saddle cinches.

Sun-reflected snow dazzled her eyes and she raised a hand to shadow her face. "You're leaving now?"

"Yep," said Gat, acting uninterested.

"You should have taken the money. You earned it." She managed a weak smile.

"Yep!" This "yep" was said with more emphasis.

Bluestocking stretched her neck and nosed India's hand for sugar. "You still have my horse."

"Yep," Gat replied, seemingly more interested in the position of Bluestocking's bit than in India's words.

"So, you think you can just take my horse?" Argument seemed to be the best way to stall for time.

"Yep." Gat climbed up on the horse.

He didn't take the bait and his "yeps" were getting on her nerves. Couldn't the man say anything else to her after all they'd gone through—after last night?

"Well, I guess it's good-bye, Mr. Ransom," she blurted out as coldly as she could. If he wasn't going to be sentimental, neither was she, no matter how much she loved him.

He took hold of Bluestocking's reins and turned her head toward the street. Then almost as an afterthought he said over his shoulder, "Too bad you ain't the marrying kind."

He touched the brim of his hat in a farewell salute. Bluestocking carried him down the snow-sloshed street. The two dogs followed faithfully. *Well*, India thought wretchedly, *if he wants unswerving devotion he certainly has it in that pair of dogs!*

Her lower lip slipped beneath her upper one and tears blurred Gat into a wavy vision. Feeling the needle's stitch and the prick of heartbreak, she turned away.

Oh, women might have the vote, but it still was a man's world. Now she understood her folly. *Never say never*, she thought miserably. If only she could call him back and admit that since certain circumstances had changed, she might be the marrying kind. She couldn't bear playing the reticent lady, too demure to demand or even to desire.

Then suddenly she reversed, seeing in the end the choice was hers! All this time she'd been the one crusading for free choice and now she must exercise those freedoms. Lifting up her skirt, she ran down the street after Gat, who by now was far ahead. She stopped, scooped some snow into an icy ball and threw it, hitting smack on the target of his broad back.

He turned, then pulled up his horse.

"Why is it too bad?" she called out to him.

"I wanted you to go with me." He was riding back to her.

By now India could hardly contain herself. "As your partner or your slave?" Her wide smile was irresistible, for she clearly knew the answer.

He muttered an oath under his breath. "You're the damnedest woman to use a soft rope! But if you want your horse back you'll have to marry me."

"Marry you . . . *again?*" she raised an eyebrow, her lips puckered in deliberation. "Will you agree to my keeping my own name and omitting the word "obey" from the wedding ceremony?"

He nodded. "I reckon we did that already. But while we're swapping' conditions let me ask, will *you* promise to step down off your soapbox at bedtime?"

She deliberated a moment and said, "I think I want that horse, Gat Ransom. My answer is yes. But where are you going?"

"Back to Colorado Territory."

Then an impish smile touched her lips. "Do women have the vote in Colorado?"

Knowing what he was in for, Gat rested his arm on the saddle horn and pushed back his hat in mock defeat. Then grinning into her dancing blue eyes he swore, but only mildly and under his breath.

AUTHOR'S NOTE

While writing *Waltz with the Lady* I drew from many sources, including Abigail Scott Duniway's autobiography, *Pathbreaking;* Elizabeth Stanton's *History of Women's Suffrage;* Elinor Rice Hay's *Lucy Stone;* and *Bill Nye's Experience* from the Annals of Wyoming. *Waltz with the Lady* closely follows the events that led to women's attainment of the right of suffrage in Wyoming in 1869. The main characters are fictional, but many of the secondary characters, such as Esther Morris, Amelia Post, Colonel Bill Bright and Governor Campbell, did live in Wyoming at this time and worked to bring about the triumph of woman suffrage. By 1896, the states of Wyoming, Utah and Colorado had joined the Union with the right of suffrage for women as well as men. Not until 1920, with the passage of the 19th Amendment, was the right of suffrage extended to all women of the United States.

Printed in the United States
By Bookmasters